Treasure Me

by CHRISTINE NOLFI

ISBN-10 146376524X

ISBN 978-1-4637-6524-8

Copyright © 2011 by Christine Nolfi

www.christinenolfi.com

CHAPTER 1

"Where are you? Give me back my wallet!"

From somewhere inside Birdie Kaminsky's apartment, the man in blue pinstripe stormed through the rooms like a long distance runner stoked on Red Bull. Flinching at the fury in his voice, she dangled from the window ledge and stared with wide-eyed fear at the pavement three stories below.

The man was seventy years old if he was a day. He probably worked out, which explained how he'd pursued her up three flights of stairs and made it into her apartment before she locked the front door.

Old men and their treadmills. It was something she should've considered before she'd picked his pocket on her way home from a light day of breaking and entering.

Birdie tried to ignore the sickening *whoosh* of fear zigzagging through her body. Her teeth were chattering, so she clamped her mouth shut. Three stories above terra firma made a straight drop a stupid idea. Like any good thief she was agile. But the last time she'd checked she hadn't sprouted wings. If she let go of the windowsill and took the plunge, she'd break her legs.

"Where are you hiding? You aren't taking my money, do you hear me?"

Something crashed to the floor inside her apartment, the sound too close for comfort. Had it come from the hallway that led from the closet-sized living room to the pea-sized bedroom? With any luck, Marathon Man would stop in the bathroom to check if she was hiding behind the shower curtain.

She gasped as her hold on the windowsill loosened. "Oh, shit!"

Pressing her long legs forward, she flattened against the building's brick façade. To her left, the drainpipe snaked down to the street. Reach for it and risk falling? Today *was* her thirty-first birthday and therefore a lucky day. On the other hand, her landlord had threatened to evict her this morning if she didn't make good on her rent and a demonic old geezer was pounding on the bedroom door she'd had the sense to lock before she'd stupidly made her escape.

The window on the other side of the drainpipe slid open with a *bang!* Fear scuttled her heart. Mr. Chen stuck his head out and relief swamped her.

"Birdie! What happened?"

"Uh . . ."

Another wave of fists pounding and Mr. Chen's mouth formed an O. "Is it the police? Did they threaten you? You didn't squeal on the Poker Kings, did you?"

Mr. Chen held Poker Kings, a Tuesday night game, in his apartment. He did a great job of seeding his hand with Aces and he was always worried the cops would find out. Birdie figured he should worry about the other tenants learning he was fleecing them. The overworked Lexington Police Department had bigger fish to fry.

She smiled at him gamely. "Um, Mr. Chen, could you help me out? I'm gonna fall if you don't."

"Oh. Right."

To her surprise, he jimmied a brick from the wall. Then another. When he'd finished, he grabbed her left foot and steered it toward the handy inverse steps he'd created. Stretching to the drainpipe, she grabbed hold then started toward his window. For all she knew, he hid his ill-gotten poker winnings behind the bricks.

No matter—his thieving heart was her salvation. She shimmied toward him with her pulse rattling inside her skull.

When she reached his window he helped her through and into the kitchen.

The fragrant scents of ginger and garlic mingled in the air. A wok sat on the counter. Evidently Mr. Chen had been preparing an early dinner while she'd been chased upstairs by the man whose pocket she'd picked.

Ignoring the rumbling in her stomach, she darted through the apartment. In the living room she found Mrs. Chen seated in the shiny new wheelchair Birdie had snagged from an assisted living facility last month. It hadn't seemed fair for Mrs. Chen to spend hours on the phone, arguing with bureaucrats in her broken English. All she'd needed was a new set of wheels. Birdie was familiar with the pricey new facility—she'd eaten a free lunch in the cafeteria on more than one occasion. So she'd dolled up in a tight-fitting nurse's uniform and set out to snatch a wheelchair.

She'd marched right into the lobby, cornered a hunky security guard lounging by the front desk, and announced she needed to assist a woman who was having trouble getting out of her car. All too eager to help, the security guard was still checking out her ass when she rolled the wheelchair out to the parking lot.

Dismissing the memory, she paused before the wheelchair. "Good afternoon, Mrs. Chen."

"Birdie, hello. You stay for dinner?"

"Naw. I have to leave the city."

"For good?"

"My time in Lexington is up."

"You a crazy white girl, but we miss you." Mrs. Chen thrust out her lower lip. "Wish you stay longer, steal a car for Yihung. His Buick is a beater."

"I'll grab him a Mercedes the next time I'm in Kentucky." Regret sifted through her and her fingers were stinging, too. Hell, her thumbs were bleeding—she nearly *had* lost her purchase on the windowsill and plummeted to the ground. "You take care of yourself, okay?"

Mrs. Chen glanced at the ceiling, where pounding footsteps sounded. "You got money?" When Birdie started rifling through the pockets of her army surplus coat, the woman reached for the purse she'd left on the couch. She handed over a wad of bills. "Not much. You take."

"Mrs. Chen . . ."

"Take!" The woman's dark eyes snapped. Mr. Chen came into the room and she looked up at her husband. "Make her take my dough from bingo. I only give back to St. Vincent's Church if I keep."

There wasn't time to argue. Birdie took the cash. Then she sighed at the sight of the large Mason jar in Mr. Chen's hands, the one he sat beside his chair on Tuesday nights. Quarters, nickels, dimes—his poker winnings over the last few weeks. His generosity was sweet, but she couldn't possibly lug a gallon jar to the Amtrak Station without drawing stares.

"Mr. Chen, I can't—" She cut off when he opened a pocket on her oversized coat and poured in coins. She found her voice as he moved to the other side, to weigh her down equally. "I won't be able to run if I'm lugging this much cargo."

"With legs like yours? You can run, Birdie. Now go. I'll keep the man upstairs busy. It'll give you time to get away."

"You'll do that for me?"

"Sure I will." Mr. Chen bounced his gaze across the pockets adorning her army coat. "Have you got the story with you?"

She'd placed the newspaper clipping from the *Akron Register* in a Ziploc bag for safekeeping. It was stashed in a zippered pocket above her heart.

Mr. Chen was the only person she'd shown it to. She didn't trust anyone else in the building, not with a potential windfall at stake. Every family had a legend or two, and while Birdie's clan also possessed stories of prison breaks and deals gone sour, a yarn from the Civil War probably didn't amount to much. It was also possible her mother, who was an expert at deceit but an amateur with the truth, had pruned important facts from the story. She wasn't above playing Birdie like a mark if it suited her purpose. And a tale of lost treasure, hidden away by a freedwoman when Abe Lincoln was in office, seemed more like a fairy tale than anything else.

But on the chance the newspaper article led to something of real worth, Birdie kept the clipping on her at all times.

She made a tapping motion over her right breast. "I've got it." When Mr. Chen nodded with satisfaction, she added, "Thanks for taking care of the guy upstairs. Oh. Give this back to him."

She pulled the man's wallet from her army coat and flipped it open. Jackpot—four hundred dollars was inside. It was more than enough to cover a quick grab-and-dash excursion to Ohio.

Pocketing the bills, she thrust the wallet at Mr. Chen. "Gotta go." The ceiling above them quaked. "I'll call sometime next week to see how you and Mrs. Chen are doing." She gave him a quick hug, then dashed out of the apartment.

A blast of November wind nearly took her off her feet as she headed down the street. The Greyhound station was only three blocks away. It was no problem to hoof it.

Thirty minutes later, she was elbowing her way through the crowded aisle to a seat in the back of the bus. The floor was wet with a slushy snow-rain mix. Somewhere up front, a baby's wail cracked the air. Newspapers rustled and someone popped open a can. As the bus lumbered from the station, she glanced out of the window at the buildings streaming past, a few parking lots, then they were outside of the city with the rolling Kentucky hills turning white beneath the falling snow.

She pressed her face to the window and blew out a breath. A moist haze settled over the countryside reflected through the glass. Sunlight pooled in orange puddles beneath the hills as the blue of night bled into the horizon. It would be dark soon, and her muscles were leaden with exhaustion.

Staying in any town for too long was never a good plan, but she'd really taken to the Chens. She didn't relish the possibility of never seeing them again. Mrs. Chen had taught her how to fold dumplings so the papery skins resembled tiny kites and Mr. Chen had become an unexpected confidant. The minor criminal tendencies that lured him to the card table enabled him to accept, if not admire, her larger transgressions. Their daily conversations about Mrs. Chen's cardiovascular health and the gossip they shared about the other tenants had provided an endearing constancy. It had been some time since she'd stayed in a city long enough to learn her way around, let alone make an acquaintance. Friendship was rare, a gem she unearthed when the Chinese immigrant lobbed questions at her every time he found her creeping down the hallway.

It might be several years before Birdie risked another friendship. By necessity, a thief avoided the gummy substance of relationships. Familiarity was dangerous leverage in an alliance if one member made her living slipping wallets from pant pockets and lifting bills from unattended purses. The threat of prison time plagued her and she'd tried to go legal.

Learning the knack was impossible.

Summoning up her mother's lessons required less discipline. In a busy department store, she'd dart through the mysterious contents of a purse swinging from a woman's shoulder while its nearly unconscious owner wandered through the silks and taffetas.

She didn't consider her targets 'marks' as her mother did. Rather she viewed the unlucky souls as members of a separate tribe. Her greatest shame came not from the money she took but from the personal mementos that found their way into the pockets of her coat: a crumpled grocery list, the cheery newsletter from an elementary school. A photograph of a family pressed close together before a mantle festooned with greenery.

Of course, she'd taken nothing from the Chens except their unprejudiced affection. For the space of nine weeks they'd been everything to her. Pulling her collar up to her ears, Birdie rocked in time with the rumbling bus. The loneliness she wore like a second skin became unbearable. She began chewing her nails.

Across the aisle, a man with a beard was devouring a cupcake with brown frosting. It dawned that her birthday was nearly over. Thirty-one years old . . . most women were settled down by now with a husband and children. Not that she understood much about family life. Her mother, the notorious Wish Kaminsky, never stayed long with any man. She'd dragged Birdie from state to state as if they could live with their roots sheared off or flourish without a sense of permanency.

The bus shook and bumped down the highway. Her mood sinking, Birdie slid low in her seat. Cupcake Man leered at her with dots of icing on his teeth. Curling her body toward the window, she drew out the Ziploc bag and unfolded the newspaper clipping with exquisite care.

Second Chance in Small-town America. A journalist named Hugh Schaffer had written the article. It was a nice feature with several photographs of the restaurant, The Second Chance Grill. The restaurant's owner had sold off everything she owned to save a local girl with leukemia. When the story broke last summer, Birdie watched the coverage on the national news. She thought nothing of it until her mother, Wish—who'd recently landed on the Fed's radar and was now scamming her way toward Mexico—mailed off the paper before hopping a bus in southern Ohio.

The article told of an auction at the restaurant. Once people learned the proceeds would be used to save the sick girl, every last item was returned.

Including a Civil War-era portrait in a shadowbox frame. Bringing the article close, Birdie gazed intently at the photograph.

Curiosity swirled through her. No, she wasn't responsible for the slaves her French ancestors had owned in the dawning years of the new republic. She'd only traveled through the South a few times and had never set foot on a plantation. Houses outside suburban Charleston now sat on the thousands of acres once owned by her forebears, the illustrious Postells. It was only fitting that their mansions had burned to the ground during the Civil War. Like slavery itself, they'd gone to ash.

Still, the story of a singular love had traveled down through the generations alongside the tales of slavery. Love between a plantation owner, who was Birdie's ancestor, and the beautiful slave who'd comforted him after his wife's death. The slave became a freedwoman and traveled north with riches given to her by her beloved. According to legend, the treasure had been stashed away for all these years.

Was any of it true? Birdie wasn't sure. The bits and pieces of lore gleaned from her mother never gave enough detail to tell.

In one of the *Akron Register* photographs, The Second Chance Grill's buxom chef stood in the foreground. But it was the portrait, clearly visible behind her, that gripped Birdie's attention.

Is the woman in the portrait the freedwoman Justice Postell?

She knew enough American history to realize a daguerreotype of a black woman, taken in the mid-1800s, was unusual. The dress she wore was elegant, the collar tightly ruffled with tiny beads—like pearls—scattered across the bodice. Could a freedwoman have owned a dress so luxurious? The portrait seemed to confirm the stories passed down in Birdie's family of how the plantation owner sent the black slave, Justice, north to freedom with hidden fortune. Once free, Justice became a successful businesswoman and wealthy in her own right. After she'd escaped slavery in South Carolina, where had she gone? In what state had she lived? The answer was shrouded in history.

Still, Birdie wouldn't have believed she was actually looking at a portrait of Justice Postell if it weren't for Hugh Schaffer's article. The feature seemed to unravel some of the mystery behind a scrap of parchment her mother kept in a safety deposit box in Santa Fe. Wish swore the parchment had once belonged to Justice and was a clue to the location of the treasure.

Liberty safeguards the cherished heart.

The parchment had been passed down through generations in Birdie's family as the once-proud plantation owners bred low and became a family of con artists and thieves. The cryptic message was never decoded. During those infrequent times when Birdie and her mother landed in the same city—and if they were getting along—they'd stay up late drinking Rum and Cokes and theorize about the meaning behind the words.

Every snippet of family lore agreed on one fact: Justice never sold whatever she'd carried north to freedom. Gold bullion? Antique French jewelry worth thousands on today's market?

Liberty safeguards . . .

So many guesses, and Birdie had never fully believed any of the stories. Until now.

The town where the portrait resided was Liberty, Ohio.

* * *

"Don't even start with the excuses, Hugh. You're fired."

Trapped inside the glass-walled office, Hugh Schaeffer planted his feet before the City Editor's desk and tried to get his bearings. Outside in the newsroom, journalists and copy editors were hard at work. He would have been too, if Bud Kresnick hadn't confronted him the moment he stepped off the elevator and ordered him into the corner office.

It was just like Bud to incinerate a relatively happy Monday by leveling threats. 'Relative' being the operative word. Hugh's latest live-in love, Melissa, had moved out of his apartment, taking his flat-screen TV with her.

Women, the thieving witches, always took something on the way out. His flat-screen TV. His microwave. Last March, Tamara Kelly made off with his entire sound system including the speakers he'd installed in every room of his condo. From the looks of the plaster, she'd used a blunt spoon to dig them out.

The weaker sex, my ass. Every last member of the *pilfering* sex should be banished to the seventh circle of hell.

Hugh grappled for a sense of calm. "You don't want to fire me." His trusty intuition warned that this time the City Editor would make good on the threat. "I'll work late. Move up the deadlines, pile on the work—I'm your man."

"Bullshit. You missed another deadline."

"An oversight."

Bud folded his hands over his expansive gut. "I went to press with a hole on page one. Know what I filled it with? Page four fluff. A ribbon cutting ceremony that'll make me the laughingstock of every respectable paper in Ohio."

"It won't happen again," Hugh said, thinking, *this is the third deadline I've missed this month.*

It wasn't his fault. Melissa had been spilling tears across his apartment, in some sort of premenstrual funk over the sculpture she couldn't finish. She blamed his vibes, claimed his energy was dark and repressive and his inability to commit thwarted her creative flow. He'd vacillated between consoling her and camping out in front of the tube to watch the Browns lose to the Steelers, with a six-pack at his elbow.

On the other side of the desk, Bud wasn't buying. "You've got an addiction, pal. Now it's cost you your job."

Hugh glowered. "I'm not a heavy drinker. Not anymore."

"I'm talking about women."

He flinched. "Okay—you're right. I need a twelve-step program."

"You also need a job since you're no longer employed by the *Akron Register*." When Hugh grumbled a protest, Bud waved the words away. "Listen, I was excited when I hired you. I knew you'd been thrown off four other newspapers. I also knew you'd once been a fine investigative reporter, one of the best in the state. I even felt bad last summer when I gave you the Liberty gig. You're a cold-hearted bastard, and writing cotton candy prose must've nearly killed you."

Which was true. Writing an upbeat feature about the money raised to pay for a kid's bone marrow transplant wasn't exactly Hugh Schaeffer material. No one had been gunned down at close range or absconded with thousands of dollars of public money. There was no sexual impropriety in high office to report or juicy grist about a corporation dumping some toxic stew into Lake Erie.

But he'd taken the assignment without complaint because Bud wanted to punish him for missing yet another deadline. *Not my fault.* Hugh was between live-in lovers at the time. When he met Zoe, a vivacious personal trainer, he left the article on union corruption in limbo.

Dodging the thought, he stuffed his pride. It was time to grovel. "If you fire me, there isn't a newspaper in Ohio that'll put me on the payroll. Not with five strikes against me." Nervous tension wound through his muscles—this would be the end of his career. What would he do? He'd be a failure, a has-been—he'd be pathetic. "I'll do anything. Give me one more chance."

At the desperation in Hugh's voice, Bud lowered his brows. But the City Editor surprised him when his expression softened. "Maybe you should try therapy."

"What?"

Bud slowly rubbed his chin. "Seriously, pal. Get a therapist. Talk about it."

"Talk about . . ." A sense of foreboding crept into his blood.

The members only club of newspaper editors was so tight knit, it was nearly incestuous. Had Bud heard through the grapevine about Hugh's involvement in the Trinity Investment scandal? Ancient history, but it was the kind of archeological dig that could bury a man for years.

Fourteen years had passed since he'd written the article that derailed his life. Had Bud learned the sordid details from a colleague? The article, written when Hugh was a rookie, brought him perilously close to his subject. Naïve and eager, he plunged into the murky world of celebrity when he was too young to comprehend the danger. Had he loved the celebrated philanthropist, Cat Seavers? Impossible to recall—the intervening years had washed away the particulars of his emotional state even if they hadn't absolved him of his sickly remorse. Her death and the subsequent uproar nearly destroyed him. He sought absolution in drink and women. He survived, barely, and his journalistic style became edgier, more in-your-face.

When he couldn't find his voice, Bud said, "What are you, two years away from forty? All you do is chase tail, which has me thinking you aren't chasing so much as running."

"I'm not running from anything," Hugh replied with enough heat to nearly convince himself. But if the City Editor had been a goddamn mystic he couldn't have been more accurate.

"Tell you what." Bud turned toward his computer and navigated through the Internet. "Remember those websites for the Perini girl? The ones where people donated cash for her bone marrow transplant?"

"Of course."

"They're still up, bringing in money."

"She had the operation months ago." Hugh's inner antenna went on alert. Why were people across the country still making donations? Blossom Perini was on the mend. "What's her father doing with all the cash?"

"Gee, Hugh, I don't know. Think he's funneling greenbacks into a vacation condo?"

"Could be."

"Lots of good people donated money for the girl's medical expenses. A real shame if Anthony Perini misappropriated the funds."

Hugh's brain whirled. "He could be doing anything—investing, buying cars—I'll bet he's already put thousands in his 401k, the bastard."

"You tell me."

"Okay, I will." It might take a few weeks to uncover the scam, but if it put him back in Bud's good graces, what the hell.

"But don't tell me on my dime because you're fired. You want to do some digging? Do it without an expense account from the *Akron Register*."

Stunned, he let out a gargled laugh. "You're telling me to spend a few weeks in Liberty without a paycheck or an expense account? Are you shitting me?" How much did he have in his checking account—a thousand dollars? Saving for a rainy day had never been his style. "If you want me to jump through hoops, I will. But not without greenbacks to make the gymnastics palatable."

"Then forget it. I'm cutting you loose."

The irritation churning Hugh's gut mixed with fury. "That's it? I'm fired unless I dig up dirt without pay?" Which wasn't the worst of it. Liberty was a time warp from the 1950s. They rolled up the sidewalks and turned out the lights at 9:00 P.M. No nightlife, nothing. "You think I'm so desperate I'd consider it?"

Bud picked up a pen and rolled it between his thumb and forefinger with galling disinterest. "I have work to do." He turned back to his computer. "And stay away from women while you're in Liberty. Who knows? You might produce decent copy if you give your gonads a rest."

"What sort of asshole demands work without pay?"

"Watch it—"

Hugh placed his palms on the desk. "I won't do it." Scowling, he leaned close. "You got it, Bud? The answer is *no*."

CHAPTER 2

Shivering on the cobblestone walk outside The Second Chance Grill, Birdie took stock of the small town.

Liberty Square was stirring to life beneath a slate colored sky. Bands of gold poked through the clouds to illuminate a scene from a bygone era, the brick buildings iced with snow and the cobblestone walks gleaming and wet, as if each shop owner on the Square had hurried out in the dawn chill with a broom and good cheer to sweep the place clean. In the window of the florist shop, bouquets of yellow daisies and shell pink carnations framed a poster from the local Girl Scouts for the father and daughter Princess Ball, to be held on Saturday night at the United Methodist Church. Cars drove by slowly to avoid the pedestrians dashing across the street, a few women with their children bundled nicely in heavy coats and thick scarves, and three elderly men with their bristled cheeks glowing in the frigid breeze. In the center green, business types in long coats streamed into the brick courthouse anchoring the north end of the Square.

An unsettling déjà vu gripped Birdie. This was her first time in Liberty . . . and yet it wasn't. She felt as if she'd been here long ago, the memory nearly a dream. The storefronts hemming in the large rectangle of the center green, the imposing brick courthouse—it was all intensely familiar. As was the restaurant with patriotic bunting festooned in the picture window, the door attractively painted Wedgwood blue.

Had she visited Liberty during her long-ago childhood? Uneasy, Birdie silently ticked off the elementary schools she'd attended, the entire depressing list. None were in Ohio.

Shrugging off the sensation, she entered the restaurant. Many of the tables were occupied: more business types, a few women with kids and several elderly couples. The counter's barstools were filled, and a waitress with a bad dye job dashed from one customer to the next.

Where was the picture of Justice? Birdie scanned the cluttered walls. The restaurant was like a museum of Americana, with pewter sconces competing for wall space with gilt-framed portraits and paintings of Colonial America. To her left, a businessman rose from his table and strode out, leaving his half-eaten omelet and his toast untouched. Birdie slipped into his seat. Snatching up the toast she ate quickly, her gaze bounding across the museum of artifacts on the walls. An odd feeling tugged again and she whirled, as if to catch someone watching her.

No one noticed her . . . and the portrait of Justice was nowhere in sight.

The feeling of being watched wouldn't abate and she hurried back out with the last of the man's toast. It was early enough to wander around Liberty without drawing stares so she strode to the back of the building. The alley lay silent beneath the soft-falling snow.

The building was large, three stories in all. Through the windows above, a swath of darkness filled the second and third floors, as if they were rarely visited and largely forgotten, and she wondered if the upper floors held nothing but supplies for the restaurant. The safest place to break into a building was usually in back. She didn't relish the thought of staying in the town any longer than necessary, and now was as good a time as any to check the place out. There was only one door, with an old-fashioned lock. She sorted through the pockets of her coat and found the two-inch file she kept on hand for this sort of occasion. The lock gave, and she dashed inside.

Noise from the restaurant's kitchen carried down the hall, a burst of impatient conversation and the clatter of pots. She skirted away from the commotion and up the shadowed steps. The second floor's narrow hallway led into a sea of black, the carpeting underfoot nothing more than waves of grey, and she stumbled forward in search of light. The corridor opened into a cozy reception area.

The walls carried the sharp scent of fresh paint. The seating arrangement appeared new. A big cutout in the opposite wall revealed a receptionist's desk on the other side. Nearing, she peered inside. By the phone, a stack of business cards read, *Dr. Mary Chance – Family Practice.*

She recalled the contents of the newspaper article. The good doctor had inherited The Second Chance Grill and resided in Liberty for just a few months when she took up the cause of paying for Blossom Perini's bone marrow transplant. Among the other antiques auctioned off then returned, the picture of a freedwoman had probably seemed insignificant. Wandering into the reception area, Birdie hoped that no one would notice when the portrait—and its hidden clue—disappeared altogether. Once she knew the portrait's location, she'd break into the building at night and carry it off. Given all the stuff in the restaurant, the loss would surely go unnoticed.

Satisfied with her plan, she studied the pretty green carpet underfoot. Two examination rooms lay ahead, and both were neatly filled with sparkling medical instruments and gleaming jars of cotton balls. Even here, the scent of new paint was strong.

Medical care wasn't something a drifter got much of, and she'd always been grateful for a hearty constitution. Life on the road meant head colds went untended and a sprained ankle was bound with tape stolen from the nearest drugstore. She frowned at the memories and the accompanying heartache. Even as a child she'd understood that complaining broke an unspoken rule. Her mother worked her scams from city to city, luring a man with her beauty, after which she'd take her ill-gotten gains and her kid and move on. Birdie saw the world as a kaleidoscope of people and events, a swirling mass of excitement that ended as quickly as it began.

She'd spent her childhood like a novice standing backstage in an adult play trying to learn the lines of her mother's script. When brought onstage she was the adorable tot of a woman down on her luck and in need of a man's protection. A certain type predictably fell for the trick, the sort of mark who joined civic groups and wore a conservative suit. There were always men to be had, innocent stooges with pathetically gallant natures.

Remembering those years feathered sadness across her heart. The child she'd been had bobbed her pigtails engagingly whenever the man called her sweet baby. She'd smiled, but her pleasure was never sincere, except for that one time when she was three or four years old, too young to understand the mistake of loving a man caught in her mother's web.

She'd paid dearly for the error.

Paw Paw.

His name, the city where he'd lived, the lines composing his face—time had erased the particulars save the affectionate timbre of his voice. If she saw him on the street today she wouldn't recognize him.

He must have been wealthy, because her mother had stayed in his city longer than usual while the temperature ground down to the single digits. Freezing rain hung from the fir trees like diamonds scattered amid the greenery and Birdie recalled a fever that left her dazed. Paw Paw, worried, took her to an emergency room where she was treated and released. He bundled her off to a house he must have rented on their behalf, the place so clean it looked new and the bed impossibly soft. He spent hours playing Go Fish with her while she recovered. The cards were made of a heavy stock easy for a child to handle and printed with vivid scenes of marine life Birdie found mesmerizing.

The cards, now worn a tired grey, were mere scraps of fleeting joy tucked inside her coat.

Drawing out of the troubling reverie, she left the office and retraced her steps down the stairwell.

* * *

Settled on a plan, Birdie left the Square and found a small hardware store a few blocks away, where she bought a pen flashlight and extra batteries, and a bag of potato chips to hold her over. She was still stiff from the long bus ride and spent the next hour strolling the streets of pretty houses. There had to be a cheap motel somewhere, even in a town as small as this one, but she couldn't find it. When her toes went numb inside her boots she started back up the hill to the Square. By the time she returned to The Second Chance Grill half of the breakfast customers had cleared out and she was able to grab a stool at the counter.

With renewed energy she surveyed the walls bursting with Americana, the large painting of George Washington astride a white horse, the brass sconces that might've been crafted in Williamsburg during the Colonial period. There was also a portrait of a man in a frock coat. Next up were a series of porcelain figurines she guessed were Pilgrims. Where was the portrait in the shadowbox frame? Frustrated, she slipped out the article from the *Akron Register* and examined the photo with painstaking interest, the heavy-set cook in the foreground and the portrait—it had to be of Justice—in the background. Had the photo been shot in the restaurant's kitchen? Was the portrait, a key to untold riches, hanging by the stove or a sink full of dishes?

"Do you need a menu?"

Startled, Birdie swung back around. "Yeah. Great." Stuffing the article back into her pocket, she gave the waitress, who looked about twenty years old, the once-over. "Nice hair."

The waitress's bubble gum-colored lips eased into a smile. "I was experimenting. Something went wrong."

Way wrong. The young woman may have started on the highlighting highway toward blonde but she'd veered off on the lime green exit. Her close-cropped hair bore a definite green hue on top of the sunny yellow color. Then again, she was young enough to pull it off.

The waitress tipped her head to the side. "I'm Delia Molek. Are you new in town?"

Birdie hesitated. She didn't have a story down yet. Was she visiting relatives? Just passing through? "Yeah, I just arrived," she hedged. "My name's Birdie Kaminsky."

"Cute name. And don't worry. All the publicity about Blossom has brought lots of newcomers to town. You aren't alone. Liberty is growing for the first time in years."

"Where's the hotel?" Birdie peered over the heads of diners, and out the large picture window. "I didn't see it on my way into town."

Delia snorted. "Are you kidding?" She slapped a menu down in front of Birdie, who'd suddenly lost her appetite. "If our population mini-boom keeps up, maybe we'll get a movie theatre. But a hotel? I wouldn't hold my breath."

"Where do people stay?"

"With relatives, where else?" The waitress rolled her tongue inside her delightfully plump cheeks. "Don't you know anyone around here?"

Since when was that a crime? Of course, Birdie usually scammed her way through cities. In a small town, a new face stood out. Cops in the sticks were best avoided and the neighbor next door might notice an afternoon burglary.

"I don't have any relatives in Liberty." The scent of bacon frying in the kitchen brought her hunger bounding back. After she ordered, she asked, "What about apartments? Is there a place I can rent by the week?"

"Mary's place is available. It's on the second floor, right above us. But I think she was hoping to rent by the month. If I were you, I'd grab it. There really isn't anywhere else."

She'd already canvassed Dr. Mary's new office upstairs—the door in the hallway she'd passed must've led into the woman's apartment. "Why is Mary renting her apartment?"

"She got hitched to Blossom's dad. Real spur of the moment."

"How much is the monthly rent?" After Delia told her, Birdie frowned. "That seems awfully steep."

"Trust me—there's nowhere else."

Which was a hassle since Birdie had no idea how long she'd be staying. She still had to locate the portrait of Justice. According to family legend, there was a clue attached to the picture, which led to the mysterious treasure. Of course, it might all be a tall tale. She might spend time in Liberty spinning her wheels for nothing.

While she ruminated, Delia returned with a plate of eggs, sunny side up, bacon, and a side of wheat toast. After the waitress poured coffee, she said, "So. Do you want to check out the apartment?"

"I don't need a tour of the place." Like it or not, she'd have to pay a month's rent. "I'll move in right after I finish breakfast."

"I'll tell Finney." Delia jerked her chin toward the swinging door, and the kitchen beyond. "She's the cook—a real nice woman as long as you don't piss her off. She'll ask for references."

"What kind?"

"The usual. Your last three places of employment, and the names of everyone you know in town." The waitress misread the horror on Birdie's face and quickly added, "It's not a big deal. Use me as a reference. We'll tell Finney you're a friend of the family."

The offer would've been suspect if it weren't for Delia's wide-eyed cheer. Stuck in this desolate town, surrounded by snow-covered cornfields, the waitress had probably lost half of her girlfriends to marriage and the rest to civilization. Yet the offer wasn't enough to put Birdie in the clear. She didn't have anything resembling an employment history. Stumped, she bit into her toast to stall for time.

When the silence grew daunting, she said, "My job history is a little sketchy." Delia puffed out her lower lip in what appeared to be a show of empathy. Emboldened, Birdie corralled her scattered thoughts and devised a plausible story. "I've been traveling. In Europe. I worked in a shoe store in London and a travel agency in Rome. Short gigs, but they paid for my Eurail pass."

Delia fiddled around inside her blouse and withdrew a stick of gum from her bra. "Sweet. I'd love to see Europe."

"I'll tell you everything once I'm settled in." She sensed triumph as the young woman's expression lit up. "I mean, Finney won't mind calling overseas to check my references, will she?"

"She'd make me walk to London to check you out before she'd pay for an overseas call."

"Then I guess I'm screwed."

"No, no—we'll think of something!" Delia raked her fingers through her hair. "There must be a way to get around the references."

Birdie was about to wholeheartedly agree.

Her optimism died when, from behind, a man said, "Delia, don't bother. You can't lease the apartment to her. I'm taking it."

CHAPTER 3

The angel in the army jacket swung around on her barstool and gave Hugh a look that needed no interpretation. Pure unadulterated loathing. He was out to steal her new digs in town. Evidently, she wasn't pleased.

Which was her tough luck. He needed a base of operations. It might take weeks to write an exposé about Anthony Perini's misuse of the money pouring into the websites for his daughter's medical bills. Those bills no longer existed. The dirt Hugh planned to dig up would make for journalistic greatness. Best of all, he'd get reinstated at the *Akron Register*.

He shrugged off her ire when Finney Smith, who'd presumably heard his voice, barreled from the kitchen and hurried around the counter.

"Hugh! What are you doing here?" The cook caught him in a bear hug, greasy apron and all. "Why didn't you tell us you were coming? Are you writing another article about Blossom? Oh, wait until Mary and Anthony find out you're back!"

Her excitement barely registered. The angel, with her white-blonde hair and eyes he'd swear were violet, hadn't stopped glaring at him. Then she spoke.

"Wait a second. You're *that* Hugh? The journalist from the Akron newspaper?"

Of course she knew who he was. The article he'd written about Blossom had been circulated far and wide. But the angel wasn't a local. He'd met nearly everyone in town last summer when he wrote the article. Not this woman. She was stunning, if bizarrely dressed in a combat coat that must have pulled duty in WWII. She was the kind of long-legged beauty whose thighs could put a man in a hip-hugging lock sure to send him into bliss.

You need to give your gonads a rest, remember?

"Hugh Shaeffer." He stuck out his hand, which she ignored. "I'm sorry about taking the apartment."

"You're not sorry. You look pleased, asshole."

"Nice mouth." Nice lips, actually—her language he could do without.

"Glad you like it." She turned back to Delia, who was snapping her gum and watching their verbal tussle. "He can't have the apartment. It's mine."

He turned to Finney and launched into a smooth series of lies. "Listen, I promised my editor I'd stay in Liberty until the feature's written. I'm doing a nice follow-up on Blossom."

Finney planted her hands on her hips. "Whatever you need, Hugh. Mary has no use for the apartment. She moved in with Anthony right before they left for their honeymoon."

"Honeymoon . . . Mary and Anthony?" If Anthony was AWOL, Hugh couldn't grill him about the websites until he returned. "When did they get married?"

"Last Sunday. Damn if we all weren't surprised."

"Where's Blossom?"

"Meade is staying with her at the house. I don't think you've met Meade." Finney grunted. "She's a real piece of work, all pomp and circumstance. The queen of cosmetics—she owns a company in Beachwood. I'm hoping Blossom will torture her and hide the evidence. I love that child."

Hugh barely heard the comment. The commando angel was digging bills out of her pocket in an attractive and growing state of agitation. "I'm taking the apartment," she announced, sorting the cash. "Delia, let me give you the rent."

Which was when Hugh realized she wasn't carrying a purse. He'd never before seen a woman without her everyday gear—a purse slung over her shoulder or a bag so large it could hold his golf clubs. And there was something else, something about her that put his inner antenna on alert. He got the sudden premonition, the one that always started his thoughts whirling. *There's a story here.*

While he tried to get a handle on what had sent up his antennae, Delia approached the cook. "Finney, she was here first. This isn't right."

The angel hopped off her barstool. "Not right at all!" She softened her tone as she cornered Finney. "Here's my rent—and an extra fifty dollars. No. Make it a hundred." She thrust the wad of bills into the cook's eager fist.

Hugh began perspiring when Finney stared at the money in a sort of rapture. Hell, if they got into a bidding war, he'd be broke when he did move in upstairs.

"I'll pay two hundred over the asking price," he said.

"Then I'll pay three hundred."

Finney whistled. "Oh, my. Now I'm in a real quandary."

Delia tugged on her sleeve. "Uh, Finney . . ."

"Not now! I'm working through my quandary."

The waitress tugged harder. "We've been running the 'Help Wanted' ad for three weeks now, haven't we? The only applicants have been teenagers. You've turned them all away." She winked at the flustered commando. "Her references are good as gold. She's an old friend of the family. I've known her forever."

The cook ran her fingers through her brassy blonde hair. "It's true I can't afford another hormonal teenager. All they do is break dishes and flirt with the customers." Finney sized up the angel. "I suppose you're old enough to be responsible, miss. I'll let you share the apartment with Hugh if you promise there'll be no misbehaving . . . and if you'll wait tables."

Hugh shouldered his way between the cook and Delia. "Hold on. I didn't agree to share the apartment." Until he was reinstated at the *Akron Register*, he was done with women. The commando angel was beautiful and hostile, a perverse combination sure to test his self control. "You can't do this. I need the apartment."

"And I have a business to run. I need a waitress to help Delia and that fool Ethel Lynn." Finney planted her hands on her hips and regarded the woman. "Well, miss? Do we have a deal?"

The angel shrank back as if she'd seen a rat scuttle past. "You mean I'd be waiting on people. Taking orders and stuff?"

Delia nodded eagerly. "We could sure use the help."

Hugh almost pitied her when she opened her mouth then closed it again. Finney, who also seemed to sense her distress, said, "We've been shorthanded for months. And Hugh's a big reporter so he gets first dibs on the apartment. He made our town famous, didn't he? Now, I can make him share the place with you. It's unorthodox, but seeing the two of you don't particularly get along I'm sure there won't be any shenanigans. Even so, if you can't wait tables you'll have to find somewhere else to stay."

The woman chewed on her lower lip. "I guess I can help you out," she finally said.

"How many hours a week do you want?"

"How many do I have to take? I don't have to work full-time, do I?"

Delia plunked her elbows on the counter. "Not if you don't want to! Part-time is great."

After they discussed hours, Finney returned to the kitchen with a load of cash—inspired by her negotiating skills, she'd hit up Hugh too. She was whistling off-key as the door swung shut behind her, leaving an uneasy silence in her wake.

Delia poured coffee and Hugh murmured his thanks. The angel glared at him with enough ire to melt sand into glass. Her fury was amusing—and damn enjoyable. Worming your way into a woman's good graces was an interesting challenge when she wanted you dead. Maybe he'd luck out and get some angry sex before she unpacked the kitchen knives.

Basking in her growing hatred, he slid onto the barstool next to hers. "Since we're stuck together, what's your name?" he said, thrilled when her gorgeous eyes flashed a deepening violet. If he brought her to full rage she'd probably resemble Helen of Troy. "We don't have to split the rent fifty-fifty. I'll talk Finney into giving some of your money back. I'll pay sixty percent, you'll pay forty."

She gave him a look that implied she was thinking about knocking him off his barstool. Then she surprised him by saying, "Let's try this—seventy-thirty. You're a hotshot reporter. You probably earn six figures. I'm a part-time waitress who only makes—" Digging into her breakfast, she looked at Delia. "What's my hourly wage?"

The waitress told her in a quick, grateful voice. Nodding with satisfaction, she threw her attention back on Hugh.

There was a whole forest fire in those violet eyes, the sort of feminine hostility a man could wrap around himself like a warm blanket of succor. *Hello, Helen.*

He dragged his attention back to his coffee. *You've sworn off women, remember?*

Then his trusty antenna went back on alert. He immediately understood why. The angel, still nameless, couldn't keep her eyes from straying to the walls of the restaurant. A reporter's inbred curiosity shivered through his veins.

She was searching for something.

* * *

"Blossom! What did you do to my dog?"

Flinging off the blankets, Meade Williams stormed to the door and yanked it open in the hopes of finding her quarry on the other side. In the corner of the guest bedroom her miniature poodle, Melbourne, yipped wildly.

The red plaid bows behind his ears were gone, no doubt snatched by the devilish thirteen-year-old she'd agreed to patrol for several days. Worse still, a gooey substance dripped from his toothpick-sized legs. Beneath the goo, his white fur was covered in an art fiend's metallic . . . sparkles. And Blossom Perini was nowhere to be seen.

Mad with rage, Meade scooped up Melbourne and stalked down the second floor hallway of the Perini house. Why, why, *why* had she agreed to watch Blossom while the kid's father and new stepmother were on their honeymoon?

Not long ago she'd wanted Blossom's father, Anthony, for herself. She'd foolishly underestimated what it would be like to raise his daughter in the bargain, especially after the media coverage launched Blossom's story onto the national news. The teen's successful battle against cancer was heartwarming, to be sure, but no one who knew her personally would describe her as a saint. Of course, folks across America thought Blossom deserved a halo—as did Dr. Mary Chance, Liberty's only town doctor and the unlikely owner of The Second Chance Grill. Mary connected with the girl in a way no one else did. Perhaps she even enjoyed the more devilish aspects of Blossom's personality.

Meade flew down the stairwell with Melbourne bouncing beneath her arm and yipping all the way. It was truly unbelievable how she and Mary had gone from being rivals for Anthony to the best of friends. On second thought, maybe it wasn't surprising. They were two professional women who had discovered a mutual love of tennis and a nearly frenzied devotion to Royal Doulton china. They'd been on a shopping expedition in search of porcelain figurines to add to their respective collections when Mary made the request: watch Blossom during the honeymoon.

Meade stormed into the kitchen. She should have said *no.*

At the stove, Blossom serenely flipped pancakes. By the back door her golden retriever, Sweetcakes, sat at attention. The rotten dog sized up Melbourne then ran her tongue across her snout.

"Oh, no you don't, Sweetcakes." Meade opened the door to shoo the dog out. "If you frighten my baby he'll piddle all over the floor."

Blossom gave an elaborate sigh. "Your dog doesn't piddle—he's marking his territory. Only this isn't his territory. You should have his thingies removed."

"I'll do nothing of the sort." Meade spun around to face the teen. "You're in hot water, young lady. Why do you keep terrorizing me? And what did you put on Melbourne?"

Shrugging, the girl flipped another pancake. "I don't know what you're talking about."

"I've had it—"

"Seriously, Meade. Chill. Want some coffee?"

The aroma wafting from the sweetly percolating pot *was* enticing. "Did you lace it with arsenic?"

Blossom slid a stack of pancakes onto a plate. "What's arsenic?"

The kid knows how to Google. Don't give her any ideas. "Never mind." She sat and lowered Melbourne to the ground. He trotted toward his food bowl shedding sparkles in a happy trail. "You're giving my dog a bath after we finish breakfast. Are you listening? You need to be punished."

"I get to bathe the gerbil?" Grinning, Blossom set the pancakes before Meade. "No problem, muchacha. I'll take care of your dog."

"Forget it. I'll bathe him."

"No, really, I'd like to."

"Cut the crap. You'd like to feed him to Sweetcakes."

"Okay—you got me." Blossom set a cup of coffee before her. "Drink. Grownups never make sense until they've been dosed with caffeine."

Meade grudgingly brought the cup to her lips. *Heavenly.* How did a thirteen year old make coffee so divine? But then, Blossom Perini was full of surprises. She'd managed to beat leukemia, hadn't she? Looking at the girl's corkscrew curls and rosy cheeks, it was hard to imagine she'd ever been ill. Yet she'd nearly died of leukemia before the bone marrow transplant saved her life. And that was the real miracle, wasn't it? Blossom's new stepmother, the valiant Dr. Mary Chance, had only been in town for a few months when she found out about the girl's struggles. When it became clear there wasn't money enough to pay for the bone marrow transplant, Mary placed all of the antiques in The Second Chance Grill on the auction block. The restaurant, which first opened in the mid-1800s, was the city's oldest historical treasure and much of the furniture, artwork and other decorations were worth thousands. People arrived from all over Ohio to put in bids.

Everything sold quickly, only to be returned once word got out as to *why* Mary was raising the money. Then the story exploded on the Internet. Websites sprang up, donations flowed in, and Blossom was soon on her way to recovery.

The phone rang, pulling Meade from her musings. Blossom sprinted across the kitchen. She exchanged pleasantries with the caller then handed over the receiver. "For you."

Not a call from a client, surely. Business colleagues wishing to reach her cosmetics importing company knew to call the office in Beachwood. Worry clenched her stomach. She'd only given the Perinis' number to one person.

Rising, she moved from the table for privacy. "Dad? What's wrong?"

For several minutes, she listened to his latest tale of woe. She'd hired a gardener to winterize the landscape surrounding her father's estate, a move that had seemed sensible—until now. "Dad, the gardener isn't peering in the windows. You're being paranoid." The anxiety in her voice brought Blossom near. "Yes, I'm sure the gardener isn't spying on you . . ."

Ten minutes and much cajoling later, she finally hung up. Unsettled, she set her plate in the sink. There wasn't time this morning to drive out to the estate. She had to get Blossom off to school and leave for work.

From behind, Blossom asked, "Is everything okay? You look sad all of a sudden."

Her voice held sudden compassion, and Meade managed a smile. "I'm fine," she lied.

"What's wrong with your dad?"

"Nothing." Another lie, but there wasn't an easy way to describe chronic depression to a child. "He likes to worry."

"Can't your mom calm him down?"

"My mother died a long time ago."

"It's tough to be without a mom. Even for someone as old as you."

Meade crossed her arms. "I'm forty-one—not exactly ancient."

"Yeah, but it's hard anyway."

The girl's voice wavered, and guilt washed through Meade. It was common knowledge that Blossom's mother had run off when she was a toddler. Which might explain why the kid got into so much trouble. Not that Meade wanted to find patches of Melbourne's fur on Sweetcakes' snout, but still.

She flicked Blossom's chin. When the girl brightened, she said, "Can we call a truce until your dad and Mary get back from their honeymoon? I'll stop making comments about your table manners if you'll take my dog off death row."

"Can I think about it? I've been working on the other tricks up my sleeve." Then Blossom surprised her when she added, "But hey, if you need to talk, I'll listen. I know what it's like to worry about a parent. Before Mary snuck into my dad's heart, I worried about him all the time."

Sorrow engulfed her. Mental illness wasn't simple, and it encompassed more than worry. Guilt, for one. A feeling of helplessness. And loss—certainly loss, of the man who'd once fathered her with gentle grace and rapt attention.

"Blossom, my situation is different." It was the most simplistic explanation she could muster. "My dad has . . . problems."

Concern puckered Blossom's brows. "He sounded confused on the phone. He must be pretty old, right?" She slipped her hand beneath the curly mass of her hair and tapped her temple with charming concern. "Is it his head?"

More like his heart, but there was no way to explain. "He's not senile, if that's what you mean."

She stared at the girl who liked to torment her, a teenager who suddenly looked older, more compassionate. Then Meade's vision began to blur and anguish filled her soul.

She looked out over the years and saw the lake. How she'd stood on the pier with desperation churning her blood and her throat hoarse from arguing. The waters were frighteningly calm beneath a sky thick with clouds. The wind rose up. The air pressure sucked the wind into a fulcrum and Meade, with a mariner's eye, looked north. Canada lay on the other side of this, the shallowest of the five Great Lakes. The waters of Lake Erie were warm, too warm, and autumn's first blast was barreling down from the north.

Please don't go out on the lake. There's a small craft advisory, a storm coming.

But her mother wouldn't listen. Cat pressed the envelope into Meade's palm, the photographs that held proof of their ruined lives, and climbed into the skiff. Two boxes lay astern. No doubt Cat, always dramatic, planned to dump their contents into the waters. It never occurred to Meade that her beautiful, self-absorbed mother might also send herself to the bottom of the lake.

"Meade?" Blossom placed tentative fingers on her arm, drawing her from the shore. "What are you thinking about?"

Speechless, she struggled away from the lake with her heartbeat ringing in her ears.

CHAPTER 4

Birdie crossed her arms and surveyed Hugh's mountain of luggage. "You sure don't travel light," she said.

He shoved another suitcase inside the door. "If you're a good girl, you can help unpack." He slid the case beside the duffel bag he'd already deposited in the growing heap of luggage. Then he dug a wad of bills from the back pocket of his jeans. "I convinced Finney to return most of your money. Feel free to show your gratitude. I'm all yours."

Taking the cash, she stared at him pointedly. "Do you always flirt this much?"

He kicked the door shut. "Only when I'm confident it'll get on a woman's nerves."

"You've hit the mark, pal."

Which wasn't exactly true. Despite herself, Birdie found his come-ons amusing. She'd visualized the reporter who'd written about Blossom as much older and nothing like the testosterone-drenched hunk before her. The word *journalist* called up an image of a man with nose hair down to his lips and a cigar clenched between his teeth. Some guy older than Andy Rooney with Mike Wallace's surly disposition. She certainly hadn't been prepared for the real Hugh Schaeffer.

With hair darker than midnight and eyes to match, he looked like Lucifer's younger brother. His easy smile and faded jeans lent a careless sexuality and his houndstooth sports coat smelled enticingly of men's cologne. Not that she'd dare have a fling with a guy who made a living exposing people's secrets. She had enough skeletons to fill three closets. And send her down the river for five to ten.

He peered in the kitchen before pausing in the living room. "We're really moving up in the world. If this place were any smaller Thumbelina would feel crowded."

Following, she studied the frayed couch and mismatched curtains. She'd stayed in dozens of places like this but he seemed disenchanted with their new digs. As if she cared. "It's not so bad."

"Whatever." He started down the hallway. From over his shoulder he asked, "Will you tell me your name? I can't stand the suspense." When she did he added, "Where are you from, Birdie?"

She heard him rattling drawers in the bedroom. "I'm from all over," she called. "My family moved around a lot."

"Is your dad in the military?"

Prison. "Something like that. Actually, I did the moving around with my mother."

When he grew silent she wandered back into the mini-foyer. A cream Nautica sweatshirt poked out of his duffel bag. It looked deliciously soft, and she'd been wearing the same clothes for twenty-four hours. Shrugging out of her coat, she donned his sweatshirt then—bingo—found a pair of men's boxer shorts further down in the bag. Peeling off her grungy jeans, she stepped into the boxers. Roomy . . . but nice.

A guy as well groomed as Hugh probably owned more bath products than a diva. Crouching, she snapped open a suitcase.

"I didn't give you permission to rummage through my things."

She looked up. Hugh stood several feet away, scowling. "Do you have something to hide, Mr. Reporter?"

"No. Do you?"

"Not today. By the way, where do you keep the bath gel and the toothpaste? It'll save time if you tell me which suitcase to check."

"Cute. You're a stand-up comic and a thief."

The last hit too close to home. "Like you said, I'm just rummaging." She started to her feet with her chin tilted haughtily. "Can't you share or what?"

Hugh wasn't listening. His devil dark gaze followed her ascent, the heat igniting in his expression making her ankles wobble. He zeroed in on her legs, naked below his skimpy boxers. Spots of color bled across his cheekbones.

He swallowed. "My mistake. Rummage away." Their gazes tangled, and a dangerously sexy grin eased onto his lips. Muttering a curse, he scrubbed his palms across his face. When he came up for air he'd replaced the grin with a look of distaste. "On second thought, stay out of my stuff and we'll get along fine."

"Don't hold back with the sweet talk."

"Cross me and there'll be hell to pay."

"Keep laying it on, dear."

Nearing, he wicked away her bravado with the advantage of height and a quiet and very masculine sort of impatience. "Ground rules," he said, backing her into the wall. "I don't have to share my stuff. We're stuck together but I don't have to like it. I don't have to like *you*." He scoured her face with disdain. "And, babe, if I decide to sweet talk you, you'll know it."

She glared at him. The man had a short fuse—she'd have to watch her step. Sharing an apartment was a no-brainer, sure. If she spent the next week padding her pockets with his cash it would be all to the good. With luck, she'd find the portrait of Justice and follow the clues to the treasure, whatever it was. She'd make off with the loot without revealing any secrets.

She'd also clean out Hugh.

By the time he figured out what hit him, she'd be halfway across the country with a fortune in gold bullion or a cache of artwork. Or she'd make off with enough jewelry to live easy for years to come. She'd also snatch the best pickings from his gear and all of his cash.

Even so, he *was* a reporter. He might start asking questions she didn't dare answer.

"Where's your luggage?" he asked, as if on cue. "Still in your car?"

* * *

Three hours later, she escaped the apartment with her secrets intact. Hugh had peppered her with questions she avoided by darting into the bathroom to shower.

When she returned, tingly and pink, they agreed they both needed a nap. Trying to earn points, she casually offered to let him have the bedroom. He was paying more rent, she said, plying him with a gracious tone so effervescent she swore her teeth might rot. Naturally, any decent guy would offer to camp on the couch while insisting the woman take the bedroom. A lady needed privacy to paint her toenails or sort through whatever items she'd stolen during the day's work.

It was a shock when he readily agreed to keep the bedroom, cementing his status as no gentleman.

Not that she was a lady. And, with chivalry dead, when she awoke to his snoring drifting down the hallway she lifted a twenty from his wallet.

From the restaurant below, tantalizing scents wafted heavenward. At the bottom of the stairwell, she hesitated. The shouting inside the kitchen would send most people fleeing but she had a heist in her future and needed to locate the portrait of Justice. Drawing up her courage she hurried forward, only to discover smoke billowing from the massive stove in the center of the room. An old woman, oddly done up in her Sunday finery, was flapping her arms.

"Hells bells! We're doomed!" The ruffled sleeves of her dress brushed across veined wrists. "Quick—put it out!"

Shoving the woman aside, Finney slammed a lid over the flames. "Didn't I tell you to stay clear of my stove?"

"You said nothing of the sort."

"You're as deaf as a post. Back off, old fool. I've got red blazing before my eyes!"

The cook's tirade brought Birdie to a standstill. Finney Smith was fiery and attractive in a heavy-set sort of way, but she didn't seem like the sort of woman to mess with. Her gaze settled on Birdie, who saluted.

Finney gave a short nod of approval. "Tell me you're working the dinner shift."

Birdie inched toward the dining room. "Um . . . I don't start until tomorrow."

"You got an appointment somewhere in town?"

She had an appointment to find the portrait of Justice, which probably didn't count. "My social calendar is empty at the moment."

"Put on an apron, get out to the dining room and help Delia." Finney grabbed the fluttering old woman by the shoulders. "Take this with you."

Birdie shrunk back. "What is it exactly?"

"A thorn in my backside." The cook prodded the woman forward. "This here is Ethel Lynn Percible. She's been waiting tables and doing the books at The Second Chance since before you were born. Get her to retire and I'll owe you."

Who worked rigged up in a daisy-dotted dress and a saucy church hat of pink velvet? "You mean she'll be helping me and Delia out front?" Of course, there was an additional problem. Birdie had never waited tables in her life.

Ethel Lynn's hat slid sideways as she approached. Birdie stepped back. "Heavens, child, don't be afraid of Finney's bad temper. Why, she's evil to the core but she won't hurt you."

Finney leaned over the stove to check a bubbling pot. "I'd like to hurt you, old bat. Come near my stove again and I will."

"Idle threats." The woman proffered her hand. "It's nice to meet you. I already know who you are, Birdie. What a delightful name."

"It's short for Bertha." Birdie grimaced. "My mother had a sick sense of humor."

"Apparently." Ethel Lynn straightened her hat. "Why don't you take your coat off, dear? Gracious, it's awfully big for a slender girl like you."

From the stove, Finney waved a spatula like a sword. "There's an extra uniform in the closet back there by the sink."

Worry rooted Birdie to the spot. Everything worth keeping was inside her coat: money sewn into the hem, tools of the criminal trade deftly hidden in secret pockets. The few private remnants of her life were also tucked inside. Complying with the command was *not* a good plan.

"Why don't I run back upstairs and leave my coat in the apartment?" As the words left her lips, she remembered Hugh, asleep upstairs. What if Mr. Reporter rifled through the pockets? "Nix that. I'll keep it on."

Finney sliced the air with the spatula. "While you work? You'll overheat."

"I'm cold—freezing, really." She checked the closet and found a white shirt with black piping. There was also a black skirt sized for a much shorter woman. She held it up. "This skirt is too small. It'll barely cover my ass."

Something in the cook's expression warned she'd take enjoyment in stringing Birdie up if she didn't get changed, and fast. Thankfully, the cook's narrowed gaze returned to Ethel Lynn. Mortal enemies, those two. Birdie made a mental note never to be caught standing in front of Ethel Lynn if Finney was throwing cutlery.

The cook marched across the room and grabbed Birdie by the shoulders. "Go. Hang up your crazy military garb. Put on the uniform. *Now.*"

Several hours later, Birdie thought she'd run enough miles to qualify for a track and field event at the Olympics. An employee-training program didn't exist at The Second Chance Grill—Delia thrust a pad into her fist and shoved her into the hungry mob.

Which wasn't so bad. Sure, she dropped a few plates and poured coffee on one of the tables. But compared to Ethel Lynn, she was the epitome of calm. The old woman screeched whenever a plate slid to the edge of her tray. She twittered when waiting by the pass-through window for an order. She dropped a bowl of tapioca into a toddler's lap and, while serving coffee at table nine, bashed into a man's head with the coffee pot.

But Liberty was a small town. The restaurant's diners seemed familiar with Ethel Lynn's high-strung constitution. The man, quietly rubbed his aching head, ducked the next time she approached. The toddler, a boy, took a daisy from the vase on the table and handed it to Ethel Lynn. It was touching to watch the diners treat the old hen with affection.

The townspeople were just as friendly with each other. Birdie slowly wiped down the counter as a middle-aged lady with a constellation of freckles sauntered from table to table bestowing kisses and hugs. Her generous spirit altered the energy in the room, smoothing over the tantrum of a toffee-skinned tot at table three, who veered from tears to rapture when she whispered sweetly in his ear, and bringing an elderly gentleman to his feet, his arms beckoning her in for a short waltz between the tables of delighted onlookers. The lady settled at table five, where a younger woman waited with a bright smile. When the women embraced and the older one planted another kiss, Birdie absently feathered her fingers across her own cheek.

She'd spent her life drifting from state to state. It had been years since anyone kissed her. The last man she dated, a gambler in Reno, stole most of her cash on his way out of the relationship. Desperation brought her a woman roommate in St. Louis, but they'd lived in wary silence. Even the Chens, who'd been her only friends in Kentucky, had known to keep their distance.

Mesmerized, Birdie wandered to the end of the counter. The two women bent their heads, deep in conversation. What did it feel like to experience such closeness? Neither woman kept an eye on her purse. In between the hushed smiles and soft laughter they could've been stealing each other blind. They weren't. Such unquestioning trust was overwhelming to behold. How did people *do* that?

When Birdie got to work picking pockets she worked with dreary intent. The anonymity of a bustling street corner was preferable to a roomful of diners whose names were becoming familiar. It was easy to work the crowded dining room, and she netted fifty dollars. She'd drop something on the floor, a spoon or a fork, and snatch a wallet on the way up. Safe behind the counter—and if both Delia and Ethel Lynn were in the center of the dining room—she'd rifle through the wallet, slip out a few dollars, and then return it to its unsuspecting owner.

Through it all she kept an eye out for the portrait of Justice. In a room so crowded it was difficult to check the walls. People stood on the sidelines, chatting with neighbors or fussing with children who wouldn't stand up or sit down, and the walls were chock full of antiques. She'd nearly given up hope when, at closing, a man beside Delia chuckled loudly.

Birdie stopped clearing dishes and lifted her head. Her legs were on fire with exhaustion and her mood low. Glumly, she glanced at the man as he moved away from the cash register.

And there, on the wall behind him, was the portrait from Hugh's article.

No wonder it had been impossible to find. People stood in front of the cash register all night paying their bills and gabbing with Ethel Lynn and Delia. Not one of the diners glanced at the picture. Of course, they weren't aware of the secrets hidden behind the freedwoman's dark eyes and regal poise. They didn't know about the clue supposedly hidden beneath the gilt frame or the promise of untold riches.

Birdie started toward the portrait with her breath catching on her lips.

CHAPTER 5

Hugh awoke on a gargled snort.

Where am I? He peered through the darkness of a bedroom that sure as hell wasn't his condo in Akron.

Christ—I'm in Liberty. He groaned, remembering: he'd lost his job at the *Akron Register* yesterday and was stuck in the boondocks seeking redemption. He needed to write a stellar exposé on Anthony Perini, the thieving bastard who was AWOL on his honeymoon.

In a best-case scenario, Anthony had thousands in ill-gotten loot. He was soaking up cash from the people sending money to the websites for the nonexistent medical expenses of his nowhealthy kid.

Scratching his belly and considering the possibilities, Hugh wandered through the apartment's cramped living room and into the even smaller kitchen. If he was trapped here for a few weeks he might as well make the best of it. He'd been furious when he'd stormed out of the *Register*. He'd fled back to his condo to throw stuff into suitcases as if he'd show the City Editor, Bud Kresnick, who was boss by packing up and leaving for good.

Hugh scrubbed his palms across his cheeks. He was a pathetic bastard, a journalist skidding toward oblivion. Too many years had been spent chasing tail instead of doing his job. He'd been a real human being once—he'd even been engaged twice. Now he was nothing more than a self-pitying, unemployed writer.

Flicking on the lights, he studied the kitchen. He liked an orderly environment, so he wiped down the counters then found the dishwashing soap beneath the sink. Within minutes he'd washed the few plates and glasses growing dusty in the cupboards.

Through it all he worked in a state of sexual frustration that brought back memories of his pining adolescence. Irritated, he stalked into the hallway to grab his luggage. What was his problem? It wasn't as if he hadn't had sex lately. Melissa had been in one of her jungle moods before everything went sour and she dumped him. So why was he mired in illicit thoughts?

Then he remembered.

He wasn't flying solo in Liberty. He was sharing his digs with the sullen commando angel, Birdie-with-no-last-name. Maybe his brainpan had shorted out on the information, but his body sure hadn't. Sharing digs with a sun goddess, even one outfitted like a guy in the army, was sure to test his self-control.

Was this his punishment for all the years he'd put women before work? If so, he'd take his lumps like a man. He'd write the Perini exposé and get the hell out of Liberty with his newfound chastity intact. Resuming work at the *Akron Register* took precedence over his gonads, hands down.

The living room couch was a twining mess of blankets. He checked his watch; it was after midnight. His inner antenna went on alert. He doubted Birdie had friends in town and there wasn't any nightlife to speak of. So where was she?

* * *

Through the picture window the streetlights threw bands of silver across the dining room. A feathery snow was falling in Liberty Square, dusting fir trees and cobblestone walks. The bell atop the county courthouse glinted in the moonlight. Turning away, Birdie padded through the shadows toward the portrait of Justice. Her heart thumped beneath her ribcage.

It had been a hassle waiting to check out the portrait. After they'd closed the restaurant, common sense warned her to stay in the apartment a reasonable amount of time before coming back downstairs. Surely the cops patrolled the Square until midnight and people might still be out on the street. Resigned to testing the boundaries of her patience, Birdie had dozed on the couch with the timer on her wristwatch set. When her watch gave out a series of rings she'd hurried downstairs and broken in through the back door.

She stared up at the portrait of the proud black woman with a sense of awe. So many stories surrounded the freedwoman. Supposedly she'd loved Birdie's ancestor, the plantation owner Lucas Postell. Had Justice gone north with a bag of gold Lucas insisted she take? With jewelry? Was the treasure gone, sold long ago, or still hidden away somewhere? Birdie's mother, convinced the world was out to screw her over, worried the treasure was lost and she'd never profit from it.

Birdie's grandfather, before he'd whittled out the end of his life in the New Jersey state penitentiary, believed Justice was pregnant when she undertook the dangerous journey to freedom. In a desperate act of love, Lucas gave her something of great worth. The way Birdie's grandfather told it, Justice never cashed out because she was generous and pure. She'd considered the treasure a legacy belonging equally to her unborn child and the white branch of the Postell family tree.

Hard to believe, since most people were driven by greed. Certainly everyone in Birdie's family was. Yet she preferred her grandfather's theory not simply because something of worth might be found. She liked to think of Justice as someone who'd risen above her base desires. Secretly she imagined the freedwoman as a paradigm of virtue.

Maybe the stories were true and Justice bore a child with Birdie's ancestor. Which meant Birdie had more family than she knew of, black relatives who might have done better with their lives than their avaricious white relations.

Hungry for the truth, she grabbed the sides of the frame to remove it from the wall. The portrait was heavy. Stumbling, she managed to lug it to the counter and set it down.

Family lore agreed on one fact: the portrait hid a clue to the location of the hidden treasure. Examining it would take time. Trying to see in the darkened room was impossible. Risk turning on a light? If Hugh woke upstairs he might notice the glow knifing across the snow. Or a cop might investigate. Finally she noticed a pewter sconce on the wall that held a candle.

Wiggling the candle free, she lit it and returned to the portrait. She dropped the candle into a juice glass and stared hard at the swirls of burnt umber and deep rose comprising the image of Justice. She half expected to find writing hidden in the deft strokes of paint but nothing looked like a clue. Frustrated, she ran her fingers across the frame's heavy scrollwork. The ornate curls were feathered with gilt paint, and she wondered if something was etched in the wood. No dice. Was the clue hidden inside the backing paper?

Turning the portrait over, she drew out her switchblade. Carefully she peeled off the tan backing paper. And felt gravity shift when a small rectangle of yellowed parchment dropped out onto the counter.

Nearly faint with excitement, she blew out the candle and returned the portrait to the wall. Stumbling through the kitchen, she nicked the corner of the stove before managing to stuff the clue in her bra. It wasn't safe to examine the contents until she'd locked herself inside the bathroom upstairs.

"Hey, there."

Her heart slammed against her ribs. Beneath the reddish glow of the kitchen's Exit sign, Hugh lounged against the wall.

"How did you get in here? I locked the door behind me!" she demanded without thinking.

He shrugged. "Fatman Berelli."

"What?"

"Fatman." Hugh strolled through the shadows toward her. "He's one of my contacts in Youngstown. Union guy, big as a Sumo wrestler. He's branched out—now he's a private investigator. Fatman taught me all of the dark arts including how to pick a lock."

Speechless, she tried to get her bearings. Did Hugh mean he knew she'd broken in too? It was unlikely he'd buy a story about Finney leaving the door ajar after closing up for the night. The cook was as territorial as a Rottweiler.

She stumbled toward the massive steel refrigerator. "I was hungry." She wrestled the door open. "Do you want something to eat? How do eggs sound?"

"That's a freezer. Are you planning to thaw the eggs, assuming you find some? Everything in there is frozen solid."

So it was. The shelves were packed with frigid bricks in white paper. Maybe she'd grab one and hit him on the head. When he came to his senses, he'd find the aggressive Finney standing over him. It would be his problem.

He came up behind her, too close. The nerve endings on the back of her neck crackled. "Do you mind?" She nailed him with a nasty look. Which must have been faulty ammunition because delight sparked his inky gaze. "Back up, Hugh. You're standing too close."

"I'm trying to see your eyes. It's dark in here."

"Stop staring at me."

"Are they really violet?" He took hold of her chin, angling her face toward the Exit sign's glow. She froze. "Wow—they are. And I'm worried your light blonde hair didn't come out of a bottle."

"Why are you worried?"

"Because if it's real, you're blonde all over. I'm having a heart attack thinking about it."

"My hair is natural." She tried to jerk free but her feet had a mind of its own. Or minds of their own, since she had two. *Think your way out of this!* "Are your eyes really black?" she asked. Obviously her brain wasn't under her powers of persuasion either.

"Dark brown, actually. Do you like them?"

"No."

What she'd like was a taste of his lips. Hugh's mouth was incredible—full lower lip, with pearly white teeth hiding underneath. She'd gone stupid all right, but it *had* been a long time between relationships.

He drew his fingers down her waist. "Do you want to have sex? A short détente before resuming hostilities?"

"Not right now. I'm making eggs." Did he get any action with lines like that?

Putting her self-control into a fist hold, she rammed into the door to the walk-in cooler, swore at it then pulled the damn thing open. "Hey, I found the eggs and some veggies. How do you feel about a spinach and Swiss omelet?"

"I'm on the fence. Am I the one cooking?"

"No."

"Then I'm off the fence. Should I find a skillet?"

"Sure."

He also found a light switch beside the massive sink. The glow wasn't much but it surely wasn't visible from out front. They'd be safe.

"So will you tell me why you broke in here?" he asked while she whisked eggs. "I'm not prying. I'm curious."

"You're more than curious."

That didn't come out quite how she'd intended, and Hugh grimaced. "You got me." He handed over the spinach. "I'm sure we'd be great in bed together. But you're right—we should skip the fireworks."

"So you're easy even when it's not the Fourth of July?" She connected with his gaze and flushed. She began chopping up the spinach with gusto. Her self-control was already mincemeat. "Listen, I wouldn't mind having a fling with you. But it wouldn't stop there. You'd talk."

He looked offended. "I would not."

"I mean you'd talk in bed and expect me to share. My business is private. I'm not stupid enough to chat beneath the covers with a newspaper reporter. All I need is to find my life story in the *Akron Register.*"

"Meaning your life *is* a story? I'm intrigued." He leaned against the stove as she poured the frothy eggs into the skillet. "Which is why I'd love to know why you broke into the restaurant. What were you hoping to find?"

Turning on the heat beneath the skillet, she was aware that her private thermostat was already rising. "I thought I left something down here. I didn't want to wait until morning to get it."

"Lies, foul lies." He smirked. "Thinking of making off with the cash in the till? I wouldn't if I were you. Finney has a temper. Think Pompeii, with people fleeing."

"I'll take it under advisement."

She split the omelet in half and slid the pieces onto plates. Handing one over, she took a moment to look at him closely. Apparently the man was hungry—his attention hung on his meal, giving her the chance to appraise him carefully. He looked tired in some indefinable yet soul-killing way.

"What are you doing up this late?" she asked suddenly. "Did bad dreams wake you?"

He surprised her when he nodded. "The same dream, actually. Only it's more like a play-by-play." He held up his plate. "Should we dine upstairs?"

"Good idea." She snapped off the light and followed him to the stairwell. "What do you mean, play-by-play?"

From over his shoulder, he gave her a long look. Nothing casual in his eyes—she was asking questions he didn't want to answer. *Touché*. But something touched her heart, a fleeting emotion. Hugh wasn't like any man she'd ever met—he seemed stable, grounded in ways she didn't understand. He might even be likeable.

Was the flirtatious and fast-talking reporter plagued by nightmares?

If so, she wanted to know why.

CHAPTER 6

Meade peered out the window with misgiving as Finney barreled across the porch of Anthony Perini's house.

Calling Finney hadn't been easy. The woman didn't talk. She stampeded through conversations. Yet at half past midnight Meade couldn't think of anyone else to call.

The cook stomped into the circular foyer without knocking.

"Are you nuts?" The words came out in a hiss, presumably to avoid waking Blossom. "Where are you going this late at night? I was asleep when you called."

"Doze on the couch until I get back." When the cook glared, Meade added, "It *is* an emergency."

Finney gave her the once-over, taking in the turquoise knit top Meade had thrown on after she'd hung up with her father. "You're dressed awfully nice for an emergency. If you're meeting someone, I'll kill you for messing with my sleep cycle."

Did Finney think she had a *date?* "I'm not seeing a man," Meade snapped, and then reconsidered. "Actually, I *am* seeing a man, but not like you think. Not that it's your affair."

"Don't use a high-and-mighty tone with me. Women like you draw men like flies to a manure heap. If you think I'll watch Blossom while you're out at all hours—"

The tirade came to an abrupt halt at the sound of the tinkling bells on Melbourne's collar. The poodle trotted into the foyer and the cook stared at him with palpable distaste.

"Is the rat staying while you're gone?" Melbourne stopped beside her, his furry ears perked, and Finney moved back. "If he tries to mark me, you won't be putting him out for stud service. Not after I'm through with him."

"I'll put him in his cage, all right?"

"With a muzzle? I don't need him yipping."

Meade prayed for patience. She'd had a long day. After escaping the office, she arrived at the house to find Blossom filling the place with ear shattering hip-hop. She nearly blew out her larynx before the music was turned down. Blossom insisted on making a strange dinner of Cocoa Puffs and fried chicken, which was probably common fare among the teen set. Once the girl trudged upstairs, Meade tried practicing yoga to regain her center. She'd been about to drag herself to bed when her father had called in such an agitated state she'd felt compelled to drive out to the town of Goose Grove to check on him.

Wrenching a promise from Finney not to harm Melbourne, Meade started on the lonely drive. An autumn moon sat above the tilled farmlands, fat and golden. This close to Lake Erie the temperature was near freezing, the sparkle of water visible between thick stands of trees. Reaching Belfair Lane, she drove with trepidation toward the mansion.

In the moonlight, the large brick Tudor looked like an abandoned fortress. Huge urns, which held massive blooms during Meade's childhood, stood empty with chips and cracks glinting in the cold light. The windows of the mansion, wrought iron between panes speckled with rust, wore a greasy film of pollen and soot. On the rolling lawn, piles of maple leaves were stiff with November frost.

Regret tightened her throat at everything lost fourteen years ago. Every year since then seemed to whittle away more of the estate's glamour and beauty. All the memories she'd held dear had collapsed into the black hole of her mother's death.

With a heavy heart, she went inside.

The housekeeper, Reenie, rose stiffly from the bottom step of the wide, curving staircase. Her white hair was knotted at the base of her skull. As she approached, Meade spotted new lines arcing from the corners of her eyes and an increasing droop to her mouth.

"Thank God you've arrived!" The housekeeper clasped Meade's fingers. "I can't find your father. I've looked everywhere. He must be somewhere on the grounds."

"Did he wear his coat?" He'd grown increasingly forgetful. Depression was like an acid eating through his mind as surely as his health. "Oh Reenie, he's not wandering outside in his pajamas, is he?"

"Good heavens, I hope not."

Meade smoothed the fear from her brow. There was no sense in upsetting Reenie further. Increasing the housekeeper's anxiety over her stubborn and unpredictable employer wouldn't solve anything.

"Go back to bed, Reenie." She strode across the foyer and stepped inside the closet. Coats were everywhere, hung haphazardly or dumped on the floor. She found a pair of hiking boots, the soles crusted with mud. She put them on. "Did you check the boathouse?"

"I didn't see any lights."

"Which means he's sitting in the dark." She ushered the housekeeper toward the staircase. "Go on. I'll find him."

At the back of the house the tiered patio floated in a sea of shadow. An owl hooted from the woods, its voice lonely and strong.

The sound of the lake, a low rumble of waves beating against rock, grew in intensity as she started down the path. She'd once loved the open expanse of blue-green water and the rush of wind in her face as her mother drove the powerboat in undulating circles too close to shore, or away from land at ferocious speed to open water. Her father never went on the lake. He preferred a life sequestered in the library surrounded by financial ledgers and dog-eared copies of *The Wall Street Journal*. A banker by profession, his days were spent shepherding the assets he'd gained through marriage and growing the legacies of Cat's illustrious friends. Meade, their only child, was pampered and spoiled. She'd tried to emulate her mother's grace and had been awed by her father's prodigious intellect.

Now the sight of the lake stabbed her with regret.

She paused on the path to rub the chill from her arms. The darkened boathouse, nestled beneath fir trees at the water's edge, was moored in silence. The cream paint was so faded the wooden slats shone through. A shutter on one of the windows hung ajar like a black flag.

She entered with her breath locked inside her lungs. The oblong table in the center of the room was heaped with fishing poles and tackle. The organic scents of marine life clung to the air, and a host of memories accosted her. She shielded herself from the blow and quickly scanned the murky dark.

The moment her eyes adjusted to the darkness she spotted her father perched beneath a window.

"Dad?" His silvered head turned. Moonlight caught the side of his face, turning his fierce blue eyes a smoky grey. "What are you doing out here?"

"Thinking." He stared at her for a long moment as if needing to reboot his brain. His expression clearing, he asked, "Why are you here? Did we have an appointment?"

"You called several hours ago. You were upset. Don't you remember? Reenie called later when she couldn't find you."

"Reenie doesn't need to look after me. Why isn't she asleep?"

Knowing how to proceed was difficult. Through the grime on the window, the lake shimmered like a galaxy of stars. Meade looked away from it, praying for strength. Her father's hair was pungent and unwashed. His pants were spotted with grease or food; it was hard to tell which, and she didn't have the courage to turn on a light. Dampness pooled beneath his eyes.

Taking care not to startle him, she stroked his arm. "Why are you upset?"

He looked out at the lake. "I'm trying to decide."

"Tell me what's going on. You're scaring me."

He sighed and the long, drawn-out sound tightened her resolve. He didn't like confrontations and his temper rose from within his agonized silences with stunning unpredictability. There wasn't a road map for depression, no sign-posts to aid with navigation. He'd be withdrawn for months before something set him off, the least little thing.

He surprised her when he checked his temper behind a thinly veiled defiance. "I saw her today," he said. When she merely stared at him, he added, "Don't try to talk me out of it. When I was in Liberty, I saw her."

"Dad—"

"No. She was there."

Did he actually think he'd seen Cat in town? The sorrow nearly swamped her. She'd lost her mother in a mishap on Lake Erie that had been relentlessly televised throughout Ohio. She'd lost her father soon after. The maelstrom of bad publicity had destroyed his career, then hurtled him into despair.

She let the heartache roll through her, allowed it overtake her for one excruciating moment. Then she tamped it down and clasped his shoulders. "Stop it. She's been gone for a long time now." She gave him a shake to impart some of her pain, to make him share the weight of an unnecessary burden. "Your mind is playing games with you."

The words fell like thunder. Her father was deaf to them. "You don't understand." He pulled away and stumbled to his feet. "I saw her in Liberty. I wasn't imagining things." His voice broke. Then he drew himself straight. "She's come back to me."

* * *

The slip of yellowed parchment—a clue to the location of the hidden treasure—was safely tucked inside Birdie's bra. Containing her excitement was a struggle. She'd have to wait to read the message until after finishing the late night supper with Hugh.

Entering the apartment with her plate balanced on one hand, she fought for patience. How easy it would be to hurry off to the bathroom, lock the door, and read the clue.

Even as she imagined ditching Hugh her attention strayed to his face. To his eyes, which were red-rimmed and framed with faint shadows. When he'd discovered her in the restaurant he'd mentioned waking from an upsetting dream. Actually it was a nightmare, something about a play by play, as if, while he slept, he'd relived some distressing event in his life. Not that it was any of her business.

If she started asking questions, she'd ramp up the intimacy between them. They were already sharing close quarters. They could bicker all they liked but the sexual attraction between them was nearly thick enough to see. The last thing she needed was a short-lived romance mucking up the works. She'd found a clue in the portrait, hadn't she?

She'd wondered her entire life if Lucas Postell had sent untold riches north with his beloved. The clue hidden in the portrait gave the story weight: At the dawn of The Civil War, something of great value was spirited out of the Deep South by the freed woman slave, Justice, who was probably his lover. She kept the treasure for safekeeping in a northern state—Ohio. The slip of parchment found inside the portrait might lead to a bag of Civil War gold bullion hidden somewhere in the restaurant. Or a cache of jewelry waited to be unearthed by a determined thief with a reporter on her tail and a plate of eggs in her hand.

Skirting around her, Hugh asked, "Where are we dining?"

"I'd rather eat alone. No offense."

"None taken. But I'm joining you."

"If there's no other choice." Birdie came to an abrupt standstill in the kitchen. "Hold the phone, Parsnip. What happened in here?"

The kitchen was immaculate. A lemony scent wafted from the linoleum floor. The countertops gleamed. Even the window above the sink looked sparkly and new. Did Mighty Maids have a satellite office in bucolic Liberty, Ohio? Doubtful, which meant Hugh had done the cleaning.

She spun around and gaped at him.

Which must have rattled his tender emotions because he blushed. "Who's Parsnip?" he asked, no doubt to steer her away from making wisecracks about his feminine side. "A friend of yours? Does he run numbers with your other pal, Mr. Potato Head?"

"It's an old joke. When I was a kid, a man who dated my mom called me vegetable names."

"How endearing."

"Not nearly as endearing as your domestic skills. You're quite the nester."

With jerky movements, he set his plate on the table. "The place was filthy. I cleaned up. So what?"

She cocked her hip against the doorjamb. "You keep a fine house, darling."

"Give it a rest, Turnip."

Grinning, she ran her fingers across the gleaming counter. "You steal my apartment, take a nap and when you wake up, you . . . clean. Like a happy housewife from one of those sixties shows on late night cable. I'm touched."

The chair made a scraping sound as he pulled it out and sat. "I'm all about order. Everything in its place."

"Will you do laundry and leave chocolates on my pillow?"

"It depends on what I get in return. For starters, tell me why you broke into the restaurant. Were you robbing the place?"

A direct assault, and there was no way to prepare for incoming. For an excruciating moment her brain turned to mush. Not the best state of affairs for a thief who survived by her wits.

She sank into a chair. "I was just looking around."

"Sure you were." He studied her with unnerving intensity. "Do you always steal from your employer? There's not much loot in a restaurant. Maybe they need a bank teller at Liberty Trust."

"I never steal from people I like." Horrified by the outburst, she backpedaled. "I mean, Finney is a little tough and Ethel Lynn is weird. But Delia is nice—they're all nice."

Hugh rubbed his jaw. "So if you didn't like them you *would* steal from them?"

She would, but it wasn't his business. "I can't chew and talk at the same time." She dived into her omelet. "Shut up and eat."

"I knew it. You *are* a thief." He dug in with relish. "It must be a hard life. Do you worry about prison?" he asked between mouthfuls. "Waiting until someone hides a file in a pastry and you can escape? I would."

Frustrated by Hugh's powers of deduction, she shrugged out of her army coat. And immediately regretted her decision when he stopped eating. Leaning sideways in his chair, he took in the skimpy waitress uniform while she squirmed. His attention danced from the gold piping embellishing her breasts to the ruffled hem, which revealed no small section of her thighs.

He pointed at her with his fork. "You'd draw rave reviews in whorehouses across Paris."

"Go to hell."

"I meant it as a compliment." He shoved eggs into his mouth, tried to swallow, and choked.

When he grabbed his throat, Birdie rushed to the sink. She filled a glass with water and thrust it at him. After the long day waiting tables she didn't need a run to the nearest emergency room. Not unless she could dump Hugh off on the curb and get away with his car. She gave him a few good thumps on the back.

Oh, why hadn't she learned the Heimlich maneuver? Concern for his welfare warred with the lure of grand larceny and she cringed when he pushed the glass away and stomped his foot.

When he finally sucked in air, she drew back. What if Hugh drove a Mercedes or a Beemer? Maybe she *should* offer to take him to the hospital.

Before she decided her position on auto theft, he began mouthing the words stuck in his throat.

"Fishnet stockings," he croaked. When she crossed her arms, he had the sense to ditch the bedazzled expression. "I mean it. All you're missing is a little whore's netting on your gams."

Searching for a hostile retort, she noticed Mr. Clean's duffel bag still propped in the corner. Given the amount of gear he'd arrived with, he'd probably run out of shelf space in the bedroom closet. Sifting through the bag, she found a pair of sweatpants and another softly worn sweatshirt like the one she'd stolen from him earlier today. This one was emerald green.

Pulling it on, she threw back the only rejoinder that came to mind. "In the restaurant, what did you mean about a play-by-play?" She sat back down and reached for her plate.

Thankfully the question doused the passion in his gaze. "I don't want to go into it."

"Why not?"

Darting his fingers through his hair, he gave himself a sexily disheveled appearance. When his ebony gaze wavered, her heart lurched. Doubt bloomed on his face.

Some cajoling was in order. "C'mon, Hugh. Your secrets are safe with me." The hesitancy in his eyes made him more likeable even if she was loath to consider why. "How bad can it be?"

"Let's just eat and hit the sack."

"I'm not sleeping with you."

"I didn't mean together. Not tonight." He stabbed repeatedly at the spinach poking out of his omelet. When the leaf was suitably impaled, he stuck it into his mouth.

Now the man was as buttoned up as a stockbroker on Wall Street. Which was fine. He liked putting her on the hot seat with questions about her line of work. Time to take as well as he gave.

She let out a theatrical sigh. "I'm waiting," she said, and immediately regretted the desire to push. The question bore down on him, curving his shoulders and sending pain flashing across his brow. The fear scuttling his features took her by surprise. He really was upset.

The silence grew full. Finally, he said, "I wrote an exposé fourteen years ago when I started out at a newspaper in Cleveland. It was my first big story, about an investment firm in the city. The guy running the place was playing fast and loose with the sweep accounts."

She tried to keep up. "What's a sweep account?"

He warmed to his story. "If a company pours millions of dollars through an account, a bank pays interest daily. Let's say you keep, on average, twenty million in the account. You rack up interest every day."

"Nice deal. Where's mine?"

He swiped his hand through the air, silencing her. "The investment firm used the sweep as a way station for client funds before putting them into the stock market, mutual funds—wherever clients were investing. The firm's owner stole from the sweep. I found out about it."

"You wrote an article about the theft?" She'd have to watch her step or he'd be writing about *her*.

"It was front page news." Hugh laughed, but the sound was hollow. "I was so proud of the scoop even though I knew the guy would only get a slap on the wrist. He had powerful friends and a crack attorney. His wife was wealthy and all the money was repaid to the investors. But it didn't end there. What I didn't expect were the repercussions the publicity had on his wife."

Dread shivered across Birdie's skin. "What happened?"

"She learned why her husband was stealing from the sweep. He was seeing another woman and had bought her a pricey condo. The works. All sadly predictable—a bored middle-aged man and a hot blonde ten years younger."

Birdie thought of her mother, how she glided through life on other people's money. But she stole from innocent men, not bastards who cheated on their wives. The bastards had it coming to them. "Please tell me the blonde took him for all he was worth."

"She did, but it gets worse. His wife had a shouting match with the other woman in the middle of a department store. Because of the wife's standing in Cleveland—she was a prominent socialite and philanthropist—it made the gossip columns. Not to mention every radio talk show from here to Cincinnati."

An awful memory edged to the corner of Birdie's mind, a fleeting image of a woman in an elegant suit. The woman smelled of roses. She was shouting and someone took Birdie by the wrist to tug her out of the way. It was impossible to grab hold of the nebulous threads of the memory but it left her feeling oddly blue.

"The wife took her boat out on Lake Erie right before a storm," Hugh continued and she wheeled her attention back to him. To his hands, which he clenched and unclenched, his knuckles white. "They said it was an accident. She drowned."

His guilt looked overwhelming, which was something she understood. Didn't she feel the same way every time she lifted money from a wallet?

Rising, he collected the plates and deposited them in the sink. Clearly he'd lost his appetite. They both had.

Absently, he dumped the eggs into the wastebasket and filled the sink with soapy water. He attacked each plate with a dishcloth, scrubbing with single-minded purpose. The set of his jaw was hard. Yet his eyes were vulnerable and Birdie found herself on her feet, walking toward him. What was it like to hold yourself responsible for a death? None of her transgressions compared, not the robberies or the petty thefts. She'd never owned a gun. If it ever came down to risking a life in the commission of a crime she'd walk away first. She'd walk away gladly.

She came up behind him, unsure of how to comfort a man who was little more than a stranger. His back was to her and she noticed his hair was too long even if he did carry it off well. His shoulder blades worked beneath his chambray shirt as he let out the water, then dumped in scouring powder and began scrubbing the sink. Why hadn't she noticed his height? Standing this close it was easy to see he had a good three inches on her, maybe four, and she was a tall woman.

Rub his back? It was how a friend offered comfort. Yet the gesture felt like an invasion. Her hand froze in mid-air, her confusion unnoticed by the man who'd dried the dishes until they squeaked and rattled them into a stack inside the cupboard. He polished the forks and flung them into a drawer. When he'd finished he gripped the edges of the counter and stared out the window above the sink. She understood suddenly what he'd meant by a play-by-play. His dream, or nightmare, rather—the image haunting him—was a play-by-play of the woman who'd drowned, the woman he believed he'd sent to her death with an article written in his youth.

Offering solace with a phrase was inadequate. *It's not your fault.*

Hugh wasn't to blame—people did all sorts of crazy things. Hadn't Birdie's own mother shaken out a handful of heart-shaped pills on the day she'd threatened suicide? The Valium looked pretty, like candy, but it threw a wall up in their tumultuous relationship. And how could a teenager convince her mother not to die? Birdie had felt responsible; she knocked the fistful of Valium from her mother's hand, sending the pills scattering across the motel's filthy bathroom floor. On hands and knees she scrambled after them. Every last pill landed in the toilet while her mother clawed at Birdie's scalp, yanking hair out by the handful. *You bitch, don't you dare throw my drugs in the toilet.* Seared by the belief she was responsible for her mother's mental state, she'd barely felt the hair wrenched from her scalp.

Did Hugh carry the same remorse?

"Hugh, it's all right." She rested her hand on his back. He tensed, a fierce little movement, and her heart clenched. "Fourteen years is a long time to punish yourself. Let it go."

His arms lowered to his sides. "If you were in my shoes, would you let it go?"

"I'd try."

"You don't know what it's like. Wondering if you could've done more. Wondering if everything would be fine if you'd done nothing at all."

Flinching, she saw herself at sixteen, when she had given up on trying to live with her mother. The canvas tote bag stolen from a boutique was stuffed full of everything she held dear. The contents were light, inconsequential, as if her life didn't matter to herself or to anyone else.

"Still, I'd try," she said, the hurt cascading over her in waves. "No one said life is simple. You keep moving. You try to forget the bad stuff and move on."

Hugh turned and regarded her. "I tried letting go." He smirked but she wasn't fooled. He was raw and didn't like showing it. "First, I broke my engagement to my college sweetheart. I screwed up the next relationship too."

"Hugh—"

"Afterward, I had a love affair with Scotch," he said, refusing to let her get in a consoling word. It seemed he needed to flail himself in front of her even if she didn't understand why. "I drank my way out of a few good jobs. Talked my way onto other newspapers. I'm beyond rehabilitation even if I have gotten myself off the sauce. Birdie, some mistakes don't go away. You live with them like a disease you manage but never cure."

He did look sick, the guilt a cancer on his soul. She couldn't cure him. It wasn't wise to try. Yet she felt compelled to do something, if only to wash the moment clean.

She went up on tiptoes like a clumsy ballerina. Pressing herself against his chest, she took his face in her hands. She kissed him full on, the way she'd kiss a man she knew intimately. Hugh shuddered. Then he jerked his hands up, splaying them across her back. Her heart tripped as he took control of the kiss as if she were his first taste of heaven.

Curving into him, she sank into sensation. The pads of her fingertips scraped across the bristle shadowing his cheeks. She let her eyes drift shut to better focus on the experience. Hugh felt like heat and tasted like glory. No hesitation, no doubt—he kissed her as if he'd done so a thousand times before.

When he'd finished, he let her go. A mistake. Her knees dissolved and she nearly slumped to the floor. Deftly, he grabbed her by the shoulders.

She blinked. "Thanks." She edged out of his grasp.

"Thanks for catching you or for kissing you?" He took a strand of her hair and rubbed it between his fingers. There was a nice flush on his cheeks and some of the light was back in his eyes. "You have incredible hair. Spun gold." He drew away. "Goodnight, Birdie."

He left without another word. No sexual innuendo trailed in his wake. Steadying herself, she leaned against the counter. Rating a man's kissing ability was silly but Hugh deserved a ten.

He'd put a lazy sort of luxury into her veins and she couldn't clear her head. It wasn't worth the effort to analyze why she'd kissed him. It would be even worse to analyze why she'd like to do so again.

Finally she remembered the parchment tucked inside her bra. At the other end of the apartment the bathroom door clicked shut. Seating herself at the table, she withdrew the parchment and unfolded it.

And read the heavy, sloping script:

A jewel beyond compare stitched tight
With red, blue and white.

CHAPTER 7

Theodora Hendricks propped her Remington pump shotgun at the snowy base of an oak, surprised to see Landon Williams making his way across the wooded acres of her property.

Worry formed a tense patchwork of lines across his long-jawed face. His shoulders, set rigidly in his tall frame, seemed posed to ward off a blow. Surely he'd arrived at daybreak without invitation not because he'd misplaced his manners—Landon was courteous to a fault—but because he required her counsel.

And although she was hard-pressed to admit it, their unlikely friendship was a cherished part of her rich and unusual life.

Nearing her eighty-first birthday, Theodora still enjoyed hunting when she wasn't piloting her sky blue Cadillac through the streets of Liberty. She was something of a fixture in town, a crusty old black woman who'd lived long enough to see it all and then some. She had more acquaintances than anyone should be cursed with, but Landon was one of her few real friends. Most of the people she'd once cared about had been whittled down to nothing more than memory while she chafed under the curse of longevity.

There was no figuring why life worked out the way it did. Squirrel stew, buttermilk biscuits and venison steaks had kept her fit and irritable for years. Or maybe the hunting kept her in shape. She'd always been irritable.

"Morning, Landon," she called when he started down the incline.

The former investment banker brightened at the sound of her hard, grating voice. He came around a poplar tree, waved, and then frowned at his boots. This far back in the woods the land was swampy, the smell of earthworms and fungus thick in the air. She chuckled as he sunk ankle-deep in a patch of mud.

Behind him the sun crested the forest in a glow of pink light. A Canada goose lifted from the lake, breaking the silence with a honk.

Landon stopped and looked around. "You didn't answer the doorbell. I assumed you were out hunting."

"I have a hankering for duck." She motioned toward the trees guarding the lake. "I'm on my way to fetch tonight's supper."

"My apologies. I shouldn't have disturbed you."

"You didn't." She rubbed her arms, silently cursing the arthritis that never abated until noon. Above, the goose arced into the sunlight, its black wings beating air. "Do you want coffee? You look damn cold."

Landon stomped his feet. "Would you mind if we walked instead? I've had too much coffee as it is."

Picking up her shotgun, she headed toward higher ground. The gun was nearly as tall as she was—the one thing aging *had* taken was her height and she'd never been tall in the first place. She drew the weapon over her right shoulder like a fishing pole. She glanced up at Landon, who looked pitifully sad, and waited.

He kicked a stone from the path. "Meade is worried about me. It was a misunderstanding, but I couldn't find a way to explain."

"It doesn't take much to worry your daughter." Of course, Landon's depression gave the girl reason to fret. "What happened?"

He cast a murky glance. "I inadvertently led her to believe I'm seeing ghosts. Cat's ghost, in fact."

"Lordy." Meade didn't much trust Landon's mental state as it was. "If she thinks you're having visions of your late wife she'll pack you off to a fine institution."

"I should've cleared up the misunderstanding." He raised his hand then wearily lowered it to his side. "Meade arrived unexpectedly. She found me in the boathouse."

Had she found him weeping? Theodora sighed. Landon was a good man, and not nearly as off-center as his daughter thought. But he'd shielded too much of his life from Meade, especially after his wife drowned in Lake Erie fourteen years ago. He was like a magician lost in his own smoke and mirrors.

"Why did she think you'd seen Cat's ghost?" Theodora asked.

"I saw someone in town, someone who left years ago. I couldn't explain."

"Why the blazes not?"

"Meade never would've believed me. I'm hoping you will. In fact, I'm sure you will."

His implicit trust slipped a latch in Theodora's brain, opening her to memories vast and distended, like a drawn-out sigh. Her oldest daughter, in first grade, insisting on the concrete fact of the tooth fairy's existence. Her husband, shortly after Kennedy's inauguration, working over her heart with soft words while she fingered the lipstick-splotched collar of his Tasty Cream uniform. The fish tales she'd heard from friends who tried marijuana in the seventies and repented the following Sunday or, in the eighties, surreptitiously bleached their skin along with their hair. Recently, the whoppers she endured came from her great niece who was between jobs and always hungry for a handout.

"I'll believe you," she heard herself say, and it wasn't a lie. She'd lived long enough to wear her skin down to a vaporous film that let her walk right out of herself and into other folks' shoes. And from Landon's point of view he *was* telling the God's honest truth.

He waited half a tick, then said, "In Liberty . . . I saw . . ."

Suddenly Theodora understood. "The Greyhart woman? After all this time—that varmint is back?" She lowered the shotgun from her shoulder, setting the butt in the snow. "It's not possible!"

"I was passing by The Second Chance Grill. I don't know why I looked in the window—a feeling, I guess. There she was, sitting at the bar. I should've gone inside to speak with her but I was overwhelmed."

"You're sure it's her?" The woman had broken Landon's heart time and again. She deserved to be horsewhipped. "Don't jump to conclusions. The world is chock-full of pretty blondes with hearts as dark as the devil's."

The blunt edge of the insult started a muscle twitching in his jaw. "You never met her. I can't expect you to understand. She's had a difficult life."

"Haven't we all."

"She's not evil. Mixed up, perhaps. She's always needed my help."

She's a swindler. Theodora wiggled her hunting cap down over her ears. Inside Landon's imagination he'd built a shrine for the Greyhart woman. Nothing she said would change his views. The toxic brew of love and libido did awful things to a man. It blunted his common sense and made him a willing participant in his own destruction. Damn it all! Landon's mental state was fragile at best. The possibility of Greyhart tangling him up again was the worst of all outcomes.

She studied him carefully. "Maybe your medication is acting up. That psychiatrist who likes to fish around in your brain—maybe she put you on something punky, something not fit for your constitution. You must've been seeing things when you moseyed on by The Second Chance."

No one else would dare to bring up mental health issues with the proud banker, but Landon trusted her. Didn't most people have acorns rattling around inside their heads? Whatever problems the man suffered, he was no more off-center than most.

"I'm not taking a hallucinogen." His voice rose like a guitar string plucked too soon. "Theodora, please try to understand. I'm sure I saw her. I stood outside the restaurant for more than five minutes watching her to ensure I wasn't mistaken."

Knowing how to proceed was damn hard. They'd never discussed the love affair in much detail, and it had been years since the black-hearted woman skipped town once and for all. She'd taken a chunk of Landon's wealth with her, and it had been enough to make him spiral into despair. The banking scandal broke soon after, sending Landon's wife, the spoiled, self-absorbed Cat Seavers, to the bottom of Lake Erie. All of it was a fine mess. No, Theodora didn't want to hear the details of the love affair. Delving into the topic would give her a three-alarm headache.

Carefully she asked, "Why would Greyhart return after all this time? After Cat drowned, half the reporters in Ohio were nosing around your affairs. It was enough to scare her away for good." If she'd returned, was she planning to dip her fingers into Landon's bank accounts? "Say you're right and she *is* here. My advice? Stay holed up in your house. Don't go into town at all."

"I have to," he said, and his eyes glowed. Age sifted from his face, making him appear frightfully young—young enough to make a fool of himself. "If there's any chance she's returned, if she's in Liberty . . . Theodora, I'd be remiss if I didn't call on her."

"You're too old to be unzipping your pants for a lover who's burned you more times than I can count."

He flinched beneath her harsh assessment. "I *must* see her."

The guitar note again, pealing out the man's desperate love. It brought Theodora to a standstill in frustration and remorse. The hank of flesh the Creator put between a man's legs was a curse. All the hardships women endured—none were so awful they brought a woman to her knees on account of lust. None broke her mind the way Landon had been broken by desire.

She gave him a hearty thump on the arm. "That woman put you in a heap of trouble," she said, and thumped again. "I'm not saying I blame her for Cat's death. Your wife was headstrong. She had no business going out on Lake Erie with God spitting thunder and pouring down enough rain to sink Noah. If you see Greyhart and call on her, what good will come of it? Better to let sleeping dogs lie."

Twigs crackled underfoot. Mention of Cat bowed Landon's shoulders. He walked on with sadness forming around him like mist. Why didn't men leave well enough alone? He was in his sixties now, old enough to shut down his mojo. Was he actually hoping to start up again with the woman who'd ruined his life?

Theodora sighed. "Here's what I'll do," she said. "I'll go into The Second Chance and ask Finney and Delia if they remember the woman. Maybe they talked to her. I'll check this out if you'll stay put."

"You'll go today?"

They were setting down terms of a wager. Landon's heart, and his sanity, were held in the balance. Apprehension curled in her belly, greasy and thick. She was getting in the middle of something she shouldn't touch with a ten-foot pole.

Finally, she gave a stiff nod. "Done."

* * *

In the back of the Liberty Municipal Library, Hugh flipped open his laptop and stared blankly at the screen.

He hadn't been himself since Birdie laid a kiss on him last night. A major blunder. She'd ambushed him by the sink and aimed one right on his mouth. Of course, he'd reacted to their sudden détente with a full-out assault, taking command of the kiss with enough fervor to send his common sense fleeing for the hills.

What made him pull back, what stopped him from surrendering to her enchanting violet gaze and sweet caresses was the bone chilling knowledge that Birdie Kaminsky was getting under his skin.

Forcing his attention back on work, he entered one of the websites raising money for the medical expenses of Anthony Perini's daughter. A collage of patriotic images blinked on the computer screen. People across America were still sending in money. The heart superimposed over the cartoon version of Uncle Sam continued to expand with each new donation.

More donations were streaming in every day. How much exactly was anyone's guess.

Exiting the site, Hugh jotted down a few notes. If he wanted his job back at the *Akron Register* he had to unlock the secrets of Anthony's perfidy. Where was all the ill-gotten cash? Anthony was still incommunicado on his honeymoon. Grilling him in person would have to wait. Hugh didn't relish the thought of staying in Liberty, not with an addiction for Birdie simmering in his veins.

Hadn't he promised Bud Kresnick, his boss—or ex-boss, if he didn't bring in the goods on Perini—that he'd stay away from women? Agreeing to share the apartment was a major blunder. Birdie was worse than liquor, a long, smooth drink of a woman. She'd have him intoxicated with lust if he didn't work on his abstinence training.

If her physical beauty weren't enough temptation, there was her complex personality to consider. Whenever he tried to pry into her life she hit back with a snitty response. Yet last night she'd displayed unexpected sensitivity. She possessed the long, leggy beauty of a woman who'd look good in mink and pearls, but she skulked around in old jeans and an army coat that had probably seen duty in the Normandy Invasion.

She seemed lonely, the type of woman who avoided serious relationships. And, for reasons unknown, he'd confided in her. He wasn't in the habit of chatting about his past debacles. He sure as hell never opened up with anyone about the Trinity Investment scandal. Why had he done so with Birdie? All it took was a little prodding and he'd willingly aired his dirtiest laundry.

Shit, he was in trouble.

Despite his determination to stay on track with the Perini exposé, he started tooling around Nexus for information on her. No data was available, not even an old address. Where was she from? Simply asking was an obvious strategy. But shucking clams was easier than getting information from the woman.

Yet he knew she was a thief. She'd lifted a few bucks from his wallet yesterday and he'd caught her red-handed in The Second Chance Grill after midnight. She didn't break into the restaurant to steal a paltry fifty dollars from the till. She was after something more valuable.

Antiques? The place was loaded with museum-quality furnishings. Still, it was impossible to visualize Birdie hawking Chippendale on eBay. Something else was the lure. What, exactly?

On impulse, he flipped open his cell and dialed Fatman Berelli. The union organizer had friends at the FBI, IRS and Interpol. He knew cops on the beat and had contacts at Homeland Security. If anyone could mine the depths for information on a mysterious thief, it was Fatman.

* * *

"Couldn't you drag yourself out of bed?" Finney barked. "It's after ten o'clock."

Birdie rubbed the sleep from her eyes. She'd woken in a bad mood, with the memory of kissing Hugh settled on her chest like a two-ton safe. A long shower and the prospect of locating more clues hadn't raised her spirits.

"I'm here, I'm dressed like a prostitute. What more do you want?" She yanked down the ruffled hem of her waitress uniform but the skirt rode up. Growling with frustration she added, "I shouldn't have to wear this thing. Delia's uniform fits her. Why am I stuck with clothes sized for a Playboy bunny?"

"I'm not buying a new uniform until I'm sure you'll stay for more than a few weeks. Will you?"

"Hell, no."

"Then you're stuck with the whore suit." The cook wagged a wooden spoon at Birdie's legs. "Besides, you're good for business. The men at the courthouse? The lawyers and the judges? Once they get an eyeful it'll be standing room only in the dining room."

"Then buy me a feather boa and find some guy to play the piano. I can't do burlesque without music."

"Now, that *would* bring in business."

Birdie fiddled with the buttons on her blouse. Sucking in air with the fabric pulling taut across her breasts was a bitch. "When do I get off work today?"

The cook slapped a plate down at the pass-through window. "Why don't you stay through the dinner rush?"

"Pass."

"How 'bout till four o'clock?"

"I'll miss my nap. I'm running a sleep deficit."

Finney stalked back to the stove with her chin jutting forward. "What are you, made of money? I'd think you'd be grateful for the work."

"Then you'd be wrong."

"You sure are mouthy, aren't you?"

"You bet."

An indefinable emotion worked across the cook's face, dousing the ire from her gaze. Uncomfortable, Birdie shifted from foot to foot. Rage she could deal with. Or lies. Was this compassion? She didn't like anything that made her feel too much or too deeply, and the cook's eyes had grown soft.

Muttering under her breath, Finney strode to the massive refrigerator and poured orange juice. "Delia says you don't have family in Ohio," she said, offering the drink. "Are you all alone, child?"

Birdie took the glass. "I'm not a child. I'm thirty-one."

"Are you alone?"

"I travel light. Only way to go."

The quip merely increased the warmth in the cook's steady gaze. "Lived through a couple grease fires, haven't you?" Birdie looked at her with confusion and she added, "When I was learning to cook there were some mistakes I only made once. Like the oil fire in Brubaker's Café. Nearly torched myself. The lead chef put out the blaze. There are scars all over my arms from the oil spatter."

She turned her arms over. Mottled scars gouged the soft skin.

Birdie flinched. "They look painful."

"I'm guessing you have scars too, that's all."

Emotion clogged Birdie's throat. Yes, she had scars, too many to count. Her mother using her in con games despite her objections. The lover in Miami who took off with her cash while she slept. The years of traveling alone without hopes or dreams to sustain her. So many scars. She hid them in her heart, stuffed them down deep. Staying fixed in the moment—on the next mark, the next theft—kept her emotions at bay and her cunning intact. It was the only way to survive.

Resignedly, she tied on an apron and tried to shake off her gloom. She only had to pretend to be a waitress until she deciphered the clue on the parchment and found the loot.

A jewel beyond compare stitched tight
With red, blue and white.

Mulling over the lines of poetry, she dropped an order pad into her apron pocket. The clue revealed, at least in part, the most pressing mystery—what *was* the hidden treasure? Was *a jewel beyond compare* a flawless diamond of rare color and impressive weight? Maybe it was a gem on par with the Hope Diamond.

All she had to do was unlock the mystery while waiting on customers and picking a few pockets. She'd find the diamond and ride out of Dodge before someone caught wind of the theft and put her in the pokey.

An exasperated Finney waved her toward the dining room and Birdie hurried out. Delia was arguing with a portly geezer beside table five while Ethel Lynn cowered before a pint-sized nemesis. The old woman was decked out in another one of her vintage outfits, a plum colored dress with tiny rosebuds spilling across the fabric in a shower of blooms. The redheaded girl hurled a handful of sugar packets at her and she warded off the barrage.

The dining room was nearly empty. Birdie leaned against the counter to watch.

Approaching, Delia said, "The brat terrorizing Ethel Lynn? Her name is Flame Sanson." The old guy Delia had been arguing with headed for the door. She flipped him the bird then resumed the conversation, unfazed. "Don't you love it? The kid is a redhead and her name is Flame. People are sickos when it comes to naming their children."

"Maybe we should rescue Ethel Lynn," Birdie said as the kid grabbed more ammo from a table.

"I hate to bug her mother. Mrs. Sanson tips like Midas. She probably thinks Ethel Lynn is babysitting the monster."

Pity for the old woman sent Birdie into the dining room. Grabbing the last of the sugar from the kid, she created enough of a diversion to allow Ethel Lynn to stumble away on her plum pumps. Mrs. Sanson's leather bag was slung on the back of her chair. If the woman tipped like Midas, she probably carried a stack of bills in her wallet.

But first, there was the issue of locating the Hope Diamond. *A jewel beyond compare stitched tight. With red, blue and white.* Maybe the jewel was stashed in one of the patriotic decorations festooned throughout the restaurant. The only way to find out? Check every one.

During the lunch shift, Birdie sidled up beside the large American flag tacked on the wall and padded her fingertips across the dusty fabric. She found nothing, so she worked her way through the rugs on the floor, dropping spoons and forks and checking underneath. Nada. The painting of George Washington astride a white horse was also a bust. So were the pilgrim figurines on the wall behind table three.

Depressed, she kept busy until the place cleared out after lunch. The gem was nowhere to be found. She'd have to risk breaking into The Second Chance tonight. The dining room merited a more thorough search. If Hugh followed her, as he'd done during the last break-in, she'd be hard pressed to come up with a believable explanation.

Just as worrisome, she hadn't lifted cash from any of the customers except wealthy Mrs. Sanson. She'd meant to work the entire room but lost the desire. Something about the small town was infecting her with a bad case of ethics. Maybe the holiday decorations going up in Liberty Square were getting to her, the evergreen garlands draped around windows at the courthouse and the pretty wreaths going up on storefronts. With Thanksgiving only a few days away an air of expectancy had crept into the town. The holiday spirit shone bright on pedestrian's faces as they peered into shop windows and bustled down the street with boxes and bags.

If she weren't flinty with the desire to snatch the Hope Diamond it would've been enough to make her go squishy inside.

Tugging down her skirt, she wandered toward Delia and Ethel Lynn. The two women stood before the picture window discussing the holiday decorations they planned to put up in the restaurant. They mentioned the storeroom where the decorations were stored. Birdie's heartbeat leapt into a gallop. Maybe the diamond wasn't hidden in the dining room after all.

She joined them by the window. "Did you say there's a storeroom?" she asked in what she hoped was a casual voice. "I've never seen it."

Delia nodded toward the kitchen. "You pass it when you go upstairs to your apartment. The door at the end of the hall?"

She'd assumed the door led to a closet for mops and cleaning supplies. "There's a room back there?"

Ethel Lynn waved her scrawny arms. "Hells bells, we could park a Mack truck in there. The room is huge."

This got Birdie's complete attention. "What's inside?"

Fluttering with excitement, Ethel Lynn stumbled back into the wall. "Why there's a treasure trove of history in the storeroom. Just like a museum!" She got her footing by grabbing onto the patriotic bunting draped around the window. When she'd steadied herself, she added, "My heavens, where do you think we keep the extra furniture and whatnots? This fine establishment opened during the Civil War. Many of the antiques are still tucked away in the storeroom."

When Ethel Lynn fluttered again, Birdie's attention shot to the patriotic bunting. The drapery swished back and forth, sending forth a loud thump. Something was banging against the wall every time Ethel Lynn batted her arms and struck the fabric. It was down low, inside the hem, jogging back and forth a few inches behind Ethel Lynn's ankles. Another distinctive thump and Birdie's heart nearly shot from her chest.

Something was *hidden inside* the hem.

From the kitchen, Finney yelled, "Ethel Lynn, have you been rearranging the walk-in cooler again? You're a dead woman!"

Delia grabbed the old bat by the sleeve. "Are you nuts? If you keep messing with Finney's kitchen, she'll pound you."

"I merely alphabetized our supplies. It's easier to find the capers if they cozy up with the cabbage."

"Yeah, and it puts Finney on the rampage. She turns into a wild boar and I'm scared shitless." Delia regarded Birdie. "Watch the dining room until we get back. We've got to soothe the savage beast."

Too excited for speech, Birdie jerked her head up and down. The women hurried to the kitchen in a flurry of snappish comments from Delia and near weeping from Ethel Lynn.

The moment they were gone she scanned the dining room. At table four a man in a suit shouted into his cell. All the barstools at the counter were empty.

She dropped to her knees. Quickly she felt along the hem of the bunting. And nearly blacked out with the thrill of discovery when her fingers bumped into the hard, square shape sewn into the corner of the hem.

CHAPTER 8

Working quickly, Birdie tugged apart the threads at the corner of the hem. A small metal box slipped out of the bunting and clattered to the floor. Cringing at the noise, she snatched it up and stumbled to her feet. The businessman at table four was still barking into his phone. Relief spilled through her.

Facing away from him, she turned the box over in her hand. The thin wedge of silver bore a swirling design of roses etched into the tight-fitting lid. Was it an earring box? It looked fancy and feminine, the sort of item a woman from an earlier era might keep in her purse.

With care, she pried off the lid. Her heart bounded at the sight of the embroidered cloth inside. Delicate loops of thread artfully rendered the two lines of poetry. Another clue!

Brick by brick, my love
My life built alone, without you—

Her exhilaration waned. Sadness curled through each word.

This wasn't merely a clue. The lines of poetry were something more, a first glimpse into a broken heart. Had Justice embroidered the fabric with the stitches of her sorrow? The fabric had been worked with unmistakable passion. Was this proof positive of her love for Lucas, the beloved she'd left behind in South Carolina?

Gently, Birdie placed the cloth inside the box and closed the lid. She slipped the box into the pocket of her apron and returned to the counter. From somewhere inside the kitchen, Ethel Lynn made a series of sputtering noises. Finney shouted.

Brick by brick, my love. Birdie wandered over to the cash register, where the portrait of Justice hung on the wall. Was it even possible to solve a riddle about bricks? The building housing The Second Chance Grill was built of bricks, thousands of them. If the diamond was hidden behind one, she could hunt from now until doomsday and never find it.

My life built alone, without you. There was real sorrow in the poem. The sorrow of lovers forced to build lives separate from each other? Perhaps Justice had loved Lucas deeply. The passage north was surely filled with hardship for a former slave. If the stories in Birdie's family were true and the freedwoman was pregnant during the journey, if she was overwhelmed with grief for the man she'd left behind, how *had* she found the courage to build a new life in Ohio?

Until now, Birdie had only thought of the hidden treasure as a means to vault her into a new life where she'd live quietly and carefully—and legally. No more picking pockets or running from state to state evading the law. She'd free herself from a painful and ugly past. She hadn't viewed the treasure for what it was—a symbol of devotion between a man and a woman torn apart by the harsh boundaries of the society in which they'd lived.

Shame brought her head up. She'd only thought of her own gain. An old habit, she'd learned little else over the years.

She'd grown up watching her mother use men then discard them at whim. And she'd experienced her own dead-end affairs.

The tenuous concord between men and women, the passion and the lies—she came of age determined never to fall prey to love. Even the spontaneous and fleeting affection she'd shown Hugh was meant to comfort, not inflame. A moment in his arms hadn't altered her pessimism toward relationships.

Her heart sinking, she found her attention straying back to the portrait. Justice appeared to regard her with haughty displeasure, her large, wide-set eyes filled with dark fire. Regret pricked Birdie. Was she waiting for Justice to miraculously come to life and issue a stern warning? The freedwoman had gone to great lengths to safeguard whatever Lucas had entrusted to her. The treasure had meant something to them both. Birdie wrapped her arms around herself, sticky with self-loathing.

She had no right to the treasure.

When did she ever stop to think about right and wrong? A good thief skimmed the surface like a dragonfly zooming above the murky pond of other lives, darting in to take whatever was coveted before flying off again. The consequences of her actions never mattered until now.

The bell above the restaurant's door jingled. Ignoring it, she grimaced. She felt sluggish with some new emotion, as if the simple act of standing before Justice was changing her internal chemistry. She couldn't shake the feeling that the freedwoman *was* eyeing her with disdain.

The clatter of pots shook her from her reverie. Through the pass-through window, Finney was growling at a whimpering Ethel Lynn. Delia leapt out of the way, allowing Ethel Lynn to flee toward the sink. The mayhem in the kitchen was accented by heavy footsteps approaching through the dining room.

"Are you getting a dose of Justice?"

The worrisome double meaning spun her around. The grating voice erupted from the throat of an old woman. Given the heavy thump of the woman's gait, she expected to find a lady of substantial girth. What she discovered rooted before the counter was a petite, scrappy-looking crone wearing a Davy Crocket-style buck-skin jacket oddly matched up with a felt hat. The hat sprouted silk roses. A few of the buds drooped over the old woman's black, beady eyes.

Their gazes connected and the woman's mouth froze. Birdie wasn't sure what to make of the surprise glinting in her expression. She appeared startled, as if the sight of a waitress dressed in a whore suit would turn her into a pillar of salt. Wary, Birdie edged away from the counter separating them.

Just as quickly the old woman blotted the strong emotion from her eyes. Her ebony features became glass, like the sea before a typhoon.

"Would you like a menu?" Birdie asked, too frightened to move toward the stack.

"I've had lunch, you fool. It's the middle of the afternoon."

No one called her a fool and got away with it. Let someone walk over you and they made it a habit. "I left my watch upstairs, which isn't as bad as you leaving your manners at home. Pack them the next time you leave the house, Parsnip."

The woman slapped her buckskin satchel onto the counter. "What did you call me?"

"Huh?" Birdie feigned confusion. Hell, the gnome was older than God. Playing with what little grey matter she had left might be fun. "I'm sorry—what did you say, Avocado?"

"Are you messin' with me?" The woman screwed her ridiculous hat further down on her brow. "I'm not much for vegetables but I can fricassee your hide if you don't watch it."

Birdie offered a saccharine smile. "My apologies." With flourish, she picked up a menu as if she were a game show host revealing the item behind door number two. "It's sensational. You won't believe what's inside, Tomato."

"Stop sassing me. There's nothing wrong with my hearing."

"What?" She widened her eyes in what she hoped was a fawn-like expression.

The gnome blinked. Baring her false teeth, she patted her satchel. "I've got a .32 caliber. Don't make me use it."

The threat drained the amusement from Birdie's face, not to mention the blood from her head.

Satisfied, the old woman settled onto a barstool. "Got anything else to say, ruffian?"

"Checkmate?"

"Game over is more like it." She broke out a devilish grin. "The name's Theodora Hendricks." She jabbed a finger toward the coffee station. "Don't keep me waiting."

Birdie sloshed coffee into a mug. Theodora Hendricks' narrowed attention stuck on her like glue, sending waves of nervous tension racing across her skin. It was the sort of hard appraisal she received from the police on those rare instances when they suspected her of snitching wallets. The urge to flee nearly got the better of her.

"Here you are." She placed the mug on the counter. "Just wave your pistol if you need anything else."

When she started to move off, Theodora snapped her fingers. "Stay put. We're not done talking." She tapped the counter with one bony finger, and Birdie visualized a fairy tale witch and an oven. "Tell me your name."

"Um . . . it's Birdie."

"Birdie?"

"Yeah."

"Your last name?"

"Kaminsky."

"Sounds Polish."

"You want to make a joke?"

"Not particularly."

Theodora's narrowed gaze stayed put, even as she rifled around her satchel and withdrew a corncob pipe. Birdie might have laughed if her stomach wasn't roiling with a queasy sort of trepidation.

"You're sure your last name is Kaminsky? You wouldn't be lying, would you?"

"Of course I'm sure, Br—" Birdie caught herself before *Broccoli* spilled out. Who knew if the Saturday night special was loaded? "Do you want to see my driver's license?"

"I do."

"I was joking." When Theodora glared, Birdie hitched up her skirt and wiggled her wallet from its hiding place on her hip.

"Funny place to keep your wallet. Come to think of it, why *are* you dressed like a painted lady? This is a farming community, not the big city."

"I'll let you know when I figure it out." She flipped open her wallet and withdrew her driver's license. "There. See? My last name is Kaminsky."

"Not Greyhart." Dragging her nose to the counter, Theodora studied the license with ill-concealed disappointment.

"Why would you think my name is Greyhart?"

Shrugging off the question, the old woman planted her pipe between her weathered lips.

Birdie returned the wallet to her hip. "You can't smoke in here. It's against the law."

"And I'll bet you follow the law to the letter, now, don't you?" The crone struck a match that seemed dull compared to the pugnacity sparking in her gaze. "You can't stop me from smoking. Whenever and wherever I please."

"I guess not. At least not while you're armed."

"Now you're talking." On a cackle, she blew a puff of smoke. Then she nodded toward the picture of Justice. "I noticed you taking an interest in one of this town's founding mothers. You like the portrait?"

"It's beautiful. *She's* beautiful."

"I do agree. You know, the portrait was lost in the storeroom. That fool, Ethel Lynn, packed it away the same year John Travolta wore those crazy white pants. Didn't matter how much I threatened to skin her hide; she couldn't recall where she'd put it. Finney dug out the portrait last summer."

It was no wonder that Birdie's mother hadn't found the portrait—and the slip of parchment hidden inside. She'd visited nearly every town named Liberty in the United States. She probably checked this town, too, but came up empty because a dotty old bag packed the portrait away and promptly forget exactly where.

"Her name was Justice Postell," Theodora said, drawing her from her thoughts. "Quite a lady, if I don't mind saying. She opened this restaurant right as The Civil War was coming to an end. First black, man or woman, to own a business in northern Ohio. When she retired, her son took over this establishment."

Justice did have a child. This tidbit of information was enough to replace the worry in Birdie's veins with heady anticipation. She was still leery of Theodora—the old bag *was* armed—but the desire to learn more about the freedwoman won out.

"I heard someone in here talking about Justice," she lied. Theodora arched a brow and she quickly added, "They said Justice was pregnant when she moved here. She was an unwed mother. Right?"

"Not exactly. Justice got hitched to the colored preacher's son after she arrived in Liberty."

Her heart sank. Maybe the story wasn't true. If Justice didn't have a child with Lucas, Birdie wasn't related to the freedwoman's descendants after all.

But her spirits immediately rose when Theodora added, "It was a kind of mercy, their marriage. Justice came to Ohio in a bad way. Nearly seven months pregnant. She left the baby's father down in the Carolinas."

In South Carolina. A feverish excitement stole through her. It was foolish to think she'd earned a reward by learning she might be related to Justice. She wanted to be. She needed to know someone in her family hadn't done time in the state pen or died in a barroom brawl. She yearned for a legacy that didn't involve duping some mark out of his hard-earned cash.

Her excitement must have been palpable because Theodora smiled. Leaning forward, she said, "Child, I don't know why, but you look as happy as a flea at a dog show. Would you like to hear the whole story?"

* * *

Returning from the library, Hugh found Birdie lounging on the sofa in a disconcerting state of bliss.

She was leafing through a scrapbook, and something in the pages delighted her. Her gaze danced across the page, her lips pursed with pouty interest. In deep concentration, she possessed a sweetly studious air. She looked beautiful, in fact, too much so. Her attire didn't help matters—she'd once again laid claim to some of his clothing. The striped boxers clung to her sumptuous thighs and the threadbare jersey gave more of a view of her breasts than was safe.

"Good reading?" He tossed his keys on the coffee table, startling her.

She snapped the scrapbook shut. "I wasn't expecting you this early," she said, as if they'd merged into the predictable schedule of a married couple.

The irritating thought put an edge to his voice. "Next time I'll call ahead. I wouldn't want to return to my apartment too early."

"*Our* apartment."

"For the record, I'm paying the lion's share of rent." When she huffed out a sigh, he added, "I'm through researching for the day, all right? I'm beat. I came back for a nap."

"Believe me, you need one."

"What's that supposed to mean?"

"You're testy." She bobbed her head in the direction of the hallway. "Night, night, Parsnip. Try not to snore. You sound like something escaping from the bowels of hell when you're overtired."

Her glib dismissal raised his cackles. Which was ridiculous since he needed to get away from her. The kiss they'd shared earlier in the week had left Hugh feeling like he was backed up against something perilous. When he looked over his shoulder to assess the danger he was staring straight down into an abyss. Of course, any red-blooded man was at risk of losing his balance when an attractive woman began stealing his clothes. Imagining Birdie stepping her long legs into his boxers, salivating over the fantasy of how she shimmied the waistband over her hips—she was tormenting him and she damn well knew it. If she was intent on scavenging his stuff she should have the decency to dig out his condoms and let him use them with her.

Frustrated, he started for the bedroom. From the corner of his eye he caught the flutter of tapered fingers slipping the scrapbook back off the table. Curiosity swung him around.

He snatched the book away. "What is this?" She yelped in protest and he stepped out of reach.

"Give it back! I promised Theodora I'd be careful with it."

"Theodora Hendricks lent this to you?"

Birdie leapt off the couch. "It's stuff on Liberty history, photocopies of old newspaper articles about The Second Chance Grill and some of the people who lived here. And yes, she lent it to me."

"You're reading *history*? I didn't think you read anything besides 'how to' books on breaking and entering."

"Kiss my ass."

He would, gladly, but that wasn't the point. "If you're so enthralled with history, I'll get you a book on Watergate from the library. You can move up from restaurants, start breaking into the headquarters of major political parties."

"I'm a pacifist," she snapped.

Hugh arched a brow. "I think you mean you're an Independent."

"Whatever."

"I used to lean toward the Democratic Party. But rooming with you, I'm heading Republican. I need a gun to protect my stuff."

She yanked the scrapbook free. Hurt swam in the depths of her violet eyes and he reeled at the possibility that he'd insulted her.

Birdie had more armor than the Marines, or so he liked to think. That she might be motivated by anything other than avarice was disconcerting. They were both jaded, twin cynics. Keeping his emotional distance was easier when he viewed her as a common criminal. Seeing her like this—open, feminine, stung by his comments—put him in peril. Their sexual attraction was enough of a complication. He needed to keep his emotions the hell out of it.

She cradled the book like a babe in her arms. "What's the big deal if I enjoy reading about the town? Theodora has been telling me stories about Liberty, about people who've lived here. The stories are pretty cool."

A superficial explanation if ever there was one. "What people?" He was sure she was hiding something.

"None of your business."

"What's in it for you?" When the question put a hard light in her eyes, he added, "There's always something in it for you, right? Theodora plays show and tell with Liberty's history but you're playing her. For what, I'd like to know."

Getting the unvarnished truth from a thief wasn't possible. So why was he irritated by the way she clamped her lips together and flung herself back on the couch? He chastised himself for his stupidity. The intimacy they'd shared with one short necking session had done more than infuse their relationship with sexual tension. Now he felt compelled to break down her barriers and find out what kind of woman she was underneath. The desire wasn't logical. But that wouldn't stop him from trying.

They spent the next days in an uneasy standoff. He tried for civility but failed miserably. Birdie's unique scent, something akin to ripening peaches, hung in the air of the apartment. She sang in the shower whenever she thought he'd gone out. Her low, throaty voice set his pulse racing. Apparently puzzled by his surly retorts and glaring silences, she doled out rude comments then followed them up with the most disconcerting peace offerings: his freshly laundered clothes appeared in neat stacks on his bed and splotches of pizza sauce vanished from his keyboard. If she cooked, she left Chicken Parmesan or stir-fry in the fridge with a note urging him to dig in. His wallet got lighter by the day, but she hung out fresh towels in the bathroom and left a vase full of daisies, undoubtedly pilfered from the restaurant, on his nightstand.

She tried to get along while they were stuck together. She made the best of an awkward situation while he was powerless to stop his attention from galloping after her whenever she passed him in the hallway or the kitchen. If she sensed the sexual conundrum he'd put himself into, she hid the knowledge behind a demure smile or a brash comment, depending on her mood.

None of which was particularly upsetting. What did torment him was the suspicion that she was merely counting down the days until he'd wrap up his stay in Liberty and return to Akron. He wasn't used to being so casually rebuffed, and certainly not after the woman in question had laid a kiss on him that haunted what little rest he got. She was a drifter. She'd invest only as much emotional coin in their relationship as required, while he grew increasingly drawn to her.

They were roomies now. She was handling it fine. He wasn't sure if he could.

CHAPTER 9

Ten days and counting after he'd started bunking with a gorgeous thief in boondock Liberty, Hugh stood shivering in the brisk November wind of the Jeffordsville Farm Park.

In the outdoor arena a glare of spotlights rose from beneath the podium. Framed in light, the *Akron Register's* Bud Kresnick smacked the cameraman on the head.

Although the next U.S. presidential election was two years away, the Farm Park swarmed with activity. Hugh wondered if the Republican contender, Senator Gabe McCutcheon of Vermont, would be on time or would leave the pre-Thanksgiving masses shivering in the cold for another thirty minutes.

Pulling his jacket closed, he suffered a moment's trepidation. He didn't know why Bud had summoned him to the park. The City Editor was in a predictably sour mood, his fleshy cheeks going red as he growled at the rookie cameraman, then shoved through the crowd to Hugh.

"Dipshit." Bud nodded toward the cameraman. "Tell me why I bother hiring them green and right out of college."

"Because you have a good heart." The smarmy compliment made Hugh's teeth ache. Hell, was he reduced to groveling to stay in Bud's good graces? Unsure, he added, "So, how's it going? Miss me at the *Register*?"

"Getting needy, Hugh? Should I send a Valentine to show my love?"

"In lieu of courtship, I'll take a paycheck. I haven't seen one of those lately."

"Earned one yet?" Bud fumbled through the pockets of his wool coat and withdrew a sub sandwich. Tearing open the cellophane, he eyed Hugh with what sure as hell looked like misgiving. "You got the goods on Anthony Perini? I haven't heard a peep out of you since you took off for Liberty."

"I'm working on it."

"Work harder." Bud dug into the sandwich and chewed thoughtfully. "Staying away from broads? You know what they do to your concentration."

Hugh visualized Birdie shrugging out of her army coat to reveal generous curves tucked inside a waitress uniform three sizes too small. "I've sworn off women. Like I promised."

"Why don't I believe you?"

"Because you're a suspicious son of a gun?" The joke fell flat.

Before his ex-boss interrogated him further, Hugh launched into a recitation of the legwork he'd done on the exposé while waiting for Anthony Perini to return from his honeymoon. Guiltily, he wondered why he'd been wasting time scouring the Internet for anything on Birdie. He'd even called Fatman, who was now digging around for the goods on the curvaceous thief. Why was he screwing around when he had an article to produce?

Finishing up, he wondered if Bud had heard a word of what he'd said. The City Editor waved at someone in the crowd.

Turning, Hugh spotted Timothy Ralston strolling past a clutch of adoring women. The warning bells in his skull started clanging.

The prissy scion to a retailing fortune, Ralston kept dental floss in his desk and had most of the power brokers in Ohio on speed dial. He highlighted his brown hair and strutted around in a physique to put Hercules on the defensive. The bastard was rich, stupid and gallingly polite. Hugh felt an allergic reaction coming on—he'd never had much tolerance for the bronzed dullard.

He thrust out his hand, which Ralston claimed in a fearsome grip. "Are you interviewing the senator after his speech?" Hugh asked.

"Already done." Ralston leaned forward conspiratorially. "McCutcheon plays tennis with my father whenever Dad is in Washington. Mean backhand. I asked for some face time, pre-speech. McCutcheon was happy to comply."

Hugh produced a Teflon smile. "Nice work. Page one spread?"

"Of course."

Bud finished his sub and belched. "Our boy here is tired of features. He wants to try his hand at investigative journalism."

Hugh feigned interest while his guts turned to jelly. "You don't say."

Until now, Ralston had carved out a few hours in his social calendar to write articles on counting carbs or making the perfect brioche. Drivel on choosing the right tattoo after the age of forty. Nothing he wrote smacked of hard journalism, yet now he wanted a seat with the big boys? Hugh struggled beneath a premonition of doom. There was only one slot open at the *Register* for an investigative journalist—his job, the job he'd lose permanently if he didn't produce a drag-them-through-the-mud piece while he camped out in Liberty like a vulture seeking prey.

The notion must have telegraphed directly to Bud. Grinning, he landed a punch on Hugh's shoulder. "You catch on quick, buddy. Think of it as motivation to stay away from chicks."

"I get it."

"When will the exposé be on my desk?"

"In a few days."

"Stay celibate and sober. Who knows what you'll produce?"

Ralston, who was predictably obtuse, looked from one man to the other. "Does Hugh have a problem with women?" The compassion in his voice made Hugh's molars throb. "Listen man, I can hook you up with a therapist and an herbalist. Combination therapy—it works."

"I've already called my astrologer," Hugh replied dryly.

"Great, great. Want the name of a good psychic too?"

"Naw. Too many people reading my tea leaves, and I won't know which way to turn."

Ralston gazed in wonderment like an idiot king. "No problem, man. And don't worry about the newspaper—I'm covering for you. By the way, I've been working at your desk and using your computer. Soaking up the vibes of the master."

"No shit."

"You don't mind, do you?"

"Are you *shitting me?*"

Ralston gave another of his shatteringly bright smiles. "It's good karma to share a productive work space."

Rage nearly struck Hugh dumb. "Don't get too comfortable, pal. I'll be back at the *Register* before you know it."

He squinted into the harsh sunlight and glimpsed failure. The kind of failure that came from ditching ethics to get ahead. He'd expose Anthony's perfidy and reveal the townspeople as fools for thinking they were contributing to Blossom's medical care. He'd wipe the sheen right off the town. Sure, some of the donations *had* saved Blossom's life. People across the U.S. now viewed the kid's story as a lesson in how goodness prevailed. Which would no longer seem true once Hugh's poison quill slashed across the *Akron Register.*

Was there any choice? Safeguarding his career required nothing less than walking right over the good people of Liberty.

* * *

Soon Theodora began appearing at the restaurant during the afternoon lull to perch on a barstool and share the century-old tales surrounding Justice Postell.

Despite Birdie's growing frustration—she still hadn't found the Hope Diamond—she looked forward to the midday coffee break when they'd share conversation. Once a cup of java appeared beneath Theodora's nose, she shelled out tidbits of the freedwoman's life.

Justice had arrived in Liberty at the dawn of the Civil War when the town was little more than an outpost carved in the forests of northeastern Ohio. At the height of a blistering August, she appeared on the steps of the Unitarian Gospel Church in a tattered dress and a pair of men's boots. She was still young, maybe late twenties, and possessed of a hunger for learning and a gaze so focused people said she wore blinders. Soon she became a fixture in town, often spotted with a book cradled in the crook of her arm. A polite, reserved quality imbued her speech. She scratched out a living as a seamstress then married the Negro preacher's son, Elijah Turner, a few weeks before giving birth to her child.

Two years later, Turner died of pneumonia during a particularly brutal winter. The preacher's son had been educated, and he'd had the foresight to teach his plucky wife how to read and to manage accounts. Turner owned several large parcels of land at the time of his death and Justice added to these holdings. By the time she opened the restaurant, which she named The Second Street Eatery, she was well established and the owner of one of the finest residences in Liberty.

Summing up, Theodora swiveled around on her barstool. "The house, the one Justice owned? It's up on North Street." She peered across the dining room to the picture window. Outside, a light snow was falling, partially obscuring the pedestrians and the cars weaving around Liberty Square. "Big house—you can't miss it.

Justice added on a few times and painted the house pink. Pink! I reckon she picked a feminine color to shock her uppity white neighbors. It's been pink ever since."

"I'd like to see the house." Birdie twisted a rag between her fists, caught herself, and tossed it aside. She still hadn't mustered up the courage to ask about Justice bringing something of value from South Carolina. "I wonder how a woman like Justice made so much money," she ventured. "I mean, her husband taught her how to manage accounts but opening a restaurant would've taken a lot of cash."

"You're wondering how she bought this building and started the restaurant?" Beneath hooded eyes, the shadow of a smile played on Theodora's mouth. "The rubies, that's how. Justice used them as collateral to start the restaurant."

"Rubies?"

"Oh, yes. Pretty gems too."

"You mean she had more than one?"

Forget the Hope Diamond. Somewhere in the building, *a cache of rubies was waiting to be unearthed.* "How many gems did she have?"

"Two bags full. They were given to her by the man in South Carolina who loved her."

My ancestor, Lucas Postell. "And she used them for collateral?"

"She was a smart woman—knew better than to part with the jewels. An abolitionist owned a farmer's bank outside Liberty. Good Henry Williams, why, he helped her. He kept the rubies for collateral until she was making money with her restaurant. He let her buy them back once the place was profitable."

"I wonder where the rubies are now," Birdie said, stupidly. When Theodora's expression grew suspicious, she clamped her mouth shut.

"Don't rightly know," the old woman replied. "Why are you so interested?"

"I'm not."

Birdie smiled gamely. Outside, Liberty Square was being festooned in Christmas decorations but she had visions of rubies dancing in her head. Gems the size of a robin's egg. Glittering facets of blood red, a whole bag worth thousands—hundreds of thousands, maybe.

Snapping out of gem lust, she deftly moved the conversation forward. "I can't wait to see the pink house," she said. "After work I'll walk down North Street and get a load of the place."

"If you do, take the nosey reporter with you." Theodora jabbed a thumb toward Hugh, hurling himself down on the next barstool. "The scoundrel looks itchy for some fresh air."

Birdie fetched the coffee pot. "Where have you been?" She forced her mind off buried treasure. Filling a mug, she cast a look of displeasure that he ignored. He'd been avoiding her all week.

"Working."

"So you say, Parsnip." Replacing the pot on its stand, she leaned against the wall to give her sore feet a rest. "I'm a firm believer in keeping my enemies close. I haven't been able to keep track of you for days. What time do you get up in the morning?"

Hugh looked at her peevishly. "Earlier than you." He exchanged pleasantries with Theodora before landing another sour glance. Bitter lemons, this one. "Why do *you* sleep in every day? Aren't you worried about losing the waitressing gig?"

"Actually, that's my strategy. Tardy today, tardy tomorrow. Keep coming in late and Finney will have to fire me."

"Why not quit? Move on, find another town." Draining his mug, Hugh set it down and tapped on the rim. "We can all agree you're mouthy. Given a chance, Finney will be happy to dump you in the nearest ditch. I'll help. My wallet is still leaking twenties and I'm sick of sharing my clothes."

"Why Hugh, greed is a deadly sin." Pot in hand, she sashayed back over.

"So sue me." Brightening, he slid his cup forward.

Ignoring his mug, she did a pretty turn and returned the pot to the coffee station. When he glowered, she batted her eyes. "Now what's wrong?" Still high on rubies, she gave a flirty look. "If I didn't know better I'd swear you're premenstrual. You aren't in one of your crappy moods, are you?"

"I am now."

"Pity." Shimmying her hips, she toyed with the hem of her midget's uniform. Hugh licked his lips, caught himself, and frowned. She smiled. "Tell you what. Leave a big tip and I'll improve my serving skills the next time you blow into my restaurant."

"Give it a rest, Tomato."

She couldn't. Having to share the apartment with a cranky roommate was intolerable, but it was something she wouldn't have to endure much longer. Now that she knew she what she was looking for—rubies—the future was golden.

And a rich, radiant red.

"Roomies should get along better than we do," she said, brimming with cheer. "Look at me. I'm the picture of sweetness and light. You, on the other hand, were planted with the demon seed. What gives?"

He muttered something nasty under his breath. She shot a look at Delia straightening chairs in the center of the dining room. The young waitress lifted her shoulders in a careless shrug.

Theodora pounded her gnat-sized fist on the counter. "Both of you, stop squabbling. If I have the desire to watch Saturday night wrestling, I'll wait until Saturday night. Let me drink my coffee in peace."

Birdie squeaked. "He started it!"

"Hogwash. You *are* sassy. If I had a bar of soap, why . . ."

"You'd what? Wash my mouth out?"

She got a visual of fending off the flea-sized woman. Not that she was in the habit of defending herself against the elderly.

"Stop grinning, missy. You're playing Cat's Cradle with the last thread of my patience."

"I'm really scared, Theodora. Shaking in my boots."

Theodora slid her buckskin satchel toward Hugh. "Use the gun if you must," she said. "A little bloodshed will make my day."

Rising, Hugh pulled on his coat. "I have a better idea." He motioned for Birdie to follow. "Tell Finney you're taking a break. We both need some air."

Any reason to leave work was a good reason. "Finney, it's slow out here," she called, poking her head into the kitchen. The cook, busy scrubbing the stove, blustered an objection. Hurriedly she added, "Delia's got it covered. I'm leaving for the day."

She donned her coat and the leggings she'd stored beneath the counter. The cook rattled off a few more choice words, then banged a pot, probably for emphasis. Delia, swabbing down a table, flinched.

The tips would be sparse for the rest of the afternoon. Birdie didn't relish the idea of horning in on the young waitress's wages. Delia had mentioned more than once that she lived on her tips. *Lived on them.* How she did it was beyond comprehension. Besides, it was a good idea to escape the confines of the restaurant before Finney came barreling out of the kitchen brandishing a skillet over her head.

In the Square, city employees were stringing holiday lights. A twenty-foot blue spruce blinked with holiday cheer. Midway up, a youth with a goatee balanced on a ladder.

Goatee Boy recognized Hugh. *Hola, Mr. Schaeffer! You back in town to give Liberty another fifteen minutes of fame?* Stepping to the curb, Hugh shouted a reply over the hoods of the cars wending around the Square.

The moment he turned away, Birdie crouched before the brick façade of the building. The putty-colored mortar was intact; none of the bricks appeared loose. Wherever the rubies were hidden it wasn't out here, on the street.

Since locating the second clue in the patriotic bunting she'd done nothing but search for loose bricks in the dining room, the hallway, and now here outside. Not the storage room, however—the damn door was kept locked.

Finding the treasure was proving far too difficult.

Tamping down her frustration, she straightened as Hugh returned from the curb.

"So what's up?" she asked. With his hands stuck deep in his pockets, he looked troubled.

"We need to talk."

"Does arguing count? We do that all the time."

"Can it, babe. We need more than a chat."

Whoa. The razor-sharp edge to his voice raised her defenses. He wasn't troubled. He was pissed off about something or someone. Probably her.

Recalling her conversation with Theodora, she clamped her self-composure in place. "Let's walk down North Street. There's a house I want to see," she said, jockeying for the upper hand. "I don't mind having a heart-to-heart as long as I can navigate."

"Why do you get to call the shots? We're heading down South Street, Carrot."

"No can do, Parsnip. North Street it is."

"I'm not walking down North. I can't."

"Why the hell not?"

He glowered, the fury rising off him like steam. What was the big deal? Shrugging, she started off. Screw him. If he needed to talk, he'd pick up his feet and follow.

The street bustled with holiday shoppers. Weaving through the crowd, she reached the northern edge of the Square and the stoplight. The light had already turned green when a blast of foul language parted the crowd.

She crossed with Hugh dogging her heels. "You're a pain in the ass, Birdie."

Venom peppered his voice, but she let it slide. There was no understanding his lousy mood or why he had an aversion to North Street, which was bizarre, given the street's beauty. The houses were spectacular, rambling Colonials with holiday candles glowing in the windows and Greek Revivals with wreaths hung on the doors. There was even a Gothic mansion of golden stone, with a grouping of life-sized tin soldiers set out on the snow-crusted lawn.

No pink house in sight. Was it further down the street? Theodora had said Justice built and then added on during her lifetime. Owners who came later might have done the same, which meant the place was large. It would be impossible to miss.

"Are you casing the houses for the perfect heist?" Hugh chided, catching up. "Bad idea, Sweet Pea. Most of these homes come equipped with burglar alarms and dogs with names like Adolph and Killer."

"I'm a waitress, not a burglar." And soon, she'd be legit. With the cache of rubies—two whole bags of rubies—she'd have enough cash and then some. "Your snarky comments are rude."

"Give it up, Potato. I'm a reporter. I read people. You've got 'criminal' written all over you."

Did she? His powers of observation were unnerving. "I do not." She skirted a boxwood hedge growing over the sidewalk. "Just yesterday, Ethel Lynn invited me over for tea. I have friends in town, Cabbage. It's more than you have."

A new experience, for sure. She still wasn't sure what to make of the affectionate way the women of The Second Chance treated her. Reluctantly, she'd begun to enjoy their company. Especially Delia's—the young woman treated Birdie like a visiting dignitary, asking for advice, lobbing compliments like so much confetti—it was hard not to become attached to her.

Not that Hugh would be impressed. He regarded her with so much contempt that acid churned in her stomach.

"You had tea with Ethel Lynn? Did you lift anything from her house?" he asked. "China, silver? Did you notice the Grandma Moses paintings in her living room? Worth thousands?"

Birdie caught her temper before it flared. It was stupid to feel anger—and hurt—because he had a bead on her true occupation.

Numbing her emotions was easy most of the time. Work the street, work a room—take what she needed without feeling a thing. Unfortunately Hugh had a way of burrowing under her skin. Like a tick.

The vibe coming off the man was dangerous. "What do you need to talk about?" The quicker they parted ways, the better.

She paused before a cream colored Victorian with a turreted roof and a kid's bicycle gathering snow in the front yard. Hugh glanced nervously down the street. For what, she couldn't imagine. He looked spooked.

"The honeymoon is over," he said, tugging her toward the Square. When she slipped free and resumed her original path, he followed, adding, "You have to move out of the apartment."

"Hell no, I don't. And you're confused about honeymoons. Mary and Anthony are on one. You and I are living a nightmare."

"Which is why we can't go on sharing the same digs."

"Then send a postcard from the road." She stopped before the next house, which boasted huge pillars twined with red ribbon and evergreen garland. The pillars resembled giant candy canes. Despite the worry churning her gut, she sighed with pleasure. "There aren't any other rentals in town. You'll have to join the ranks of the homeless."

"Damn it, I'm a reporter! I need a place to work. You don't need the apartment."

"Oh, yeah? Because I'm *not* working? For the record, I have calluses on my feet the size of waffles. I work my ass off."

Hugh grunted. "You're full of shit. You didn't come to Liberty to wait tables. You're here for something. To steal something or bribe someone—maybe you *are* planning a heist. I should warn the bank manager over at Liberty Trust."

Gooseflesh prickled her arms. Was this a threat?

She never should have kissed him the night she broke into the restaurant. A momentary and incredibly stupid feeling of compassion had overridden her instinct for self-preservation. She'd felt sorry for the guy. Okay, so lust had also worked a number on her brain. It happened, especially when a woman went too long between relationships.

And he *was* attracted to her. Even now, he was sending out enough pheromones to have her thinking about doing it in the road. Quickly she ran through the men she'd had relationships with during the last few years, the entire seedy lot.

Fear made her shiver. Any one of them would've sold her out. Hugh would, too.

"Get real, Hugh." A trickle of sweat ran down between her breasts. She was grateful her coat hid her distress. "I'm an innocent waitress trying to make my way in the world."

"Don't head for the stage lights just yet. Your routine needs work. Now listen—"

She pressed her fingers to his lips to shut him up. Wrong move, since touching him sent her gooseflesh fleeing and started her skin tingling.

"For roomies, I thought we got along okay," she said, snatching her hand back. But not before her touch dilated his eyes and a needy sensation filled her belly. "If you're making me throw you out of the apartment, at least tell me why. Is it something I said?"

"More like something you wear. Or, more precisely, what you *don't* wear when you're lounging around." He pulled back an inch, far enough to allow his gaze to roam free across her features in a way that pooled heat in her hips. "Modesty isn't your strong suit. You walk around in satin panties under my Rugby shirt. Or you watch the tube in your purple bra and my gym shorts."

"They're both winning combinations."

"So they are. If *Sports Illustrated* ever produces a lingerie-with-guy-skivvies issue, they're sure to give you a call."

"You're making a big deal out of nothing." So what if she liked mixing his clothes with her lingerie like a mad scientist out to test the limits of his self-control? The reactions she'd catch simmering on his face were the sort of ego boost every woman needed. "I thought you enjoyed the show."

"It's killing me." He yanked his attention away and looked off down the street. "Satisfied? I have an addiction."

A goofy delight sugared over her cynical heart. "You're addicted . . . to me?"

"Get your facts straight, Potato Head. I have an addiction to women *in general*. It's nothing to be proud of."

A swift kick of disappointment, then she drew herself tall. "You're saying you can't room with *any* woman because the temptation is too great?"

"That's what I'm saying. Until my job's safe I can't risk it."

"Then take off. You live in Akron, right? Go back to your place."

"Not until I finish my work here." He ground his teeth. "I'm on probation with my boss. If I don't write a sensational article while I'm in Liberty he'll fire me for good."

"Meaning he *has* fired you?"

Hugh grunted. "Something like that."

"Your boss is a taskmaster. Even if you do a lousy job on the feature you're writing about Blossom, it shouldn't nix your job."

He shrugged, his gaze hooded.

She almost pitied him. "Then we're at an impasse," she said, dragging her attention from his eyes. They'd widened enough to let her glimpse pride battling fear.

Hugh was such a hassle. Why did he get to her whenever she caught sight of his vulnerable side? She was still trying to figure it out when his head snapped up. The color bled from his face. Confused, Birdie swung around and zeroed in on the voice—a kid's singsong voice with laughter at the edges.

From across the street someone was calling to Hugh.

* * *

Hugh's emotions went into a skid. If only he'd avoided North Street he wouldn't be in this dilemma. Despite his best efforts to dodge the Liberty teen who had captured America's heart, Blossom Perini had found him.

Which was both upsetting and inevitable. News traveled fast in a town this small. No doubt the thirteen year old believed the bald-faced lie he'd been low enough to spread around town—he was back to interview her about her successful battle against leukemia.

Now the kid had found him. And not even the brisk November air could erase the beads of perspiration sprouting on his brow.

Last summer he'd featured Blossom in the most out-of-character article he'd ever produced. He wrote about how the entire town—and shortly thereafter, the entire country—raised the money needed for the bone marrow transplant that cured her leukemia and saved her life.

The damn article was actually heartwarming.

Usually he got hate mail after exposing a corrupt local politician or debunking a new fad. The screeds flowed into the *Akron Register* like a glorious stench.

Not this time. After Blossom's story hit the newsstands Hugh started receiving . . . fan mail. Lavender-scented cards and smarmy letters. He even received flowers—white tea roses in a china cup as big as a salad bowl—from a Mrs. Richard Snickles of Pepper Pike. She said the article renewed her faith in the world.

The other reporters at the *Register*, accustomed to his jaundiced view of humanity, nearly laughed him out of the newsroom.

And he took a hammer to the china cup.

Now he'd returned to Liberty, pretending he'd arrived to write a follow-up. As the girl waved joyously from across the street, the fabrication sickened him. Who stooped so low they lied to a kid?

He chewed on his eroding self-respect. *A cold bastard like me.*

Blossom approached with her corkscrew curls bouncing and her brown eyes sparkling. Soon, he'd expose her father and earn her loathing.

So why worry about the kid's feelings? A journalist's ethics demanded service to the higher good. Everyone from folks on fixed incomes to soft-hearted teens had been sending cash to the websites for Blossom's nonexistent medical bills. Once the story hit the newsstands, the flow of greenbacks would stop.

Regret took a swing at Hugh's sense of honor. He'd turn off the spigot of cash. In the process, he'd bury Blossom's dad under a mountain of dirt.

"Mr. Shaeffer!" She skidded to a halt before him. "I was wondering when you'd come over to interview me. Will I be on the front page of your newspaper like the last time?" She glanced shyly at Birdie. "Hey."

"Hey yourself."

Birdie was still brewing with emotions he refused to analyze. She looked hurt. The crack about her being a burglar wasn't his best moment, and it was surely a low blow to evict her from the apartment. Not that he was sure he'd won that argument.

He didn't like wounding her. Problem was, he spent too much time thinking about her thighs and the pouty thing she did with her lips. He spent most of his time imagining what she'd feel like pinned beneath him, and here he was with his ass on the line at the *Register*.

They still hadn't resolved who'd stay in the apartment and who'd go. Now he'd run into Blossom. Frustrated and sick-hearted, Hugh swabbed at his brow.

Somehow Birdie stuffed the hurt and winked at Blossom. "We got in a new shipment of ice cream this morning—Cherry Chunk, Chocolate-Marshmallow Madness, Coconut Crush. You like coconut, don't you?"

"I love it!"

Birdie gave him a knowledgeable look, as if they hadn't squabbled and he hadn't cut her deep. "The kid here is crazy for ice cream, any flavor," she said, unaware he knew all about Blossom's dairy obsession. He'd spent a week interviewing the kid last August. "I asked Finney to put Coconut Crush on the order list, just out of curiosity. I wasn't sure if you'd go for it, Blossom. Some kids won't eat coconut."

"*Other* kids." The teen bounced on the toes of her sneakers. "Hey, did you order anything else tropical? Pineapple Passion or Mookie's Macadamian Cookie?"

"Mookie's Macadamian Cookie? I don't remember seeing it on the list . . ."

They launched into a discussion of ice cream flavors. Hugh tried to put his game face on. So Birdie was not only acquainted with Blossom, she'd befriended the girl. No surprise, given Blossom's penchant for banana splits with all the trimmings. The kid probably hit the restaurant every day after school.

What *was* surprising was the easy-going camaraderie flowing between them, and Birdie's obvious affection for the girl. The defensive commando angel with the sharp tongue and sassy comebacks gave way to a breathtaking vision whose laughter brightened the crisp, late autumn day.

He gave himself a mental kick in the keister. Maybe he should be the one to move out of the apartment.

"So you're friends with Mr. Shaeffer?" Blossom was saying.

Birdie's eyes refused to meet his. "Mr. Reporter? Yeah . . . we're great friends." A lie, and his heart squeezed. Was this a reprieve? "Which house is yours, Blossom?"

"It's way down, past those big pine trees. Do you want to see it?"

"Sure."

Blossom hooked her arm through Birdie's. Greasy shame filled Hugh's gut. How to get out of here? After Blossom invited them inside she'd give Birdie a tour of the mansion Anthony was forever remodeling. They'd end up in the kitchen. Blossom would make hot chocolate. She'd hurry around the room heating water, fetching the chocolate, grabbing marshmallows; she'd sprinkle cinnamon on top to impress them.

Trapped, Hugh would finish the ruse. He'd interview her for an article he'd never write.

Soon, she'd open the *Akron Register* with her young heart soaring. She'd call through the house. *Dad, come look!* But she wouldn't find an article about her recovery from leukemia. She'd drop into a chair and read about how her father had stolen thousands from the websites set up for her medical care. The bald facts would sweep her innocence away.

It would be Hugh's fault. All because he'd needed to destroy her world for the sole and regrettable fact that he'd screwed off long enough to lose his job.

"Hugh? Are you coming or not?"

Blinking, he looked up to find Birdie retracing her steps. Damned if he wasn't standing in the center of the road with the sky opening up above him. Snow hurtled down from the blue-grey heavens. A layer of white was burying him alive.

"Are you trying to become road kill?" Birdie looked genuinely concerned, and he felt sick. After the way he'd treated her, he didn't deserve kindness. Besides, she'd do better to save her concern for Blossom once the article hit. "What's wrong? You don't look so great."

"I'm fine."

"Come on, then. I skipped lunch. Maybe Blossom will feed us."

"Count on it. She's Italian. In her world, food and hospitality go hand in hand."

"Good to know." They rejoined the teenager, and Birdie said, "So, Blossom. Ethel Lynn says your Dad is on his honeymoon . . ." Trailing off, she squinted over Blossom's shoulder. "Hey! A pink house!"

On a *whoop,* she leapt into the air. Startled, Hugh flinched. Blossom giggled.

At full throttle, she sprinted down the street toward the Victorian mansion that, in Hugh's estimation, was painted a stately brownish-rose, not pink.

She halted before the long, rectangular lawn. Snow gathered on her sunlit hair and oversized army coat, and the way she looked—her hair flying, her expression brimming with childish wonderment—sucked the air right out of Hugh's lungs. Longing curled in his chest beside his cold self-loathing. The longing won out, and he started toward her.

Flecks of white caught on the filigreed, wraparound porch and the gingerbread latticework trimming the roof. Angels in cream lace flew around a wreath tacked on the door.

"This is the house. The one Theodora told me about." Birdie pulled Blossom into a hug. "Isn't it beautiful?"

Blossom chortled. "Do you want to come inside?"

"Come in . . . you live here?" Birdie gaped at her. Then she turned to Hugh with enough delight to render him speechless. She really *was* beautiful. "Can you believe it? This is the house Justice Postell built. The kid lives here."

"With her father," Hugh supplied.

He was about to add, *and her new mother*, when his cell phone vibrated. He checked the display bar—Fatman Berelli.

Probably the PI had dug something up on Birdie. With a twinge of guilt Hugh stuffed the phone back into his pocket.

Blossom led Birdie toward the front porch. "My bedroom's a little messy," the kid was saying. "The rest of the house looks okay. Well, Meade's stupid poodle has probably peed in a corner somewhere. But don't worry. I'll have Sweetcakes chase him back into his cage."

Grinning, Birdie let the kid drag her forward. "Is Meade your babysitter?"

"Yeah, and she's working late. I've got the place to myself. I'll give you a tour."

Hugh paused on the walk, shame rooting him to the spot. In the midst of their girl bonding he hoped they'd forgotten him.

Blossom sprinted down the steps. "Mr. Shaeffer, come on!"

She clasped his hand. She'd always been an affectionate kid.

Hugh closed his eyes.

When he found the courage to open them he caught her darting glance. The trust burnishing her face was its own form of punishment.

"I've got an idea," she said, and he knew with depressing clarity what would come next.

"What's that, Blossom?"

"After I show Birdie around I'll make hot chocolate. You like hot chocolate, don't you?"

"Sure I do."

She gave his fingers a squeeze. "And you'll interview me, right? I'll tell you everything that's been going on since I got healthy. It'll make a great story in your newspaper."

"Sure it will," he said.

It took a moment then he swallowed down his shame.

CHAPTER 10

Meade tossed the mail on the kitchen counter.

She'd spent the better part of the afternoon with the cosmetics buyer at Saks and had dodged two calls from her father. On the drive back to Liberty she'd foolishly snapped open her cell phone only to discover Theodora, of all people, on the line. The old battleaxe said she'd be visiting the Williams estate tomorrow morning to discuss important matters. The prospect of spending even a few hours of Thanksgiving with her was unpleasant. Meade had been about to press further when Theodora abruptly ended the conversation.

And now this. A filthy kitchen. Meade set her face like someone with lockjaw. Setting down her briefcase, she fingered the stack of instant chocolate packets strewn across the counter. Three mugs sat on the table with marshmallows surrounding them like so many snowballs.

"Blossom, where are you?" No reply. Sighing, she retrieved Melbourne from his cage in the corner of the kitchen. "Blossom? I know you can hear me!"

The teen appeared in the doorway. "What?" She cradled an algebra book in one hand and a bag of chips in the other.

"Did you have friends over this afternoon?" Probably some of the girls from Liberty High had stopped by. Which wasn't a crisis even if they *had* left trash all over the countertops. "I don't mind if you entertain friends while I'm working. I simply wish you'd pick up after yourself."

"I'll clean the kitchen when Dad and Mary get back tomorrow night."

"You'll do it *now*. I'm dropping you off at your grandparents' house in the morning." Where the girl would spend the holiday, thank God. "It looks like Huns invaded. Your new stepmother doesn't want to come home to this mess."

"Okay, okay—I'll clean the kitchen."

Melbourne yipped and Meade lowered him to the floor. He trotted over to his food bowl, which was empty, and eyed her plaintively. "Who was hanging around with you this afternoon?" she asked, pulling the dog chow from the cupboard.

"Mr. Shaeffer was here."

"You let a *man* in the house? While I was at work?"

"It's okay. He's the reporter from Akron. He interviewed me last summer."

The newspaper article, now framed, hung above the desk in Blossom's bedroom. "He's back?" Meade asked warily. She hated reporters. Bad publicity had destroyed her father and sent her mother to her death. "Is Mr. Shaeffer writing about you?"

"Another feature. A really big one."

"How long did he stay?"

"About an hour. Birdie came with him. They've gone back to the restaurant."

Anxiety tripped up her spine. She'd offered to take her father to the restaurant last night. He'd refused, mumbling something about a promise not to visit The Second Chance for several days. Baffled, she'd dropped the invitation.

"Who's Birdie?"

"The new waitress at The Second Chance."

Had the new waitress insulted her father? Landon's depression was hard for some people to take. Filling the dog's bowl, Meade wondered if he'd had a run-in with the new employee. Yet her sense of unease warned that something more was going on here.

The silence lengthened, and the niggling sensation increased. At the sink, Blossom had turned on the tap. But the girl wasn't washing the dishes. She was staring at Meade with her eyes growing wide.

Nearing, the teen tipped her head to the side. "You know what? Gosh, I don't know why I didn't notice earlier."

Sighing, Meade stared longingly at the door. A hot bath. A drink. She was exhausted, and in no mood for small talk. "Notice what earlier?"

Blossom hesitated, and the uncomfortable sensation brought Meade's attention back to her. "Birdie is a blonde, like you," Blossom said. "I mean, her hair's longer and she wears funny clothes, but . . ."

"But *what?*"

The teen blew out a stream of air. "Never mind." She returned to the sink. "It's stupid. Forget it."

Meade opened her mouth, reconsidered. The sensation pooling inside her warned not to press Blossom further.

* * *

On a leather couch in the Deer Creek hunting lodge, Fatman Berelli sprawled out like he owned the place.

At well over six feet in height and weighing in at two hundred and eighty pounds, the private investigator looked like a big game hunter in his canvas shirt. In fact, if he told Hugh that he was leaving on safari tonight, the announcement would be utterly believable.

"Hey, Fatman." Seating himself, Hugh clasped the PI's beefy fist. He surveyed the wall, attractively built of stone. Above the blaze in the fireplace the stuffed heads of moose, rhino and zebra stared down with baleful glass eyes. "We could've met at a fast food joint, but this works too. Out of the way, but the drive was scenic. Are you a member?"

"Have been for years. You should join."

"I'm not into hunting."

"Unless we're talking women, right? With your rep, you're always on the hunt." Fatman drained his glass and motioned to the waiter. "What are you drinking, man?"

"Whatever you're having."

"Chivas Regal it is." The liveried waiter approached and Fatman handed over his glass. After they were alone, the PI gave the room a quick scan. He appeared pleased they had the place to themselves. "The woman you wanted me to check out? Birdie Kaminsky wasn't easy to track. In cyberspace, she's a ghost. But I got lucky."

"Then you found something?" At minimum, Hugh wanted basic information.

He'd nearly convinced himself it was right to dig. They were still sharing the apartment, albeit in an increasingly tense standoff.

"I might have come up empty if I hadn't checked with a colleague. Remember DeWayne Simpson?"

Hugh recalled the rude Jamaican from an interview with gang bangers he'd conducted nearly a decade ago. "Isn't he doing five-to-ten for armed robbery?"

"He's out. And you won't believe this. DeWayne works at a Big Brother outfit in Toledo. Remember his dreadlocks? Gone, man. He got religion in the joint. I nearly shit when I met up with him."

Trying to visualize the sullen Jamaican as pious was impossible. Thanking the waiter, who'd returned with their drinks, Hugh asked, "Has DeWayne met Birdie?"

"Not Birdie—her mother."

"I didn't know she had a mother." A chat about their respective families never came up. Most of the time, they merely traded insults.

"Everyone has a mother, even a cynical bastard like yourself." Fatman took a sip of his drink. "Turns out Wish Kaminsky is a real player, the type who'll clean you out then skin you alive for fun."

"Sounds like a real charmer. I'm beginning to feel sorry for Birdie."

"You should. Wish doesn't have a soul. And she rarely uses her legal name. The FBI's recently put her up on their radar."

"Is Birdie also wanted by the Feds?" God, he hoped not. For her sake, and his. If he was falling for a felon—

Falling?

No. Birdie was simply a beautiful woman. He was a red-blooded male, which meant he was hardwired with the need to bed her. So his programming was infected with a bad case of lust. Emotionally, he was the Sahara Desert.

Until Fatman said, "Personally, I hope the Feds bag Wish. Any woman who'll use her kid in scams deserves more than a visitor's pass to Purgatory."

"Are we talking recently?"

"Long time ago. She started using Birdie when the kid was four or five years old. A helpless mother-and-child routine. No motherly love there—Birdie was just another tool Wish used to scam men."

The comment nailed him in the chest—hard. Hugh took a healthy slug of his Scotch. Staring into the glass, he tried to process the ramifications. Life on the run. A felon you called mommy.

Child abuse.

He drained his glass. Given his track record with booze, he shouldn't be drinking. Hoarsely, he called over to the waiter and ordered another.

A navy briefcase sat on the stone floor beside Fatman. Hoisting it into his lap, the PI said, "According to DeWayne, Wish brought him in on a few jobs around fifteen years ago. One of the jobs was in Pennsylvania. Several others were in Florida. In one of the Florida games, Wish set herself up selling catastrophic health insurance to seniors. DeWayne was her sidekick. He said they made thousands working retirement communities."

"Where was Birdie in all this?"

"Long gone by then, living on her own."

"Tell me about the scams involving her."

Fatman snapped open the briefcase. "The first one I tracked was a poor widow routine in Chattanooga. Birdie was the bait. Wish dressed the kid in ratty clothes and planted her in churches on Sundays near an upstanding type. The dupe was usually someone who'd lost his family in a car wreck or something equally grim."

A clammy sickness rolled through Hugh. "A man eager to replace the family he'd lost." Eager to replace love.

"In the Chattanooga scam, the kid was five years old. Check out this photo. Is this her?"

Fatman dropped a five-by-seven glossy into Hugh's lap. Slowly, Hugh picked up the photo of a young girl in pigtails. She sat stiffly on the lap of a man with haunted eyes. The man, who certainly looked like he was in mourning, hunched forward in his brown corduroy blazer.

Hugh's stomach did a painful flip. The girl's matchless violet eyes, her high cheekbones and heart-shaped mouth—every feature was intensely familiar.

"It's Birdie." He tossed the photo back as if it carried typhus. "Who's the man?"

"Name's Sam Brinkley. His wife died of breast cancer five months before Wish arrived in Chattanooga. She probably read the obits."

"Easy enough to do. What line of work was Brinkley in?"

"He owned a jewelry store. He really fell for Wish. Those wedding bells were ringing hard in his ears."

"They married?"

"Are you kidding? She cleared out the cash and a fistful of gems from his store before he waltzed her up the aisle. The chump was even looking into adopting the kid—he thought she'd lost her daddy. I've found three other instances of men swallowing Wish's poor widow routine. All were lonely. Seems they fell for Birdie as much as they fell for her mother."

Pity for the child she'd been nearly swamped Hugh. Had she loved any of those men like a father? A child couldn't possibly understand that it was only about draining some poor bastard's bank account.

"Who *is* Birdie's father?" He felt weightless, like an observer floating above the sordid debris of a ruined life.

"Tanek Kaminsky, a small time loan shark and something of a bumbler. A decent man when it came to his kid. During her childhood he was in and out of the pen."

"So they had a relationship?"

"Tanek raised her part of the time. Wish, great gal that she is, dumped Birdie on whoever was nearby. Relatives, friends—Tanek whenever he wasn't incarcerated. She only kept the kid around when a new scam popped up."

"Jesus."

"Tanek's back in the pen. The chump writes to her pretty frequently."

Fatman handed over more photos, of Birdie at the ages of ten or twelve. Birdie in the lanky and awkward stages of puberty. School yearbook photos, and a newspaper clipping of her ninth grade class at a natural history museum in Trenton, New Jersey. She stood at the end of the front row with her blonde hair flowing like rain down her shoulders. She looked desolate, a hollow-eyed teen out of place in her torn jeans and rumpled tee shirt. By contrast the other students were dressed up for the school trip, the girls in skirts and blouses, the boys in slacks and long-sleeved shirts. One boy even sported a tie.

Fatman rifled through the briefcase. Predictably efficient, the PI had typed up a rough chronology of Birdie's life, which he handed over. The depressing list detailed Wish's fraudulent activities and infrequent scrapes with the law. Gutted, Hugh noticed how many of the scams involved Birdie.

"Why did you want background on this Birdie character?" Fatman asked, drawing him from his troubled thoughts. "Are you writing about her family?"

"Thinking about it." Which was bullshit. Yet he couldn't bring himself to admit the personal reasons. Fatman would think he'd lost his sanity. Or worse, make jokes about taking the dive for a female criminal.

Was sexual attraction ever logical?

There *was* a story here. A professional thief was preying on the unsuspecting citizens of a small town. If he didn't have a tangle of emotions for Birdie, he'd set to work. It would be the type of reporting sure to win accolades at the *Akron Register.*

"The kid tried to go legit in her early twenties. It didn't stick," Fatman said. "Her type doesn't get it together. Not after she's been raised on the kind of mother's milk a broad like Wish Kaminsky doles out."

"Probably not." The thought of Birdie destined for life as a criminal was a goddamn tragedy. "Is there anything else?"

The PI withdrew a sheaf of documents from his briefcase— school transcripts. "Your little Birdie attended college."

"You're shitting me."

"Stayed two whole years before dropping out."

Hugh's pity turned to sorrow. Birdie was a bright woman. She could be anything. He was still imagining the possibilities when Fatman elbowed him in the ribs.

"You'll love this." The PI's grin grew sickeningly wide. "Want to guess what our girl studied before heading back down the low road? I'll give you a hint. She took a lot of English classes before declaring her major."

The sorrow in Hugh's chest became an oppressive weight. "And her major was what?"

Fatman looked inordinately pleased. "Journalism." He slapped Hugh on the knee. "The kid aced news writing. The little pigeon wanted to grow up and become a newspaper reporter. Just like you."

* * *

Thanksgiving morning arrived in a swirl of snowfall.

Liberty Square lay in shadow with a flinty thread of orange light rising above the courthouse. Hugh parked in front of The Second Chance Grill. The restaurant was dark; the faint chords of Christmas music, rising from the surrounding streets, echoed through the lonely Square.

Climbing the stairwell to the apartment, he wondered if he should've called to explain he'd be gone all night. A call would've seemed intimate, and Birdie wasn't his lover. He wasn't even sure they were friends.

Inside the apartment, he spotted her sleeping form curled beneath blankets on the couch. He paused, startled by the nest of Wal-Mart bags on the floor. A rustling of plastic, and he withdrew a woman's nightgown from the nearest bag. The fabric was covered with flowers and had a ruffled collar. It looked like something straight out of his grandmother's closet.

The gown was painfully similar to the one Birdie was sleeping in.

He recalled their conversation about her lack of modesty, how she mixed her skimpy lingerie with his clothes. Had she gone shopping to make herself less of a lure? She shouldn't have. She wasn't responsible for his lousy self-control or his carnal thoughts.

Shame wrestled his heart. He tamped it down. Careful not to wake her, he pulled the blanket to her chin. Fingers of daylight caressed the sweet curve of her cheek. Her lips were rosy with sleep, her warm breath whispering across his knuckles. Gently, he tucked the blanket around her shoulders.

Satisfied, he tiptoed into the kitchen. Brew coffee? He'd hardly slept at the lodge. The drive back to Liberty had been long. He was still deciding when he noticed Birdie's army coat flung over a chair.

Searching the pockets was an invasion of privacy. Doing so broke a basic code of decency. Lifting the coat, Hugh stood transfixed. Given Birdie's unlucky past, there was no telling what she carried around. Switchblades, fake credit cards—he was sharing an apartment with a criminal. She was a petty criminal, to be sure. Birdie wasn't a hardened case. She was young and fresh and funny, really, when she let down her defenses. But he had a right to know who he was dealing with.

Fatman had revealed enough facts to make the future excruciatingly clear. She'd leave, and Hugh would spend months wondering where she was. Years, maybe. Fate had only thrown them together for a few short weeks.

Wavering with indecision, he let his thoughts tumble back to a childhood unlike the world where Birdie had grown up. His pop, an insurance adjuster. Mom, a homemaker and part-time secretary. Both were emotionally distant, sure. Still, he'd never doubted their love.

Not every kid grew up in a world that was predictable and safe. Had anyone cheered Birdie's small successes, her good grades or her athleticism?

An odd pull of emotion made him spread the army coat out on the table. It looked like a scarecrow missing its straw. With the breath locked in his lungs, he searched the front pocket. There was a pack of gum inside, and a tube of lip gloss.

Other pockets held surprises. Wads of bills neatly banded. An ivory bracelet exquisitely carved with a design of lilies. He withdrew a musty volume, *Miss Patti's Etiquette for Ladies*, with the awful knowledge that he didn't know Birdie at all. The book's copyright was 1912. Not the sort of thing he'd expect a petty thief to cherish. The other book, a paperback, sent a stinging warmth into his eyes—*The Portrait of a Lady*.

Hugh fingered the dog-eared pages. Birdie read Henry James? What had he found? Whimsy and dreams . . . and the evidence of hope. Did Birdie dream of becoming a lady? She'd mentioned visiting Ethel Lynn's house. Did she forget the harrows of her past while sipping tea? Did she find safety in Ethel Lynn's dining room, a moment of peace as she gazed appreciatively at the vintage tablecloth and the balloon lamps?

God, he hoped so.

A sickly remorse brushed across his lips. Soon she'd be gone. He should've cherished her company. He should've enjoyed what little she was able to give. She was a singular woman. Calculating, sure. But she was warm and witty too.

With regret, he draped the coat back over the chair. A pack of cards fell out with a *thunk*.

Not playing cards—a child's deck of *Go Fish*. A cherished memory from a horrific childhood? His throat tight, Hugh picked up the deck. Some instinct made him turn the box over. On the back, in blue crayon, was a child's clumsy scrawl.

I lov Paw Paw

Reverently, he slipped the cards back into her coat.

* * *

"What smells so good?" Struggling onto her elbows, Birdie lifted her nose.

A feast of scents lingered in the air. The savory aroma of poultry mixed delectably with the bite of cloves and the sweet of cinnamon. Her stomach rumbled.

From the kitchen, Hugh called, "The turkey's already in the oven. There's a grocery store on Fifth open twenty-four-seven. Lucky for us, they had a fourteen-pound bird left."

"You're cooking a turkey?"

She threw off the blanket then hesitated. His domestic skills might be a peace offering. Even so, he *had* tried to kick her out of the apartment. Was he softening her up before trying another stab at eviction? A pity. She'd gladly chow down on his grub but she wasn't leaving. Now that she'd discovered what she was looking for—rubies!—she wasn't going anywhere until she'd snagged them.

Getting to her feet, she decided to play nice. "Need help?"

"*You* know how to cook?"

She made a beeline for the coffee pot wafting out its own enticing scents. "I once shared an apartment with another woman in Phoenix, a chef. She taught me a lot." She neglected to add that Felicia Perez had learned her culinary skills in several of Arizona's finest correctional facilities. "I'd never had much experience with home cooking. I was happy to learn."

"No one taught you Cooking 101 while you were growing up?"

Hugh was cutting up carrots for a salad and she grabbed one. "Not really." During childhood she'd been dragged through seedy motel rooms that were never equipped with kitchens. If it weren't for grocery store salad bars, she'd have been stuck with her mother's disgusting faves—burgers and fries. "Dinnertime wasn't a high priority in my family."

"What *was* a high priority?"

She caught the strain in his voice. "What's with the twenty questions?" In response he bent his head to the task of slicing carrots in an efficient row. "And why do I get the feeling you're trying not to look at me?"

The question put color in his cheeks. Then he caught her gaze and held it. "Birdie, what happens after Liberty?"

"What do you mean?"

"Where will you go?"

"I haven't decided." West, probably. Once she found the rubies she'd put lots of miles between herself and Ohio.

"When are you leaving?"

"I don't know. Soon, I suppose."

He pushed the cutting board away and nearing, cupped the side of her face. She froze. Was this a new ploy? The angry routine hadn't forced her from the apartment. But she couldn't detect artifice on his face. The unabashed sincerity softening his features was confusing *and* distressing. She tried to back away but couldn't.

His eyes held a fierce agony. "You move around a lot, don't you? Footloose and fancy free." He frowned, considering. "I don't want you to leave the apartment."

"But you said—"

"I've reconsidered."

"What *do* you want?"

He drew her close enough to melt the reservations warring in her soul for one perfect moment. She was still sleepy, not fully in control of her senses, and he tugged her close easily. She allowed herself to savor his embrace.

"Birdie, I want to enjoy you while you're here. Is that all right?" This time he grinned, and the fire banking in his gaze was irresistible.

She felt breathless. "I'm not sure." He'd been treating her like a pariah for days.

"You're a complication I don't need, but I want to make love to you. Every day and often. Until you leave."

"We can't."

"Why not?" He trailed his palm down her spine and she trembled. "Maybe we'll get along better if we drop the celibacy routine and admit the facts. We've both got it bad."

They did. *She* did. Floundering, she tried voicing the long list of reasons why they shouldn't become intimate. She couldn't think, not with his languid caresses feathering heat across her hips. Her hunger grew stronger by the day, and the physical pleasure Hugh would supply was as potent a lure as the rubies she was desperate to find. What if their passion became uncontrollable?

He cradled the base of her skull to keep her attention planted on him. "Try letting me in. Trust me, as much as you're able."

His entreaty sent a dull ache into her chest. Trusting anyone was emotional suicide. People used each other. Sooner or later, the best intentions were forgotten. Hugh appeared sincere and maybe he was for this one moment. But eventually he'd walk right over her heart. Men always did.

Everyone did.

"I'm not good at trust," she said, dreading his reaction.

"Give it a try. You might surprise yourself."

Letting her go, he resumed cutting up the salad. He was giving her space. Allowing her to think.

He wasn't asking for much. A relationship until they both left town. Not much at all.

They were sharing a certain level of intimacy, which emboldened her. "Where were you last night? You left me hunkered down in the Perini kitchen with Blossom and two dogs that were definitely *not* made for each other. I thought Fido would eat Fifi the moment you left."

"Blossom's dog is Sweetcakes. The poodle . . . didn't Blossom say the poodle belonged to the babysitter?"

"You're avoiding the question." She took the knife from his hand and placed it on the counter. "And since we're on the subject, tell me what's going on with Blossom. I saw you making doodles on your notepad."

His gaze scuttled and she knew she was on to something. "Sometimes I doodle when conducting an interview."

"You sure don't lie well."

"Stay out of it, Birdie."

The resignation in his voice piqued her curiosity. Maybe he'd changed his mind about writing another feature on the kid. Sad for Blossom, but she'd survive. How many teens got front-page coverage even once?

"Blossom's a good kid," she said reasonably. "Why not play straight with her?"

He was spared replying. Her cell phone gave out a series of rings. Wandering from the kitchen, she checked the display. It was Delia.

She liked Delia, and hoped they were becoming friends. The young woman looked up to her, like a big sister, and it was silly and uncalled for and thrilling.

The ache returned. *I'll leave soon. We won't become friends.*

She went into the bathroom and closed the door. "What's up?" She grabbed the hairbrush by the sink and dragged it through her hair.

"I've got a favor to ask."

"Sure, whatever you need."

"Can you meet me in the restaurant in half an hour? I forgot to get out the Christmas decorations for the dining room. I promised Finney I'd get them organized. She's coming in early tomorrow morning to start putting them up."

Birdie had never owned holiday decorations. No doubt there was heavy lifting involved. "Are you bringing the boxes over in your car?"

"The stuff is in the storeroom, about twenty boxes of ornaments and lights."

The wheels in her mind spun. "Don't drive in," she replied breathlessly. With Delia out of the way, she could check every inch of the room. "I can get the boxes without your help."

"You'd do that for me?" Delia's voice was thick with pleasure. "Gosh, that'd be great."

"Just tell me where Finney keeps the key."

CHAPTER 11

Landon's daughter swept the door open.

Entering the grand foyer, Theodora plunked down her satchel. Her galoshes were slippery black eels in her weathered hands and she pulled them off with a struggle. Perversity being one of her finer traits, she'd worn the galoshes over her high heels for the shock value. Old age didn't offer many gifts, but throwing Landon's daughter for a loop was always a thrill.

Meade toyed with her strand of pearls. "Why are you wearing those . . . things? They're far too large."

"My galoshes? They're just a little roomy." Big enough for a man twice her size, but she'd stuffed the heels with balled up pantyhose. "I'll ask you to keep your comments to yourself."

"I'm merely saying—oh! What's under your dress?"

Handing over her coat, Theodora hauled up the pleated hem of the crepe de chine number. "These are ballet pants. Nice, stretchy ones. I bought them online."

"How convenient."

Bending, she snapped the skin-hugging fabric. "Why, if elasticized fabrics hadn't been invented, the lower half of my body would rearrange itself."

Meade gasped with horror.

Satisfaction spread through Theodora like oil, and she switched topics. "How's your father this morning?"

"Just fine. I asked him what this was about. He won't explain, not without you present. What's going on?"

"Patience, missy." Landon had asked Theodora to come, mostly for moral support. He'd never make his daughter understand about the woman he'd seen in town without an ally by his side. "Come along and we'll get to the bottom of this."

They entered the library. Theodora was greeted by the pleasing sight of cherry wood shelves stuffed full of books. Landon stood with his back to the fireplace. His attention tracked his daughter as she gracefully seated herself on the couch.

How different they were. Landon never put on airs, yet Meade believed window-dressing was the end-all to life. Outwardly, she resembled him. But on the inside? She was the spitting image of Cat. If Meade's house ever caught fire she'd walk past the family heirlooms and rescue her chinchilla coat.

Landon approached. "Theodora! Thank you for coming."

"It was no bother. I'm not due at my daughter's house for Thanksgiving dinner until this afternoon."

"Should I have tea brought?" He steered her to a deeply cushioned chair.

"Let's not dilly-dally." Pausing, she waited as he sat on the couch. "The top of your daughter's pretty head might blast clean off if we do."

Meade stared haughtily at Theodora, then her father. "I don't know what secrets you've both kept from me, but I'm not a child. Dad, are you listening? Stop coddling me."

The girl looked at her father with exasperation. The urge to protect him rose quickly within Theodora. She smiled at her foolishness. It was darn ridiculous when an old black woman viewed a white, middle-aged banker as something of a son, but there it was in a nutshell.

She pulled from her musings as Meade said, "I believe my father is tongue-tied."

Landon wavered. "I'm not sure how to begin."

"Dad, tell me!"

"I'm trying, darling."

Theodora jumped in. "This is about fornication and the foolishness of men. It's about sex."

Landon blanched and she pitied him—they *were* about to discuss his imprudent behavior. It was an old topic. Only this time they'd embark on a sordid discussion with his daughter passing judgment like Solomon on high. Hell and damnation. Throwing a harsh light on a man's predilections first thing Thanksgiving morning was *not* the proper way to spend the holiday.

She nailed her sights on Meade. "Let me speak plainly. Your father led you astray when you spoke with him a few days ago in the boathouse."

"He did? How?"

"He didn't see your mother's ghost. He knows Cat is dead."

"Of all the . . . Dad, why didn't you explain?"

Landon bowed his silvered head. "I was too ashamed to explain. It was easier to let you think I was talking about your mother."

Meade brought her hand to her throat. Theodora frowned. Hearing about Landon's infidelities wouldn't sit well with the girl.

"Oh, Dad. Why were you ashamed?" She clasped his wrist. "I thought you were hallucinating. I nearly called your psychiatrist."

"I'm glad you didn't."

"I'm sure I don't want to hear this. Who *did* you think you saw?"

The question hung in the air. Carefully, Landon smoothed his palms down the creases of his pants. If the foolish sod were searching for the right words, he'd never find them. What language existed to allow a man to discuss such matters with his child? Even with an adult child?

Theodora wondered why she'd declined his offer of tea. She was suddenly parched and more nervous than she dared to reveal. "Meade, how much do you know about your father's relationship with the Greyhart woman?" she asked, pushing forward.

Something hard and defensive worked through the girl's features. "The woman he ran around with while my mother was alive? I've never asked for the details. I didn't have the stomach to hear them." She pressed her hand on top of her father's. "Dad, you didn't actually think you saw her, did you?"

"Well, I thought—"

"What? That the woman who'd robbed you to the tune of six figures was back with open arms? She won't dare come to Liberty! I'll have her arrested, I'll—"

Theodora interrupted. "Girl, calm down! Lord above, didn't I go into The Second Chance to check her out? Well, I did."

Clearly Meade's patience was wearing thin. "And what did you find?" she asked.

"She's the new waitress Finney's hired. Trust me, she isn't the black-hearted witch who came between your parents."

"You're sure she's not that awful woman?"

"Dang it, of course I am!"

"Then why am I still worried? When my father was involved with . . . Theodora, did you know her?"

"Can't say I did. But she must be past fifty by now. The new waitress at The Second Chance, why, she's young."

Meade's lips tightened with distaste. "I've heard about her."

"She's not half bad," Theodora shot back, surprised by her ready defense.

True, Birdie had the manners of a goat, strutting around in a waitress's uniform so small it showed half her bosom and most of her butt. But she didn't take much guff, which might explain why Theodora secretly admired her. Not to mention Birdie wasn't the type to lure a man from his marriage bed. She wasn't church-going folk, and the devil himself knew she enjoyed spitting hurtful words from her pretty mouth. Even so, Theodora could spot a decent soul from twenty paces.

She didn't like most people, but she was starting to like Birdie. The way the child listened to the stories of Justice Postell, with her eyes aglitter . . . why, if it wasn't evidence of bone-deep goodness, what was?

There was decency in the child even if she couldn't recognize it in herself. No surprise there—people knew so little about themselves. Most people didn't know themselves at all. And what to make of Birdie falling in love with the story of Justice, the story of a black woman who'd lived during awful times? Slave times, and the Civil War to boot.

Theodora wasn't sure what to make of the child at all.

* * *

For twenty minutes, Meade interrogated her father about his relationship with the Greyhart woman. Among other sordid facts, she was horrified to learn that by the time he'd reached forty-one—the age she was now—he'd already spent years living two parallel lives. In one life, he was the quiet and dignified investment banker. In the other, he was a man bewitched.

By the time she'd finished her line of questioning, his pallid face wore a mask of tension. Mumbling about going upstairs to lie down, he left her standing before the bookshelves.

When he'd gone, Theodora said, "Let him sleep for an hour, but no longer. It does no good for a man to hide beneath the covers with the new day risen."

"I'll take care of it."

Meade ran her fingers across the books on one of the shelves, the rippling touch of leather-covered spines a surprising comfort. Now *that* was a common interest her parents had enjoyed—rare books. They'd made a disaster of their marriage, but they had shared some pursuits.

"Do you need a drink?" Theodora asked, moving to the bar.

"I'm not sure."

With a *harrumph,* the old woman mixed a martini and grabbed a beer from the fridge.

"I should thank you for intervening in all of this," Meade said, taking the martini. "The night in the boathouse . . . it's no wonder my father couldn't explain. He dreaded my reaction."

"No man wants to discuss such matters with his daughter."

Meade returned to the couch. "You *are* sure she wasn't the Greyhart woman?"

"Of course!"

"But you've never met Greyhart." Meade knew she was fishing.

"Never did."

The memory of her mother climbing into the skiff grew vivid. The argument they had on the pier was heated. Cat, always headstrong, climbed into the skiff to cut off the battle, but not before she'd handed over the packet of photos that altered Meade's world forever.

"I have some photographs of my father's mistress that I managed not to burn or cut into pieces," she said, willing a steadiness to her voice that didn't sink into her bones. "You might want to look them over to be certain."

Theodora approached, her eyes narrowing. "Lordy! How did you come by pictures of the devil herself?"

"On that day, right before Cat took the boat out on the lake, she handed me a large envelope. She was crying and slightly intoxicated, but she was determined to go. I was so upset, watching her steer toward the thunderclouds. I didn't realize she'd given me an envelope of photographs."

"I'd like to see them someday." The old battleaxe surprised Meade by sitting down beside her. Light snapped in Theodora's dark eyes as she placed her glass of beer on the coffee table and cleared her throat. "Is there anything else you're hankering to know?"

Meade rubbed her thumb down the stem of her martini glass. Did Theodora know the specifics of the years-long affair? How peculiar that her father would share his secrets with anyone, much less Theodora. Maybe it was because they'd known each other for so long. Or perhaps compassion lurked beneath her crusty, short-tempered exterior.

"I'm trying to understand why my father . . ." The words lodged in her throat. How to discuss something this awful? Perplexed, she took a sip of her drink.

"Spit it out, missy."

A frisson of impatience leapt through Meade. She set her martini down. "Why did my father cheat on my mother for so many years? I can understand how a man stumbles into a one night stand. He's out of town on business, he has too much to drink—Theodora, I *can* understand. What's so difficult is why Dad continued. Didn't he feel guilt? Remorse?"

"He's depressed, isn't he?"

"And my mother is dead."

"If your mother had taken better care of him, he would've ended the affair right quick."

"Now it's her fault? My father was a liar and a cheat. He ran around on my mother for years. Given everything he's done, he deserved to be brought low by a woman like the Greyhart bitch."

The outburst brought a low rumble from Theodora, a nearly imperceptible rasp. Her sparrow's breast quivered with buckling fury. Age couldn't diminish some people; frailty was a mere inconvenience to an overpowering personality. The lines carved into the sides of her mouth deepened and Meade drew back with alarm when their gazes locked.

"You want the truth?" Theodora slapped her hand against her thigh. "Now, I don't like speaking ill of the dead. Of course there was good in your mother—Cat drew rich folks to good causes like a buck drawing doe to the rut. Women's shelters, the arts—I was proud to work on any foundation she chaired."

"You were involved with her philanthropy?"

"Most of the time I was willing to oblige."

Cat's association with Theodora made sense. Theodora struck a low profile in public, but she owned huge tracts of land in Jeffordsville County. The depths of her wealth went back generations. Any foundation would covet her as a benefactor.

Meade looked at her squarely. "Are you saying you were friends with my mother?"

Theodora drew a gnarled finger in lazy circles on the fabric of her dress. "I was your father's friend. When he fell in love, I was happy for him. Cat was a young thing the first time we worked together—your parents were newlyweds. Not that anyone saw much of your father on the social circuit."

Unlike her mother, he hadn't come from money. "The world she grew up in . . . he probably found it overwhelming."

"I'm sure he thought she was quite a catch. People loved Cat, loved the way she'd float down a staircase in her Tiffany jewels and sweet-smelling perfume." Theodora frowned. "Your father, on the other hand, was a quiet man. He worked hard investing her inheritance and building a fortune in his own right while Cat, why, she had more than enough beaux to squire her around to the charity balls."

Beaux?

A bitter taste bloomed in Meade's throat. Had Cat also been unfaithful? So many secrets, and she didn't have the stomach to hear the awful details. Yet she couldn't stop herself from saying, "For the record, my mother was a great philanthropist. She did a lot of good in Ohio."

"Stop thinking with your heart! Those charities—do you think she cared a hoot about homeless women or the art museum? She worked the circuit for the men."

"Stop it." Meade stumbled to her feet.

"Cat, then the Greyhart woman—your father got himself bound up with two great performers. Each knew how to use him for her own gain."

"How dare you compare my mother to her! Greyhart's a criminal. She took everything from my father. *Everything*."

"And your mother didn't?" Theodora stared at her as placidly as a Sphinx. "Cat and Greyhart were both alley cats. Don't you know they could've come from the same litter?"

CHAPTER 12

Praying the rubies were in the storeroom, Birdie hung up with Delia and slipped out of the apartment.

Hurrying down the stairwell, she recalled the clue found in the bunting draped across the restaurant's picture window. *Brick by brick, my love. My life built alone without you.* The building was built of bricks. For days, she'd tapped on bricks in the dining room searching for loose spots and chipped at mortar in the kitchen when Finney went on break. She'd thought she'd checked every blasted one.

But she hadn't checked the storeroom.

Excitement quickened her stride, and she reached the first floor in record time. And to think she'd had to pick the lock the night she'd entered the restaurant on the sly. Who knew the key was hidden in plain sight? Giddy, she looked up.

Just as Delia had described, the heavy molding around the door was loose. On tiptoes, Birdie removed the sliver of wood. The key tumbled into her palm.

She opened the door to the kitchen and flicked on the lights. According to Delia, the second key, used to unlock the storeroom, was in a silverware drawer near the grill, where Finney usually stood cooking and barking orders. She wrenched open the drawer. A large, old-fashioned brass key clattered forward.

It was pretty, really, with a heart-shaped head and large gleaming teeth.

Drawing it close, she gasped.

The clue, the one hidden in the bunting, spoke of building a life alone without the one you loved. *And the head of the key was shaped like a heart.*

Would it lead directly to the rubies?

Retracing her steps, she reentered the hallway. The storeroom lay at the end, past the stairwell. She unlocked the door and stepped inside.

The musty scent of dust peppered the air. On an involuntary sneeze, she found the light switch.

Spellbound, she blinked. The storeroom was *huge.*

The place brimmed with a treasure trove of boxes and furniture and plastic-wrapped dishes. Aisles cut through the heirlooms in a sensible grid fashion that made perusing the antiques a simple task. Absently, she ran her fingers across the smooth mahogany of an antique sideboard. The furniture alone was worth thousands, and it was hard to imagine the wealth tucked away in the hundreds of boxes. Clearly nothing of worth had ever been thrown out in the restaurant's history.

She was itching to investigate all of it when the sound of footfalls on the stairwell brought her up short.

"Birdie? Where are you?"

Hugh appeared in the hallway with a dishtowel flung over his shoulder, his black hair mussed. Despite her irritation at the interruption, she laughed at the orange glop speckling his blue oxford shirt.

"What did you get all over yourself?" she asked. He approached, and she instinctively blocked the door like a pirate protecting her booty. "You have some of it on your shoes, too."

"I do?" Bending, he swiped a finger through the orange muck on the toe of his loafer. She cringed when he stuck his finger in his mouth. Noticing her disgust, he added, "What? You got something against pumpkin pie? It's Thanksgiving. Everyone has pie after they chow down on the bird."

"A man doesn't have the skill set needed to bake a pie. It's a multi-task event. Men aren't multi-taskers."

"For the record, I baked two pies."

It was clearly the truth. Spots of flour dusted his all-too attractive features. "So we both get a pie? We don't have to share?" The urge to push him from the doorway competed with her penchant for home-baked goods. "When do they come out of the oven?"

"You have to eat dinner before you have dessert." He angled his head to peer over her shoulder. "What are you doing down here, cupcake?"

"Vegetable names, Hugh. If you want to call up sweeter memories from my childhood, stick to vegetables. Don't forget to lay on the affection when you do."

"Whatever you say, Tomato."

"Shouldn't you be upstairs basting the turkey?"

"Probably." He pushed her aside and strolled into the room. Pausing beside an oblong table draped in plastic, he added, "I heard you on the phone with Delia."

"You mean you were eavesdropping."

Shrugging, he lifted the edge of the plastic. He let go and it fluttered downward in a puff of dust. "Do you need help moving the Christmas decorations or not?"

Covering her nose, Birdie shoved past him. "Don't do that again. I hate dust." She made a beeline through a clump of furniture and headed toward the nearest wall—which was, naturally, made of brick. "I can manage on my own."

"I'll wager some of the boxes weigh fifty pounds. Think crystal and ceramics. Lots of the holiday decorations are from the 1800s. They aren't made of plastic."

"Delia said there's a dolly in here." Birdie noticed the contraption beside a stack of boxes. She wheeled it toward the center of the room in a hasty, zig-zag route. If he didn't leave, she wouldn't be able to search for the gems. "See? I can manage. Now go away."

He stood fast, but there wasn't time to argue. She caught something out of the corner of her eye and abruptly surveyed the walls. The bricks were different here. They weren't all of the same fire red color used in the rest of the building. Some were a muddy brown. Others were a bright orange like the pumpkin Hugh had spattered all over himself. She remembered something Ethel Lynn had said: the storeroom was part of the original building, which had been added onto several times.

Excitement tripped up her spine. *Brick by brick, my love. My life built alone without you.* Bricks of many colors . . . she must be close.

"What are you up to?" Hugh joined her at the wall, his intelligent gaze traversing the bricks like a hound pursuing quarry. "You don't care about getting the Christmas stuff out of storage. You agreed to do the dirty work for something else."

"Stop sweet-talking me. You know how it goes to my head."

"Then let me lay on more sugar. I'll help if you'll tell me what's going on."

Dragging her attention from the wall was nearly impossible, but she managed to glare at him. Help her? Was he kidding? The rubies were her ticket to a better life. She wasn't sharing them, least of all with a reporter who was as irritating as he was sexy. She had to find the boxes of holiday decorations, start moving them, and get him off her tail.

"I mean it," he said softly. "Let me help you."

The entreaty in his voice was sudden and sincere. His expression was infused with a gentleness she hadn't thought him capable of. For a reckless moment, she wondered if maybe he wasn't trying to horn in on the loot at all. He wanted *her*.

Impulsively, she brushed the lock of hair falling across his brow. "I'm fine on my own," she replied. He took her by the wrist to stop her from moving off, and her emotions cartwheeled. "Go back upstairs. I have work to do."

"And I shouldn't watch you in the commission of a crime?"

"Hugh—"

"I'm only trying to help. Maybe it'll give me a better understanding of the woman I'm sharing an apartment with since she's also the woman who's getting under my skin."

"Being under your skin doesn't sound so bad," she replied, lured by the soft lights in his eyes. She couldn't look away.

"Birdie, I'm not perfect, and I won't judge you. We've both made mistakes."

His voice, like his expression, went fluid. "What kind of mistakes?" she asked, his sincerity pouring something new and wonderful into her heart. He did understand how much she'd messed up her life because he'd messed up his own. It wasn't easy to pass judgment if you were able to call up the long, dreary list of your own errors, the people you'd hurt through anger or neglect, and the actions taken that were petty and self-serving. Hugh was better than most people—he possessed fortitude, enough to view himself with clarity and recognize his transgressions.

Still, it was crazy to stand here and drink in the enticing scent of his cologne and the misgiving in his eyes. But her feet were glued to the spot even as her thoughts sped forward and became focused. He'd also made mistakes. Whoppers, probably. Had he made a few recently?

Blossom.

Why had he sat in the kid's house pretending to interview her if he wasn't writing an article?

"Is Blossom one of your mistakes?" she asked. "You aren't going to hurt her, are you?"

"Probably." He tried to smile but his expression collapsed. "Yes, I will hurt her. I don't want to. I didn't come back to make her famous all over again."

"Why are you here?"

He scrubbed his palms across his face. "I'm investigating her father."

Anthony Perini owned the Gas & Go on the other side of the Square. He'd just wed Mary Chance, the doctor who owned the Second Chance Grill. The way Finney spoke of him, Anthony was nothing if not decent. Why would a hard-edged reporter like Hugh be interested in such a regular guy?

Noting her confusion, Hugh said, "Last summer, Blossom's leukemia progressed to the point where she needed a bone marrow transplant. Anthony's insurance didn't cover the procedure."

"I remember. I read the article you wrote about the auction that raised money for Blossom's care."

"It was the same with the websites. They went up and brought in money by the truckload. Problem is, those sites are still up, still bringing in cash."

What he'd described was sad and common, and her lower nature told her exactly where this was headed. She thought of her mother scamming marks and reeling in cash. Wish never used websites. She was a klutz on a computer and had never learned how to use the Internet. But Birdie could imagine the possibilities.

She whistled softly. "Anthony kept the sites up to make himself rich?" Even in small town America, people weren't as decent as they seemed. The realization hit hard—she wanted to believe the people of Liberty were better than most. She'd grown to like so many of them. "How much cash are we talking?"

"Thousands."

Her thoughts turned to Blossom, a sweet kid with a potential felon for a parent.

The thought jogged a memory from childhood, one she despised. Cold, cement walls, and her mother dragging her forward by the hand. She'd been five or six years old. The sinister noises of the penitentiary had terrified her—metal doors slamming, and a man shouting in the distance. With her feet tripping forward, her attention hung on the glinting silver of the guard's sidearm.

The guard moved off, leaving them trapped in a room that felt like a tomb. Birdie scrambled onto a chair and pressed her hands to the glass separating her from her father.

Why he'd been in the pen, when he'd be released—she no longer recalled the specifics. What she *had* carried through childhood was the humiliation. Unlike most kids, her dad was usually behind bars.

Bleakly, she drew from the reverie. "Will Anthony go to prison?" Sick at heart, she stepped back. "Get real, Mr. Reporter. If you report this, you'll send him to the pen. You know that, right?"

"He'll get a fine and have to return the funds. He won't serve time."

"Yeah, and who gave you that guarantee?" For a reporter, he sure didn't understand how the world worked.

Hugh looked as sick as she felt. "I don't think Anthony will do time."

"If you're wrong, it'll destroy Blossom. Is it worth it?"

He took her by the shoulders and spun her toward the wall. "Is *this* worth it? Why are you studying the bricks? Thinking of switching jobs and going into construction?"

"I can't explain."

"Can't or won't?" When she pressed her lips together, he added, "I told you about Anthony to prove I'm trustworthy. You know my secret. Now tell me yours."

Indecision wound through her. Given Hugh's occupation, he was good at unraveling mysteries. Could he help find the gems? It wasn't like she'd done so great on her own.

But she didn't trust him. The dark, painful truth threatened to shut down her heart. She didn't trust anyone.

A little depressed, she tried to kick-start her cunning. No easy feat with Hugh looking at her with enough sincerity to make her feel like hell. But she couldn't bring herself to tell him exactly what she was looking for. A better ploy? Hide the specifics behind a hill of lies.

Maybe he'd buy a story about a family heirloom she'd come to Liberty to seek out. It was a half-truth, really. She *was* related to Justice through the child the freedwoman had with Lucas. Of course, Justice's direct descendants had more right to the rubies, assuming the gems could be found. Still . . .

In the past, skirting the truth had been easy. Since arriving in Liberty, her conscience had risen from a deep slumber. Something in the water was getting to her. Or the people were. Whatever it was, she didn't relish lying, even if there was no other choice.

Would Hugh buy some bullshit she made up on the fly?

Birdie managed to lift her head to regard him. The truth knocked around in her throat, trying to get out. But it was professional suicide for a petty thief to trust a newspaper reporter.

CHAPTER 13

Hugh lounged against the plastic-wrapped table as a battle waged in Birdie's eyes. The Greeks and the Trojans going at it inside her skull, and it was anyone's bet which side was winning.

Odds were, she didn't want to come clean. But from the looks of her, she wasn't comfortable lying either. He recalled the sad bits Fatman had told him about her life, a childhood that had been damn abusive. Wish Kaminsky, a grifter more interested in lining her pockets than in raising her daughter. A father in prison.

Making the slog to the moral high ground wasn't second nature for Birdie.

"Why not play straight with me?" he asked, frustrated. Even if he couldn't alter the trajectory of her life, he could offer friendship. "The bricks have something to do with your search, don't they? The way you keep studying them, they must be important."

"They are." She rolled her lower lip beneath her teeth, her violet eyes smoky with doubt.

"Tell me why."

"I'm still deciding if it would be a smart move or a dumb-ass one."

"It's a good move, a winning move. If you don't have someone to trust, what have you got?"

"Peace of mind," she said, but she grinned. Kneeling, she dragged a box close. "I have to find the holiday decorations and move them into the dining room. You want to help? Then help."

"You've got it."

Anxious to gain her trust, he scanned the notes written on the top of each box she pushed forward. The cursive was thin and wavery, rather difficult to read. Ethel Lynn's handwriting? The first two boxes were labeled 'linens' and 'Wedgwood China'. The third was marked 'holiday.'

"Birdie, the contents are listed on top. Good for us, or we'll never find all the stuff." The enormous room was filled to overflowing with boxes, furniture, and bric-a-brac. Hugh nodded toward the next aisle. "Why don't you look over there? I've got this row covered."

Moving away, she hunted for several minutes in silence. When she made a whooping noise, Hugh nearly jumped out of his skin.

"Jackpot!" She did a quick count. "Eighteen boxes. Delia said most of the decorations were stacked together."

"I'll get the dolly."

They worked in silence for twenty minutes. After the last of the boxes were deposited inside the restaurant, they returned to the storeroom. He expected her to douse the lights and lock up. Instead she weaved through the clumps of furniture, halting before an overstuffed chair. Peeling off the plastic sheeting, she tossed it to the cement floor and sat.

With her elbows on her knees, she knitted her fingers together. "I came to Liberty because I'm trying to find something," she said, and a surge of satisfaction brought Hugh to a standstill. She'd decided to trust him. "I'm not having much luck. It's a puzzle, really."

"I'm good with puzzles." Scanning the room, he spotted a chair upholstered in green cloth. Whipping off the sheeting, he dragged it close enough to sit knee to knee. "It's all about problem solving."

"What if I don't tell you what I'm looking for? Will you still help?"

"Sure." Stung, he kept his expression neutral. Apparently her trust had limits. He'd take what little she'd give. "Tell me what you've got so far."

"It's kind of like a family heirloom, and it's hidden."

"Why would something owned by your family be hidden in Liberty?"

"Not in the town. Somewhere in this building." She made a sweeping motion to encompass the room. "This place was built during the Civil War. Believe it or not, a former slave built the place and operated the restaurant."

"Justice Postell," he supplied.

Her brows shot up. "You know about her?"

"She was an important figure in Liberty." He'd read up on Justice last August during a week interviewing Blossom. "The historical society has an archive on her. Justice was the first woman, black or white, to operate a business in Jeffordsville County."

"I know. Theodora told me."

"The Chamber of Commerce manages a foundation in her name. Grant money is given out each year to small businesses, but it's done anonymously. Whoever the benefactor is, he's publicity shy."

"Or *she's* publicity shy. Maybe a successful business*woman* is the anonymous benefactor."

A playful light entered Birdie's matchless eyes, and Hugh toyed with the idea of kissing her. Seated this close, it would be easy to lean in and lay one on her. Outside, snow was blanketing the town. The lazy Thanksgiving holiday was upon them. They'd spend the rest of the day in the sack . . .

"I'm glad someone thinks enough of Justice to honor her memory," Birdie said, drawing him from his salacious thoughts. She reclined against the chair's soft padding and he was grateful for the distance. "She's always been like a . . . well, like a hero to me. My mother was a lousy storyteller, but my grandfather's stories made Justice sound noble. Noble and beautiful. You've probably seen her portrait in the dining room so you know what I mean."

"I have seen it."

Birdie's eyes grew dreamy and he was entranced. "Tell me about your grandfather's stories," he prodded.

"They were about one of our French ancestors, a wealthy plantation owner from Charleston, South Carolina. Justice was a slave on his plantation. She worked inside the mansion, helping with the housekeeping and tending to his daughter."

"Lucas Postell. I'll take you over to the historical society whenever you'd like. They have a sketchy background on Lucas, including several love letters he wrote to Justice. The letters were hidden away for decades—someone bequeathed them to the society around the same time The Beatles took America by storm. Are you sure you're one of his descendants?"

"My mother's maiden name was Postell. The plantation burned to the ground during the Civil War, but a painting of Lucas survived. You'd laugh—my grandfather was his spitting image. I'm positive I'm related."

"I'll be damned."

No wonder she admired Justice. Birdie's parents were reprobates. Neither one deserved a daughter who could make so much more of her life if given half a chance. In Justice, she probably saw an example of how someone could overcome the worst of circumstances. The freedwoman *was* a hero.

"Your grandfather, were you close to him?" he asked, desperate to find one example of decency in her harrowing life.

On a sigh, Birdie smoothed her palms over her jeans and his heart sank. "I loved him," she said. "He wasn't around much."

Was her grandfather another con artist? Anger shot through him. For Chrissake, were *all* her relatives criminals?

"Did his job keep him on the road?" he asked, needing to push her to tell more—tell all of it, if she had the courage.

"Grandpa was usually in prison." She looked at him squarely, her defiance colored by something deeper. Hurt? "He drank too much and he had a temper, but he liked to eat. No one in our family was into cooking except me. If I made an omelet or spaghetti, Grandpa paid up by telling a story about Justice."

"How old were you when you became the family chef?"

"Seven or eight." She tapped the porcelain curve of her cheek, a line he often dreamt of kissing. "Grease spatter is a real bitch when you're four feet tall. I probably burned myself a dozen times before I snagged a step stool from a drugstore."

"Someone should've been watching you." Rage at her parent's negligence made him clench his fists. "It's wrong to leave a kid alone at a stove. You could've been injured."

"Hey, I was glad when we had a stove. My mother never stayed in one place long. Most of the time, we lived in motel rooms."

"The stories of Justice carried you through?"

She looked at him with wonderment. "I guess they did."

Now her special kinship with a freedwoman from the 1800s seemed entirely logical. Hadn't they both lived in bondage? Justice overcame impossible odds to reach the North and build a new life. Did Birdie dream of escaping the shackles of a world with nothing but the criminal arts to guide her?

Yearning spiraled into Hugh's chest. It wasn't sexual in nature; it certainly wasn't love. *Empathy*. He wanted the same things, to escape the prison of his past, the doubts and the regrets.

He recalled the etiquette book and the novel, *Portrait of a Lady,* Birdie carried around in her army coat. "I'm sure Justice was quite a lady," he said, acutely aware of the emotion burnishing his voice. "Pregnant with Lucas's child, traveling north. She married a preacher's son and carried on after his death. She raised her son alone and managed a business right alongside the men in Liberty."

"She was an amazing woman." Birdie drew her legs up onto the chair and cradled her knees. She looked sweet, animated, nothing like the hard woman who launched brusque comments like grenades. "After Lucas lost his wife, Justice was there for him. She comforted him and helped raise his daughter, Molly."

Hugh was familiar with the story. "He sent Justice north and promised to follow after he sold his land holdings. But The Civil War erupted. She arrived in Liberty, pregnant—" He stopped, the rest clicking into place. "Do you realize you're related to the son Justice had with Lucas? You might have relatives here in Ohio. Maybe even some in Liberty."

Birdie's expression grew wistful. "I'd like to search for them . . ."

Disappointment flooded him. "But you can't stick around long enough to meet them? You'll find what you came for, and leave?"

Wearily, she rose from the chair and approached the nearest wall. With fingertips she traced a line of grey mortar, her movements oddly sad. "Lucas, my great-great grandfather, gave Justice something before she left South Carolina. Something valuable. She was supposed to trade it for cash and use the money to start a new life. She never did cash it—them—in."

His memory was nearly photographic and he didn't recall anything of the sort in the historical record. "Is that what your grandfather told you?"

Nodding, Birdie moved her hand in a swirling motion across the wall, her expression distant. "Lucas died soon after the war, and Molly was destitute. She was raised by someone else. Cousins, or an uncle—I'm not sure. Justice wanted to return the valuables. Somehow, she got a letter to Molly. There was a clue inside."

Hugh joined her. "What was it?" he asked, brushing his knuckles across her forearm.

A nervous smile lifted the corners of her mouth. "Liberty safeguards the cherished heart." She tried to catch his gaze but her eyes scuttled. "Theodora says Justice brought rubies to Liberty."

"Did you say *rubies*?" Lucas had been a wealthy plantation owner. The possibility he'd owned precious gems was entirely plausible. "What are we talking about? A few small stones or something larger?"

"I'm not sure exactly." She grabbed hold of his shirt. Which was nice, because he was able to steer her into his arms. "Hugh, I'm trusting you. Don't tell anyone."

"Not a soul."

"I'm serious. And don't try to steal the rubies from me once we find them. I'll hunt you down if you do."

Wasn't *he* the one on the hunt? "Tomato, you can follow me wherever you like. There's a nice fat bird roasting in the oven upstairs. I'll serve dinner. Have me for dessert."

She tried to struggle free. "Stop joking. This is my life we're talking about—my future." Her eyes blazed. Yet he noted with satisfaction the mirth flickering on her full, thoroughly kissable mouth. "I shouldn't have told you about the gems. Obviously your brain is clogged with thoughts of sex. What I really need to know is if your heart pumps with avarice."

"What do you take me for?" Sure, he'd like to seduce her. Nothing more. "I'm honorable to the bone."

"Of course you are."

She tried to shoot him the evil eye. She grinned, ruining the effect and giving him the opportunity to nibble on her neck. *Luscious.*

He grazed his teeth across her collarbone. "I'm a born and bred gentleman." She trembled, and his thermostat skyrocketed. "You need to follow the clues to the rubies? I'm your man. I'll help you unravel the mystery. Honorable chump that I am, I'll ask nothing in return."

"If you're so honorable, why are your hands on my ass?"

"That's not honor, Eggplant. That's human need." Palming the silky curve, he was aroused in an instant. "Kiss me, Birdie. I'm willing to help you, but I'll work better with an incentive."

"Wait a second. Aren't you the guy who asked me to move out of the apartment? Something about my lack of modesty interfering with your ability to meet deadlines? I thought your job was on the line."

"No one worries about job security on Thanksgiving. We're supposed to be eating too much and enjoying ourselves."

Her jeans were damn tight, but he managed to inch his fingers toward her pelvis. Birdie shuddered, and the fire in his groin leapt higher. "We've shared secrets," he murmured against the tasty curve of her collarbone. He steered her away from the wall and toward the nearest table. "We've bonded. I'm not into sealing our pact with blood, but I *can* think of a way we can form a more perfect union."

"You aren't planning to recite The Declaration of Independence while we're doing it, are you?" Giggling, she flattened her palms on his pecs. He watched, dizzy, as her eyes dilated with an unexpected and thoroughly greedy passion. "Scratch that. We're not doing it. Get off me! We need to check the wall, the bricks—"

Pinning her on the table, he swooped in and caught her lips in a hungering kiss. She stilled and the taste of her sent his heart into a gallop. Then she was returning his kiss with equal heat, a whimpering moan escaping her throat. Victorious, he eased back enough to better position her on the table.

She delighted him when, impatient, she grabbed him by the shoulders and dragged his mouth back down to hers.

CHAPTER 14

The number of relationships Birdie had enjoyed with men roughly equaled the number of U.S. presidents elected during her adulthood. Pathetically few. And there was something every relationship shared. A drifter or a grifter, the man held her emotions for ransom then stole her cash on his way out.

Sliding her arms around Hugh's neck, she knew this time was different.

Oh, Hugh was all wrong for her. The man had *mistake* written across his devil-dark eyes. It didn't help that he tasted good and smelled even better. The way he was fondling her hips was sheer heaven—no, that wasn't the problem. What was?

He was the first man she'd ever known who wasn't planning to clean her out. He truly was honorable in a cocky, take-no-prisoners way.

His decency put her heart at risk.

"This is a mistake," she murmured against his ear. She considered protesting further, sank beneath the sensations, and arched her back. On a groan, he grabbed the hem of her turtleneck and rolled it up. "This isn't the right time for a relationship. Your job is on the line, and I have to find the rubies."

Hugh lifted his head, his black hair engagingly mussed. Had she been running her fingers through his locks? It was hard to be sure with her attention zooming in on the hot journey his hands were making up her ribcage.

His fingers shaking, he wrenched her turtleneck over her bra. "We all make mistakes. Live and learn." He let out a moan that rippled straight up her spine. "Birdie, you're gorgeous. Thirty-six double D. My God."

She stilled. "How the hell do you know my bra size?"

"Some things a man learns."

She reloaded with a comeback, which fizzled when he flipped up her bra. His palms landed on the base of her back, hauling her closer. Dizzy with pleasure, she was dimly aware of his eyes drifting open as hers drifted shut.

"If that isn't strange. Birdie, look." The provocative feeling of his mouth on her skin withdrew. "See the design on the wall?"

She wrenched her eyes open. "Design?" She had designs on *him*, actually.

"Over there," he said, nipping at her ear.

"Huh?" Her bra was twisted around her turtleneck. She looked like a lust-bitten whore on her way to the gallows.

Hugh struggled into a standing position. "Look at the wall. See the bricks? They're darker than the others. They make a pattern."

"How can you talk about patterns at a time like this?" Yanking her shirt down, she craned her neck. No easy feat when you were lying on your back. "Next you'll admit you edit news articles while doing the nasty."

"Are you planning on doing the nasty with me, babe? God, that makes me happy."

"Vegetables, Hugh. Stick with the program."

"Whatever you say, Carrot." He scratched his head, grinning. Then he bent and nibbled on her collarbone. "And by the way, I'm an investigative journalist. I get paid to notice something out of the ordinary." He started toward the wall. "This will sound crazy, but I swear the pattern looks like a big . . . heart."

A heart?

She clambered from the table. Her blood was still thick with longing, but she managed to clear her head. The clue, the one she'd found in the patriotic bunting, rang in her ears.

Brick by brick, my love
My life built alone without you

"It's the clue, the last one I found!" She stumbled past a cluster of end tables for a better look. "It was about love. Love, hearts— wow. Look at that!"

Hugh was right—the pattern *did* form a heart. The wall was made of bricks in many colors, but the rust-colored bricks stood out visibly against the rest. On instinct, she dropped to her knees beneath the heart's arrowed base.

Blood pounded in her ears. The brick, the one right beneath the heart, was loose. She jiggled it and chips of mortar pinged off the floor. Tension wound across her shoulders. With a gentle tug, she worked the brick out.

Hugh was at her side in an instant. "What is it? What's inside?"

Boyish delight flooded his voice. Smiling up at him, she reached inside. "Give me a sec, will you? I don't feel anything, just empty space." An involuntary shiver bounced through her shoulder blades. "I hope there aren't any spiders. I hate anything that moves faster than I do, especially if it has eight legs."

"Fear not, Turnip. Move back. I'll search the portal."

"And ruin my fun?" She giggled. "Get away!"

The edges of the brick were rough, and cool to the touch. Straining, she reached in further and let out a gasp. Her fingers connected with something soft, a cloth of some kind. What if she'd found ten rubies? A dozen? She'd pawn the gems in Atlanta or Dallas and use the money to go legal. She'd buy a house, a sweet bungalow with flower boxes on the windowsills. . .

"Birdie, come on already!"

"Got it." With exquisite care, she drew the bag out.

It was purple, the color of royalty, and made of velvet.

"Are the rubies inside?" Hugh crouched beside her, a lock of hair brushing his brows. He looked like a boy on a treasure hunt. "Open it up!"

"Give me a kiss for luck," she replied, steering his lips to hers. He obligingly darted his tongue into her mouth and reached for her breasts. She squirmed away.

She'd swear he was holding his breath. As she was, as she took the heavy yellow cord between her fingertips and drew the bag open. No rubies inside. Disappointed, she withdrew a brass key. It was similar to the key for the storeroom, with a heart-shaped head and four teeth.

She looked closer and her emotions rebounded. "Do you see that?" Awestruck, she traced her fingers across the base of the heart. Across the stone residing there.

It was a glittering, blood red gem. A ruby.

CHAPTER 15

"This is ridiculous," Birdie said. "Answer your cell."

Beside the empty bowl of mashed potatoes, Hugh's cell phone vibrated across the table like a Mexican jumping bean. Yanking his arms from the soapy water in the sink, he stalked over and read the display panel. He tossed the phone down.

It was the third call he'd ignored.

"Why not pick up?" she asked. "It might be important."

"It's not." He motioned toward her plate. "Are you done?"

"I'm stuffed. The plate's yours."

He'd gone all out serving Thanksgiving dinner. They'd eaten in a bubbly delirium after the discovery in the storage room. The meal would've been perfect if not for the phone calls he'd refused to pick up.

Propping her chair against the wall, Birdie lifted the key and turned it in the light. She tried to appreciate the scintillating blood-red ruby at the base of its heart-shaped head even as her attention strayed to Hugh.

Discovering the key had brought a new, if tenuous, intimacy to their relationship. She'd confided in him about the hidden rubies, and he seemed worthy of her trust. Throughout dinner, they'd kept the conversation centered on the treasure hunt even as the air grew thick with sexual longing. And no wonder. They'd nearly made love on top of one of the tables in the storeroom. If Hugh hadn't noticed the heart-shaped design in the wall, they would have gone at it like rabbits.

A close call. Birdie twirled the key between her fingers. With the thrill of discovery now passed, she was riddled with second thoughts. Turning their normally combative relationship into something more was a stupid move. She was starting to like Hugh—the boyish side he'd displayed in the storeroom, the sensitivity he unleashed at unpredictable moments. Why muck up the works by sleeping with him? Sex was supposed to be a mindless release, a few hours' diversion from the loneliness of her days. This time was different. There was more at play here than mere lust.

If she slept with Hugh she wouldn't be able to keep her emotions safe. Risking an entanglement, with the rubies at stake, was *not* a good plan.

Once she found the gems she'd leave Ohio. It was a cardinal rule. Do the crime and get out. Only, she'd leave part of her heart with Hugh—a man she'd never see again.

Worried, she brought the key near. There hadn't been a clue this time, no poetry to lead her forward. The velvet pouch had contained only the key. What did it open?

At the sink, Hugh lifted a serving platter from the suds. "Want to give me a hand with the dishes?"

She traced the key's heavy brass teeth. "Thanks, but I'll pass."

"When I was growing up, we had a rule. The cook never cleaned up the mess."

"Good thing I didn't grow up in your house." She rolled her eyes when his cell phone did the *fandango* across the tablecloth. "Why don't you answer it?"

"Thanks, but I'll pass."

"Who calls four times on Thanksgiving? I'd go with 'parents' but most give up on the third try." Not that her mother ever got in touch. Her father . . . maybe. If Tanek wasn't too wrapped up in a prison poker game he'd ask the guards for the phone.

"It's not my parents," Hugh said. "It's Timothy Ralston, a reporter at the *Register*."

"You've never mentioned him."

"I try not to think about him."

The venom in Hugh's voice got her complete attention. Or maybe it was the attractive way his eyes flashed. His version of anger was far too sexy.

"What have you got against the guy?" she asked, putting her libido into a fist-hold.

"Think Hercules without a brain. The guy writes fluff. He consults his astrologer before doing an interview. He picked up these weird crystals in Sedona on his last vacation, and keeps them on his desk like a strange rock formation growing beside his keyboard. He's into yoga."

"So Ralston has a mystical side," she replied, amused by his petulance. "No danger there."

"The family's loaded. Ralston buys a new Maserati every April. This year's baby is cherry red."

"He's rich. What's the big deal?"

"Daddy's furniture chain pours thousands into advertising at the *Register,* which is why Ralston was hired. The City Editor is happy to feed him ideas. Rich boy's job will always be secure."

"Unlike yours?"

Hugh's face clouded. "Ralston is vying for my job." He thrust a pot into the water and scrubbed with a vengeance. "If I can't dig up enough scum for the Perini exposé, I'll be in the unemployment line permanently."

"Stop being dramatic. Someone else will hire you."

"I've been thrown off five newspapers. Think leprosy. No one will touch me."

She'd love to touch him and the thought sent warmth leaping across her skin. Struggling away from the salacious possibilities, she slipped the key back into the pouch. The war between her urge to comfort Hugh and her libido sure wasn't comfortable. Who was she kidding? She didn't want to offer friendly affection—she wanted more.

Of course, his livelihood wasn't simply at risk. If he didn't publicize the theft of the website money, he'd lose his job to a journalist he apparently despised. Rough break.

And what about Anthony Perini? The guy might have a perfectly good reason for taking the money. Uncomfortable with her line of thinking, Birdie rose from her chair. There were all sorts of reasons why someone stole cash. A guy might be desperate. Or maybe he didn't understand how to live a straight and narrow life. It didn't mean he was bad. He might be a good person, deep down.

She might be a good person.

"How can I help?" she asked, tentatively stroking his back. "If Ralston calls again, I'll shout obscenities into the phone. Or threaten him—whatever you need. I'll steal the tires off his Maserati. That'll clip his wings."

Hugh dried his hands and eased her into his arms. "You'd do that for me?" He stroked her cheek, his fingertips damp from the dishwater. His touch was gentle and sweet, a balm for the doubt shuttling through her soul. "I've never been with a professional thief. Most of the women I know think of it as a hobby."

"I can set up classes, give your dates some pointers."

"You have a cruel streak, Birdie." He rubbed his nose across hers, a leisurely movement. Her pulse tripped. The irreverent turn of the conversation appeared to lift his spirits, which was a relief. "How do you feel about breaking and entering? Make off with Ralston's astrology books and it'll derail him."

"Whatever you want."

He cupped her face, suddenly serious. "I want to make love to you."

"I want that, too," she said, and her heart overturned.

He kissed her deeply to drive the point home. Mired between lust and common sense, she slid her hands from his shoulders. If they made love, she'd be at risk of falling for him—

He drew back an inch. "What is it? If I'm going too fast—"

"You're not." She rested her palms on his chest. The heavy staccato of his heartbeat warmed her blood. "What happens after we sleep together? I mean . . . I don't know what I mean."

"Are you asking if we'll keep seeing each other?" He pressed his thumb to the side of her mouth then slowly rubbed her lower lip. The movement was heady, erotic, and her knees threatened to dissolve. "I'm not the one living on the road. I can handle seeing you on a day-to-day basis."

"So we'd have a relationship?" Hugh wasn't the type to stick with a lover for more than a few weeks, which should've been fine.

It wasn't.

"We can try," He said. "If you're asking for a show of hands, I vote you stick around Liberty."

"I can't. Not after I find the rubies."

"Stop looking for them." He tried for a light note, but his hold on her ribcage tightened. "Problem solved."

"It's better if you don't fall for me."

"Because you're leaving? Or because you aren't worth it?"

Harsh questions, they were distressingly accurate. Anger scalded her cheeks, but she held it in check. She wasn't worth it. She could pretend he was the problem, a guy closing in on forty who was married to his job. But she knew better.

"I don't stick." With shaky movements, she withdrew his hands from her waist. "To people, places—I leave. If I get bored or scared, I take off."

"You can change."

"No one changes, Hugh. People bullshit you into thinking they'll try, but they never pull it off."

The comment stole the fire from his eyes. Gauging his reaction, she felt nervous and wavery. In some awful way, she'd revealed the essence of her life's creed. Her take on life was small-minded and cruel.

Hugh rocked back on his heels. Behind tightly clenched lips, he rolled his tongue. He looked at her like she was something he'd found on the sole of his shoe, something sticky and foul.

"Jesus, you're cold. Where's the end-game, Birdie?"

"The end-game?"

"Think you'll always get away?" He put ice in his voice, enough to urge her to flee. "One day, you'll get caught. Three strikes and you're out. Or didn't you get the memo?"

Somehow she stood her ground. "I know how the law works."

"For other criminals. You don't get how it applies to you."

"This time is different," she snapped, and immediately regretted the words.

"Oh, man." Hugh dug his fingers into his scalp. "Let me guess. This is the big heist that'll make you go straight."

She wanted to agree, but her throat closed. What right did he have to mock her? The rubies were worth thousands. In one theft, she'd make more than she earned in a year. In five years. She'd pawn the gems and start over.

Not over. She'd begin. A new life. She'd become a new person. *People never change.*

She'd stumbled into an abyss. Frightened, she wondered if he was right. She'd live off the rubies for a few months or a year. Then she'd go back to the only life she knew, the habits of a lifetime impossible to break.

Sick to the bone, she was spared raising a flimsy defense by the light rap on the door. Hugh flinched. Then he tore his gaze from hers and went to answer.

A man's voice tumbled into the living room. Hugh joined in, his conversation tight and unsettled. The tension rising off his voice was no comparison to the anxiety churning her thoughts. Analyzing her dreams too closely put them at risk of disappearing. If they were a mirage, what *did* she have?

Clumsily, she pushed herself off the edge of the counter. She glanced at the sink, then the door. Leave for an hour? Maybe while she walked around town, Hugh would cool off. Maybe they both would.

She was halfway across the kitchen when a man entered.

He was a little younger than Hugh, with curly brown hair and an easy smile. "Birdie, right?" He offered his hand. "I'm Anthony. Blossom's father."

She felt weightless, but she managed to shake his hand.

They made small talk for a moment about Blossom's penchant for hanging around the restaurant after school. "If she ever gets in your hair, tell her to go home," Anthony said.

"She's never a problem. We like having her around." Birdie tried for a smile but her mouth was parched and her lips stuck to her teeth. Hugh was managing not to look at her, and his displeasure cut her deep. "Congratulations, by the way. I hear your wedding was lovely."

"Thanks." He turned back to Hugh. "Blossom says you're in a hurry to write the article and I don't want to hold you up. I'd do it now, but I'm on a beer run. There are forty people at my parents' house, and we ran out of brew. Tomorrow's a wash, but what about Saturday? We can meet after I help set up the Festival of Lights."

Hugh shrugged, his expression edgy. "There's no hurry. You just got back from your honeymoon."

Anthony grinned. "Mary's spending the weekend rearranging the house while I help with the festival."

"Take your time. We'll do the interview on Monday." Clearly Hugh was stalling, even if Anthony couldn't see it. "I'll call you."

"You're sure it can wait?"

"Positive."

Needing to prolong the conversation, Birdie asked, "What's the Festival of Lights?" Once Anthony left, she'd be alone with Hugh and his painfully dead-on observations of her.

"It's the Liberty holiday parade. You're going, aren't you? It's this Sunday in the Square."

"Maybe I'll go with Delia." She'd do anything to stay out of the apartment and away from Hugh.

The men talked for a few minutes then Anthony headed out. Birdie wavered in the foyer before following Hugh into the living room. They stared at each other in an uneasy silence.

When it seemed he'd had enough, he grabbed his coat off the couch. "I'm going out for a drink."

"Then go."

For a second he hesitated, a hint of apology on his face. She quashed it by starting back to the kitchen.

He walked out, leaving a sad little silence in his wake.

* * *

The dim lighting of Bongo's on Route 6 offered a welcome anonymity. Grabbing a stool, Hugh motioned to the bartender. The redhead was about six months pregnant and appeared none too happy about it.

"Scotch on the rocks." He reconsidered. "Make it a double."

From the poolroom in back, the jukebox sent a whiny ballad through the walnut paneled room. At the other end of the counter, a balding security guard nursed his beer.

When the Scotch appeared, Hugh downed it. The scalding kick burned the back of his throat. A quick and fleeting relief followed. Not enough to dull his wits, but the alcohol *did* help him face the facts: he'd screwed himself completely when he came back to Liberty.

If he didn't write about Anthony, he was out of a job. And if he didn't get the hell away from Birdie, he'd be in thick with a woman who'd burn him, and good.

What she'd said—she was correct. People never changed. You came into the world battered and bruised and that's how you stayed. Birdie had suffered more blows than most. Raised by grifters, she spent her life on the run. She was beautiful and sensitive but tough in ways he didn't understand. He might pity her but he was a fool if he let himself love her.

Grimly, he stared into his glass. And therein lay the problem. He didn't like her choice of career. He sure as hell didn't care for the way she compartmentalized her emotions. But she knew how to be tender, and he was already starting to love her a little.

He flagged down the bartender. "I'd like another, please."

Like many redheads, the woman sported freckles from her chin to her brow. "Maybe you should slow down," she replied, the light ochre spots dancing. She settled her elbows on the bar. "The last guy in here drinking as fast as you? A State Trooper nailed him half a mile up the road. I've got coffee in back—"

"A double. *Now.*"

Muttering under her breath, she reached for the bottle and poured generously. "Suit yourself." She slid the glass forward and stalked off.

The urge to get smashed was nearly overwhelming. Somehow, Hugh managed to sip the drink. He'd had a problem with booze for a long time even if he didn't like to think of himself as an alcoholic. His thirties had been riddled with binges and periods of abstinence. The dry periods were now more frequent, and he'd even assured Bud that his days of hitting the bottle were over.

Most of the time it was true.

Finishing his drink, he stared at the empty glass with the need for more alcohol gnawing at his gut. When life flowed along it was easy to stay sober. If the currents were choppy it took every ounce of self-control to resist the mind-numbing habit begun fourteen years ago.

"Darling boy, have a drink."

Hugh stiffened as the memory rolled toward him.

"Ms. Seavers——"

"How many times must I insist? Call me Cat. I despise formality."

He stared, unseeing, as the memory pulled him under.

"Cat, I don't drink."

"Today you'll start," she said, lifting the crystal decanter. "We're celebrating the rise and fall of a great philanthropist. I'm a bit of a monument, don't you think? Soon I'll be nothing more than an artifact."

Her eyes were puffy. Yet she laughed, a sparkling twitter of sound, and poured the honey colored liquid into the goblets. The noon sun, streaming in through the glass wall of the hotel suite, touched the crystal with hot fingers of light. Prisms of color tore across Hugh's field of vision. He welcomed the momentary blindness.

"I should go," he said.

"And leave me alone to brood? Why, haven't you read the paper? As of today, I'm a bit of a tragedy."

"I didn't write the article to make your life difficult. I was simply . . . I was doing my job."

Mortified, he realized beads of sweat were trickling down his back. He couldn't find his internal balance. There'd been no time to prepare for the private appointment—she'd summoned him to the swanky hotel within hours of the *Cleveland Post* hitting the stands. Before the day was out, newspapers and television stations throughout Ohio would pick up the story.

The news might even go national, a coup for a young reporter. Yet Hugh had felt oddly saddened when he rode the elevator to top floor of the hotel. Reaching the suite, he'd been shocked to find the inimitable Cat Seavers dressed in a negligee as thin as dreams. Desperate for a sense of normalcy, he tried to remain aloof even as his attention strayed to her breasts.

Embarrassed, he pulled his gaze toward the fierce sunlight pouring through the windows. "You aren't responsible for what your husband did. If you'll give me a quote, I promise to include it in the follow-up article."

She took a sip of her drink then placed the goblet on the bar. "A quote?" More laughter, and it was a lonely trill of sound.

"I want to help. You shouldn't suffer."

Cat drifted toward him. "Women always suffer, darling."

He hadn't meant to hurt her even though he'd thrown himself into this, his first big story. He'd dug deep and come up with enough evidence of impropriety at Trinity Investments to send Cat's husband, Landon Williams, to prison. The story was sure to earn him a raise at the *Post*.

"If you give me something for the follow-up article . . ." His voice broke, and he tried again. "People want to hear your side. You'll have the chance to set the record straight."

"Every word you wrote is true. Landon has a mistress. He's kept her in high style with money from his company." She pursed her lips. "I have no choice but to protect him—and my good name. Of course, I'll hire the finest legal team in Ohio. Now, let's have our drinks in peace."

Beneath the negligee's gauzy material, her breasts were large and surprisingly pert for a woman in middle age. Her golden hair was pulled back loosely at the nape of her neck and her eyes—large, dewy—were mesmerizing. How could a woman nearly twice his age be such a lure?

With horror he felt the stirring of an erection and froze beneath her attentive gaze.

Cat pressed her hand against his throbbing flesh, sending him into freefall.

"You're sorry you've hurt me, aren't you?" She placed the goblet into his fist. Hugh took the glass, the silence broken by his sudden, horrible groan of pleasure when she stroked him. He didn't want to succumb but her lips were red and her hands carried magic . . .

"Drink up, darling boy. Hurry. I've been wallowing in tears all morning. Make me feel good again."

Repulsed by the memory, he dragged himself back to the present. At the other end of the bar, the security guard dropped a twenty and rose to his feet. Shutting his eyes tight, Hugh let the shame roll through his chest. *You should have left the suite.* He hadn't, and the moment he was freed of the barrier of clothing, his veneer of civility dissolved.

The conservative life he'd led, the general hazing he'd been subjected to by the older journalists at the *Cleveland Post*, every battle he'd fought to achieve a better life—all of it drove his actions the moment Cat laid her hands on him. She represented everything he wanted in life. Her wealth and beauty were sirens calling him to a destruction he willingly met.

She was in so much pain.

The bartender approached, and Hugh tried to smile.

I destroyed a man's career and slept with his wife within hours of her death. I could have saved her.

He'd spent the last fourteen years mired in guilt and remorse.

"I'll take you up on the coffee," he said.

The bartender tipped her head to the side. "I thought you'd come around. You look like a smart man."

"I'm not." He was damned by his actions. "I'm the biggest asshole you'll ever meet."

The waitress chuckled. "I've seen worse."

She hadn't, but he didn't argue. The potential for decency was there—his father had been respectable—but Hugh was a mere caricature of a man.

He'd brushed against fame in his youth. The experience had brought out his base nature. He slept with Cat mere hours before she summoned her daughter, Meade, to the dock and stepped into the skiff.

Meade contacted the police soon after, fearing her mother lost in the storm pummeling the dark waves of Lake Erie. For a week, the Coast Guard searched. Then the call to the newsroom and Hugh stumbled to his car with the sickly fear settling in his bones. The dusk moved in as he waited on shore with the police and the paramedics. Her body, heaved from the surf like so much drift-wood, her sinewy frame bloated, her face little more than a shell.

The fish had been feeding on her for days.

Hugh struggled against his self-loathing. And the questions—always the questions, burning down to his soul. Would Cat still be the toast of Ohio if he'd shown compassion? If he'd squelched his physical desires, if he'd led her to a chair and simply *listened* while she cried, would she be alive today?

Yes.

Startled, he looked up. The bartender had returned with the coffee. He murmured his thanks.

Cradling the cup, he tucked the memories away. He'd meet with Anthony first thing Monday morning. He'd corner the guy with the facts, maybe even get a confession. Then he'd write the article, like he'd written the piece on Cat. It was sure to destroy what little good was left inside him.

His despair was nearly overwhelming but he managed to organize his thoughts. Go back to the apartment? He wasn't sure he could face Birdie.

Not that either of them deserved a relationship worth its mettle. They were both damaged goods.

Darling boy.

Pulling off the barstool, he tossed a few bills on the counter. So they hadn't slept together. Did it matter? He'd do anything to save his job and she was a thief—a professional thief who wouldn't stick around long enough to let their relationship deepen.

Neither would he.

CHAPTER 16

Birdie stared bleakly at the crowd.

The townspeople were converging on Liberty Square for the Festival of Lights with the celebratory fervor of spectators at the Macy's Thanksgiving Day Parade. The curb was a string of wool coats and striped scarves, and a gangly Santa Claus was shoving candy canes at the children in the crowd.

Easy marks.

Every eye was trained on the street, waiting for the parade to begin. The pickings were plentiful. Women carelessly dangled purses from their shoulders. Men's coats flapped open in invitation. She could steal half of them blind and they'd never know what hit them.

Uncomfortable with her thoughts, she huddled against the harsh brick of the restaurant. This wasn't an anonymous crowd in Atlanta or Los Angeles. Many of the people were regulars at The Second Chance. She knew them by name. Zip Dekins, a mechanic down on Third Street. Natasha Jones, the baker who ran a shop on the other side of the Square. Mrs. Samuels, Greg Surrey, Bo Waverly—she enjoyed sharing conversation with them in the restaurant, even knew the names of their kids.

She yanked up the collar of her coat. According to Hugh, she had the moral compass of a flea. All she cared about was snatching a few bills and living by her wits. But she was trying to change.

Even though she was pretty damn sure he was still at the library, she scanned the crowd for him. He was doing everything in his power to avoid the apartment.

To avoid her.

Landing on his shit list didn't matter. Why waste so much energy feeling angry? Of course the hurt was far worse. The way he'd looked at her when they'd argued had inflicted a whole series of bruises on her heart. Worse still, he'd made her question herself.

At the curb, Natasha Jones elbowed her way through the crowd. Her family appeared behind her—first her husband, next her father, then the three kids. The boys were close in age, and Birdie guessed the oldest was eight. They were great diversions, all three of them, if she *were* planning a light day of work. Grandpa was an easy mark as he bent over the middle boy, his wallet peeking out of the back pocket of his trousers. Natasha, too. Her husband pressed his cheek to hers. Her purse swung free.

No. A gust of wind kicked by, nearly taking Birdie off her feet. *They're a nice family out to see the parade.* Instinctively she fished around her pocket, winding her fingers around the ruby-studded key. It felt heavy and complete. Substantial. Unlike her dreams, which Hugh had cruelly pointed out were an illusion.

Had he foretold the future? Finding the rubies and believing she'd go legal wasn't the same as doing it. Wandering from city to city and praying for her luck to hold were habits ground deep under her skin. It was all she'd ever learned. It was how her parents lived. Not much comfort to a man doing a long stretch in Arizona. And her mother? The Feds were determined to take down Wish. Their pursuit had probably driven her deep into Mexico by now. How normal people lived, people like Natasha, with her arm linked through her husband's and the boys darting around like fireflies—it was incomprehensible and unfair.

Despair swamped her. Why pretend she was anything more than a two-bit thief? She carried Tanek's blood in her veins. If she dared to look in a mirror she glimpsed a replica of her mother, a younger version of Wish with too-long hair and a hard certainty around her mouth.

Natasha swung around to peer at the courthouse, her red leather purse bobbing like a ripe cherry. On instinct, Birdie shot forward.

Bumping into the woman, she worked fast. It was a ballet really, her practiced apology and Natasha's honeyed eyes sparkling, and the way the boys laughed at Birdie's deceptively clumsy moves. They didn't see the lightning in her fingertips. They missed the joggle of their mother's purse and the flash of green. It was over in seconds.

Returning to her perch in front of the restaurant, Birdie stuffed the bills into her pocket. The usual, self-congratulatory high didn't surface. Holiday music burst from the center green, *Rudolph the Red-Nosed Reindeer*. She listened in numb confusion. The crowd heaved forward even though the street was still empty. Unable to get a fix on her emotions, she watched them with the detachment of an observer on the moon.

"Birdie, wipe that sour expression off your face. It's the holiday season."

The scrape of Theodora's voice snapped her to attention. The fringe on the old woman's cowhide jacket whipped through the air like rust-colored snakes. Beneath a cowboy hat trimmed with red and green lights she screwed up her face with palpable displeasure.

One of the hat's green lights stuttered out. Birdie tapped it and the bright flashing resumed. "Where's your tinsel?" Tipping her head, she took in Theodora's brown and white leather boots. Obviously the pint-sized retiree was itching for a cowboy

Christmas. "Nice. If we find you a mask, you can hand out presents dressed like the Lone Ranger."

"Are you casting aspersions on my clothes?"

"Why not?" She flicked at Theodora's satchel. "You can't shoot me in public. It'd ruin the parade."

"Or start it off with a bang." Theodora stuck out her chin. "Why are you hiding over here by yourself?" She bounced a thumb at Finney, creating all sorts of mayhem further down the street. "Why aren't you helping her?"

Evidently the volunteer fire department was trying to raise money. Their members flanked a bent Christmas tree with cheery smiles. They'd stuffed the trunk of the tree inside a garbage can and dotted a few branches with tinsel. Finney stood in the center of the men, clanging a bell in front of a red lacquer bucket. Whenever someone approached, she charged with her bell singing and her face tilted at a bullish angle.

"She doesn't need my help." What Finney *did* need was a sedative.

Furtively, Birdie's gaze drifted back to Natasha. Taking the baker's money wasn't merely stupid. It was mean. Cruel. What had she been thinking? Natasha's coat looked ten years old. True, her purse had been polished to a nice luster but there were spidery cracks in the fake leather.

Theodora poked her in the stomach. "Pay attention!" Then she barked at Delia, who was flirting with a biker. The girl trotted over and she added, "If you lazy asses don't have anything better to do, come and help with the parade."

Delia's nose crinkled. "Oh, man. What's wrong this time?"

This time? Birdie looked at them with confusion. "Are you talking about the floats for the parade?" Surely they were ready to go.

Delia chortled. "This is a small town, Birdie. We rig up vans and trucks for the Festival of Lights. There aren't any floats. We have enough problems convincing the farmers not to dress up their chickens and add them to the convoy."

"And how's that my problem?"

Theodora thwacked her arm. "You're in a beastly mood. Now, get moving. The trucks are behind the courthouse. There aren't enough folks getting them fancied up. Where's Hugh?"

Delia popped a stick of gum into her mouth. "He's laid claim to one of the tables at the library. He's got a homemade 'Do Not Disturb' sign."

Theodora did the angry-shimmy thing with her shoulders. "What does he think he is? North Korea? Delia, trot over there and haul him out. There's work to be done."

After Delia trudged off, Theodora latched onto Birdie's wrist and dragged her forward. The old woman was an angry bee zipping through the crowd. Even as her hat blinked holiday cheer, the scowl on her face sent the swarm of parade-goers scattering.

Breaking free, Birdie set herself a mulish gait. She nodded in greeting to Finney, busy emptying the pockets of anyone unlucky enough to pass within earshot of her clanging bell. The pail was already full of bills. Tens, twenties, a Ben Franklin—no, two. The citizens of Liberty weren't rich, but they were certainly generous.

Still, there must be limits. If there *was* a parade committee, they operated on a budget of fifty dollars . . . or less. The trucks idling bumper to bumper behind the courthouse sported plastic poinsettias stuffed into rust spots and cheap tinsel taped on greasy windshields. A silver Ford was pathetically adorned with cardboard bells a five-year-old must have cut out. Behind it, a pockmarked Chevy revved beneath a twisted clump of twinkle lights. Half of the lights were dead.

"Give them your hat, Theodora." Birdie nodded toward the men heaping greenery on the Chevy. "They need all the help they can get."

"Like hell I will." The old woman went up on the toes of her cowboy boots. "Hugh! Over here!"

Birdie tried to steel herself as he strode forward. Hugh was in fine form. His eyes were slitted and he was working the muscles in his jaw. His irritation went unnoticed by Theodora, who put them both to work on the third truck in line—another Ford. They strung lights in an uneasy silence while their cowboy general barked orders at Blossom, who'd eagerly appeared with her friends. Delia ran off to fetch aluminum garlands. Anthony was already pouring sweat from the flatbed of a truck near the end of the procession. Several men Birdie recognized as regulars at the restaurant were helping him.

Nervous energy galvanized her into action. The faster she got away from Hugh, the better. She peered back at the crowd for Natasha, who'd disappeared.

"Working out your next heist?" he asked when they'd tugged a gaudy length of aluminum garland around the front bumper and faced each other. He snatched the duct tape from her quivering fingers and tore off a strip. "If you're watching Finney, you've picked the wrong target. She'll never let you near enough to the fireman's fund to grab a fistful of bills."

"Go to hell."

The retort jerked him upright. "It's nice to see you too, Eggplant. Been minding the apartment while I've been away?"

Did he think she cared if he avoided her? "Let's get this done, all right? I left my boxing gloves at the homestead. Find someone else to go a few rounds with."

"I'm not fighting."

"Then what *are* you doing?"

"Trying to get you to admit you need morality training. Not to mention a new line of work."

"Leave me alone."

Horrified at the tremor in her voice, she bit her mouth shut. Pressure built behind her eyes. Her heart flung against her sternum like a fledgling thrown from the nest. *Tears?* No way. Tears were reserved for cataclysmic events. If she were evicted from an apartment for skipping rent, or another drifter stole her stuff— maybe she'd bring on the waterworks. But not for Hugh.

She drew a deep breath in a desperate attempt to stabilize her emotions. "Will you lay off?" Because he was right, mostly. She hadn't been able to resist looking at the fireman's fund, and she *had* lifted cash from Natasha. She'd earned his loathing . . . and her own.

She'd stayed too long in this little town, long enough to grow used to the scent of cinnamon sweetening the air every morning as Natasha got to work at the bakery, long enough to wait with anticipation to hear about Delia's weekend social life every Monday. Miss Betty greeted Birdie with a wink and a nod whenever delivering the mail, and Blossom Perini took over The Second Chance most afternoons with her teenage friends. They asked for advice about boys while they slurped root beer floats and fiddled with their iPods. Birdie liked the way they took in her words as if they were valuable gems. But she'd donned the townspeople's affection like an ill-fitting pair of jeans. Trying to fit into their company was impossible.

Approaching, Hugh seemed to sense an opening. "How 'bout this. I'll back off if you'll admit I'm right."

"Then here goes. I'm everything you think I am. A loser, a drifter—I'll never get it together. Satisfied?"

His expression froze. "If you agree, why not change?"

The question ate through her eroding composure. "Gee, I don't know. Because I don't have any real job skills? Or maybe it's because I can't deal with people, their expectations. You should've seen how pissed I made Finney yesterday. A customer grabbed me by the arm, to take his order. I nearly sent his ass to the floor. I reacted like he'd come at me in an alley."

"Get off the street and you won't have to be streetwise. There are other ways to live."

And what would that involve? Monthly bills, a car payment—*responsibilities*. "You make it sound simple. It's not," she replied. "No one taught me the basics. How to keep a schedule. Hold down a job. Pay bills."

"You have a job. You do pay bills—rent at least."

"I can handle a short stint. Then it falls apart. I don't get it."

"Sure you do." He drilled her with a hard stare. "It takes perseverance to change, but you want it easy. You'll grab the rubies and go. When the money runs out, you'll go back to drifting."

Christ, she *did* want to cry. "And you're an expert on change? I should follow your lead?"

"I can help you rehabilitate."

"I manage fine on my own."

"Oh, yeah? Seems like you need something before you manage your life straight into jail."

He'd tapped her deepest fear and the harsh tenor of his voice made the horror vivid. The steel cage. Miles of cement, like a tomb. If she was ever forced to spend time in prison, locked up like an animal, she wouldn't survive.

He grunted. "So you are scared." He blocked her path when she tried to flee. "You should be. The U.S. has grown a conservative hide. Most people think criminals like you should be warehoused for the long haul. They aren't big on rehabilitation, Birdie. They'd just as soon incarcerate your ass and throw away the key."

"Why won't you lay off?"

"I can't. Not while you're screwing up your life."

She wasn't taking it. "Aren't you the guy who derailed his life when he wrote about some do-gooder's cheating husband? Didn't the woman drown?" She got into his face, enough so he flinched. It was an awful victory. "Isn't it your fault she died? Oh, and you've been doing so well ever since."

The accusations sucked the air from Hugh's lungs. She was taking gutter swipes and she knew it. No glory in winning, not with the pain in his eyes mainlining straight to her heart. She wanted to double over and wallow in the body blow she'd doled out to them both.

Theodora trotted up. "Cain and Jezebel! What are you fools arguing about?" She planted herself between them. "Hugh, you're not fixing to faint, are you?"

The question drew his shoulders up. "Stand off, buckaroo. I'm all right." He scraped his hand through his hair, unwilling or unable to draw his eyes away from Birdie's. The pain in his face ebbed to low tide, with gale winds rising.

Theodora screwed down her hat. "Make another comment about my Western wear and you won't be fainting. You'll be dead." She grabbed the duct tape dangling from his hand. "We'll finish together. Birdie, get the lights. Move!"

Stiffly Birdie swung onto the ice-crusted lawn, where decorations were heaped in boxes. When she returned with her arms full, Hugh lobbed fiery glances. Enough so that Theodora noticed. Her mouth worked silently while the air between them congealed. When she'd had enough, she stamped her foot.

"All this high emotion is poisoning my disposition. What were you rascals discussing?" She thumped Hugh on the hip, as if he were the one more prone to honesty. Glowering, he was as mute as marble.

Theodora's mistrust stung but it was manageable. "We weren't discussing anything important," Birdie snapped. She flung one end of the string at his chest. She ached from her ankles to her neck, as if his displeasure were a virus running rampant in her system.

"Horse manure. Hugh, tell me what's going on."

He glanced at Birdie, the hurt extinguished from his face. His predatory smile pooled fear in her belly. "We were arguing about Justice Postell," he said, and her blood ran cold. "Birdie swears the freedwoman brought rubies to Liberty. I wasn't buying it."

"The story is true. I told Birdie myself."

"Yeah, but you weren't the first. She'd already heard about the gems."

His announcement coiled the moment so tight it came to a standstill. Birdie considered strangling him even if it wasn't in keeping with the holiday spirit. What was he doing? She'd told him about the clues in the strictest confidence. How dare he betray her?

There wasn't time to figure it out, not with Theodora regarding her. "You don't say." She stared unblinking, an owl spotting prey. "Birdie, who told you about the rubies?"

She tried to think past the terror shorting out her brain. No dice.

Hugh obligingly spoke up. "She heard a rumor—she's not sure where. Something about Justice leaving behind a clue to the location of the rubies."

Oh, God. He was about to reveal the clue handed down in her family. It was part of her family lore she treasured. He paused before her, his devil-dark gaze churning with an indecipherable flood of emotion.

"I'm not sure I remember the lines. How do they go, Birdie?"

His voice became mellow, like wine, diffusing the anger between them. The change came too quickly, so quickly that Birdie couldn't protect herself by drawing her gaze from his. The lines of poetry were sacred. He knew they were important to her. All of the emotions she'd hidden away moved swiftly through her expression and she couldn't halt the peeling back of her hard exterior or hide what was revealed underneath. Hugh muttered a curse as her lower lip trembled and her eyes grew wet. Then he cradled her face between his palms. His scent wove around her, musky and deep, and she swayed toward him as if he'd become her center of gravity.

Bending, he nearly brushed her lips with his. "What were the words?" His eyes were dark and inviting. She dived in willingly. "Liberty safeguards the cherished heart?"

He said the words sweetly, in a low voice that thrummed across her skin. Longing stole through her, unwanted and potent. He was traitorous and cruel.

He was the only man she'd ever needed.

Behind them, Theodora made a tiny sound of surprise. Inside her cowboy boot, her left ankle wobbled. Her knees gave way.

Hugh lurched sideways, catching her in mid-swoon. With a gargled cry, she snatched for his shirt. The moment she was anchored by his sturdy arms, she tried to find her feet.

"Theodora?" Birdie grabbed her other arm.

Above the cowboy hat, Birdie connected with Hugh's worried gaze. A heart attack? It wasn't possible. Nothing shook the old woman. She was indomitable. *Please—not a heart attack*. The prospect of Theodora in real danger filled Birdie with fear. The old woman had only recently come into her life. She wasn't ready to lose her.

Surprisingly, Theodora lurched away from Hugh and toward her instead. Startled, Birdie grabbed hold. Their entwined hands were oddly mesmerizing, the raisin-skinned fingers with arthritic knobs at their base wrapped firmly around Birdie's pale hands. Theodora murmured something like a prayer, low and sweet.

Her hat fluttered to the ground. Hugh let go, allowing Theodora to rest her head on Birdie's shoulder.

Thrilled she'd been chosen, Birdie protectively steered her to the nearest truck. "Do you need to sit down?"

"No, no—just give me a moment." Theodora released a flutter of air.

"Take all the time you need."

They stood together for long minutes. Hugh sprinted off, returning quickly with a glass of water that Theodora waved away. A man trudged past dragging a small fir tree, his cheeks shiny with perspiration, and hoisted it onto the hood of a truck farther down in the convoy. With a few strips of electrical tape he attached the tree to the windshield. How the driver of the truck would see in traffic with his view obstructed was anyone's guess.

Appraising his ridiculous stab at decorating, Theodora murmured choice words. She appeared to regain some of her usual vigor.

She glanced suddenly at Birdie. "How much do you know about the Civil War, child?"

"Not much," Birdie admitted, relieved to see she was doing better. "I'd love to hear whatever you're willing to share."

The comment must have pleased the old woman because she hurried on. "It was a dark time in our great nation's history. Good folk torn asunder by the war. White folks, too."

Hugh retrieved her hat and handed it to her. "For the record, the abolitionists were white. They helped Justice."

"Yes, but she didn't tell anyone about the rubies. Not right away. She had two bags of gems, more jewels than you can imagine. My, how they sparkled! Worth more than the average man makes in a lifetime, I figure."

Transfixed, Birdie shut out the clang of Finney's bell charging up the street and the impatience oozing from the waiting crowd. The rubies must be worth tens of thousands. No. Hundreds of thousands. Maybe half the jewels of France were buried right here in Liberty.

"Now, Justice understood the value of the gems entrusted to her," Theodora continued. "Those rubies were the foundation of her new life, a life of freedom. She didn't squander them buying useless notions or fancy dresses."

"Did she sell them?" Birdie asked, unable to stop the words from bounding forth.

A speculative gleam lit Theodora's eyes. "Justice was a clever woman. Like Hugh mentioned, an abolitionist helped her. His name was Henry Williams."

Birdie recalled the first time Theodora mentioned the rubies, in the restaurant. "Henry Williams owned a farmer's bank around here, right?"

"That's right. His kin still live in these parts. Landon Williams?"

Theodora leaned close, as if Birdie's reply held some importance. The name wasn't familiar. But Hugh must have heard of Landon, because he looked distressed. Quickly, he donned a poker face.

"Henry let Justice use the gems for collateral," Theodora continued. "The money she borrowed paid for every brick in The Second Chance Grill."

"Every brick," Birdie murmured, recalling the clue she'd found in the patriotic bunting. *Brick by brick, my love. My life built alone, without you.*

"When the restaurant became profitable, she repaid Henry and got the rubies back."

"So she didn't sell them?" Hugh asked Theodora. He stared pointedly at Birdie. "She didn't sell them to a pawn shop or anything like that?"

"Only a fool would do such a thing! Those rubies were a bond between her and the man she loved. To even think such a thing!"

Chagrined, Birdie licked her lips. If she found the rubies she wouldn't hesitate to sell them. They were merely a tool she'd use to build a new life. What they'd once represented to Justice wouldn't matter.

No—it would matter. It did matter.

A tumult of emotion poured through her. What if she could build a new life right here in Liberty? Given half a chance she'd like to stay near Theodora. Maybe she'd convince Hugh to stay too. Everything Justice represented—her goodness and her pride, the way she'd arrived in town with nothing but her hopes for a better life—Birdie thought for a fleeting moment that she'd do the same. She'd make more of herself than she'd ever dreamed.

Foolish hopes. She didn't possess Justice's strength of character or her ability to transcend the lot she'd been assigned in life. Only a person of worth deserved such a chance. Justice had earned a better life through a thousand unimaginable struggles. And Birdie? She'd come into the world the child of thieves, grasping and wanting and taking. She'd go out the same way.

Thankfully, she was spared hearing any more of the story.

Blossom ran toward them. "Hey! Dad says you've all got to get out of the way. The parade is about to begin."

* * *

From her bedroom window, Theodora watched the night steal the last of the sunlight from the sky.

Though the parade was long over, she couldn't calm the hornets swarming through her insides. She pulled the ruffled curtain across her bedroom window, closing out the darkness. One by one she turned on the lights, then smoothed the lace coverlet on her four-poster bed. Her thoughts were still jumbled as she entered the walk-in closet, where she kept the safe.

Liberty safeguards the cherished heart.

Where could Birdie have heard the words?

For a long moment she stared at the safe, her mind leaping and running in a fitful way. Working herself into a state wouldn't do. One way or another, she'd get to the bottom of it.

Finally, she calmed down enough to work the dial on the safe. The heavy door swung open with a groan and she removed the leather bound volume.

Returning to her bedroom, she sat in the rocking chair and placed the book in her lap.

Tenderly, she ran her fingers across the buttery leather. A world's worth of pain was encased inside. And love—there was certainly love. Every question she'd ever struggled with in her long life, every hope and every dream—these pages spoke to them all.

Liberty safeguards—

Until now, they'd been her words alone. Hers, and the babies she'd brought into the world, and the babies who'd come from them. Pride was stamped on every page. And reasons. There were so many reasons to live honorably and with dignity. These words anchored her, and her kin.

But Justice's diary belonged to them all. The wisdom on each page was meant for her entire family, black and white. She opened the book and let her vision blur above the pretty handwriting.

Until now, she'd thought of Birdie Kaminsky as both an irritation and a pleasure. A cocksure child who liked to hear stories about the past when she wasn't hurling zingers like firebombs at anyone who stepped on her toes. And she knew with a deep, unshakeable certainty that there was more to Birdie than she'd imagined.

CHAPTER 17

Hugh closed the file on the Kaminsky family that Fatman had given him at the hunting lodge. He was still shaken after his run-in with Birdie yesterday at the parade and didn't relish another upset, this one with Anthony. To top it all off, the librarian was glaring at him as if she knew he was stalling. The library was about to close. He was already late for the interview.

Steering his car through the Square, he tensed beneath the guilt gnawing at his guts—guilt put there by the questions Birdie had thrown at him at the Festival of Lights. What she'd said was true. The article he'd written fourteen years ago about Landon Williams had led to Cat Seaver's death. Now Hugh was again writing an article sure to destroy another family.

And what of Theodora's comments? She'd tossed out a real stunner when she'd mentioned Landon still lived in the area. Given the publicity he'd endured, he should've moved away. Negative media exposure uprooted people, sent them scuttling from the limelight. Yet Landon was still in town.

Night shadows pooled on North Street. Slowing his car, Hugh tried to pull himself together. Lights from the row of houses flung a diamond-sharp brilliance across the hard-crusted snow. Birdie had been right to get in his face—he was the last person capable of rehabilitating her. Hell, he couldn't even keep his own life together. He kept repeating the same mistakes.

For a long moment, he wrestled with his reservations about investigating one of Liberty's most cherished citizens.

Problem was, he liked Anthony. It was a stretch to say they were friends but he admired the type, a man who was steadfast and decent. What if Birdie was correct? Anthony's reasons for taking the cash might be understandable, if not quite legal. During the interviews Hugh conducted last summer, he recalled the entire Perini clan going into hock to save Blossom during her long battle with leukemia. The donations flowing into the websites from people across the States . . . would anyone care if some of the cash repaid the mountain of debt Anthony carried?

In the strictest sense, there's no crime here. He pulled into the Perini's driveway and cut the engine. *I won't be writing an exposé. It'll be a public lynching of a good man.* Wearily, he climbed the porch steps and rang the doorbell.

Blossom threw open the door as if she'd been waiting for him. "Mr. Shaeffer, come in!" She pulled him inside. "Dad says we can't vote until you hear the choices. Democracy in action. Don't worry—you get to vote, too."

What was the kid talking about? Handing over his coat, Hugh looked around. "Where's your dad?"

"In the living room with Mary. C'mon. They'll give you the lowdown while I go back upstairs. I have a gazillion emails to return."

"Then you'd better get to it." Following the girl to the living room, his guilt morphed into a soul-killing agony.

Leave now. He spotted Anthony and Mary together on the couch. Anthony was hunched over a sheaf of papers on the coffee table. *Call Bud at the Register. Quit.*

CHAPTER 17

Mary looked up at Hugh and smiled. "Aren't journalists supposed to be punctual?" Rising, she gave him a quick hug. "I have calls from patients to return. If you'd been much later, I would have missed this."

"Sorry for the delay." Uneasy, he chose a chair across from them. "How's your medical practice?"

Mary returned to the couch. "Growing by leaps and bounds. People were going out of town for basic medical care. The drive was especially hard on my older patients."

"I'm glad it's working out."

Oblivious to their conversation, Anthony pulled a document from the pile. "Found it." He handed it to Hugh. "Mary created a spreadsheet before we left on our honeymoon. We should've organized the deposits earlier. At least we finally got to it."

Curious, Hugh glanced at the neat columns of numbers cramming the page.

"Blossom helped Mary put it together. Most of the cash went into short-term CDs."

Mary added, "With three banks involved, there's been a lot to track."

Floundering, Hugh looked from one to the other. Banks? CDs? "You've lost me," he admitted.

Anthony took back the document. "Remember the websites we put up to help my daughter?"

Hugh kept his face blank even as his heart raced. "Of course."

"Well, we didn't," Mary interjected, laughing.

Anthony slung an arm across her shoulders. "Between Blossom's bone marrow transplant and our decision to elope . . . heck, we completely forgot about the websites. You find out your kid is going to live and the woman you love has agreed to marry you—"

"And you lose track of everything else?"

"Yeah, and I mean *everything*. Once Mary started talking about a trip to the Bahamas, you know where my head was at."

A miserable sort of longing seized Hugh. "I've got an idea."

An alluring image of Birdie accosted him, Birdie leaning close when he'd nearly kissed her before the parade. They'd been fighting, but they always fought. It certainly never dampened his desire for her, and the hungry expression on her face had stoked his need. He'd already spent too many years ravaged by disappointment and self-recrimination. Somehow, she could find a way past his defenses.

He tamped down her image, but not before it spilled pain into his chest.

"What happened when you remembered the websites were still live?" he finally asked.

"At first, we were shocked. Man, you wouldn't believe how much money was still coming in." Anthony shook his head with bemusement. "You don't expect people you've never met to be so generous."

"They thought Blossom was still fighting for her life," Mary said. "We had to do something, and fast. But we'd already eloped and booked the flight for our honeymoon. The tickets were non-refundable."

"We figured, 'no harm, no foul' if we waited until we returned to rectify the situation." Anthony nodded toward the ceiling. Several voices were audible. "Blossom is posting on all the sites, explaining she's doing fine. The news will put a stopper in the cash flow."

Hugh recalled meeting one of Blossom's girlfriends last summer. Snoops was a geek with purple-framed glasses and a penchant for computers. "Is Snoops helping her with the posts?"

"Yeah, and they're rebuilding some of the web pages, dropping in new pictures of Blossom, how she looks now. The guest book on each site is filled with notes from well-wishers. Everyone is glad she's doing so well."

"I am, too." Hugh's throat tightened with unexpected emotion.

"We've also had a family discussion to decide how to put the money to good use."

"What did you come up with?" For once, he bypassed his natural cynicism and said a silent prayer of gratitude. Anthony hadn't misappropriated the money.

Why do I always expect the worst from people? He suffered a jab of remorse. *Because I'm a distrusting bastard.*

But the Perinis *were* decent. They'd come up with something worthy, something that didn't involve buying vacation property in the Florida Keys with the retirement checks sent in by old ladies from Topeka, Kansas. Anthony hadn't lined his bank account with cash garnered from good-hearted souls in Seattle or Houston.

He was startled from his thoughts when Mary said, "Anthony, spell it out for Hugh. I'd like to hear what he thinks."

Anthony lowered his elbows to his knees. "Here's the deal. We've collected more than half a million dollars through the websites. We've banked every penny."

Half a million dollars? Stunned, Hugh leaned forward in his chair. "It's all in the bank? *All of it?*"

"You bet." There was no missing the pride in Anthony's voice. "We're shutting down the websites, but now we have to figure out what to do with the money we've already collected."

"What if the people who donated want a refund?"

"We're way ahead of you, pal. Snoops has it covered."

When it came to computers, Snoops was Steve Jobs and Bill Gates combined. "I'm guessing she compiled a mass emailing to everyone who made a donation," Hugh said, putting the rest together. It was impressive work for a kid in junior high. "Is she asking if the money can be used for another worthy cause?"

"It's amazing how many people have already given the go-ahead." Anthony angled his neck toward the ceiling. "Blossom! What's the count?"

Blossom thundered down the stairwell and hung over the banister. "Closing in on two thousand responses, Dad. We're still at eighty percent."

"Which means what, exactly?" Hugh asked, caught between amusement and self-pity.

From the looks of it he'd need to stop in at the *Register*, but not to give notice. Bud would fire him because he hadn't delivered a scathing article destroying the myth of goodness in small-town America. Something was happening in Liberty—it was taking place right here, in front of him—but it wasn't ugly or shocking or bloody. For once it was something good. Something *marvelous*.

For the sliver of a moment, he reveled in the pleasure of the Perinis' generosity of spirit. "Anthony, what do you have eighty percent of?"

"That's how many people have agreed to let us use the money to help other sick kids." Anthony grew serious. "So we have to choose. Start a foundation for kids with leukemia and help families pay for uninsured services? Or do something more inclusive by aiding kids with any type of cancer? There's a lot to think about."

Hugh swallowed down the emotion welling in his chest. Anthony pressed the spreadsheet back on him, adding, "We're hoping you'll help us decide what to do."

CHAPTER 18

"Stop talking so much," Delia said with thick sarcasm.

Brushing past her, Birdie entered the kitchen and deposited the tray of dirty dishes in the sink. At the massive stove, Finney attacked a steak with her spatula. Grease sizzled and snapped.

Birdie glared at Delia, who was stuck to her heels like a hound dog. "Don't badger me. How many times do I have to ask you to drop it?"

"Drop what?" Finney asked, flipping the steak.

Delia pouted. "Something's had her blue for days."

Birdie yanked open the dishwasher. Every time the baker, Natasha Jones, came into The Second Chance for a meal, she suffered through the woman's friendly conversation—something she didn't deserve, not after what she'd done at the parade. She'd lifted forty bucks from the woman's purse. For the first time ever, she was seized by the urge to return something she'd stolen. Her newfound conscience was like a bratty kid throwing tantrums whenever Natasha crept into her thoughts.

Tough break, and the baker wasn't the only issue waging war on her peace of mind. Not by a long shot.

Delia noisily chewed her gum. "Enough already. What's going on?"

"I haven't seen Hugh for days, all right?" His gear was still lying around the apartment but some of his clothing and most of his toiletries were missing. If he'd gone back to Akron, he should've left a note explaining when he'd return. "He took off without telling me where he's going."

"Today is Monday," Delia said, as if they were all too dumb to know the day of the week. "So you're saying he's been gone for a whole week? You don't think something happened to him, do you?"

"If I had to guess I'd say he's off . . . sulking. He's a brooder."

Finney pounded the steak into submission. "Have you two been fighting?"

"A lover's quarrel?" Delia added, clearly delighted with the prospect.

"*No.*" Birdie stacked the dishwasher with jerky movements. It was a good use of her nervous energy because she *was* concerned about him. Not that it gave Delia the right to imply she was, hell, lovesick. "He could've at least left a message on my cell. It's not a big deal."

Finney snorted. "Hogwash. The man leaves without giving you a way to track him? You're angry."

"Not me. I never let a man throw me off my game."

"C'mon, now. You like him. And he likes you. I'm betting you can't keep your hands off of each other." The cook reconsidered. "Not that I condone shenanigans between an unmarried couple, mind you."

"Do tell," Delia said, ignoring Finney's trek to the moral high ground. "It's been a month since I've hooked up with a guy. I can live through you until the dry spell's over."

"My dry spell's gone on a tad longer." Finney slid the steak onto a plate. "Five years. Heaven help me."

Delia twirled her lime-tinted hair. "C'mon, Birdie. Share the juicy details. Or share Hugh. I go into meltdown just looking at him."

"There aren't any juicy details. We aren't lovers!"

Not yet, anyway. Chances were, they would've consummated their relationship on Thanksgiving if not for the argument. No opportunity since then. He was practically living at the library.

Now he'd disappeared altogether. Not that she cared.

"Finney, you ought to check out one of those online dating services if you want to find a man," she said. "And Delia—stop bugging me!"

The young waitress's face fell. "I'm only trying to help. It's what friends do."

Birdie closed the dishwasher, touched by the comment. They *were* becoming friends. True, she couldn't remain in Liberty, not after she found the rubies. Even so, was there any harm in enjoying Delia's company for now?

Pulling out of her funk, she ran a hank of the girl's lime-and-blonde hair through her fingertips. "You're the one who needs help. Remind me to pick up some hair coloring at the drugstore. I can fix this mess."

"You can?"

"As long as you remember to *mind your own business*."

Delia flounced toward the counter and snatched up a serving tray. "Whatever." She slid the steak on top and headed for the dining room. The door had barely swung shut when it swung back open and she reappeared. "Uh, Birdie . . . your one o'clock is here."

"Theodora?" The news lifted her spirits for the first time in days.

Since the Festival of Lights, Theodora was increasingly forthcoming with her stories about Justice. Now that Birdie had found the ruby-studded key in the storeroom—a key without a clue attached—she hoped one of those stories would lead to the rubies. She tried not to think about what the gems had meant to Justice.

And she certainly didn't like considering how finding them would bring her stay in Liberty to a close. She'd have to leave the friends she'd made . . . and Hugh.

She'd already spent too much time pacing the apartment and worrying about him.

I'm starting to act like a wife. The thought gave her the shivers. She didn't love him. Some days, she didn't even like him. She'd never consider marrying him or any man. Her parents' idea of marriage was shouting insults across a seedy hotel room, and she'd seen what her mother did whenever her father was in the lockup. *Thanks, but no thanks.* She was concerned for Hugh's welfare, but she certainly didn't care about him. Not much, anyway.

In the dining room, Theodora sat at the counter in a holiday dress of red and green stripes. She was casting her beady stare on a nervous Ethel Lynn, taking a dessert order in the center of the dining room. When Ethel Lynn became rattled and dropped the ordering pad, Theodora bared her fake incisors. A low growl rumbled from her throat, and Ethel Lynn shrieked.

"Why do you like scaring her half to death?" Birdie filled a cup with coffee and placed it before Theodora. "Are you two sworn enemies, or what?"

"It's my duty to keep her in line."

"What the hell did she ever do to you?"

Theodora grunted. "Our families have bad blood—bad blood going back more than a century. There's no trusting the Percibles, not one of them." She peered across the dining room like a fox with a hen in its sights. "Ethel Lynn comes from a witless and cruel tribe."

"You don't say." The witless part *did* make sense. Ethel Lynn bent to retrieve the order pad she'd dropped, knocking a little girl's milk to the floor. But *cruel?* "She doesn't have a cruel bone in her body."

Theodora pounded her gnat-sized fist on the counter. "It doesn't make an ounce of difference! Some insults are never forgotten. She deserves to suffer for all the wrongs of her ancestors. Vermin, all of them!"

"Talk about holding a grudge." Birdie patted the old woman's forearm in the hopes of calming her down. Theodora's laser vision shot to her, and she snatched her hand away. "Hey, don't take it out on me. I'm already having a bad day."

"Hugh still isn't back, is he?"

"How did you know he was gone?"

"Do I look like an idiot?" The old woman leaned close, her face collapsing into an expression of concern. "Stop worrying yourself into a tizzy. He's a man. All men are fools, but the stupidest among them can find his way home. You waste too much time fretting about the darnedest things."

"How did you know I was . . ." Birdie pressed her lips together. *Theodora's a goddamn psychic.* How she even knew he'd taken off was anyone's guess.

"Has the rotten man called?"

"No. Why do you care?" *Why do I care?*

"I don't. Love's a foolish business."

Birdie yanked down the micro skirt of her uniform. "I'm not in love with him. Do *I* look like an idiot?"

Theodora gave an appraising look. "Sometimes."

"Thanks a lot." She gave up on straightening her skirt and let loose a curse. "Why are you asking about Hugh anyway?"

"I merely ask because now he's got time on his hands for romance. He won't be penning acid prose about Anthony, that's for sure." When Birdie stared, slack-jawed, she added, "What? You think I couldn't figure out why he slunk back into town? Came here to write about Blossom, my ass. He thought he'd tar and feather Anthony."

"So Hugh won't be writing the article?" *Never let Theodora out of my sight. She's tricky.*

"Haven't you heard? Anthony is using the website money to start a foundation for youngsters with cancer."

"Geez, that's great." So Hugh must have gone back to Akron to resign from the *Register*. He *was* out of a job. "Listen, I have to get back to work," she added, her desire to hear another story losing out to her worry over Hugh. He needed her help. Which would be easy to supply if he'd pick up his cell phone.

I'm not in love with him, am I? Lifting the serving tray, she prayed she wasn't.

"You don't want to badger me with questions about Justice?" Theodora demanded, bringing her to a standstill. "I reckon it's a first."

"Not today. But thanks."

"Truth be told, there isn't time for a walk down memory lane." She took a quick sip of her coffee before rising. Jabbing a finger toward the kitchen, she added, "Tell Finney you're coming with me."

"I'm not going anywhere. Did you load your Saturday Night Special?"

Theodora clenched her buckskin satchel to her sagging breasts. "None of your beeswax." She lowered what was left of her brows. "Now, skedaddle. Tell Finney I won't keep you long."

What was the use of arguing? It wouldn't stop Theodora from using deadly force. Some people didn't soften with age. "Where are we going?"

"There's a lady who insists on meeting you. Awful timing, too. I'd been planning to hunt this afternoon, but some things can't wait. Tell Finney to make do until you get back."

Wary, Birdie started toward the kitchen. A thief never trusted the unexpected—it usually meant the mark had noticed his wallet slipping from his pocket or the cops were in pursuit. Surprises were best avoided.

What was this about? She entered the kitchen toying with the idea of making a run for it.

Remembering the old woman's gun and take-no-prisoners stare, she pulled on her army coat instead.

* * *

Wavering midway across the marble lobby, Birdie hissed, "This is an office. I thought you were taking me around the corner, not to the Cleveland suburbs. Who the hell *are* we meeting with?"

Everything in the lobby wore an intimidating patina, from the silk prints on the walls to the mile-high arrangement of African daisies beneath the skylights. The place was a haven for stylish women with disdainful expressions and too much jewelry.

"We're here to see Meade. She's been badgering me for days about making your acquaintance." Theodora dragged Birdie to the wall, where they stood like jailbirds in a lineup. "She imports cosmetics and whatnots. Does well by it, too."

"She owns the place?" *She must be loaded.*

"Lock, stock and barrel. She's a thorn in my behind, but I can't quibble with her success." Theodora dumped her mohair coat into Birdie's arms. "She demanded to meet you because she doesn't believe me. The fool's got you mixed up with someone else, which is why she asked to eyeball you for herself."

The explanation didn't sit well. "If someone's nabbed her boyfriend, don't point fingers at me."

"This isn't about love gone astray. Her last name's Williams."

"Like the abolitionist who helped Justice? You said his family still lives around here."

"Meade is Landon Williams's daughter." Theodora frowned. "You're sure you've never heard of him?"

The question had already come up during the Festival of Lights. "I really haven't."

"Then you've got nothing to worry about."

Not exactly a reassuring comment. "Then what's going on? Can I at least have a hint?" she asked, unsure if she wanted to play along.

"No."

"Have it your way." Spotting a coat tree, she hung up Theodora's coat but decided to keep hers on. She didn't need some nosy secretary rifling through the pockets of her most cherished possession. "If I were Meade, I'd believe you. I don't know what we're talking about but, hey, you're no one to mess with. Theodora's law is just one short rung below God's law, I always say."

The assessment pleased her. "Now that you mention it, I am uncommonly astute. Honest, too." She squared her shoulders and seemed to grow taller. With a few more compliments, she might reach five feet in height. "Meade is too pigheaded to trust my opinion. Damn fool."

"I trust you," Birdie replied, and stopped in surprise. It wasn't a lie.

Theodora's wrinkles eased into a grin. "You should. The way I see it, you don't have many friends in Liberty. Not yet anyway." She gave her satchel a pat. "And let's not forget—there are good reasons to mind me."

There wasn't time for a comeback. The secretary spoke into the intercom then motioned them through the gold door she'd been guarding.

Birdie followed Theodora into the office. The door shut with a soft click.

The room was large, the walls an oyster grey that matched the carpeting. Everything was sleek and minimalist. No personal mementos, nothing. There wasn't even a framed photo on the desk or a cheesy montage on the wall. The spacious room would suit an amnesiac whose personal history was lost to the sands of time.

"Nice digs," she said to the woman behind the desk. She felt edgy and defensive, mostly because the woman was loaded down with gold jewelry and enough eye makeup to do a geisha proud. Or maybe it was her expression of disapproval. "This place is like walking inside an oyster shell. Me, I'm into bright colors. I guess you go for neutrals."

Theodora elbowed her in the ribs. "Settle down." She approached the desk. "Meade, you got your wish. Here she is in the flesh."

Her forehead damp, Birdie stepped forward. The moment she did, the nerves plaguing her vanished.

Why, she couldn't fathom. A sensation of expectancy swept through her like a warm summer wind. Nothing in Meade's expression warranted the sensation. Yet Birdie couldn't stop the euphoria from expanding out, irrepressible and sudden.

Here. This is it.

Throwing her shoulders back, she realized she wanted to make a good impression. A first. Since when did she give a damn what anyone thought? Yet *this* woman . . . she mattered. She mattered a lot.

The thought was crazy. Still, she couldn't shake it.

"You're not the Greyhart woman," Meade was saying. She came around the desk. "Theodora was right. You're too young."

Birdie opened her palms. "A case of mistaken identity. Happens all the time."

"Not to me it doesn't."

A note of impatience came across in the retort, and Birdie's apprehension returned. *Why doesn't she like me?* "Tough break," she said. "This Greyhart woman must be on your shit list."

"She is." Approaching, Meade narrowed her regard. "How old are you, Birdie?"

"Thirty-one." She stared into the woman's eyes. *Hello.* Nervous laughter nearly leapt from her throat. Maybe it was time for the straight approach. "You're giving me a feeling of déjà vu. Have we met before?"

"I'd remember if we had." Meade nodded toward Theodora, who'd lowered herself into one of the chairs before the desk. "Theodora says you're new in Liberty. Is the move permanent?"

"I'm only here for a few weeks. I'm not really cut out to be a waitress."

"Is your family here?"

"No."

"You don't have anyone in Ohio?"

Like the laughter she'd barely suppressed, Birdie resisted the urge to go on the defensive. "I'm sorry," she said, remembering her manners. "I don't mean to sound like a bitch, but why do you care about my pedigree?"

"I'm merely curious." Returning to her chair, Meade opened a drawer and produced a manila envelope. "My father has been ill. He saw you in The Second Chance and mistook you for a woman he once knew."

Birdie's pulse scuttled. "Did she break his heart?" *Oh God, my mother didn't scam him, did she?*

"She conned him out of a lot of money. Here." Opening the envelope, Meade removed a series of photographs. "This is the woman." She tried to smile but failed miserably. "Why don't you take off your coat? No? I can have Siki bring coffee, if you'd like."

Theodora fiddled with the hem of her dress. "Do you have beer?"

"I don't. I'm sorry."

Birdie sank into a chair. "I'll pass on the coffee." Miserable, she kept her eyes straight ahead and the air locked in her lungs.

But Meade was persistent, sliding the photographs across the desk and lining them up, side by side. Fire burned in Birdie's lungs and she took a quick breath. Gripping the armrests, she tried to stay rooted in the conversation. No easy task—the urge to run nearly brought her to her feet.

"As you can see, you do resemble her," Meade said in a danger-ously steady voice. The tension in her eyes was now accompanied by deepening lines on the sides of her mouth. "Probably a coinci-dence . . . but then, she does have a daughter. Right here. The little girl beside my father."

Please don't let it be Wish. "This is your father?" Birdie man-aged to pick up a photograph of the man without trembling.

In the close-up, he wore a tuxedo and a bow tie. "He has a nice face."

"He's a nice man. You'd like him. Everyone does." The lightest hint of anxiety wove through her voice but this time, Meade smiled. It didn't reach her eyes, which clouded with sadness. "Look at the next picture. It was taken a long time ago. I believe the girl was about four years old, which would make her near your age today."

Blackness threatened. Birdie found an inner reserve of strength. "Lots of women are my age. Thousands of women."

"Go on—look at it."

Relenting, she picked up the photograph. The room spun in a sickening whirl. When it steadied, she took in the image of the child she'd once been. Then her gaze latched onto the image of the man standing with his arm across the little girl's shoulders.

Paw Paw?

He wasn't familiar. No shred of memory emerged to assure her that he was the man she'd loved like a father. The man who'd played Go Fish with her while she ran a high fever and her throat burned with infection. He'd been a fleeting, stable figure in her tumultuous childhood.

Her ears buzzing, she handed the photo back.

And was immediately accosted by the third photograph Meade slid forward. The man, Landon, was standing in a ballroom with his arm around a scintillating blonde. In the background, party streamers burst from the ceiling in a kaleidoscope of color. Diamonds glittered at the woman's throat, her practiced look of adoration bestowed on Landon.

Stunned beyond speech, Birdie set down the photo of her mother, the brilliant and immoral Wish Postell Kaminsky.

CHAPTER 19

Leaning close, Theodora asked, "Birdie, do you recognize the woman in the photograph? Take your time, child."

The bellyful of bees in Theodora's stomach was pinging tension all the way from her tummy to her feet. The boots she'd worn with her Christmas dress were tight, and she wiggled her toes. Her feet had gone numb, but why wouldn't they? Meade had sprayed as much tension in the room as a skunk rousted from its nest. Nasty business, all of this.

"I've never seen her before," Birdie finally said, the words little more than a whisper.

Theodora pushed the stack of photos back across the desk. "I figured as much. Meade, I hope you're satisfied."

Oh, Birdie was lying, all right. Not that a touch of dishonesty meant she deserved the third degree. Let the child hold to her lies for now. What was the harm? The truth would eventually win out. In Theodora's estimation, the harder people tried to bury their secrets the easier it was to dig them up.

Which made her wonder: was Birdie the child in the photograph with Landon?

Parsnip.

Theodora settled her bones deep in the chair. When Landon had been at his worst in the years after Cat drowned, Meade had placed him in a psychiatric lockdown. The normally taciturn man talked incessantly—but only to Theodora. The moment she came through the door, bearing a picnic basket of goodies in one hand and pack of playing cards in the other, he rose from the chair by the window and padded across the room. His hair was every which way and his bathrobe speckled with coffee stains, but his face would regain a shred of its former composure. Watching the transformation was like seeing clay shaped into the semblance of a man.

She'd always suspected the playing cards were the catalyst, bringing him out of depression in short bursts of disjointed, yet vivid, conversation. For reasons beyond comprehension, the cards loosened the memories from wherever he'd buried them, loosened them like so much silt scratched from the side of a hill and sent rolling down into the riverbed of his emotions. *Parsnip* he'd say, the word encompassing all the joy the world contained, and he'd described a little girl as blonde as an angel, a child he'd loved like his own. Clasping Theodora's hands in a death grip, he took her far from shore, into dreams. She gathered enough from his words to finally understand. The child had been the daughter of Wish Greyhart, the woman who'd wrecked his soul.

Was Birdie the child? Dang it all—was she Wish Greyhart's child? If so, and Meade ever found out, there'd be a hornet's nest of trouble.

Meade collected the photographs with the faintest hue of misgiving whispering across her features. "I didn't mean to waste your afternoon, Birdie. If I've been rude, please accept my apology. I've been under a lot of stress at work and now my father . . . the situation is difficult."

"It's not like I was doing much—just waiting tables back at the ranch."

"Should I pay you for the time you've missed?"

"We'll call it even if you'll get the maid to bring me a Coke." Birdie laughed shortly, her eyes skittering like violet wrens afraid to land. "I'm awfully thirsty."

"The maid indeed." Meade spoke quickly into the intercom. "Siki would kill you if she heard you say that."

Gingerly, Birdie drew her long legs out and crossed her ankles. She rested her hands in her lap. The normally uncouth girl was sitting as pretty as a lady and the sight was startling. "How is your father?" she asked. "The woman in the photos . . . does he still see her?"

"God, no." Lazily Meade brushed a wisp of hair from her cheek, lost in thought.

"When did it end?" Birdie prodded, making Theodora wonder if the child recognized fire when she played with it.

"It's been years. He doesn't talk about it and I don't ask."

"You thought she'd come back to make trouble for him?"

"Trouble he can't survive. He suffers from depression."

Siki brought in sodas, ending the conversation about Landon as abruptly as it had begun. Theodora waved her glass away. Settling back, she let the others make small talk for a few minutes, the conversation stilted. When she grew tired, she announced it was time to go.

In the parking lot, Jack Frost had put a sheet of ice on the windshield of her Cadillac. Scraping it off would take time. She stomped her foot to rid her body of the jangly irritation.

"I'll take care of it," Birdie said, her voice breezy. She rooted around on the floor of the Cadillac and found the scraper. "Just give me a sec."

"You can do better than that." Theodora slapped the keys into her hand. "I don't take well to heavy traffic. It's almost five o'clock."

"You want me to drive?" Birdie stared at the keys as if she'd never seen anything like them before. "Are you sure?"

Nodding, Theodora climbed into the passenger seat and stared at the white-crusted windshield. A shuffling outside the truck, then the child got her ass in gear and started scraping. When she'd finished, she slid into the driver's seat and sat motionless.

"What's the matter with you?" Theodora rapped her knuckles on the steering wheel. The sun was setting and her stomach was making a fuss. "You hold onto this and *drive*. Don't you know how?"

"I'm not sure I remember. It's been awhile."

"Since you've driven a vehicle? Of all the . . . how long?"

Birdie worked her jaw. "I'm not sure, all right?" She found the ignition and jammed the key in. Bringing the engine to life, she added, "It's been five years. No—seven. I've never owned a car but I had a friend who used to loan me hers. When I lived in Sante Fe. Crapsticks. Maybe it was eight years ago."

"Get out." Theodora flung open the door and hopped to the ground. Cain and Jezebel! She wasn't allowing the child to drive anywhere in the trusty old Cadillac if she couldn't remember the last time she'd been behind the wheel. "Trade places. And I mean right quick! Don't know how long it's been. What's the world coming to?"

They switched off and she pulled out of the parking lot. On the seat beside her, Birdie slouched low with her white-gold hair spilling out across the ugly green fabric of her military coat. The sun, dipping low, sent flashes of red across her shuttered face as they made their way onto the highway.

If the girl was the spawn of the no good grifter, Wish Greyhart, she sure as hell wasn't anything like the devil. Can't drive a car, heaven above!

"There are worse things than not being able to drive," Birdie said, breaking the silence with a defensive jerk of her chin. "It's not exactly the end of the world."

"In America, it is. It's your God-given right to own a car and take it out on the road. *Route 66, Ventura Highway*—don't those songs mean anything to you?"

"Not really," Birdie replied, slouching lower. "Face it, Theodora. Culturally, we're from different time zones."

"Like I give a rat's ass. Don't you *want* to own a car?" She banged on the horn, blaring a Honda Civic from the passing lane. The thought of what the child was missing made her angry and she flipped the other motorist the finger. When Birdie gaped at her, she added, "The idiot was in the passing lane."

Birdie raised her hands in an act of surrender. "Like I've said before, I don't argue with old ladies who're packin'."

"Smart of you, too." Softening, Theodora glanced across the seat. Birdie was examining her cuticles as if they unlocked the mysteries of the universe. "Is it true what you told Meade? You don't have kin nearby?"

"Kin. You mean family?" Birdie shrugged, the nasty show of disinterest she did with her shoulders. Theodora wasn't fooled. The child looked beaten down, about a hair's breath from tears even if she was good at holding them in. "I'm better off by myself. Family can be a real hassle."

"Not always. Not when your people love you."

"Mine don't." Birdie stared at her fiercely before looking away.

When she tried to add something but the words wouldn't come, Theodora said, "The cavalry has arrived. Consider me family. You're spending the night at my house."

* * *

Computer monitors blinked and keyboards clacked in the busy newsroom of the *Akron Register*.

Standing before the City Editor's desk with a feeling of hopelessness grinding down his shoulders, Hugh looked out at the humming room with a sense of longing. He'd miss the people and the general chaos of the place.

After meeting with Anthony last week he'd driven around for hours, finally ending up at his digs in Akron. In a truly undignified show, he'd spent days ignoring Birdie's calls and drinking too much beer, watching the tube and sleeping in late. None of it constituted R & R. In a state of exhaustion, he'd finally shown up at the *Register* to fight for his job.

Once he explained the Perini story was a no-go, Bud said, "I wish I had better news for you." The bastard almost looked sincere. "I don't want to cut you loose but I'm feeling pressure from upstairs. You've missed too many deadlines. Now the Perini story is a bust. My hands are tied."

"They wouldn't be if I'd come back with the dirt. Is that it? Anthony should be skimming thousands from the websites, not putting together a foundation to help kids with cancer?" Hugh was unable to halt the sarcasm seeping into his voice. "True, good news doesn't grab headlines like avarice and gore but I can stay in Liberty and write about the foundation."

"Since when are you interested in reporting on the good side of humanity? You don't think there *is* a good side to humanity."

"Maybe I'm seeing things differently now."

An image of Birdie spilled before his eyesight, the excitement and sheer joy on her face when they discovered the key in the storeroom. The way she fought back when he battled with her at the festival. She didn't believe she could put her life straight but damn it, she tried. She tried because in the deepest part of her heart, at her essence, she was an optimist. Her life was harrowing and harsh, yet she found an inner reserve of goodness that had allowed her to make friends in Liberty. She tried to appeal to her higher angels.

Hope.

Was that what set her apart? She was cocky and irritating and rude, but underneath it all, she possessed enough hope to rise above her lousy lot in life.

Pulling from his thoughts, Hugh said, "A feature about the foundation won't carry the front page but it *is* news. Why not give it a shot?"

Bud stared at him with a jaundiced eye. "You want to drive back up to Liberty? Why? A guy like you can't see the good stuff in life even if it hits him like a two-by-four."

"You'd be surprised by what I can do." Hugh grappled with his self-doubt, which was mixing with rising anger. What right did an editor from a second-rate newspaper have to tell him what he was capable of? "I'm writing the story. If you're cutting me loose, I'll sell it to a magazine."

"Good luck." Bud jerked his chin toward the newsroom. "If I want fluff, I'll send Ralston out to Liberty. The story's dead, pal."

"How is our boy?" Looking across the newsroom he peered over the heads of journalists to the desk where he'd worked the last five years. Ralston sat with a Starbucks in one hand and the telephone in the other. "He almost looks like a real journalist. Did the ad department send you flowers when you gave him my job?"

"You brought this on yourself. Ralston thinks he can handle investigative journalism."

"Cut the bullshit. You're buttering up his father. If daddy's furniture chain pours enough ad dollars into this dump, you might turn the *Register* into a real newspaper."

"Out." Swinging from his chair, Bud jabbed a finger toward the door. "Clear out your desk and see Cummings. Good guy that I am, I had him cut you a check even though I officially canned your ass before you went to Liberty."

"Well thanks a helluva a lot," Hugh said, reeling. The payroll department had written his last paycheck *before* he'd arrived to plead his case? No judge, no jury—Bud had already decided to cut him loose.

Furious, he stalked from the office. Reaching the desk he thought of as his own, he discovered Ralston making eye contact with a blushing Sarah Blake, the paper's movie critic, two desks away.

Coming up from behind, Hugh pleased himself by startling the big oaf. "Keep away from Sarah. Her boyfriend is into kick-boxing."

Ralston stumbled to his feet. "Hugh. I didn't know you'd be in."

"I'm collecting my stuff."

"You're fired?" A hint of glee marked Ralston's voice. "Bad break, man. I'm sorry."

Hugh resisted the urge to shove him out of the way. "Sure you are."

Pausing, he noticed Fatman's name and number scrawled on a slip of paper in Ralston's bold hand. It was a stunning breach of ethics. No journalist used a colleague's source without permission. A contact of Fatman's caliber was guarded like a state secret.

Then he thought of something else, and the ramifications sucker punched him in the gut.

Fatman had dug up a landfill on Birdie and her family. If Ralston ever learned about it, he wouldn't think twice. He'd write about her. A real charmer about how a pretty thief was preying on unsuspecting folks in small towns.

Rage bolted through him. "Where did you get this name?" He snatched up the paper.

"I took Fatman's call on Tuesday." Ralston shrugged. "He was looking for you."

Perfect. Fatman probably called with more information on Birdie. Hugh mentally flailed himself. He wasn't merely dodging Birdie's calls. He'd inadvertently missed a few from the PI.

"I didn't give you permission to use one of my sources. Do your own legwork, pal."

"If you've been bagged, why do you care?"

Hugh went nose to nose with the bastard. "I care," he growled. "Why the hell do you need Fatman's expertise?"

"I got his take on the UAW strike."

"Since when does the UAW rate a piece in the Features section?"

"Piss off, Hugh. It's hard news, and I needed Fatman's help."

Hugh prayed Ralston was telling truth. He couldn't ask Fatman what they'd discussed. The PI was clever and resourceful, but honest? In his vernacular, the word didn't exist.

"Stay away from him. He's my source."

For a long moment, Ralston stared at him. Then in a surprisingly strong voice, he said "I don't take orders from you, *pal.*" He stepped forward. "Bud's fired your ass. So Fatman isn't your source. Not anymore. He's mine."

Hugh froze. He didn't have any leverage and Ralston knew it. If he was off the paper, there was no stopping Fatman from changing allegiance. The PI was always hungry for cash. And in the final analysis, Hugh was responsible for the mess. He'd asked Fatman to poke around in Birdie's background. The goods would go up on the auction block if he didn't think of something, and fast.

"Bud hasn't fired me so Fatman is off limits," he said, grabbing the big oaf by the shoulders and shoving him against the desk. The computer twitched and Ralston's cactus joggled. "Get your trash off my desk *now*. I don't share my territory."

"But you said—"

Ralston never got the chance to finish the thought. Hugh drove his fist into the man's face with all the force of his fury. Ralston spun backwards, meeting the floor with a thud and bringing the newsroom to a standstill.

Seething, Hugh cleared a wide path through the newsroom. Losing his job after years of work for the *Register* was bad enough. Somehow, he'd manage. But now Birdie's privacy was at stake. It would only be a matter of time before Fatman invited Ralston to the hunting lodge. They'd talk, drink too much—Hugh would enter the conversation. And Ralston, curious, would quiz the PI on what Hugh had been working on. Birdie would come up.

That was one reason for what he was about to do. The other one undermined what little dignity he had left.

By writing about the rubies, he'd stop her from searching for them. No rubies, no reason to leave Ohio. There'd be time to talk her into staying, time enough to build a relationship—assuming he found a way to gain her forgiveness. After her treasure hunt graced the front page, the odds weren't good.

A fleeting image of her swept through his mind and his heart seized. *No choice here.* He'd write about her treasure hunt or Ralston would write about her. Either way, her secrets were about to meet the glaring limelight.

He strode through the newsroom on autopilot, forcing his thoughts away from her. It was easier to focus on Ralston growing rock formations out of the desk where Hugh had interviewed mob bosses and captains of industry, uncovering scams and putting corrupt politicians in the spotlight. *I can protect her if I save my job.*

He'd barely come to a scudding halt before the City Editor's desk when Bud's mouth curled. Hugh cut him off.

"There's buried treasure in Liberty," he said.

Bud looked at him like he'd grown a tail. "What? Like in a pirate movie?" He pointed toward the door. *"Leave."*

"I'm serious. There are rubies hidden in Liberty."

Queasy, he rattled off everything he knew. How Justice Postell hid the rubies during the Civil War. The clues Birdie had found in The Second Chance Grill. Then he went for the jugular—Birdie's, and his own.

Guilt seeped under his skin, but he hurried on. "There's a key with a ruby in it—I've seen it."

"What does it unlock?"

"I'm not sure yet. Probably a safe, with the rubies inside."

"And this Birdie—what's she like?"

"Just a woman who found the clues."

Bud leaned across the desk. "You aren't sleeping with her, are you?" When Hugh reddened, a foul retort on his lips, the City Editor waved him off, asking, "How much are the gems worth?"

"Six figures, I'd guess." Remorse welled up, nearly shattering his heart. Steadying himself, he added, "Birdie says they were owned by one of her ancestors, a Rhett Butler type from South Carolina. I think she knows what she's talking about."

"If she does, that would be some story."

"She's close to finding the gems. I'll be there when she does." He paused for effect, relishing how Bud hung on every word. "If you're not interested, I'll take the story elsewhere."

"No, no—I want it!" Bud shot from his chair. He bellowed across the newsroom. When Ralston neared, Bud said, "Get your stuff off Hugh's desk. It's the sacred territory of this paper's finest investigative reporter. You've got a desk in Features—use it."

Ralston flapped his gums like a fish out of water. After he sulked off, Bud swung back around. He was glowing like a goddamn holiday wreath and Hugh reveled in an involuntary spurt of self-congratulation.

It was snuffed out by a growing sense of doom.

CHAPTER 20

Arguing with Theodora about where to spend the night wasn't much of a plan.

Privately Birdie didn't relish the thought of being alone, not after learning her mother had conned the sweet-looking Landon Williams. His ancestor, Henry Williams, was the abolitionist who'd helped Justice open the restaurant after she arrived in Ohio. So Landon came from good stock. Probably Meade was nice too, if she didn't have reason to hate you because your mother had taken her father for all he was worth.

Her pulse rattling in her ears, Birdie stared out the passenger window of the Cadillac. What if she ran into Landon at the restaurant? She had no memory of him. She'd been young when her mother arrived in Liberty to shake him down. If he walked into The Second Chance, would he take one look and remember her as the child he must have known?

Or worse, what if Meade found out? A woman so powerful made for a lethal enemy.

Worried, she rubbed her arms. Yeah, she was glad for the invitation to bunk at Theodora's place tonight.

There were other reasons to skip a night alone. With Hugh incommunicado—he still wasn't answering his cell—she doubted he was back at the apartment. Besides, Finney was probably livid. Birdie hadn't returned to work as promised after taking off with Theodora.

Waiting until morning to deal with the cook's wrath *was* a good plan.

The Cadillac rumbled past Liberty Square. Birdie caught a glimpse of The Second Chance behind a speckling of falling snow. The place was aglow with light. Pretty Mrs. Daniels was framed in the picture window with a mountain of shopping bags at her feet and her adoring husband, Garrett, seated to her left. They were holding hands, grinning as their third-grader, Tilly, spun in a circle in a red velvet dress. The Liberty Elementary School holiday concert would be held next week and Tilly had captured a lead role. Birdie enjoyed the Daniels family, especially when Tilly clambered onto a chair, her ice cream sundae forgotten, and burst into song. The kid was a perfect-pitch soprano and the other diners always rewarded her efforts with hearty applause. At those moments, the restaurant seemed more like a private gathering, as if all the diners were family with Tilly a precocious delight, and Birdie, a distant relation, was able to warm herself in the room's easy affection and good cheer.

She'd begun looking forward to her time spent at The Second Chance. Sure, she hated waiting tables even if the tips were getting larger with the holiday season in full swing. She didn't plan to spend a lifetime taking orders and running miles. Even Delia talked of moving on once she figured out what she wanted to do with her life.

She huffed a breath on the frosty white of the passenger window. She didn't enjoy the job so much as the people. Finney expected to see her at work. Delia looked forward to gossiping. Ethel Lynn, who was so scatterbrained she probably had marbles rolling around in her head, calmed down once Birdie tied on an apron.

In an unexpected way, she experienced a sense of welcome every time she arrived. For the first time in memory, her presence in a room mattered to someone. It mattered to the three women of The Second Chance.

And Theodora makes four.

Straightening, Birdie peered through the windshield. "We're in the woods." The branch of a fir tree smacked the side of the Cadillac, and she jumped. There was nothing to see but pines so thick they kept the falling snow from reaching the ground. "Hire a lumberjack, Theodora. Your place is buried in trees."

Looking pleased, Theodora made a sound with her nose. *Snickety, snickety.* "I like it this way. There's lots of privacy and enough wildlife to feed a nation. It clears out a ways up."

"You live back in the woods?" *In a hut, in a tree house?* "Don't you get scared out here, all by yourself?"

"I require my solitude."

"I'd be scared shitless."

"Nonsense." Theodora gave her satchel a pat. "I can take care of myself."

Up ahead, the trees parted like the curtains in an old-time cinema. Snow brushed the gentle clearing. The log cabin, cut into the side of the hill, was surprisingly large. The sturdy dwelling featured a wraparound porch.

"Your house is big." Taken aback, she leaned toward the windshield for a better look. "You live here alone?"

"Since my husband died, a long time ago." Theodora parked in the garage and cut the engine. "Come inside. I'll get supper on."

While she bustled around the kitchen, Birdie wandered through rooms cluttered with hunting gear and memorabilia. The walls were chock-full of photographs—family shots with Theodora proudly seated in the middle, older pictures of her as an attractive young woman. There were five children, all now in middle age—

two sons with long legs they hadn't inherited from their mother and a daughter who was younger than the rest.

"That's Belinda," Theodora said, finding Birdie in the dining room holding a silver-framed portrait. "Ornery thing when she was small. Always into something. She still carries a compass in her purse, one of those gadgets they used to put in Cracker Jack boxes. Do they still make Cracker Jack? I wonder."

"She doesn't look much older than Meade."

"Born the same year. Belinda just turned forty-one."

Which meant Theodora had been well into middle age before bringing her last child into the world. Birdie's respect for her grew.

Birdie's own mother had never let her forget what a hassle it was to drag one kid around. And here Theodora had five children, all of whom had sprouted children themselves like so many wild-flowers. There must be fifty people in her extended family, most black, some white, a petite Asian girl hanging on the arm of a young man who was probably a grandson.

Birdie turned toward the long dining room table. Seated on a gold pedestal in the middle of the gleaming walnut expanse sat a . . . thing. A squat, furry animal that had experienced the misfortune of meeting up with a taxidermist.

"What's that?" she asked.

Mischief waltzed through the old woman's gaze. "That's Alice."

"No, it's a rodent."

"She's a groundhog." Theodora gave the beast, which was as big as a terrier, a gentle stroke. "We started out as friends, but Alice upped the ante by digging around in my carrots. Soon enough, she was uprooting the tomatoes and taking bites out of the rhododendron. Oh, I warned her. But if a shot in the air won't make a varmint listen, then a shot to the head will." She patted the groundhog's ear. "The taxidermist was pleased with my handiwork. I did this with a BB gun. Less mess that way."

"*Good God.*"

What about Ethel Lynn? She was defenseless, and she got on Theodora's nerves. The old thing wouldn't hurt a fly. What if she upped the ante, purely by accident, and rooted around Theodora's proverbial garden?

Ethel Lynn had been kind enough to invite Birdie over for tea. Sure, the old bat dropped china in the restaurant and squealed like a siren, but she had her good points. She never took the last slice of Finney's homemade pecan pie. She replaced the toilet paper in the john. When a button came loose on Birdie's coat, she produced a needle and thread from her enormous purse and sewed it back on.

"I need to know what the bad blood is between you and Ethel Lynn," she said, following Theodora back into the kitchen.

The old woman lifted the lid from a pot and scooped some kind of stew into bowls. "Watch your tone." She handed them off and they returned to the dining room. "My business with Ethel Lynn is none of your affair."

"I really need to know."

Seating herself at the head of the table, Theodora nodded for Birdie to sit on her right. When she had, Theodora said, "I'll tell you this much. Her great aunt jilted my great granddaddy. Nasty business." She lifted her spoon. "Now, wouldn't you rather hear another story about Justice?"

"Sure." Birdie lowered her nose to the bowl and sniffed. "What is this? It smells funny."

"Squirrel stew."

"Made with real squirrels? The kind that hide acorns?"

Theodora feathered a hand across her brow. "What other kind of squirrel is there?"

"Can I order a pizza?"

"When Justice came north, you can't imagine what she ate to survive. Foraging through the woods, with ne'er a pot to cook a decent meal or a weapon to bring in game. Now, eat your stew." Theodora waited with her dark gaze snapping until Birdie brought a spoonful to her lips. After she'd gulped it down, the old woman said, "Now, where was I? Justice came to Liberty with nothing but the clothes on her back. A kind woman on the Underground Railroad outside Columbus wrapped the slave's bleeding feet with strips of cotton. Those were her shoes."

Birdie spooned around the chunks of squirrel meat and captured a wedge of potato. "I couldn't survive without my shoes." A good thief didn't trust much but her instincts and a fast pair of Nikes. With her feet bleeding, Justice would've been in a lot of pain. "She walked all the way from Columbus?"

"A man picked her up in Marion and hid her in the back of his wagon. Like the woman on the Railroad, he was the right type of white folk. He took her all the way to Liberty." Pausing, Theodora looked off into the past. "Imagine, child. You're a young woman and you arrive in a town without a soul to welcome you. Lonesome, tired—imagine how you'd feel."

Birdie's heart shifted. Had it been any different on her first day in town? There'd been the overwhelming déjà vu, the feeling she'd stood in Liberty Square at some time in the past. The sensation had made her irrepressibly sad. She'd been lonely and tired, a stranger in a small town. *Like Justice.*

"The man Justice loved was still down south," Theodora said. "She was heartbroken, wondering if she'd ever see him again."

What if I never see Hugh again? Birdie lowered her spoon. "How did she go on?"

"The way our kind always does. She found other women to cling to, women who befriended her. They put food in her belly and hope in her heart. They made her laugh when she was down and they found her work—honest work that didn't pay much, but it was enough to help Justice take root in a new life. A better life than the one she'd known."

Birdie lifted her spoon. *I'm eating rat. The kind of rat that lives in a tree.*

It wasn't bad. The meat was spicy and wild, with a tart after-taste. She swallowed it down.

"And if you think Justice was some kind of saint, think again," Theodora said. "Before she met the preacher's son and settled into a respectable life—even before she learned to trust the women who became her friends she was . . . Lordy."

The old woman hung her head, revealing thinning wisps of hair on her scalp. She lowered her palms to the linen tablecloth and heaved a sigh replete with shame. Birdie grabbed Theodora's wrist as her fingers curled with agony. The tablecloth bunched in rippling waves.

"What? What did she do? Was she a prostitute? No. Not Justice."

"Worse," Theodora croaked, the top of her head bobbing with the word.

What would be . . ? "No way." Birdie yanked her hand back. "If you think I'll believe she murdered someone, I won't!"

The sound was terrible, from the bowels of hell. *"Worse."*

"Oh, man." Birdie wracked her brain for possibilities. Floundering, she glanced at Theodora. If the old woman bent her neck any lower, she'd put her nose right into her stew. Was she crying? "I give. What did Justice do?"

The gnarled hands flew off the table, scuttling Birdie's pulse.

Theodora lifted her head with a snap. "She betrayed the people who loved her the most. She was a *thief.*"

CHAPTER 21

"Birdie, are you here?"

Placing his laptop on the coffee table, Hugh scanned the silent apartment. The Second Chance was already closed for the night. Where was she?

He'd driven straight in from the *Register*, where he'd spent most of the day tooling around the paper's archives for background on Justice Postell. He'd found some material but it didn't lift his mood. If his rationalizations had made him sick earlier today, he was now emotionally at death's door. He was a reporter selling out the woman he cared deeply about.

He tried to assure himself it was the right thing to do. If Ralston wrote about Birdie's true occupation as a thief, she'd suffer the indignity of being exposed before the people of Liberty. She'd made friends here, maybe the only friends she'd ever had.

Opening his laptop, he wrote, *Hidden Treasure in a Small Town*. He completed a few paragraphs before abandoning the work. Deleting the file, he started over.

While he worked he wrestled an image of her, how her eyes grew soft during those rare instances when motive met opportunity and he'd kissed her. Struggling to keep his attention on the task at hand, he plodded on. A rap on the door broke his concentration.

Delia stood in the hallway. On the lapel of her leather coat, a pathetically joyous Frosty the Snowman pin—some electronic gizmo—blinked on and off.

"It's December," she said when he stared. "I get into the spirit early. Has Birdie come back?"

"She's not here."

"She took off with Theodora yesterday. She never came back to work." Absently, Delia fiddled with the paper bag in her hands. "What's going on? You look bad. Like a guy on his way to the gallows."

"Don't hold back, Delia. I have a soft spot for women who tell me I look like shit."

Giggling, she lifted her shoulders in a flirty shrug. "I'm just saying you need rest. Maybe you're working too hard."

"Maybe." On impulse, he took a stab at bolstering his rationalizations about betraying Birdie's trust. "Have you noticed any cash missing from your wallet?" He nodded toward Delia's purse, one of those blue jean things covered in spangles. "A few bills, or a twenty missing? Anything like that?"

The waitress brought a stick of gum from her pocket and slowly unwrapped it. "Not lately." She chewed, considering. "But a few weeks ago, I was missing ten bucks. Really pissed me off. Of course, I'd been to Bongo's. You know how it goes when you're drinking."

Hugh flinched. "I have an idea." An extended drinking spree, the type to leave him unconscious for hours, was tempting about now.

"Maybe I spent the money there. But I don't think so. See, I preorder my Jell-O shots to make sure I don't overspend. Only way I know how to stick to a budget."

"Sensible."

"How'd you know I was missing cash?"

"I didn't." *Birdie.* "I'm just asking." *She's a common criminal, which is why I'm justified in breaking my word.* Hugh dug into his magic and smiled in a way that made women melt. "What about Ethel Lynn and Finney? Have they been coming up short?"

"No . . . but one of the customers complained right before Thanksgiving. She swore someone took twenty bucks from her wallet while she was in the ladies' room."

"Do you remember her name?" He should be writing this down.

"She was someone's niece—Mrs. Park's? I can't remember. She was in town visiting relatives."

"Anyone else?"

"I don't think so." The waitress rose from the spell he'd cast. "What's with the questions? A robber wouldn't come to Liberty, at least not to The Second Chance. Finney would pound him with her skillet."

Her quaint assessment was amusing. "Then let's hope there isn't a robber in town."

Maybe he was doing Birdie a favor by sparing her the danger of Finney's skillet. But with the hunt for the rubies off, would she stay? Bad odds, that. He stifled his anguish, but not before it knotted his heart.

"Give this to Birdie." Delia said, drawing his attention back to her. She handed over the bag. "Everything she asked for is in there."

Opening the bag, he was accosted by the photo of a simpering blond on a purple and gold carton. "What is this?"

"Hair coloring, dufus. Birdie promised to fix me up." The waitress twirled a lock of her lime-blond hair. "I keep trying for something golden but I screw it up. She's going to get rid of the green."

"You think she can color hair? Don't count on it, sweetheart."

Grinning, Delia smacked his forearm. "She says she can. I believe her." Angling her hip, the waitress added, "By the way, have you called her? She's left a zillion messages on your cell. She's really worried about you."

"It's on my 'to do' list."

Returning her calls meant hearing her voice. It would be enough to make him question his motives, something he couldn't afford. Not that putting off the inevitable made much sense either. Eventually there'd be a confrontation. They *were* roomies.

"Put it at the top of your list," Delia said. "She needs to hear from you."

* * *

Birdie tightened her seatbelt as the Cadillac swerved into the snow-packed Square. "Everything you said about Justice last night . . . it was a lie," she said, and the stringy muscles along Theodora's jaw twitched. "You made it all up, didn't you?"

The Cadillac coasted to a stop before the darkened restaurant. Rosy threads of daylight spread across the hood of the car. A giant plow swept past, hurling sheets of white like so much ice spun from a snow cone machine.

"Are you referring to the story of her thievery?" Theodora opened her satchel and withdrew her corncob pipe. "You skedaddled from the table so fast, I thought you weren't enthralled with my story."

"I was sleepy."

In truth she'd been dumbstruck when Theodora made the announcement about Justice. A thief wasn't worse than a murderer, no matter what the old woman thought. Yet a sticky sort of guilt had clung to her all night while she tossed in bed and wrestled the question: If a thief betrayed the people who trusted her, was that worse than cold-blooded murder?

Not possible. Still, the old woman's assessment bothered her.

Now she'd ditched the hurt and was just plain suspicious. The story dovetailed too closely with her life of petty crime. It must be a sailor's yarn.

Theodora struck a match, and Birdie waved her hands like a traffic cop. "Don't smoke in here. I can't open the window. It's freezing outside."

"I always smoke in the morning."

"It's not a good plan. It'll kill you one day."

Theodora leered, the rising sun catching the hills and valleys of her face. "Bring it on."

Annoyed, Birdie rolled down her window. "About Justice. You were telling me a fable." She dared a glance through the plume of smoke. "It was some kind of a Sunday school lesson. You made up the story to fit what you thought I needed to learn."

"Justice *was* a thief." Theodora turned up the heat in the Cadillac then settled back. "The man who picked her up outside Marion and gave her a ride to Liberty? He was a notions seller. She hid in the back of his covered wagon."

"What's a notions seller?"

"A man who sells everything from bolts of fabric to hammers and nails. Small towns didn't have hardware stores back then. He traveled through Ohio selling his wares. He sold clothing too. While they were bumping along those country roads, Justice noticed shoes in one of the crates. Nice, sturdy leather shoes."

Who'd blame a runaway slave for snagging a pair of shoes? "She walked hundreds of miles in her bare feet. Lifting a pair of shoes doesn't qualify as theft. She was desperate."

"Stealing is stealing, child. Mind you, Justice was burnin' with guilt over what she'd done. Once she was earning a living in Liberty, she sent money back to the man to pay for the shoes."

Uneasy Birdie crossed her arms, as if the action might shield her from the remorse dogging her whenever she lifted money from a wallet. Especially after she'd snitched cash from the baker, Natasha Jones. She was still trying to figure out how to return it.

If that wasn't bad enough, she'd learned at Meade's office that Wish had oozed her way through Liberty. Her mother had done a number on Landon Williams, and good. Birdie tugged her coat tighter, but she couldn't banish the icy realization—she was a thief like her mother and just as loathsome.

"The point is," Theodora was saying, "folks make mistakes all the time. They can put things straight."

"You *were* trying to teach me a lesson." Shame tweaked her false indignation. "Not that I'm a thief."

Theodora sucked languidly on her pipe. "Of course not."

She huffed out a breath. "So Justice took something. So what? Someone who steals isn't so bad," she blurted, the words gushing out in a nervous ramble. "I'm not talking about holdup men. They don't care who they hurt. But your everyday pickpocket? Maybe he's tried going straight, but he's not sure how to pull it off. Try sticking to a nine-to-five life after you've grown up in a world without alarm clocks. It's a bitch."

Theodora cocked her pipe in the corner of her mouth. "See this?" She rubbed her index finger and thumb together. "I'm playing the world's smallest violin."

Offended, Birdie shifted in her seat, the sticky feeling returning. "So you aren't big on sympathy. All things considered, it's no surprise."

"No surprise at all."

"Just admit a guy who steals to get by is light years better than someone who'd kill. I mean, if you kill someone, they're dead."

"Obviously."

"You killed Alice. Did the beast deserve it?" She was firmly on the groundhog's side. "She ate some carrots and nipped your bushes. Is it enough reason to spill blood?"

"Alice had it coming to her." A smoke ring popped from Theodora's lips. "She'd been warned."

"Great! Clear the woods of wildlife! Just don't aim your BB gun in my direction. *My* glass house is just fine, thank you very much."

"So you say."

"I'm not a thief!"

Not for much longer, anyway. She'd find the rubies and cash them in. Afterward she'd ditch life on the run. *Won't I?* Greasy doubt settled in her stomach, banishing her self-confidence.

Frustrated, she yanked open the passenger door. "Thanks for the ride, and dinner last night. You've destroyed my image of squirrels as cute little creatures. Now I've got them stuck in my head as a chunky kind of stew."

With that, she marched toward the door of the restaurant and banged on the glass. The crunching of snow beneath tires, and the Cadillac hydroplaned away into the white.

Finney should've answered by now. Her teeth chattering, Birdie snapped up her wrist. Shit—it wasn't even seven A.M.

She marched around back with her darkening mood making her strides uneven. Sliding through a thick layer of slush, she stumbled into the hallway. By the time she trudged upstairs, she'd worked herself into a fine fury.

To her surprise, Hugh was camped out in bed with his attention glued to his laptop. He looked like he'd been working there for days. Notepads and balled up sheets of paper were tossed out across the comforter.

He gave no reaction when she stood fuming at the base of the bed. If she'd been an ax murderer, he would've blissfully gone to his death typing away on his friggin' laptop.

Hurling her coat on a chair, she searched for patience and came up empty. "Where the hell have you been?" Not the best greeting, but there was a bottle of Scotch on the nightstand beside a coffee mug and Hugh looked woozy. "I thought you were in a car wreck. I was thinking about calling every hospital in the area. Would it really have put you out to let me know where you were?"

He topped off his mug then sipped. "It's nice to see you too, Celery," he replied, flourishing the mug in the air.

"You're a shit, Hugh."

"I try. Thanks for noticing."

"I notice you're starting your day with eighty-proof."

"Lay off." His flannel pants were endearingly rumpled and his tee-shirt showed off his pecs to good effect. Not that it mattered. "If you're curious, I got back last night."

"Why didn't you return my calls?"

"Because you're not my mother." He smiled devilishly, then resumed typing.

Fine. So he was playing the mystery card. No skin off her back.

Shivering, she stared at the bed with longing. She'd spent weeks bunking on the apartment's couch with Old Man Winter rattling the windows. The night at Theodora's, nestled in a bed she'd swear was stuffed with feathers, made her appreciate the finer things in life. Like a mattress large enough to sprawl out on and a comforter big enough to burrow down in.

"How's it going with the hunt for the rubies?" he asked, and something in his tone put her on alert. Or maybe it was the way his gaze refused to meet hers. "Found them yet?"

"Not yet."

"Have you gone back down to the storeroom?"

"Twice," she admitted, kicking off her shoes and shrugging out of her jeans. "I don't think I'll find anything else down there. The key must be it. Maybe there's a clue on the key, something I've overlooked."

"You heard what Theodora said. Justice used the rubies for collateral to build the restaurant. She didn't bury them."

"She buried them later. There were two bags of rubies, remember? I think she buried one of the bags for Molly."

"Who's Molly?"

"My great-grandmother. Or great-great grandmother." She gave up trying to figure it out. "Lucas Postell's daughter."

"Your theory about Justice's motives is pure speculation."

"Think what you will." She stalked around the side of the bed and yanked back the comforter. Balls of paper toppled to the floor. "The rubies *are* buried. I'll find them."

Hugh darted a sideways glance when she slid beneath the covers. "What are you doing?"

"Getting some rest. I don't have to wait tables for another four hours."

"Sleep on the couch. You're distracting me."

Now he was able to look at her fully. Or rather her breasts, outlined beneath her camisole, since she'd tugged off her sweatshirt and flung it to the floor.

She gave the pillow a few good jabs and lowered her head. "I'm sick of the couch. If I try to roll over, I fall off." He gulped down a slug of booze and she added, "Why are you drinking at first light? It's not a good plan."

Grimacing, he yanked his attention from her breasts. "It was a good idea at the time."

"You lost your job, didn't you?"

Stone-faced, he returned the mug to the nightstand. The muscles in his back tensed and she caught his scent—musky, warm. It was enough to lure her fingers down the hard bumps of his spine. Her touch froze him for the fraction of a second. Then he drew his back rigid.

"I'm serious, Birdie," he growled ridiculously at the nightstand. "Sleep on the couch. I'm not making love to you. Given the booze I've ingested, it might not even be possible."

She pulled the comforter to her chin, realized she was too warm, and threw it off. "You're not drunk. For some reason, you're avoiding me. But I'm the one who should be angry. You never returned my calls." She punched low on his spine so he'd turn around. When he did, his brows lowering, she flopped her hand through the air. "How many fingers am I holding up?"

"Seventeen."

"You're the most perverse man I ever met." She rolled onto her side, away from him. "Keep the typing down. I'm going to sleep."

She waited for the clackety clack of his obstinacy, but it wasn't forthcoming. With something between a snarl and a curse, he reached down and rolled her onto her back.

CHAPTER 22

Hugh looked like a man suspended between St. Peter's gate and Dante's inferno. Fuming after he'd flopped her onto her back, Birdie wondered at the conflict waging on his face. Doubt warred with the desire warming his features.

To her horror, it appeared the desire had won out.

Placing his laptop on the nightstand, he pinioned her with sober regard. "What are you doing?" he asked, his voice so unexpectedly gentle it wicked the anger from her blood. He rolled on top of her. "You'll never be able to sleep here. You won't be able to keep your hands off me."

"I have more self-control than you think." *His* hands were already fast at work, teasing fire down her neck, whispering feather light caresses across her jawbone. "You should get some sleep, too."

"I have work to do."

"So you have to find a new job. Work on your resume later."

The comment stamped regret on his features. She couldn't stop to analyze it, not with his fingers making a fiery excursion across the tender skin beneath her ear. Lowering his head, he brushed his lips across her temple. Her heart tumbled.

"You have to do something for me," he murmured, nipping her ear. He eased himself fully on top of her; sinew and bone, and she trembled. "No arguments."

The sincerity in his voice loosened her defenses. "What do you want?"

"Stop searching for the rubies." He lifted his head to petition her with a look fraught with entreaty. "Stop looking, stop running. Move away . . . move to Akron."

"Why would I do that?"

"Live with me. Give our relationship a test run."

The suggestion was stunning. Flabbergasted, she tried to marshal her objections. No easy feat with his hands skimming her shoulders and his breathing becoming choppy. The signs of his arousal kicked up her own need and she shifted pleasurably beneath him.

"We'd never make it work," she said, unable to come up with anything better.

She certainly couldn't share the more painful reservation— Ohio was proving to be one of the states her mother had conned her way through. Wish oozed her way through Liberty sometime during Birdie's childhood. Landon Williams was one of her marks. What if Wish had also done some of her more destructive work in the city of Akron, where Hugh lived?

Better to leave Ohio, and quickly. Find a state Wish had never worked in. Even the friendships Birdie had made here wouldn't amount to much if people learned she was the child of a notorious swindler.

"We have as good a shot at a relationship as anyone else," Hugh said.

"We argue all the time. We'd screw it up."

"How can you be sure?"

"We aren't built for relationships," she said, hating the truth. "I leave the minute I get bored. You're just as shallow. You've probably gone through dozens of women."

"I'm not willing to give you up." He dipped his mouth to hers. He smelled of Scotch and something else, something earthy and good and she ached for his kiss. "You're scared because you've lived too much of your life on the surface. You can change."

"But not overnight." She tried to slide out from beneath him, caught between pleasure and the pain of self-doubt. "You're asking too much."

"This time is different. Different from the world you came from."

A niggling unease seeped through the desire pulling her under. "You don't know anything about my world."

"I know about your mother. Your father, in prison. You're better than them. You deserve a fresh start. We both do."

"*How* do you know about my parents?" Oh, God—a reporter could find out anything. Tanek's record of arrests. The humiliating backlog of crimes Wish never paid for. "Damn it, Hugh—have you been doing research on me? You wouldn't dare."

"I have, yes."

"If there's something you wanted to know, you could've asked."

"You would've lied."

"It's not easy talking about my life." Too painful really. "What did you find out?"

"A lot about your childhood, how your mother dragged you around. How she used you in her cons, usually whenever your father was incarcerated. How she mistreated you."

"Not always," she replied, suddenly defensive of the woman who was coldhearted and cunning but her mother nonetheless. "Sometimes she was okay."

Hugh dipped his nose to hers and slowly rubbed, an Eskimo kiss potent with yearning and something sweet enough to grab hold of her senses. "When did you last see her?"

"We almost ran into each other here in Ohio." Wish sent the newspaper clipping of his article along with a short note. "I was hoping we'd hook up in Columbus."

"How long, Birdie?"

His persistence started her lips quivering. "A while, all right?" she replied, wishing he'd drop the interrogation. Her mother was a sore spot in her life, a perpetual torment.

"Tell me," he urged, cradling her face.

The hurt she'd bottled up tore through her. "It's been four years, all right?" Handling the overload of pain was unbearable. "Stay out of my business."

"I can't. I care about you."

She struggled to break free and he clamped onto her shoulders. Furious, she met his unwavering gaze. He was stronger than she'd realized, a lot stronger, and the determination tensing his jaw was frightening.

"Get off!"

"Like hell I will." He looked wolfish, enraged. "I didn't invite you into my bed. But you're here and I'm making love to you. I'm not settling for a fling, or a weekend romance. I need more. Give it to me."

"Hugh, I don't know how to make this—"

"You'll try," he said, cutting her off. "We both need redemption."

Could they find it together? Hope whispered across her heart. And something else, a sweet heaviness, as their gazes tangled.

A dart of pain skimmed his beautifully carved mouth. "I'm falling in love with you," he said. "It sure as hell isn't convenient, but I am."

He captured her lips in a hard kiss, as if to demonstrate the potency of his love. She strained against him, angry and frustrated, returning his ardor with matching heat. No, love wasn't convenient. Love was messy, unpredictable, and she liked to keep her life simple.

Could she trust in his love? Lowering the walls she'd built around her heart was a terrifying prospect. She'd never before tied herself to a place—or a man.

None of her reservations stopped her from shimmying his pajamas down his thighs, increasing the fury of his kiss, his tongue darting and tempting, driving her higher until his lovemaking vanquished all of her doubts. Suspended in joy, with the past too murky to grieve and the future too blinding to fear, she let him tease her ever higher. They made love until the sunlight blazed across the floor of the bedroom, a frenzied coupling followed by a leisurely exploration. Replete, Birdie rested her cheek against the shuddering wall of his chest. Hugh sifted the lengths of her hair through his fingertips, examining the locks with boyish curiosity as the morning light burned bright in every strand.

* * *

Theodora bristled when the interloper walked into The Second Chance.

According to Miss Betty, the mailwoman, he'd been sneaking around town all day, starting at the library after Hugh drove off. Then the well-dressed loafer went into the courthouse. Revving her Cadillac in the no parking zone, Theodora sat fuming when he came out scribbling so furiously in a notebook he nearly marched into a tree.

What was another reporter doing in Liberty? This was Hugh's turf. He wasn't the sort of man who shared his domain.

Next the stranger visited the police station. Anxiety pinged through her as she put two and two together. She considered going in after he strolled off, to ask Officer Tim what the fool wanted, but she had a hankering for Finney's lunch special.

Now he was darkening the door of the Second Chance and ruining her taste for her pastrami and rye.

She had a bad feeling about him. He was tall, too handsome, even if he did have a purpling bruise on his chin. And the look in his eyes, why, most folks would read that look as idiocy but she knew it hid cunning. Delia and Birdie had left right after the lunch rush—something about preparations for fixing the mess Delia called her hair. Ethel Lynn was manning the nearly empty dining room.

"Good afternoon, ladies." He sat down on the barstool next to Theodora and picked up a menu. "What's the lunch special?"

"The food here's crap," she said, drawing a gasp from Ethel Lynn.

"Oh. Okay. How 'bout a cup of coffee?" Fumbling with his necktie, he regarded Ethel Lynn. "Miss . . ?" Wary, he turned around and glanced at Theodora. "I'm looking for a drifter. I understand she works here."

Theodora grunted. "This fine establishment doesn't employ drifters."

"She's about thirty years old, new in town."

"Never heard of her."

The man frowned. "I haven't given her name. How do you know if you've heard of her?"

Approaching on a flutter, Ethel Lynn banged into the coffee station. "Do you mean Birdie?"

Theodora lobbed a venomous warning look. Ethel Lynn was as dumb as a doorpost! There was something oily and self-serving about the man. Couldn't she see he was a threat?

"Yeah. Birdie Kaminsky," the man replied. "I'd like to talk to her. Is she around?"

Ethel Lynn hurried forward to pass more secrets across enemy lines. Staring her into silence, Theodora said, "Birdie's moved on. Last I heard she's in Miami." To accent her words, she withdrew her pistol and cocked the hammer. Aiming for his nose, she added, "Now, why don't you skedaddle before I send you a sight farther than Florida?"

* * *

Uneasy, Hugh started across the parking lot when Birdie came out of the drugstore with Delia.

She looked happy. The nice blush on her cheeks was no doubt put there by the hours he'd spent with her in the sack this morning. Afterward there had been ample time to confess he was writing an article about her hunt for the rubies. Instead he took the easy way out, steering the conversation to safe topics. Birdie was considering his offer to move to Akron, he was sure, and she stayed in bed with him most of the morning. When she'd left for work, he'd chastised himself for not telling her the truth.

With misgiving, he organized his thoughts. She'd be furious once she learned the truth.

Looking up, she noticed him and beamed.

He shoved his hands deep into his pockets. "Can we talk?"

"I have to get back to the restaurant," she said, smoothing her palms across the front of his jacket.

Torn between affection and regret, he steered her toward the sidewalk. "This can't wait." He glanced at Delia, who took the hint and started for her car. "I'm writing an article."

Mention of an article was enough to bring her naturally guarded nature to the fore. She withdrew from his embrace, a terrible loss, but he knew enough to give her space.

Only a coward prevaricated, so he launched in. "I told the City Editor I found another story in Liberty." To stop her from bolting he gently clasped her wrist. "I'm writing about your treasure hunt for the rubies."

The admission didn't register immediately. She stared at him blankly, her luscious mouth falling open. When her lower lip trembled, guilt seared him to the bone. He cared about her. Hell, he loved her, more than he should. More than was sensible, given her career choice. The last thing he wanted to do was hurt her.

"I told you about the rubies in confidence," she said, rising from her stupor. "I trusted you. Why did you tell your editor?"

"I have to protect you. Writing about the rubies is the only way to keep you safe."

"How does betraying my trust protect me? You have no right—"

"I used a PI to look into your background," he cut in. "Fatman Berelli."

"*What?*"

"He's not loyal." Hugh soldiered on, refusing to consider the depths of his betrayal. "I shouldn't have asked Fatman to look into your life. I'd just moved into the apartment with you and I thought . . . hell, I don't know what I was thinking. I'm sorry."

"You're *sorry?*"

"If I lose my job at the *Register*, Fatman will become one of Ralston's sources. There's no telling what'll come up in conversation."

"They'll talk about me? Oh, God."

"And your parents. Fatman put together a whole file on Wish and Tanek . . . and you. If I'm gone, something might come out."

Fear tripped through her violet gaze, gutting him. "How can you do this to me?"

"I was only trying to—"

He stopped, despising himself, despising the trade he'd made with Bud. He'd write the story about the rubies to safeguard his job while he secretly grappled for a way to keep Birdie in Ohio. If she didn't steal the rubies, there was no reason to leave. He raked his hand through his hair. Except now, she'd go for sure. She had every right to despise him.

"I was in a corner," he said as her contempt hit him in a rush. "Ralston got his hands on Fatman's number. I had to think on my feet."

"You weren't thinking at all!"

Was there any sense in arguing? "Now I'm not sure what to do." He reached for her hand but she slapped him away. "Please, Birdie. Try to forgive me. We can decide what to do together."

Tears brimmed in her eyes. "Why do you care what I think?"

"I love you. Can't you understand? I love you, Birdie, and I don't ever want to stop."

The words dropped out before he checked them. Too much, too fast, especially since he'd already broached the subject this morning. Wide-eyed, she stared at him with her chest heaving. The wind scattered her hair, and a tendril of gilt clung to her lips. Gently, he hooked the lock of hair behind her ear. He cupped her cheek, relieved when she didn't push him away. Did she love him too? Her silence sure wasn't filling him with confidence.

"I'll do whatever you ask," he said, too hurt to get a fix on why he was also angry. "It's your call."

"I don't have much choice, do I? Give up the rubies or my privacy." She glanced quickly at Delia, tapping her fingers on the steering wheel of her Mustang. "You can't let Ralston write about me. If anyone in Liberty found out about my life . . ."

"Can you give up the rubies?"

The question drove sadness into her gaze. "I've dreamt about them my whole life. Maybe they don't belong to me, but . . . Hugh, I think Justice tried to return the rubies to Molly. To my side of the family—why else would she leave the clues? *Liberty safeguards the cherished heart.* She left them for Molly . . . and, in a way, for me. We meant something to her."

Was this grief? Sorrow tore down the last of his pride—Birdie cared about the rubies a lot more than she cared about him. It was painfully difficult, but he set his emotions aside. She didn't love him. Why had he believed that she did? He'd let his emotions curtail the normally cynical streak that warned him that a woman like Birdie didn't possess enough depth to love anyone. Life on the street, picking pockets and drifting from city to city—the life she'd led had destroyed some elemental facet of her personality. She wasn't the woman he wanted her to be. Life had shorn away the possibility.

Bruised, he set his mouth grimly. Of course, he was forgetting something. She was giving up more than the gems. She was letting go of her connection to Justice.

Maybe he was losing her but she'd lose something too. She'd lose her connection to Justice, a freed slave who'd been her guiding light. Even if Birdie couldn't see it, she'd craved something belonging to the only woman she'd ever admired.

It struck him suddenly that despite her avarice she wouldn't pawn the jewels. The gems carried the rich history of a life lived well. They represented the potential for dreams to evolve into reality when the dreamer lived with integrity.

Everything Justice became in her life—a free woman, a loving mother and wealthy businesswoman—every triumph sprung from her ability to *believe* in herself and others. To Birdie, who survived with her emotions dulled and her mistrust of people dragging her down—Birdie wanted no less from her own life. The rubies were a roadmap to her own heart. Now he was forcing her to abandon the hunt, and the only connection to another human being that mattered to her.

He'd let her grieve.

"Tonight we'll make a decision about what to do," he said, moving off before she could glimpse his disappointment. "What time will you be done with Delia?"

"We're going to Ethel Lynn's after work. We should finish by nine o'clock."

When she returned to the apartment, he'd offer more apologies. They wouldn't heal the rift, but he'd try to earn her forgiveness.

He nodded. "I'll wait for you."

CHAPTER 23

Stalking into the City Editor's office, Hugh demanded, "You got something against phones? Why do you need to see me in person?"

The two-hour drive to the *Register* had been bumper-to-bumper. Now it was past five o'clock. Agonizing on how to set things straight with Birdie, he'd barely started on the article about the rubies. And he needed to be at the apartment when she finished messing around with Delia's hair. Face-time with Bud was one hell of an inconvenience.

Not that the City Editor cared. "Holding out on me?" Bud asked.

The question drilled past Hugh's rising temper. "What are you talking about?"

"The woman looking for the rubies? Her mother is connected to the Trinity Investment scandal." Bud glowered. "You forgot to mention it."

He reeled with disbelief. "Check your facts. They're wrong."

Jesus, he hoped they were. He lowered himself into a chair. Dread had him gripping the armrests.

Nothing in Fatman's report on the nefarious Kaminsky clan had mentioned Trinity Investments or Landon Williams and his late wife, the philanthropist, Cat Seavers. Could Birdie's mother be connected to the scandal that had nearly destroyed him? Not the sort of odds favored in Vegas, but the City Editor looked smugly confident. A bad sign.

Bud shook his head, amused. "For Chrissake, what kind of a reporter are you? Wish Kaminsky is the babe Landon Williams was running around with, genius. She went by the name Wish Greyhart. Your pal, Fatman, told Ralston all about it. Fatman would've told you directly if you'd been answering your cell."

"I never interviewed Landon's lover. He sent her away before the story broke. Or Cat did."

"Well, they're one and the same."

"Birdie doesn't know about Trinity."

"You sure about that?"

Hell, he was positive. She didn't have much contact with her mother. According to Fatman's report, Birdie had been fending for herself since she was teenager. Worse still, her mother was a hardened criminal. Wish Kaminsky didn't care about her daughter. She certainly wouldn't care if she'd sent Birdie to Liberty into a perilous situation. But Landon wasn't the risk—his daughter was. If Meade ever ran into Birdie there was no telling what she'd do to protect her father.

Bud tapped a pen against his teeth, considering. "Seems Liberty is a big draw for both of the Kaminsky women. I wonder if Landon Williams has met this Birdie character. By the way, Ralston says he's suing you for nailing him in the kisser."

"Let him."

"Pull another stunt like that and I'll do one better. I'll make it so you never work on another newspaper. Not that any of my colleagues are eager to hire you as it is." Bud smiled malevolently.

"Since your bloodhound instincts have gone punky, I sent Ralston to Liberty. He's wrapping up the story on the infamous Kaminsky broads."

Hugh surged from his seat. "You dragged me here to get me out of his way?"

"You catch on fast."

"I told you I'd give you the story about the rubies. You're not writing about Birdie. She's off-limits. Do you understand?"

"Are you threatening me?"

Rage nearly hurtled him across the desk. Somehow he contained it. "You bet I am."

The City Editor chuckled. "I'm the one calling the shots. For starters, you'll help Ralston finish the article tonight. If he can't track down Birdie, you'll lay on the charm and get a few quotes from her. I hear she's an accomplished thief. Talk to anyone in Liberty who's been taken by her. Ralston tried to land a few interviews but a crazy old hag drew a pistol on him."

Theodora.

His gratitude was quickly replaced by fear. Birdie cared what Theodora and the other women thought of her. If the story hit, she'd never survive the humiliation.

When the story hit.

Hugh choked down the emotion barreling into his throat. She'd do what she did best—run. He'd never see her again. It was an unbearable possibility.

Bud slammed his fist on his desk. "Wake up, Einstein! I'm telling you how to play this so I won't throw your ass on the street—"

Hugh never heard the rest. *The street.* Birdie would return to a pathetic semblance of a life roaming from city to city. She deserved so much more. He'd only begun to imagine the life they'd build together. Bud was snuffing out the dreams before they took shape.

Fury and heartbreak sent him lunging across the desk. He grabbed Bud by the collar and brought his face close.

"Tell Ralston if I find him in Liberty, I'll kill him," he growled. "And by the way—*I quit.*"

* * *

"Delia, hold still."

Drawing back from the bathroom mirror, Birdie turned on the egg timer for another five minutes. According to the directions on the hair coloring kit, she needed to give the mess a little longer to work.

The wait was enjoyable. Ethel Lynn had graciously offered to let them conduct their beauty regimen in the spacious guest bathroom of her home. Touched by the offer, Birdie had readily agreed.

Dodging Hugh for a few more hours was a good plan. She should be furious with him and she was. He'd write about the rubies even though he'd promised to keep her secret safe. Giving up the search wasn't easy, but for days now she'd been plagued by an undeniable fact: she should've found the gems by now. And the announcement he'd made about loving her—she'd been stunned and thrilled and frightened, a tangle of emotions she still hadn't found the courage to unravel. After she gave him the go-ahead for the article, would he ask her again to move in with him? The invitation wasn't something she should seriously consider, but she kept coming back to it.

Elation, unbidden, swept through her. *Am I in love with him?*

The emotion died beneath the pessimism anchoring her. She'd never seen love thrive. Her parents and grandparents, every member of her extended family—wanderers all. Not one of them was capable of lasting commitment.

"Birdie, the timer beeped."

Jarred from her thoughts, she peeled the plastic cap from Delia's head and led her to the sink.

Ethel Lynn opened the bathroom door. "Would you girls like tea?"

"Sounds great." Birdie turned on the tap. "Hey, Ethel Lynn— I'm dying to know something." She started washing the goo from Delia's hair. "I couldn't get a straight answer from Theodora. Why did your great-aunt jilt Theodora's great-grandfather? Did it really start the bad blood between your families?"

"Hells bells. She *would* say that." Indignant, Ethel Lynn flew into the bathroom. "For the record, Lucas never cared for my great-aunt. Once he arrived in Liberty, he couldn't keep himself away from his true love."

Lucas.

Ethel Lynn couldn't possibly be talking about Lucas Postell. Dazed, Birdie regarded her.

It's a coincidence. Family lore held that Lucas Postell died in South Carolina, either in the waning years of the Civil War or right after. No one had ever mentioned the plantation owner coming north to Ohio.

Still, she couldn't suppress the excitement in her voice when she asked, "Lucas wasn't from Liberty? Where'd he come from?"

A silence rich in expectancy filled the air. Even Delia, bent over the sink with the water streaming over her head, seemed to sense it. She lifted her gaze in tandem with Birdie's to regard the old woman. Which appeared to please Ethel Lynn, who was seldom the center of attention.

Delighted with their fevered interest, she said, "Lucas was born and bred in the Carolinas. He lost everything in the Civil War. He came north to search for the woman he'd loved before the war tore them apart."

Reeling, Birdie abandoned Delia at the sink. "What was his last name?" Joy started a clamorous ringing in her ears.

Delia flailed her arms. "Come back! Get this stuff out of my hair!"

Her distress sent Ethel Lynn banging into the wall. "Heavens to Betsy—the child's drowning!"

"Oh. Right." In her confusion, Birdie had turned the faucet on full blast. She decreased the flow and, grabbing Delia's head, thrust her into the sink. "About Lucas," Birdie said, deaf to the young woman's cries. "What was his last name?"

"Why, it was Postell. French, dear. The woman he loved was a slave on his plantation before the war."

"Justice. Her name was Justice."

"Yes, and they had a child together. A boy." Ethel Lynn daubed at her eyes. "Theodora is a stubborn old goat. My great-aunt never was able to win Lucas's affections. If he hadn't died of a heart attack after coming to Liberty, he would've carried on with Justice until they were old and gray. Certainly Theodora's grandfather wouldn't have been their only child."

"Theodora is descended from Justice and Lucas? You're sure?"

"Hell's bells!" Ethel Lynn stumbled toward the door. "Everyone in town knows Theodora is descended from those tragic lovers. It's no secret."

I'm related to Theodora. A dizzy sort of glee brought her across the room.

Scaring the jittery old woman with too many questions was not a good plan. She might faint from over-stimulation. The doorbell rang and Ethel Lynn turned toward the sound with unmistakable relief.

"Goodness! I'd better see who it is." She hurried off.

It was well after nine, lights out in a town that rolled up the sidewalks at dusk. "I wonder who's here so late," Birdie said.

Dripping water, Delia tripped toward her. "A towel salesman?" she growled.

"Right. Sorry." Birdie rummaged beneath the sink and came back up with a fluffy pink towel. She tossed it over. *Why didn't Theodora tell me she's related to Justice?* There were some things in life you couldn't control, like the family you were born into. Birdie was coded with the DNA of criminals and drifters, a sordid lot of humanity built on the biology of greed. Back in Lucas Postell's time it hadn't been so; Lucas was made of something better, as was the slave who became his lover. Through them another line of Postells were born, Theodora's line, and the prospect that she was related to Theodora filled Birdie with hope. They shared blood, good blood, a fine mix that wasn't defective. Why hadn't Theodora mentioned her relationship to Justice? She should've known how much the news would've meant to Birdie.

Far too excited to figure it out, Birdie asked, "Do you like your family?"

Delia feigned a shudder. "My father walks around town in golf shorts all winter. My mother? When I was in high school, she worked in the cafeteria. I'd be standing in line with my friends and she'd spoon peas onto my plate. I mean, who eats peas with tacos? Parents should be outlawed."

"Some parents *are* outlaws. It's even more humiliating."

Delia giggled. Clearly, she thought Birdie was joking. "We should lock them all up and throw away the key." She blew a bubble and popped it. "Do you like your parents?"

Sadness darted through Birdie, along with tentative wisps of love. "My father is okay. My mother . . . she thinks parenting is a contact sport."

"She's a hitter?"

"She likes to argue. Grow an opinion and she chops it down. When I was a kid, I'm sure my parents were as embarrassing as yours." Especially when the police pounded on the door or her father was headed back to prison. He never made it on the outside for very long. "We moved around a lot, and I wanted . . . I wanted to be related to someone I wasn't ashamed of."

"I'm not ashamed of my Uncle Gil." Delia sat in the wicker chair in the corner, her turban shifting precariously. "He's really cool. He's the manager of an Apple store near Cleveland. He doesn't look like a nerd. He's GQ all the way."

"He sounds nice." *Theodora is nice, in her own way, and she's family.*

From the parlor, Ethel Lynn called, "Birdie! You have a gentleman caller."

Hugh? She pointed to Delia's turban. "Leave it up. I'll be back to dry your hair."

* * *

In a parlor straight out of the Victorian era, Hugh paced before the maroon couch.

He still wasn't sure why he'd tracked Birdie down. Letting her murder him in the privacy of their apartment made more sense.

From what Bud had indicated, Ralston was reporting on more than Birdie's nefarious family. He'd connected Wish Kaminsky to Landon Williams and The Trinity Investment scandal.

The vicious irony brought Hugh full circle.

Writing about the scandal put him in a tailspin fourteen years ago. During the investigation he slept with Cat, an unforgivable breach of ethics he was sure played a role in sending her to her death. Now he'd put Birdie in a situation equally perilous.

Once again he'd recklessly blurred the line between his private and professional worlds.

No question, Birdie wasn't prepared for the firestorm. The anonymity she enjoyed in Liberty, the friendships she'd made—the sudden notoriety would destroy every hard-won achievement.

Oblivious to the danger, she waltzed into the room grinning like a kid who'd won Christmas presents for life. Spots of water speckled her tank top, and her eyes were bright. She looked breathtaking.

"Hugh! You'll never guess what I found out about Theodora. Well, about me and Theodora, actually." Pausing, she took a swipe at his head. "Did you forget to brush your hair? You're a wreck."

He raked his hand across his scalp. "It's almost ten o'clock. You said you'd be home by nine." He flinched at his harsh greeting and the ridiculously cozy way he'd referred to the apartment as *home*. "All hell's about to break loose."

"Maybe on your corner of the globe but not here. I'm bonding with other women." Her saucy grin kick-started his desire. "Of course, I still haven't forgiven you. If we engage in a more intimate type of bonding later, I might consider it."

Once he laid it all out, she'd never trust him again. She wouldn't return to the apartment for sex. She'd pack her bags.

Just as he'd done an hour ago.

From the kitchen, the teapot whistled. Ethel Lynn called, "Earl Grey or Oolong, dears?"

"Whiskey," Hugh bellowed. "Make it a double, no ice." Frustrated—he still wasn't sure how to proceed—he steered Birdie toward the fireplace. "This can't wait. I have a confession to make."

"Find a priest. I can't absolve you of your sins." She smiled broadly, and the urge to capture her mouth in a kiss was nearly overwhelming. "I have enough trouble dealing with my own sins, Parsnip."

He noticed the andirons beside the fireplace and edged her away from them. Only a lunatic would put her within reach of a weapon. "This isn't easy."

"What, you've made a decision without me? Listen, I don't want you to write about the rubies but I get it. I have to trade them for my privacy. No contest."

"This isn't about the rubies." He clasped her shoulders to hold her still.

"Then what?"

"I'm a self serving bastard, but I'll do anything in my power to protect you." He needed a compass to navigate the conversation. He was traveling blind. "I don't mean to walk over people. Certainly not you."

"As of this moment, you're walking over my feet. Let go!"

Frustrated, he swooped in and kissed her feverishly. She tasted good, too good, and the way she squirmed against his chest was a nice bonus. There wasn't much glue to their relationship, not yet, but they did have a combustible form of sexual attraction. He prayed it held the power to bind her to him despite what he had to say.

Satisfaction brimmed in him when she flung her arms around his neck and returned his ardor. Which would have increased tenfold if not for the sound of china clattering from the doorway.

"Gracious me!" Ethel Lynn nearly toppled the silver platter in her grasp.

Abruptly, Hugh let Birdie go. She careened backward and bounced off the arm of the sofa.

Regaining her balance, she glared. "I'll admit the sex is good. Work on the foreplay." Turning on her heel, she approached a quivering Ethel Lynn and jabbed a finger toward the large tumbler of amber liquid. "What is this?"

"Bourbon. Men like bourbon." Patting her brow, Ethel Lynn stared at Hugh like he was a grizzly bear set loose in her parlor. "He needs a calming influence."

"Not as much as I do." With a toss of her head, Birdie downed half the glass. Flinching, she smiled maniacally at Ethel Lynn before finishing the drink. Then she turned the flustered old woman in the direction of the kitchen. "Off you go. Don't come back until I call you."

Ethel Lynn scurried off with her tray rattling.

Birdie planted her hands on her hips. "Okay—out with it," she said, freezing Hugh with an arctic stare. "What's going on and why should I care?"

CHAPTER 24

A shriek rang out from the bathroom.

Hugh flinched. "What was that?"

"Delia." Birdie planted her hands on his chest, stopping him from heading off to investigate. He'd done something stupid and she damn well wanted to know what it was. "Not so fast. We aren't done talking."

"Sounds like someone's hacking off her arm."

"She's fine." Birdie pushed him back a step. "Out with it. I'm getting a bad feeling."

Hugh muttered a curse. Swinging away, he gripped the edge of the mantle.

A sudden, queasy doubt settled in the pit of her stomach.

He turned around and faced her. "There's a story coming out in the morning edition of the *Register* about you and your family."

"Ralston talked to your friend, the PI?" Numb, she tried to formulate her thoughts. "You said my story was safe if you kept your job at the *Register*."

"I was wrong. Ralston was already working on the article."

"Stop him!"

"I quit this afternoon when my editor told me the article is going forward."

"Fix it, Hugh." Hurt and anger wrestled for prominence in her heart. "I don't care what you have to do. Keep my family out of the paper."

"I can't. But I'll protect you. We'll go to my place in Akron, ride it out."

Was he kidding? She was about to object when Delia stormed into the room flinging water droplets from her soggy head.

"Look at my hair!" The waitress grabbed at her close-cropped locks, which were a vibrant shade of . . . green.

Hugh cocked his head. "If you were going for honey blonde you missed the mark."

Birdie held up her hand to halt Delia from lunging toward her. "One second." She wheeled on Hugh. "Tell me how you'll fix this."

"We'll weather it together," he said, sidestepping the question. She considered knocking him off his feet. "You were never meant to be a criminal."

Delia frowned, trying to keep up. "It *is* criminal to screw up another woman's hair. But she doesn't deserve jail time. A stiff fine, maybe."

Ignoring the comment, Hugh zeroed in on Birdie. "You knew you'd have to give up the search for the rubies. And I wish I could make it so you won't be on the front page of the *Register*. Now we have to deal with it."

Delia stopped fiddling with her hair. "Did you say *rubies?*" She grabbed Birdie. "You'll be on the front page of Hugh's paper? Like a celebrity?"

Hugh scratched his temple. "Think *America's Most Wanted.*"

"Oh. That's not good." Considering, Delia slicked back the hair plastered to her forehead. "Birdie, you're a wanted woman?"

"*I* want her," Hugh said, "but for personal reasons." He regarded Birdie with a faint smile. "I'll find a way to make this up to you. Can you forgive me, Eggplant?"

"Not in this lifetime."

Delia rolled her eyes. "Will someone tell me what's going on?"

Birdie nudged her toward the bathroom. "No offense, but this is private. I'll explain later."

After the waitress marched off, she cornered Hugh by the fireplace. At least the man was perspiring—little beads of moisture were collecting on his brow. Not much, but enough to imply the discomfort he richly deserved.

Grimacing, he tried reaching for her. "Birdie, there's something else." She moved away and he let his hand fall to his side. "Trinity investments will be featured in Ralston's article, front and center."

"The investment firm Landon Williams owned?"

The wheels in her brain clattered to a standstill. Then her thoughts tumbled forward in a terrifying whirl as the awful pieces fell into place. She recalled Hugh telling her about Trinity and a woman who drowned in Lake Erie. Then she remembered what Meade had said about Landon's destructive love affair. She hadn't connected the two events. In a state of shock, she did so now.

Wish.

"The woman, the one Landon gave all the money to," she whispered, "it was my mother."

"I didn't know. I never interviewed her."

"Of course you didn't. She's a pro. She knows when to get out." Apprehension curled in her belly. "How much did my mother steal from Landon?"

Dragging his hand through his hair, Hugh seemed disinclined to say. "Several hundred thousand," he finally got out.

The numbers were staggering. Wish had made a major kill. My God, no wonder the Feds were after her—she'd earned a seat in the major leagues long ago, when Birdie was still a kid. Of course, Wish never bragged about her exploits. She trusted no one.

Ruefully, Birdie shook her head. "I didn't know about the money. I'm sure my dad didn't either. Wish must've stashed it somewhere away from us."

This brought a startled glance from Hugh. "Your mother was rich. She never told you?"

"Never told me, never used the money when I was around. I went to school in clothes scavenged from Goodwill." Hugh stared at her with pity and it was too much, an additional burden she couldn't bear. With savage honesty, she added, "Hey, who am I to complain? If I'd found the rubies I wouldn't have shared them with her either."

Wretched self-loathing brought her head up. What right did she have to feel betrayed? Greed ran thick in her family. It was foolish to think she could be like Theodora. She was just like Wish.

Dragging her gaze from his, she said, "By the way, I knew about my mother and Landon Williams." Wearily, she explained how Theodora had taken her to meet his daughter, Meade. Wrapping up, she added, "From what I gathered, my mother had an on and off relationship with Landon for years. She probably went to him whenever my dad was in the pen. Tanek never stayed on the outside for very long."

"Why didn't you tell me you met with Meade?"

"It wasn't important."

"Like hell it's not."

His accusatory tone sent her despair fleeing. "What? And give you more material to write about?" A cheap shot, but she was hurt and frightened and only just beginning to understand everything she'd lose. "What am I supposed to do when Meade sees the story? She'll be gunning for me. I shouldn't stand here talking—I should be getting the hell out of here."

"I didn't write the story, Ralston did!"

"Then find him," she snapped. "Take his laptop and break it into a million pieces. If he's already delivered the story, sneak into the *Register*. Do something to the computers. Trash them, crash them—I don't care."

"They're already running the presses," Hugh said with surprising calm. Anguish creased his face. "It's over, Birdie."

"Do you have any idea what will happen to me?"

He stared at her.

"I'll go to prison."

Hugh grimaced. "Possibly. It's something every criminal has to consider."

The noncommittal reply sent fury whipping through her. "I'm not going to prison." She pushed him, hard, but he didn't budge. His obstinacy merely increased her rage. "I'll break into the *Register*, take a hammer to the presses—

Spinning on her heel, she felt Hugh's arms clamp around her sides. Her feet lifted wildly into the air.

"Don't touch me!" She tried to break free as he spun her to face him. His hold tightened. "Damn it—let go!"

"I'm not letting you go off and do something crazy. You need my help. You need *me.*"

"I don't need anyone."

His dark eyes glittered. "What have you got without me? A shallow, pathetic life skipping from town to town? This is your chance to turn it around. Take it."

Sorrow punched through her pride. "My life was set the day I was born." She was nothing like Lucas or Theodora. What was she, really? A thief like her mother. A fumbling criminal who'd spend time in the pen like her father. "You can't help me. No one can."

The explanation stole the heat from his eyes. "Then you're leaving." He released her. Frowning, he pulled a wad of bills from the pocket of his jeans. "My last paycheck. It's yours."

"I don't want your money." The urge to rush into his arms collided with her pride. None of this would've happened if he hadn't asked a PI to pry into her life. Brutally, she added, "Why in God's name did I ever trust you?"

The words struck him like a glancing blow. She hadn't meant to hurt him, not this deeply. The urge to cry swept through her, a sudden, painful rush of emotion.

"I didn't mean . . ." The apology on her lips evaporated beneath his hooded gaze. Regret sent pinpricks of pain through her chest. She had no right to wound him so deeply. He was an easy target. She was angry with herself.

He scrubbed his palms across his face. "You never did trust me." He shook his head ruefully. "Jesus. Why am I surprised? I don't trust you, either. Not really. Not the way I should if I want to make something real with you."

Birdie sank down on the couch. When she couldn't find her voice, he glanced around the room. Patches of grey covered the grizzled skin of his cheeks. Noticing his coat where he'd tossed it on a chair, he stalked past her and put it on.

He gazed at her with chilly regard, and the sorrow in her heart increased. "I've already moved my stuff out of the apartment. If I were you, I'd get packed."

"Hugh, I didn't mean—"

"Take a bus out of Liberty first thing tomorrow," he said, cutting her off. His voice, utterly void of emotion, made her blood ran cold. "Set up shop on the other side of the country. It won't buy you freedom but it might buy time."

"Hugh—"

The words died in her throat. He was already gone.

CHAPTER 25

The intercom buzzed. Sighing, Meade closed her eyes.

With the holiday season in full swing, department stores in Cleveland were reordering at a hectic pace. Two of her customer reps were out with the flu and a shipment of cosmetics was lost somewhere between New York and Ohio.

None of which was a catastrophe. Still, she was frazzled and it was still early.

The intercom went blessedly silent. She hadn't been herself since her meeting with Birdie. She still wasn't sure if Theodora's young friend was telling the truth or was in fact Wish Greyhart's daughter. Meade resolved to get to the bottom of it after the holiday rush.

The light knock on her office door brought her from her musings. Her assistant entered.

"I buzzed you," Siki said. "You didn't pick up."

No doubt the lost shipment of cosmetics had been found. "Tell me good news."

"It's not the shipment. Zelda, the new secretary from Akron—"

"What happened?" Unease slithered through Meade's veins. Something was terribly wrong. Siki looked nervous and she was usually the epitome of calm. "Was the secretary in an accident driving to work?"

"She's fine." Siki glanced over her shoulder. "Something else has come up."

Meade realized the door was ajar. An arm decorated with chunky gold bracelets popped into view, and something was handed off to Siki. A newspaper.

Approaching, she held the paper away from her body as if it carried the plague. "There's an article in the *Akron Register* about you and your father," she said, kicking out the foundation of Meade's world, "and some criminal named Birdie Kaminsky. You're on the front page."

* * *

Everything was packed.

With misgiving, Birdie dropped the tips she'd earned during the last week into a plastic bag and stuffed it into a pocket of her coat. She'd already filled a duffel bag with everything she'd bought during her short stay in Liberty—clothing and a few toiletries. A soft hum of music drifted from the opposite end of the second floor where Mary had reopened her medical practice. Threads of conversation drifted down the hallway—probably more of her staff coming in to work. Farther off a thumping rose from the kitchen followed by the banging of pots. Finney, in the middle of the breakfast rush.

The cook expected Birdie to clock in at noon. She'd be disappointed. The Greyhound to Indiana left in twenty-five minutes.

With the *Akron Register* on newsstands this morning, it was only a matter of time before the news would travel north. Best to leave before anyone in Liberty read the paper.

With regret, Birdie took one last look at the apartment. The kitchen was tidy and the pillows on the couch nicely plumped. Hugh had already cleared out—by the time she'd returned from Ethel Lynn's house last night he'd stripped the place of his belongings.

A gloomy lethargy accompanied her to the stairwell. It was all for the best. If she saw Hugh again she wouldn't know what to say. She was a thief who'd never learned the first thing about trust. He was better off without her.

"Going somewhere?"

Startled, she halted midway down the steps. The duffel bag tumbled past her, landing with a thud beside Blossom Perini.

Where the kid sat eating, of all things, a chocolate sundae.

"Nice breakfast choice." Birdie picked up her duffel bag and brushed past.

Blossom latched onto the hem of her coat. "Birdie, don't go." The teen put her sundae on the step and got to her feet. "You're running away, aren't you?"

"I have some errands before my shift." Lousy move to lie to a thirteen year old, but she didn't have a choice. "Why aren't you in school?"

Now it was Blossom's turn to look uncomfortable. "I cut first period."

"You shouldn't skip school. There's nothing more important than an education."

"I wanted to see you." Hesitating, Blossom wrinkled her nose. "This morning, when I woke up? The weather was pretty bad. I thought there'd be a snow day so I checked the television for school closings . . . and there was your photo."

Birdie went rigid with fear. "My photo's on the tube?" She got a distressing image of a raging mob from a Frankenstein movie chasing her with raised torches. "Geez, Blossom. Which channel?"

"It was on the early morning program. The show with the old guy and the stupid quote of the day?"

"Oh, no."

"Is it true you steal things?"

"Oh, *God*."

"Hey, I'm just curious. You're kind of like Catwoman only without the black tights." Grinning, Blossom twirled one of her corkscrew curls. "Did you really come to Liberty because of some goofy fairy tale about jewelry?"

"Jewels," Birdie corrected. Absently, she dug her hand into her pocket and drew her fingers across the velvet sack. The ruby-studded key had led her exactly nowhere. *Except to America's Most Wanted.* And to think, Hugh had been joking when he'd made the crack to Delia.

Blossom giggled. "Rubies, right?"

"You got it. And no, I didn't find them." She stared yearningly at the daylight spreading rapidly down the hallway. *Get out now.* "Well, gotta go."

A dash to freedom never materialized. At the other end of the hallway, the door from the kitchen banged open.

Delia wheeled forward, her face stony and her green hair nicely tinseled in gold and silver. "Blossom—grab her!"

The kid put her own spin on the command by hugging Birdie around the waist. Not exactly your typical apprehension of a criminal.

"You aren't going anywhere!" the waitress sputtered. "We're in this mess because of you. Theodora is in the dining room beating people back with a broom. If I hadn't stowed her satchel, she would've shot someone by now."

Scared and stunned, Birdie gently disengaged from Blossom's embrace. "Where's Ethel Lynn?"

"Back home, changing into nice rags. Her words, not mine. A photographer from one of the Cleveland newspapers is snapping pictures, and she wants to look her best. Meaning I'm stuck alone in nutcase central."

Birdie's newly discovered familial tie to Theodora brought up her defenses. "Take a chill pill. Theodora's eccentric but she's not a nutcase."

"I'm talking about the customers—the ones *you'll* help me handle."

With that, she dragged Birdie into the kitchen. The place was a shambles. Dirty dishes stood a mile high beside the sink. Clumps of oatmeal dotted the floor. Three sausage links, uncooked, hung off the edge of a counter.

Finney barreled across the room with her spatula at the ready. Sheer terror seized Birdie.

"Say you've never so much as stolen a dime from my purse and you'll live." The cook whipped the spatula around like a machete. Birdie leapt back, cowering. "Shame, Birdie—shame! How a nice young thing like you—I gave you a job, didn't I?"

Meeting the cook's eyes was impossible. "Finney, I swear I never stole anything from you. I'm not crazy. You'd scare the mafia."

Delia rubbed at her nose. "Did you take anything from me?"

The hurt quivering across her face was worse than the cook's fury. Heartsick, Birdie fumbled around the inside of her coat and withdrew a ten-dollar note. "I took it weeks ago," she admitted, mired in self-loathing. Delia was her friend. No more. "I never took anything else. Once we got to know each other—"

"You stopped stealing from me? Gee, I feel so much better." The waitress snatched the bill from her fingertips and stormed off.

After she disappeared into the dining room, Birdie managed to regard Finney.

"I'm guessing Officer Tim will be looking for you," the cook said with surprising compassion.

"He won't have to." Hesitating, Birdie came to a decision. "I'm going to the police station." For once she wouldn't run.

"You will, now? I don't mind saying I'm surprised."

"Don't be. I'm not exactly courageous."

Birdie pushed down her fear. She was tired of running. God, she was tired. If going to the police meant doing time then she'd do it. Pay her debts and call it even.

The cook lifted her spatula toward the humming crescendo of the dining room. "There's mayhem out there, thanks to you. Go and help Delia."

"Please don't make me go out there." She dreaded walking into the dining room with all eyes settling on her in excruciating judgment. Exactly what she deserved, but it was like entering a shooting gallery with every customer gunning for her.

"You can't hide forever, young lady. Say your apologies nicely. Let folks shout at you if they've got a bellyful of anger. If anyone is too harsh, I'll come out with my skillet. You'll do fine."

The gently issued words filled Birdie's eyes with stinging tears. "I'm a crook—I admit it," she said, her throat clogging with emotion. "I'll do jail time if I have to. Just don't ask me to face everyone. They hate me."

"Hate's a mighty strong word." In a mothering gesture, the cook brushed the hair from Birdie's eyes. Which only increased the tears. "The money you took from purses and wallets. Did you spend it?"

"What?"

Finney released a labored sigh. "Do you still have the money you took from people in town? Lord knows you've been earning a living wage waiting tables. You didn't need anyone's cash to get by."

"I haven't spent a dime of it. My paycheck covered my expenses." Birdie realized where this was headed. "I'll return all the cash, but I'm not sure what I stole from everyone. How will I figure it out?"

"I have an idea." The cook went into the walk-in cooler and reappeared with a massive jar of pickles. "Dump these. Clean the jar. Put it on the counter with a sign telling people to take whatever they're missing."

"What if someone takes more than they're owed?" Birdie cringed at her bone-deep cynicism. The way the cook was looking at her, you'd think she'd announced the town was filled with criminals.

Blossom, forgotten in the corner, approached. "No one will take money if it doesn't belong to them, will they?" she asked, breaking the uncomfortable silent. Which also hurt. If Birdie infected the kid with her cynicism she'd never forgive herself. "Right, Finney?"

"Of course not, child." Blinking, the cook glanced at the clock above the sink. "Blossom, are you cutting class again? If you are, I'm telling Mary."

"If Birdie has to take her lumps from the customers and Officer Tim, I'll take my chances with my mom." Winding an arm around Birdie's waist, Blossom planted her feet. "C'mon, Finney—have a heart. Birdie needs a friend out there."

Delia stuck her head through the pass-through window. Some of the tinsel in her hair drifted to the floor but she appeared too livid to notice. "Someone get out here!"

With her insides turning to jelly, Birdie shuffled across the kitchen. She flinched as a shout erupted from the dining room. It was followed by a *whack!* There was a moment of deadly silence, then a shuffling of feet, and the shriek of a banshee.

Theodora?

At Birdie's elbow, the kid with the corkscrew curls grinned like a Cheshire cat. "After you," Blossom said.

CHAPTER 26

Birdie stared at the dining room, aghast. Mayhem didn't begin to describe it.

Every table overflowed with loud, impatient customers. Many of the faces were unfamiliar, people from Akron who'd obviously seen the *Register*. A crowd teemed outside, puffing in the frigid air and waiting to enter.

A balled up napkin whizzed through the air. Delia, scribbling an order at table six, ducked. A man tall enough to brush the ceiling snapped photos of the antique furnishings, the fidgeting people—even of Theodora, patrolling the perimeter with a broom held before her like an oversized nightstick.

"Don't worry about the reporters," Blossom said. "Every time one comes in asking for you, Theodora gets pushy. She gave a woman from the Cleveland paper a goose egg." The kid tapped the left side of her forehead. "Right here."

"She didn't."

"Honest. The lady said she was lawyering up—"

"And Theodora told her to bring it on." It was easy to admire the old woman's chutzpah. "By the way, what's Theodora doing with the broom?"

Blossom smirked. "You'll see."

And Birdie did. At table nine, a stranger in a scruffy jean jacket slowly rose from his chair. Slinking toward the wall, he reached for a painting—George Washington astride a horse, Ethel Lynn's favorite.

The moment his fingers touched the frame, Theodora lunged down the aisle. With a *thwack* from her broom, mere inches from his loafers, she sent him stumbling back to his seat.

Birdie groaned. "The man is looking for clues behind the paintings. He's trying to retrace my steps." Apparently Ralston had spared no details in the article "I need to get my hands on a copy of the newspaper."

"No one's got one yet. My dad, over at the Gas & Go? I called him on my cell, and he said Mayor Ryan sent someone down to Akron to get a bunch of copies."

"You called your dad? Does he know you're skipping school?"

"No way. I made it sound noisy, like I was in the hallway between classes." With a sly grin, the teen produced a notepad from beneath the counter, tore off a sheet, and noisily crumpled the paper between her hands. "It's easy to fake my dad out. Nothing personal, but grownups aren't too smart."

Birdie cringed. *She* was an adult who'd managed to pit herself against an entire town. Not smart at all. "Are all of these people from Akron?" she asked, preferring not to think about what lay ahead.

"Most of them. They read the article. Not that I believe it—Finney says the story about the rubies is hogwash. But everyone here thinks they'll find clues."

It was true. A woman in a rust colored parka eased out of her chair and tiptoed up to a set of pewter sconces on the walls. *Thwack* went Theodora's broom, and the woman fled back to her chair.

At table one, two men, shifty-eyed twins with matching goatees, squinted lustfully at the vintage American flag on the wall. Nearing, Theodora growled.

The pint-sized general was a one-woman army protecting The Second Chance from marauders. Birdie smiled despite her depressed mood. *Theodora is family. My family.* True, they didn't have anything in common but their common blood.

Pride bloomed inside her. It was enough.

Delia slapped an order on the pass-through window. "Blossom—stop gabbing. Work the counter until Ethel Lynn gets back. And you—" she poked Birdie hard in the chest, "get over to table five. Mrs. Sanson wants a word with you."

Birdie paled. Mrs. Sanson, who owned the craft store on Route 44, was so deeply crimson she looked like her ears would explode off her head. *I snitched a twenty from her purse right before Thanksgiving.* Glaring, the woman swept her manicured fingers across her silverware, pausing at the knife.

Delia shoved Birdie forward. "It's only a butter knife. She's trying to scare you."

"It's working."

Humiliated, Birdie suffered through enough of Mrs. Sanson's insults to scar her for life. During the next hour, she endured more of the same as locals fought their way past the treasure hunters from Akron. One by one they confronted her with raised voices and scowling looks.

Beaten down, she kept her tone polite and her pencil moving. To her relief, Finney placed the massive pickle jar on the counter for locals to take what they were owed; she must have rifled through the pockets of Birdie's army coat as well. All the cash the cook found—all of it, including Birdie's hard-earned tips and weekly pay—were stuffed into the jar.

No less than she deserved. If she was broke at day's end, so what? She'd betrayed the entire town, making herself a pariah in the process.

"Want something to drink?" Blossom asked when Birdie, exhausted, dropped onto a barstool behind the counter. The teen waved the coffee pot through the air. "You look like you need a jolt."

"Only if there's something stronger than coffee in there."

Theodora came around the counter. "This is a dry establishment, missy," she said, but she winked.

Until now, she'd ignored Birdie. Oddly, her gravelly voice was a surprising balm. Or her expression was—she didn't look angry.

But she did look strange. Theodora sported a tall fur hat, which matched the distressing fur collar on her herringbone suit. The suit was straight out of the 1950s, a ghoulish creation with the head of a mink sewn into the collar of the jacket. Birdie prayed it wasn't a real mink—the disembodied creature gave her the shivers. Knowing Theodora, it probably was.

Birdie rubbed her temples. "I guess I'm stuck with coffee."

"You need something better. Come here." Theodora walked to the corner behind the counter. "I'll fix you up right quick."

"Fix me up how?"

The old woman produced a gold flask from the side pocket of her skirt. "Drink this," she said, unscrewing the flask and sending diesel fumes into the air. "It's moonshine. My special blend."

The fumes bleached Birdie's nasal passages. "Not a good plan. Your brew'll kill me."

"You should be more worried about Mr. Berkins killing you. He just sat down at table eleven. Damn fool's shooting fire at the back of your head."

"I've run out of ways to say I'm sorry."

"Next time try flowers."

"You're a laugh a minute, Theodora." Birdie grabbed the flask and swigged. Lava scorched her esophagus then hit her belly. "Now *this* is how you grow an ulcer."

Theodora took back the flask. "You're welcome."

"I can't take much more of this. Everyone screams at me. I'm a cockroach. Can't Mr. Berkins simply get his money from the pickle jar? Will you ask him?"

"I can't right now. I have bigger fish to fry." Theodora's wrinkles collapsed into revulsion. "Look what the cat dragged in. Leaving the restaurant to get all gussied up! It's time to give Ethel Lynn a piece of my mind."

A blast of arctic air blew in through the opened door. Startled, Birdie looked up.

Posing with a movie star's panache, Ethel Lynn let her velvet coat drop and shimmied her feathered shoulders.

Feathers?

CHAPTER 27

Batting her eyes at the photographer, Ethel Lynn oozed an aged and heavily feathered femininity. Across the dining room, necks craned.

Her gold sequined cocktail dress had arrived from the Roaring Twenties with peacock feathers on the shoulders and a line of vibrant plumage running down the low-cut bodice.

Delia careened with her tray into the counter. Dishes crashed to the floor.

Stepping over them, she tipped her head to the side. "Not bad for an old broad of seventy," she murmured—her first civil comment all morning. Grateful, Birdie smiled. "If her boobs didn't look like empty Hot Pockets, she'd actually look good."

Birdie nodded. "She looks pretty," she agreed, wanting to prolong the conversation. Delia was coming around. "More glitter than necessary . . . but it is the holiday season."

Theodora banged her fist on the counter. "It's an abomination. Ethel Lynn, hightail it over here and explain yourself!"

She did, trailing sequins like fairy dust. She'd done her face up—sapphire eyelids and crimson lips. Even her wispy, silvered hair was pulled into a chignon.

"Theodora, must you yell?" Patting her hair, Ethel Lynn favored the gawking photographer, struck dumb beside table nine, with a flutter of her lashes. "This is my first brush with fame. Don't spoil it."

"You old coot. How will you wait tables dressed like a hussy?"

"With elegance and finesse."

"Fool."

Sashaying closer, Ethel Lynn halted suddenly. "Hells bells! Theodora, there's a beaver at your throat!"

"It's a mink." Theodora tugged her collar and the little head bobbed up and down, its spooky glass eyes catching light. "Granite isn't as thick as you. Can't you tell one kind of animal from another?"

"Whatever it is, it's awful."

Delia stuffed gum into her mouth. "It is," she agreed between chews. "I feel like those little eyes are following me."

Ethel Lynn waved dismissively. "Cover it up." She was probably channeling Joan Crawford. She wasn't usually this bold.

One of the feathers on her shoulder poked Theodora in the cheek. Birdie smelled danger. If someone didn't separate them, they'd soon come to blows.

"Is there any ribbon in back?" Ethel Lynn was saying. "Someone ask Finney. Let's blindfold the beheaded pet so it doesn't stare at us."

"How dare you," Theodora hissed. She threw down the broom, her attention skittering across the counter. "Where's my gun? Insulting my clothing—you've gone too far."

Delia shook her head. "There's gonna be nothing left but fur and feathers." She grimaced, and Birdie followed her gaze across the dining room. "Uh oh. Tilly Solomon just walked in. Birdie, how much did you take from her?"

Unsure, Birdie leapt back as Theodora threw her tiny fist at Ethel Lynn's face. "Gosh, I don't know. She's a regular. I hit her more than once."

"Looks like she knows it, too."

Avoiding a left hook, Ethel Lynn shrieked. She came to her senses and raised her spindly arms in a defensive pose. The boxing match would've been entertaining to watch if Tilly hadn't dropped her Gucci bag on the counter.

"Birdie Kaminsky, I hope they put you behind bars! I've lived in Liberty all my life and I've never had to worry about someone stealing from me." The woman's hazel eyes spit fire, and Birdie's stomach hit the floor. "How much did you take from me?"

Birdie grabbed the huge pickle jar and slid it forward. "I can't remember." Behind her, the old women tussled. An aimless blue feather drifted past. "Will fifty cover it?"

"You aren't sure what you took?"

"I'm sorry." Miserable, she dug into the jar.

"Then give me forty. I can't take more if you aren't sure." Tilly snatched the two twenties from Birdie's outstretched hand. "And do something about your friends. They're both too old to be roughhousing."

My friends? Touched by the comment, Birdie regarded the scuffle behind her.

Amazingly, Ethel Lynn had Theodora by the arms and was turning her around in a clumsy circle. Both sets of legs were spinning. Since all four were as old as dry tinder, she leapt into action. If she didn't break up the fight, there'd be more than fur and feathers on the floor. There'd be blood.

"Stop it!" She flung herself between them. From the corner of her eye, she noticed the photographer snapping away. "If you're both dreaming about the ER, I'll get Finney to come out here with her skillet."

More scuffling and Ethel Lynn screamed, "I'm sending her straight into surgery! Get back—I'm taking aim!"

"Like hell you are." Birdie grabbed the fist whizzing past her nose. "You're both too old to settle your differences this way."

Theodora quivered with rage. "Then fetch my gun. We'll settle this like men."

"Oh, Theodora—shut up. You probably load your gun with rock salt. You don't have the balls to shoot anyone. Well, anyone bigger than Alice." Despite her despair, Birdie grinned. "Assuming you *did* have balls."

Delia rolled her gum between her teeth. "Who's Alice?"

Birdie waved her into silence then wagged a finger at Ethel Lynn. "And stop shrieking. The sound goes straight to my molars."

Theodora glared at the cameraman. "Isn't it time you skedaddled out of here?"

When he shrugged, she lunged for her broom. He bolted out the door.

Birdie rubbed her temples. She was starting into a headache. By the time she finished doling out apologies to the people of Liberty, she'd be working on a migraine.

"If we all calm down, the day will go faster," she said, helping Ethel Lynn adjust her feathers. "Can we please try? Yes? Good. Now, I'll wait the tables in the front of—"

Someone grabbed her from behind, sending her order pad hurtling through the air. Struggling for balance, she righted herself and spun around.

She came face to face with Natasha Jones.

Hatred glittered in the woman's eyes. "I'm amazed Finney hasn't thrown you out."

Screwing on her fur hat, Theodora rushed forward. "Calm down, Natasha. You'll get back every cent she stole from you."

"It won't make things right. My daddy went without his blood pressure medicine. He had to wait until the day after the Festival of Lights for me to come up with the money. I was scared he'd have a stroke before I got the prescription refilled."

Birdie's heart plummeted with horror. In all her years of taking petty cash, she'd never considered how her actions might affect someone. Had she put a life at risk? The prospect chilled her to the bone.

"Is your father all right?" she whispered.

Natasha released a bitter laugh. "No thanks to you. My bakery is small. It's all I can do to make ends meet. I work hard, Birdie, too damn hard to allow the likes of you to put my family in jeopardy."

"If there's anything I can do—"

"There is. Take your filthy predilections elsewhere. Leave the good town of Liberty."

The baker started off, then reconsidered. She wheeled back around and, swift as the wind, slapped Birdie across the face.

The blunt force of her fury sent a wave of blackness through Birdie's vision. Sharp pinpricks of pain followed, and a crushing shame. Natasha stormed off.

The silence left in her wake was deafening. One by one, the other women drifted back to work. Abandoned, Birdie pressed her palm to her stinging cheek.

For the remainder of the day, she worked in a miserable stupor. No one else physically accosted her but with each new apology, another bit of her soul disappeared. Natasha was right—she wasn't fit to live in a world where neighbors sat on front porches and met for coffee in the town's only restaurant. If she'd ever been foolish enough to dream about staying in Liberty, those hopes were now dashed.

She was a misfit, a con artist. No better than her conniving mother and blundering father.

By closing time, her feet were swollen like lava-filled balloons and her jaw ached from gritting her teeth. With her order pad shaking in her hands, she'd taken insults and orders in equal measure. It was no less than her due.

One more duty lay ahead. She'd promised to see Officer Tim at the police station on Elm.

* * *

At the southeast corner of Liberty Square, the sorrowful thief paused long enough for a layer of snow to gather on her army coat. The flowing gilt of her hair hung in stringy cords and her shoulders sagged.

Moved beyond speech, Theodora watched the child turn east toward Elm and resume walking.

Approaching, Finney joined her at the window. "Should we follow her?" the cook asked.

"Don't fret. She'll go straight to the police station."

Finney slowly wiped her hands on her apron. "I went through her coat this morning looking for all the cash she'd stolen." She drew in a quivering breath. "There was a sight more than money in her pockets."

"What else did you find?"

"Good grief—all sorts of stuff. I found a novel, a pocketknife, three candy canes and a church bulletin. There was also a sewing kit. She probably stole it from Ethel Lynn."

"Which church was the bulletin for?"

"New Faith Congregational in Lexington, Kentucky. Imagine—our sassy girl attending church, in Lexington no less." The cook shook her head. "None of it broke my heart, though."

"What did?" Theodora asked, curious.

"Birdie's got an old-fashioned book—must've come from an antique shop. There are the prettiest pictures of ladies inside. The text is full of instruction for all sorts of social situations, how to make a proper introduction or write a thank you note—" The cook paused, her generous bosom heaving with shuddering emotion. "A pretty book hidden beside all the stolen money. An etiquette book! Why would a pickpocket carry around such a thing?"

"She wants to be a lady," Theodora replied, amazed that Finney couldn't see what was so patently obvious. "What a person does and what they dream of becoming doesn't always match up." She grunted. "I put my faith in the dreamers. You don't become something better if you can't see it first."

"I suppose."

"Birdie was raised by vermin. Doesn't matter. She hankers to become something better. Fights the urge, but it grows thick as ivy in her."

Finney seemed to chew this around for a moment. "She also has an old pack of children's cards in one of her pockets. *Go Fish*. Mind telling me why a grown woman carries around *Go Fish* even if she dreams of becoming respectable?"

"I expect it reminds her of something pleasant from her childhood."

"I'd like to think she's known some happiness, all evidence to the contrary." The cook leaned toward the window as if searching the darkness for clues. "Are you sure she'll go to the police station? She might hitchhike out of town. If I were in her shoes, it'd be more than a passing thought."

"She said she'd go straight to Officer Tim. She will." Theodora paused, considering. "Birdie's stronger than you think. She'll do what's right."

"I can't imagine why." Finney retrieved the front page of the *Register* from where she'd hidden it in her apron pocket. "With a family like hers, who can blame her for going astray?"

Dog-tired from worry, Theodora returned to the counter. Delia poured her a cup of coffee. Sipping the brew, she suffered through her worry. While Birdie took heat from customers they'd all read the article on the sly.

Showing her the *Register* had seemed an added cruelty, and they'd decided against it. The shocking connection between Birdie's mother and Landon Williams—to think, Birdie's mother was the Greyhart woman. Which wasn't the worst part.

Timothy Ralston had written with heartbreaking detail about the life Birdie led with her mother. Sticking a child in a wheelchair and pretending she was an invalid! Only a viper would use a defenseless child in such a manner.

A vile hatred for Wish Kaminsky filled Theodora, forehead to toe.

Taking a seat at the counter, Finney gently asked, "How's Landon taking the news?"

The question put sadness in Theodora's heart. Landon was her closest friend. Even seeing the name Greyhart was enough to upset him.

"He doesn't know," she replied. "I spoke to his housekeeper, Reenie. She's kept him away from the television and is screening his calls. Tommorow is the bigger problem. The story comes out in the Cleveland paper. Landon *will* see it."

"And Meade?"

"She saw the *Register* this morning. I called her office this afternoon. She was mighty upset. She's at her father's house by now."

Delia looked up sharply. "Are you sure Meade is with her dad?"

A dark and menacing sensation crept across Theodora's shoulders. "Why do you ask?"

The waitress frowned. "I'd swear I just saw her Mercedes driving down Elm Street."

* * *

"Miss Kaminsky, I don't care if you've been searching for a pot of gold at the end of the rainbow," Officer Tim Corrigan said. "What concerns me is the money you've stolen."

The other police officers, bored on what appeared to be a slow night for the Liberty force, stood nearby eavesdropping. They chuckled every time Birdie's original reason for coming to town—the search of the rubies—came up during her interrogation.

She wasn't sure what was worse, the grilling she endured over her activities as a pickpocket or how the officers regarded her as if she needed a straitjacket, not a jail cell. They didn't believe the story of the treasure hunt they'd read about in the *Register.*

Who could blame them? The story *was* outlandish. The clues she'd unearthed, even the key in the storeroom—where had they led her? Exactly nowhere.

They'd led her nowhere because the rubies weren't hidden. Justice must've sold them during her lifetime. The story handed down in Birdie's family was nonsense—a fable, and nothing more.

"I've returned all the money I took," Birdie said, praying it would be enough to satisfy Officer Tim.

"I'll have to interview each of your victims."

She nodded. "Sure. No problem. Why should you believe me?"

"I don't," the officer replied flatly.

Swallowing, she kept her attention planted on her tennis shoes. In the corridor beyond, she'd glimpsed an intimidating row of jail cells. Was she headed for a stint behind bars? She'd seen what jail did to her father, how it took away his dignity. Suffering the same fate was terrifying—something she should've considered before recklessly following her parents into a life of crime. In retrospect, it seemed a miracle that she'd managed to avoid prosecution for so many years.

Well, she was caught now, in Officer Tim's viselike stare, while the other officers, chuckling at the story of the rubies, studied her as if she were a flea.

"We've been receiving complaints about you all day," Officer Tim said, drawing her attention back to him. "It'll take time to sort through this mess so you'll remain in town. You won't leave for any reason. Understood?"

"Yes, officer."

He picked up the *Register* and gleaned the front page. Birdie wished she had the courage to ask to read the story. Hugh had only given her the basics of her mother's involvement in the Trinity

Investment scandal and she wanted a more thorough understanding of the damage Wish had done.

Or maybe it was better not to know. Either way, it seemed wiser to wait until she'd returned to The Second Chance to see the article. Surely Finney had a copy by now.

"About your mother." Officer Tim tossed down the newspaper. "She's wanted for questioning in nine jurisdictions, including this one. There are warrants out for her arrest in Alabama and Minnesota. Do you know her whereabouts?"

"She's somewhere in Mexico. I don't have an address."

"A phone number?"

If she weren't so scared, Birdie might have laughed. Her mother was too cunning to allow the authorities to track her down through a phone number. "My mother only calls from public phones," she explained, trembling as the officer's mouth formed a thin line of impatience. "We don't have much contact."

"How do you get in contact?"

"Through my father." She hated bringing Tanek into this; he only had three more years on his present stint before being released. Hurriedly, she added, "He doesn't like to do it, but sometimes I give him my phone number to pass along to my mother in case she gets in touch with him. If she does—and it's not often—she uses the number I've left."

Officer Tim leafed through the police report. "Tanek Kaminsky, Arizona State Penitentiary. Car theft." He grunted. "Small time, compared to your mother. When she's apprehended—and we *will* find her—she'll face a long incarceration."

"Then I hope you don't find her." The officer frowned, and she added, "She *is* my mother. Would *you* want your mother doing time?"

He set the report aside. "Your loyalty, misplaced as it is, is understandable. From what Finney tells me, you've been trying to go straight. She says you're a reliable employee."

Finney had come to her defense? "I'm trying." Appreciation for the cook's loyalty washed through her. Finney's skillet might be dangerous but she was true-blue.

"Continue to abide by the law."

"Yes, officer."

"Frankly, I'd like to see you prosecuted. Finney's good word alone wouldn't be enough to sway me. If it weren't for Mrs. Hendricks, the county prosecutor would've drawn up charges. Given the letter she's written, he won't."

"Theodora wrote a letter . . . defending me?"

"She sent copies to this department, the prosecutor, and Mayor Ryan. First thing this morning."

"We spent all day together. She never mentioned a letter." Love for the old woman spilled through her ravaged heart.

"Thank her the next time you see her. Mrs. Hendricks has a lot of clout in Liberty." Officer Tim escorted her to the door. "If she hadn't stepped forward, every one of your victims would press charges. They haven't out of respect for her."

It was past ten o'clock. The moonless street was glazed with ice. Lights from the police station cast a muddy glow on the silent storefronts of Elm Street and, further up the hill rising to Liberty Square, many of the houses lay in darkness.

With the frigid wind at her back, Birdie listened to the doors of the station swing shut. She didn't relish a long trek back up Elm, to where a rumpled bed awaited her throbbing head and overworked emotions. Only the promise of escaping her woes in the blessed relief of sleep started her feet moving.

She'd barely stepped forward when Meade Williams climbed out of a white Mercedes.

Approaching, she narrowed her regard with unmistakable contempt. "Wish sent you back to Liberty, didn't she? Don't waste your time lying. I've read the paper."

Nervously, Birdie backed up against the frosty concrete of the building. "I haven't seen the *Register* yet." Exhaustion made her movements clumsy. She wasn't prepared for the confrontation.

"Well, if it's true what they say and Hugh Shaeffer has a crush on you, it's quite evident in his reporting. He made your childhood sound like Dickens. Was it rough, being raised by thieves?"

Mention of Hugh pummeled her heart. "Hugh didn't write the article. Someone else did."

But Meade wasn't listening. "You little bitch. Do you still have my father's money? Or have you and your mother run through it?"

"Look. I've only learned about Trinity Investments the other day. Whatever my mother did to your father—I'm sorry." Scared, Birdie tried brushing past. "I'm tired. I need to get some rest."

"Wait." Meade blocked her path. "Do you mean you *don't* have the money?"

"No, I don't. Now, get out of my way."

"Didn't your mother send you back here to scam my father again?"

Birdie tamped down her irritation. The emotionally trying events of the day had lowered her normally impregnable defenses. And there was something else, the incomprehensible yet deep, nagging regret. When they'd first met she'd tried to make a good impression on Meade. She'd hoped they'd become friends. The reasons were as unfathomable as Birdie's own heart.

And because she sensed the same indefinable emotions churning inside Meade, the same unanswerable questions, she said, "The pictures you showed me in your office . . . I was the little girl with your father."

"So you lied to me."

"I don't remember any of it. I was so young. I don't remember him."

"My mother gave me the photos." In her expression something died, something long-held and coveted. "She was a wonderful person. Important. Your mother destroyed her world."

"What happened to your father's investment firm . . . after?"

"He closed it." Meade studied the sky. The ash-colored clouds blotting out the starlight were as grim and unwelcoming as the pain canvassing her features. "Your mother carried on with him for years. He couldn't resist her. She took so much—two hundred thousand dollars and change. My father gave it to her willingly, by the way."

Astonished, Birdie rested her head against the wall of the station. Her knees dissolved and she locked them tight, to stop from falling. Bending, she clamped her palms to her thighs and took deep, steadying breaths of winter air. Her mother had stolen thousands of dollars and sent a woman to her death on the waters of Lake Erie. Hugh blamed himself for Cat's death but he wasn't at fault. Her mother was. She'd known Wish was cruel and grasping. But she was malevolent—

"You must know about the money," Meade prodded, breaking into her thoughts. "Fourteen years ago you were in high school. You must have accompanied Wish back to Liberty. The money would've altered your life radically."

"I left my mother when I was sixteen. We were heading through New Mexico and we fought. It was our last fight. She moved on, and I stayed. If she came back to Liberty, I never heard about it."

"Oh, please. You were on your own at sixteen?"

"I swear it's true. I got an apartment in Santa Fe. I dropped out . . . of school, life, everything."

They'd been rollercoaster years, a disheartening spiral of dead-end jobs and nights alone in the spare apartment, with her stomach empty and the cockroaches sending a wicked clatter across the floor. She held down low-paying jobs until the month when, despondent, she couldn't make the rent. Then she went back to doing what she did best, hanging around street corners while the legal types hurried by on their way to happier lives. Darting through their pockets like a hummingbird starving for nectar, she clung to her adolescent logic: if she only took enough to tide her over she wasn't really breaking the law.

By the age of twenty-one, she'd somehow managed to earn her GED and enroll at New Mexico State University. The ridiculous stint ended when bill collectors started calling and she'd restricted herself to one meal a day. She found her landlord outside her apartment, swearing in Spanish. He'd hauled her meager belongings into the hallway and would've thrown them on the street if she hadn't come up with her rent within hours.

She thought she was a failure for relying on the tricks learned after years of coaching by her mother. It didn't matter if she'd left Wish's side. Birdie finally understood. She was like her mother—worthless.

After awhile, she had stopped thinking at all.

"You dropped out of high school and left your mother?" Meade was saying with bitter disbelief. "Do you practice this stuff? Or does it come naturally?"

She'd had enough. "Get out of my way." Heartache clogged her throat.

Meade caught her by the arm. "I don't care if Theodora has it in her head to befriend you. She's always collecting strays. If you stay here, I'll make your life miserable." She pushed Birdie against the wall with enough force to knock the air from her lungs. "My father will never run into you. He'll never suffer the pain of seeing you and remembering the heartless bitch he loved."

"Get off!"

"Leave, Birdie." Sealing the threat, Meade added "If you don't, I'll make it so you wish you had."

CHAPTER 28

The eddying pool of moon glow retreated across the floor. Giving up on the pretense of sleep, Birdie showered then turned on the coffee pot.

Despite her exhaustion she'd slept fitfully, her dreams marred by despair. Frowning, she watched the coffee drip into the pot. She felt no better now; in fact, she felt worse. Facing the truth was awful, but she wasn't having much success evading the facts. She was losing everything she'd come to hold dear.

Meade had warned her to leave. Dismissing the threat was reckless. Running afoul of Officer Tim's mandate to stay in town meant the police would follow, but what choice was there? A woman as powerful as Meade could easily make Birdie's life miserable.

Where to go? Seated at the kitchen table, she opened her army coat and unzipped the secret pocket sewn into the hem. Withdrawing the U.S. road map, she considered the possibilities. Given the unwanted publicity in the *Register* and Officer Tim's mandate, she'd put as much road between herself and Ohio as possible.

Head for Utah? She'd never been to Salt Lake. Southern California? The authorities would have trouble finding her in a city the size of Los Angeles. Or she could follow her mother's cue and head for Mexico. Quit the U.S. entirely.

Sorrow budded in her chest. She'd never return to Liberty—it was too dangerous.

Which meant she'd never see the women of The Second Chance again. Finney, with her fiery temper and generous heart. Delia, who'd become like a kid sister. Ethel Lynn, with her fluttering, ridiculously feminine airs. Worst of all, she hadn't shared with Theodora the discovery she'd made—they were family.

And Hugh. Once she left Ohio, he'd become a poignant memory of her squandered dreams.

What if they'd overcome their differences and built a life together? Lulled by the beautiful and fragile possibilities, Birdie lowered her head and wept.

By the time the last sobs abated, dawn was turning the windowsill a blushing pink. Liberty Square lay in shadow, the streetlights dimming in the approaching light. She wiped her face, carefully folded up the map, and slipped it back inside the lining of her coat. As she did, her knuckles brushed against the velvet sack that held the ruby-studded key.

Her fingers caught on the thick, silky cord. The key dropped from the sack and clattered to the floor.

Worried, she checked the key for damage. The brass gleamed; the ruby at the base of the head glinted with crimson fire. Pulling the sack from her coat, she started tucking the key back inside.

She stopped. There was something on the heavy gold cord.

Black markings dotted the twining threads. Why hadn't she noticed them before? They were tiny and easy to miss. Squinting, she brought the velvet sack near.

The scratches of printing were hard to make out. They appeared to be letters set down in black ink by an impossibly steady hand. The letter in the center was faded, little more than a smudge.

Excited, she rummaged through the pockets of her coat and found her magnifying glass, a useful tool no thief did without.

Peering through the thick lens, she read:

M P

Initials? Justice's married name had been Turner.

Birdie's pulse scuttled. Before Justice married, she'd carried the surname of Birdie's forebears—Postell. Was 'M – P' someone's initials? If so, what did the 'M' stand for? She didn't know the name of Justice's son—Theodora's grandfather. Perhaps it was Mathew or Mark. Or maybe it wasn't a name at all. Her hands shaking, she tried to make it out.

She'd never unlock the mystery without deciphering the letter in between. With painstaking care, she smoothed down the cord's shiny threads. Drawing the magnifying glass near she looked again, and read:

M A P

"Map," she said aloud.

Map!

With a yelp, she dropped the magnifying glass and turned the velvet sack inside out. How could she have overlooked such an obvious clue? She hid loads of stuff in the lining of her army coat. Justice had used the same strategy with the lining of the velvet sack.

Birdie expected to find a hidden zipper or a pocket with a map tucked inside. Her heart beat in a dizzying rush as she realized the truth was far simpler.

The cream fabric was covered with a clean, legible script. Roads and the southern edge of Lake Erie were clearly depicted.

Spreading the sack flat on the table, she studied the map with the thrill of discovery bubbling through her veins. There was a pretty star in the middle at Rock Island Cove. She'd heard about the place—Rock Island was a stretch of beach on the lake where teenagers went for privacy. Delia had told her dozens of amusing stories about her antics at Rock Island. The map indicated there was a cave nearby, which Delia had never mentioned. Even so, it should be easy to find.

Hitchhike to the cove? If the Liberty police spotted her on the highway, they'd know she was making a run for it. They'd toss her in jail. Forget the letter Theodora wrote on Birdie's behalf. The county prosecutor *would* press charges.

Yet it was early, barely six o'clock. Traffic on Route 44 would be minimal, just truckers ferrying cargo across the state. And there was another, more pressing consideration—Finney had cleaned out her pockets yesterday. If the gems *were* hidden at the cove, at least she'd have the means to leave Ohio, and quickly. She'd cash in one or two of the rubies at a pawnshop. Once she reached the West, she'd give up her life as a pickpocket and find legal work.

A sweet ache of misgiving stole through her. There wasn't time to wallow in tears even though it was unbearably difficult to leave the people she'd grown to love.

Settled on her dreary choice, she walked the two miles to the highway with her teeth chattering and her heart turning to stone. The highway was a ribbon of black weaving toward the horizon, where fingers of daylight were reaching into the dome of stars. She didn't dare think about leaving Hugh—later, when she was settled in a new life, she'd examine their short romance in excruciating detail. The grinding noise of gears shifting pulled her from her thoughts. Caught in the blinding glare of headlights, she stuck out her thumb. The rig ground to a halt.

Her luck held when the trucker, a middle-aged man with a tattoo of a snake on his neck, agreed to take her all the way to the lake. "It's on my way," he said, withdrawing a pack of Camels from beneath his bandanna.

By the time they reached the heavy forest near Rock Cove the day was rising bright and stark. Miserably cold, Birdie walked toward the sound of waves crashing while she studied the map. There was a drawing of a hill with pine trees, due north of the beach, with a cave above it. The shoreline smelled of marine life and rotting driftwood, and the wind pounded the water into angry waves. Whitecaps thundered toward shore. She looked north.

A seagull alighted on the sand, its wings snapping shut. The lake roiled and churned. A sense of misgiving stole through her as she thought of Meade, losing her mother to the treacherous waters. The pain she must have endured was difficult to grasp, the shock and the horror.

The sorrow was all consuming; Birdie stood in its harsh embrace as the gull hopped through the sand. Even if it was wrong to break her promise to Officer Tim to stay put, it was a boon for Meade. She'd never again suffer the torment of seeing Birdie. Reason enough to cast her doubts aside.

Icy wind tore at her cheeks. The toes of her tennis shoes sank deep and were brushed by the tide. Turning away from the beach, she forced her attention on the trees to the north where the land rose gently from the lake.

The incline was dotted with fir trees, which grew dense as the sandy beach gave way to the ice-crusted floor of the forest. She made it to the top of the first hill and realized she still had a good fifty yards to go. She got her bearings and pushed forward. Peering skyward, she spotted a jagged outcropping of rock.

The mouth of the cave was barely visible behind a curtain of vines and brambles. Without the map, she never would've found it. But now the journey proved easy—large wedges of slate jutted out of the side of the hill, as if nature provided steps for her ascent. Climbing ever higher, Birdie paused at the small clearing on top, where heavy vines crackled at the touch. Before the cave's dark portal delicate brambles covered in ice glittered like strands of frozen pearls. It was frighteningly black inside, the scent of dampness reaching her nostrils and putting a tremor in her blood. Fumbling inside her pocket, she withdrew her flashlight and walked inside.

The plop of water echoed off the walls. With bated breath, she swung the flashlight in a wide arc. She was standing in some sort of alcove, with the larger cave still ahead. Rechecking the map, she noted the carefully drawn heart and the words:

ten paces forward, from the heart

She found the heart within minutes; a chiseled slab of granite set into the wall, it was reminiscent of the brick heart she'd found in the storeroom with Hugh. She sent a silent prayer of gratitude to Justice, who'd wisely used a similar clue.

Starting at the heart, she strode carefully toward the center of the cave. At the tenth step, she dropped to her knees. A bat fluttered overhead, startling her. Pondering where it had come from put gooseflesh on her arms. She laid the flashlight on the ground, the narrowed beam providing sufficient illumination to examine the dry, silty earth.

She hadn't thought to bring a trowel, and she looked around desperately for something to use. She spotted a flat rock bigger than her hand and snatched it up. With growing excitement, she began to dig.

Sweat was trickling into her eyes by the time she gave up on the first hole. She'd dug down nearly two feet and found nothing. Thankfully, the dirt was soft, easy to dislodge. Repositioning the flashlight, she started again.

And within moments heard the scrape of rock against metal.

She nearly blacked out from excitement. Flinging down the rock and using her hands, she clawed out clumps of loose dirt that clouded the air and started her nose itching. On a gasp, she uncovered the edges of a grey metal box. It was constructed of hammered tin, the corners marred by rust.

Wedging the box from the ground, she lowered it gingerly onto her knees. The extraordinary quality of the moment struck her full force and she sat staring at the treasure in her hands with growing awe. The rubies *were* as real as the undying passion between Justice and Lucas. The gems were here, safely tucked inside this box. Shaking, she dug the key from her pocket and pushed it into the lock. A soft click as it turned, and she opened the lid with her heart pounding in her ears.

And found nothing.

No sack, like the one protecting the key. No gems spitting fire. Nothing. Disappointment lanced through her. Groaning, she sat down with a thump.

The box joggled in her grasp. A slip of paper wedged in the corner slid out.

She snatched it up. What the hell? Quickly, she read this newest and by far most frustrating clue:

Liberty safeguards the cherished heart.

Wait a second. She knew this clue. Hadn't she been raised on its promise? These were the words written on the slip of parchment her mother kept in the safety deposit box in New Mexico.

Liberty safeguards . . .

Birdie drew in a shuddering breath. What did Liberty safeguard? Why, a cherished heart.

Cherished. Tears blinded her. They came in a torrent—she couldn't stop them. She didn't even try. For what did it mean to be cherished? It meant you were held dear. You were protected.

Loved.

Hadn't Hugh shown his love when he'd asked her to come back with him to Akron? He'd said they'd weather the bad publicity together. Sure, if he'd never hired a PI to look into her background there wouldn't have been a story in the first place. But people screwed up all the time. Most of them left you high and dry after they'd hurt you.

Not Hugh. He'd shown how much he cared by offering to protect her until the publicity died down.

He loved her.

And what about Theodora? She was well respected in Liberty, the town's leading citizen. She had risked her good name to protect a common thief. Without her intervention, the county prosecutor would've pressed charges. The letter she'd written was proof of her love.

Finney, murmuring encouragement as Birdie took her lumps from the citizens in town. Delia, managing to forgive the thief who'd stolen from her but who was also her friend. Maybe Ethel Lynn hadn't come through in some monumental way. But she offered tea and, with sewing needle posed at the ready, ministered to loose buttons with tenderness and care. And who could blame the old lady for rushing, brightly feathered, into the limelight?

Delight trembled up Birdie's ribcage and out of her mouth in a spurt of laughter. She loved them all. She cherished them.

Grinning, she snapped the box shut. She'd keep it as a trophy. Not of all she'd lost—of all she'd gained.

She was going back to Liberty. Even the threat of Meade's wrath wouldn't keep her from the people she loved.

Someday she'd tell Theodora about the ridiculous hunt for the jewels. They'd enjoy the story over shots of moonshine and bowls of squirrel stew.

On a sigh, she got to her feet and marched out of the clammy darkness. The sun was blinding, cutting across the ledge in a wide arc.

Her vision clearing, she let out a yelp of surprise.

Theodora sat perched on a boulder. Impatience brewed on her deeply lined face. Dressed properly for the frigid weather, she wore a sporty down coat, a knit cap, and leather gloves.

Birdie flapped her arms, unsure whether to be nervous or relieved. "What are you doing here?"

"What a foolish question. I'm waiting for you." Theodora sighed. "I figured after Meade cornered you last night, you'd come here at first light for the rubies. Make a run for it." She hesitated, frowning. "I talked to Meade. She admitted to threatening you."

"She told me to leave town or else."

"Or else what?"

Birdie shrugged. "I don't know. It didn't sound good."

"You fret over the damnedest things. Don't you know Meade's bark is worse than her bite?" Theodora made a swiping motion toward the cave. "Well? Did you get a dose of Justice or not?"

Birdie gaped at her.

"Lord and Jezebel—didn't you find the last clue?"

Birdie shook her head with amusement. Geez, how could she be so stupid? The box she'd dug up was old, an antique from Justice's time. But the message inside? She withdrew the slip of paper from her pocket.

The damn clue was written on a Post-it note.

"I don't know about Justice," she said, handing it over, "But I'm pretty sure I got a dose of Theodora. Nice work."

The old woman stuck her corncob pipe in her mouth, struck a match . . . and winked.

Delighted, Birdie motioned for the pipe and took a long drag. Smoke poured down her throat.

Gagging, she thrust the pipe back. "There are some things we'll *never* share. Yuck."

"At least share one secret. How did you know about Liberty and the cherished heart?"

"From the slip of parchment handed down in my family—*Liberty safeguards the cherished heart*. How do *you* know about it?"

"From Justice, of course." Theodora blew out a puff of smoke, her dark eyes awash with merriment. "Birdie, your branch of the family tree got bits and pieces of the story. My branch got a sight more—her diary. Damn informative book."

"Justice left a diary?"

"With a request on the last page she hoped her descendants— me and my kin—would one day fulfill. She was mighty upset when Lucas came to Liberty, half dead from the war and a weakening constitution."

"Why was Justice upset that he'd followed her to Liberty?"

"Molly, of course."

"My great-grandmother?"

Theodora nodded. "Molly was a wee thing when Lucas enlisted with the Confederates. He left her with kin when Southern pride sent him off to fight in a war he never believed in. He'd given Justice two bags of rubies to take north. Two bags—understand? 'Course you know Justice loved Molly. She'd helped Lucas raise the child after his wife died."

Birdie hung on every word. "One of the bags of rubies was meant for Molly?" A wave of affection for Justice swept through her.

"Justice promised Lucas she'd get the jewels to his daughter if he didn't survive the war. He *did* make it through and died right here, in Liberty." Sorrow filtered across Theodora's face. "Afterward, Justice spent years trying to find the girl, but people were displaced. The South was a shambles. Safe here in Ohio, Justice grew wealthy in her own right. By the time she found the girl's whereabouts, my granddaddy, Theodore, was a young man."

"Theodore went looking for Molly?"

"With a letter written in a sort of code by his mother."

Breathless, Birdie neared. "A letter filled with clues so Molly would know where the rubies were buried."

"She was a young woman by then, living with an uncle in Savannah—a despicable man. He took one look at the Negro calling on his niece and tore up the letter." Theodora glanced at her appraisingly. "I suspect your great-grandma was a mite resourceful. She must've got hold of a scrap of the letter—the slip of parchment handed down in your family."

Stunned, Birdie stepped away to look off over the trees. What if Justice's portrait and the remaining clues had been lost? Molly's bit of parchment wouldn't have been enough to find the rubies. She recalled what Theodora had told her on the day they met—just last year, Finney dug the portrait out of the storeroom and put it back up in the restaurant with the clue safely tucked inside—

She spun on her heel. "If you knew about the clues, why didn't you follow them to the rubies?"

Theodora snorted. "Have you gone stupid? I found the loot when Eisenhower was president."

"But the clues were left in place. I found them all—"

"You found them because of my daughter, Belinda," Theodora cut in. "The one they call Ruby? When she was a wee thing, she begged me to put the clues back. She was sure a lost relation would arrive someday in search of the gems."

"Wasn't she worried about sharing them?"

"You fool, she didn't care about the rubies. She cared about finding our lost kin."

Something heavy and surprisingly sweet wove through the old woman's voice, and Birdie's heart overturned. Even if Theodora had cashed in the gems long ago, did it matter? The clues were put back in place in hopes of reuniting the family. Theodora's daughter, Ruby, had dreamt of finding her long-lost relatives—of finding Birdie.

What did she get for her troubles? She'd been rewarded with a relative who'd arrived in Liberty with greed in her heart and as much family feeling as you'd find in a slug. Embarrassed, Birdie turned back toward the trees and the dawn filtering over the forest. Ruby deserved better. She deserved a relation she could be proud of, not a petty thief who'd arrived merely for financial gain.

Theodora, as wise and noble as a goddamn Sphinx, seemed aware of the shame washing over her. With a grunt, she said, "Stop beating yourself up—don't you know that's my job? Not that I'm of the mind to do so presently. Maybe you're not what I had in mind for a relative but you aren't half bad."

"I'm *all* bad. I don't have the right to be part of a family as nice as yours."

Considering, Theodora tamped out the ash smoldering in her pipe. "Where's the key?" she asked suddenly.

Birdie dug it from her pocket. She tried to hand it over but was waved off.

"About keys," Theodora said, screwing her hat down on her forehead, "they unlock more than doors and the occasional safebox. Keep it, child. There's all sort of things inside yourself you might unlock. Good things."

Birdie tried for a cheeky comeback but she couldn't speak around the lump in her throat. Yes, she wanted to find her better angels. She wanted to find them even if they were buried so deep it would take a lifetime to unearth them. The path her parents had taken through life was filled with sorrow. She wanted something better.

She brushed at her eyes, which were suddenly damp. "How do you start?" she asked, her voice little more than a whisper. "I'm not sure how."

Theodora approached. "I'll help you. We all will—me and my kin. Your kin." She gazed up at Birdie with the map-work of lines on her face easing and the gleam in her eyes increasing. "You are a treasure, child. Bad-mouthed and sassy and more fun than a woman my age ought to have. But there it is."

A breezy anticipation rushed through Birdie, a sudden, startling sensation that she was *soaring*, high above the treetops and the oppressive worries of her life. "Thanks."

"Welcome to the family. My kids are itchin' to meet you. Plan on coming this Sunday for dinner, okay?" Taking her by the hand, Theodora started down the incline. "By the way, I keep both bags of rubies in a safety deposit box at Liberty Trust."

Birdie scudded to a halt. "You do?"

Theodora tugged her forward. "We'll stop on our way to Landon's house. He's expecting us."

"He is?"

"I hope he's got an ice cold Bud with my name on it. Lord, I'm thirsty."

"It's not even eight o'clock. How can you think about beer?" A wave of apprehension brought her to a standstill. "What about Meade? I'm not going to Landon's house if his daughter—"

"Stop fretting!" Theodora stomped her foot. "Don't you know it jangles my nerves? Let's mosey down to the bank and fetch your inheritance."

Birdie's eyes rounded.

Inheritance?

A smile lit Theodora's face, her fake teeth poking out with the extent of her glee. "Birdie, one of the bags of rubies is yours. Justice would've given anything to get them to your great-grandmother. She died hoping that one day Molly would get a fresh start in life."

She paused long enough for the elation swimming through Birdie to lift skyward, like a song. "Funny how life works out," she added. "Fact is you'll be the one using the gems to start your life over."

CHAPTER 29

Clumps of snow landed on the library's carpet as Theodora brushed the white from her shoulders. "Reenie, do you have beer?" she asked the housekeeper while Birdie looked around at the rich furnishings with amazement.

Reenie nodded. "I took the liberty of pouring a Bud for you when I heard your car." She paused at the French doors. "I'll tell Mr. Williams you've arrived."

After she'd gone, Theodora spied the frothy glass on an end table beside a Queen Anne chair. "Thank the Lord. And Reenie, of course. The world would be a sorry place if the road wasn't paved with beer."

"If the road *were* paved with beer, you'd be standing in it."

"Settle down, girl. Have a little patience."

Patience?

The morning had already provided a roller coaster of emotional experiences. The biggest so far occurred at the bank, when Theodora rented a second safety deposit box then placed the heavy bag in Birdie's hands. The rubies, recently appraised, were worth a quarter of a million dollars.

The number was impossible to comprehend. Birdie was still trying to grapple with the sea change in her circumstances. Yet her elation vanished the moment Theodora parked her Cadillac before the brick mansion where Landon Williams lived.

Now she was terrified. Maybe she could handle running into the man, but his daughter? Contrary to Theodora's opinion, Meade *was* a dangerous enemy.

"I still don't have any idea why we're here." Birdie shifted from foot to foot. "I'll apologize to Landon for everything my mother did. Or I'll try—after I go home and wash up. I'm covered in dirt from the cave."

Under her breath, Theodora murmured, "Bitch, bitch, bitch."

Birdie tried to calm down. She was stuck here and she knew it.

Reluctantly, she recalled the photographs she'd glimpsed at Meade's office. At some time during her childhood, she'd known Landon. The fretful child she'd once been had contentedly sat on his lap and smiled up into his beaming face. Was he Paw Paw, the man who'd shown her kindness during the dawning years of her life?

Pacing before the mile-high shelves of books, she frowned at the confusing mix of emotions welling in her chest. Delight at the possibilities for the better life the gems represented. Trepidation over the reception she'd receive from Landon. And bone-deep terror over the prospect of running into Meade.

She picked up a crystal vase from one of the shelves and turned it over in her hands. "I take it Landon is rich," she said, her stomach twisting in knots. She returned the surprisingly heavy crystal to the shelf.

"He's done well for himself." Cocking a brow, Theodora lifted her glass and sipped. The line of foam on her lips made a none-too-attractive mustache. "Would you like a drink?"

"At ten in the morning? Pass."

"You sound like Meade, griping about the hour and whether it's a proper time for libations. Why can't young people *relax?* Would you at least sit down?"

"I'm safer on my feet." She smiled gamely. "If Meade shows up and hurls something in my direction, I'll need to move fast."

"How ridiculous," Theodora said, as if Meade wasn't a clear and present danger. Raising her glass, she added, "Fine drink, beer. Won't you join me?"

"No!"

From the doorway, a silvery voice said, "I'll have a beer with you, Theodora."

Birdie's guts swam with fear as Meade swept into the room. A bizarre yipping followed her stiletto heels, and a miniature white poodle trotted close behind. Some maniac had outfitted the pooch in a doll-size green jacket, red pants and bow tie. He was a pint-sized Christmas elf, with fur.

"What the hell is that?" Birdie asked before she had the sense to stop herself.

Meade paused by the wet bar and gave her the once over. "On second thought, a martini is in order." She reached for the bottle of Skyy.

Somehow Birdie found the courage to ditch her fear. "It's nice to see you too. Should we pick up where we left off last night? Got any boxing gloves in the house?" If rudeness was the game of the day, two could play as easily as one. "What the hell's in a martini anyway?"

"Vodka, vermouth—need one? You can show me your right hook later."

"Count on it. And yeah—fix me up. Are those olives? Load my glass with five or six." The dog sniffed at Birdie's muddy tennis shoes and she leapt back. "Call your beast off me. He can't have sex with my Nikes."

Theodora belched. "The dog isn't particular. The scoundrel will hump anything that's not moving."

"He's merely enthusiastic." Meade flourished a crystal goblet beneath Birdie's nose. "Your drink."

She walked to the couch with the poodle hot on her trail. "Beat it," she muttered, seating herself. The demand brought a *yip* of protest. The dog leapt into her lap, nearly spilling her drink. "Sweet baby," Birdie cooed, and the rakish dog tipped his head to the side. "Are you only allowed to play with doggies from the right side of town?"

Meade stiffened. "I'm not a snob even if I do prefer to avoid the undesirable element. People like you—and your mother."

"Leave my mother out of this," Birdie said, steering the poodle from her lap. He obediently sat on the cushion next to hers and licked her hand. Maybe she'd knock Meade down, and keep the damn poodle out of spite. He *was* cute. "I don't excuse Wish. I'm sorry for everything she did to your family, but I won't sit here and let you insult her."

"Enough already," Theodora put in.

Scowling, Meade took a sip of her martini. "Theodora, I'll grant you've been a good friend to my father. While I have no idea what you discussed with him last night, I'm willing to wait for his so-called news. Just don't expect me to feel anything but contempt for . . . her." She jerked her drink toward Birdie, who was beginning to feel as small as the poodle.

"Don't get your panties in a twist," Theodora snapped. "This meeting was his idea."

Birdie looked from one to the other. "Why are we having a meeting?"

But no one heard the question. Meade placed her drink on the wet bar and rushed across the room.

Landon Williams paused in the doorway looking broken and worn. Pity swept through Birdie. His grey suit was roomy and dated. The silk cravat at his neck seemed a sweetly overdone gesture as pathetic as the poodle's bow tie.

When his daughter reached him, he gripped her forearm like a lifeline. A muscle in his jaw twitched, and Birdie's heart went out to him. He didn't look well. He appeared as nervous as she was.

Frantically, she searched her memory for an inkling of him. If he was Paw Paw, surely the sight of him would bring something to the surface. It didn't, and she brushed away her disappointment.

Acutely conscious of her manners, she rose as Meade steered him toward the couch. Silence weighed down the proceedings as if they'd all been plunged deep beneath the ocean.

His tawny gaze found Birdie.

Something whirled through the stifled atmosphere of the library. Landon's expression shifted. Birdie snatched in a breath, nervously assessing the change coming over him.

Meade noticed too. Gripping his arm tightly, her attention tracked with his. Heat spread across Birdie's cheeks as they all stared at her, Theodora included, as if she held a secret as rich as the rubies.

"Dad, I'd like you to meet Birdie," Meade was saying.

"Birdie . . . you mean Bertha, darling. Her formal name is Bertha."

The statement was issued in little more than a whisper. It was enough. Transfixed, Birdie let his voice sink deep into her soul.

Open your mouth, Bertha. The doctor won't hurt you, darling. He simply needs to check your throat.

His voice. She knew his voice. It was as familiar as the beat of her heart.

Lost in his gaze, she was blinded by the disjointed images flung across her eyesight. Paw Paw, seated on the bed shuffling *Go Fish* cards while he checked her temperature. Paw Paw, buying her ice cream in the park and helping her load vegetables into a grocery cart.

Carrot, potato, parsnip, she'd recited, the difficult words sticking to her lips like glue. But he'd clapped his hands, delighted with her efforts.

The tang of citrus and spice—the cologne he wore, even now—breathed life into her memories. Birdie visualized him as he'd been years ago, a young man with a snap in his step. How he'd clasped her tiny hands and spun her around with a hearty laugh as delightful and dizzying as his love.

The visions raining down weren't hers alone. Landon's quivering mouth drew open with surprise. Stepping away from his wide-eyed daughter, he clasped Birdie's hands and brought her close.

And whispered in the sweetly impish voice she adored, "Parsnip, is that you?"

* * *

Birdie spent the next hour in a daze of discovery.

Under Theodora's gentle prodding, the man she'd known as Paw Paw fit together the missing pieces of her life. Landon came to life, growing more determined, even confident, as he delved further into the particulars of Birdie's childhood. The details regarding his ill-fated love affair with Wish Kaminsky stamped regret on his face. Yet he soldiered on, as if he couldn't find peace until he'd given Birdie every remnant of a stolen past.

"When I fell in love with your mother, I was unaware of her marriage to Tanek," he explained. He'd seated himself in the center of the couch between Birdie and Meade, no doubt sensing the wisdom in separating them. "Tanek was in prison at the time. In Minnesota if memory serves. I didn't find out about him until much later."

"What about *your* marriage?" Meade drained her glass. "You were cheating on my mother."

He brushed his fingers across her knuckles. "My affair wasn't a secret. Your mother didn't care." Landon's mouth was grim, and Birdie suffered a deep sadness. What did it cost to reveal the contents of his failed marriage? "After we married I chose to believe we were happy. You were born and for a while your mother seemed content to play with you, to dress you . . . she'd dreamt of having a daughter. You brought her so much joy."

"It wasn't enough?" Despite the haughty pose, Meade's voice grew whisper-soft. She was suddenly less formidable, and the comfort Birdie desperately wanted to bestow on Landon flowed on to his daughter. "Daddy, are you saying Mother regretted marrying you?"

"I managed her assets well, which pleased her. It was more her restless nature. I doubt one man could have ever satisfied Cat. She was . . . high spirited."

Meade's polished veneer slipped away. "She—she ran around on you?"

Some of the light faded from Landon's gaze as well. "Your mother craved excitement. She quickly lost interest in people, charities—she rarely stood still."

"Like my mother," Birdie said, needing to rescue him before Meade forced a more graphic explanation. His gaze drew to hers with palpable relief. "Landon wasn't the only man she took advantage of. My mother never stayed in a relationship very long. I'm not even sure she knew how much she hurt people. Relationships were a game. She kept a scorecard. If you didn't pay up or play by her rules, she cut you out."

Remarkably, Meade's gaze softened. "Do you mean her relationships with men . . . or with you?" she asked, and Birdie was suddenly aware of the hurt needling her heart. "Last night, at the police station, you said you were living on your own at sixteen."

Horror whipped across Landon's face. "Is it true, Birdie?" She nodded meekly, and a fine rage climbed his cheeks until it blazed in his eyes. "What about the money I gave Wish for your education? I put money in your college fund, and set up a money market account. It was put in place to protect you!"

He'd provided for her education? "My mother was always broke," she whispered, afraid. Anger transformed him before her eyes.

"She wasn't! She had thousands—hundreds of thousands."

"There wasn't any money." Dry-mouthed, she watched him grapple for self-control. "We lived day-to-day. In motels. On the road. Landon, she must have hid the money you gave her."

"Don't call me that!"

Swiftly rising, he strode to the wet bar where he stood with his back to them. Fury rode a tremor up his spine. His grief left a taste in the air, like ash from the fire that had consumed him years ago.

Theodora approached, but he warded her off. "No. Let me do this." Turning, he held Birdie's gaze like a fist. "Tanek was in prison when I met your mother."

"I get it." She tried to smile but her lips were frozen in place. "My mother gave you the widow routine. You fell for it."

"She left soon after," he continued, as if she hadn't spoken. "Four years went by. I was mad with grief. She returned with you. Your eyes—"

"Yeah—violet. It's unusual."

With a gasp, Meade turned toward her. "Grandma's eyes," she whispered, and the moment uncoiled in a rush of ungovernable emotion.

Landon neared, his gait even. "Birdie, you were four years old when you ran a fever. I took you into Cleveland General. I told Wish you'd be seen by a specialist I trusted." He knelt before her and took her hands in his. "The doctor ran the test, so I'd be sure. I had to make it right even if I couldn't divorce Cat. She . . . took up with men. So many, and I had to protect Meade as well."

"You tried to do what's right." Birdie replied, skimming his words, unable to see into their depths.

"I had proof you were mine," he said, and his voice broke. "The paternity test—"

He cut off. The world shook.

And she finally understood. Oh, God—she did.

On a sob, Landon pulled her into his arms. "Birdie," he said, shaking them both to the core, "I'm your father."

CHAPTER 30

Slouching on the recliner, Hugh growled at the insistent ringing of the doorbell. Glowering, he lobbed pretzels at the jarring sound.

"Go away!" A three-alarm fire couldn't pry him from where he'd camped for a week in an undignified bout of self-pity.

Heroic, he wasn't. An overrated virtue if ever there was one.

The ringing persisted, catapulting him to his feet. The television remote and several beer cans went flying.

"This better be good!" He yanked open the door to his condo with the sheer force of his impotent rage.

Leaping back, Anthony Perini raised his hands in surrender. "I'm unarmed. Don't shoot."

"Hell, it's you." Perplexed, Hugh scratched his groin. He really did need a shower. "What the hell are you doing here?"

"Looking for you, idiot." With a lopsided grin, Anthony surveyed his grizzled face. "Man, you smell like shit. Ever hear of deodorant?"

"Not lately. Go away."

"Cut me some slack. Mary sent me to talk to you. She's worried about you—everyone is."

Including Birdie? Hugh's chest throbbed, and he gave himself a mental kick in the keister. He'd be damned if he'd ask about her. *She's long gone, asshole. She probably left Ohio ten minutes after the story broke.*

"I called the *Register*. Your boss said you quit."

"Last week." Planting his feet, Hugh blocked the door. "Listen, I'm busy. There's a boxing match on the tube in ten minutes."

"I thought football was your game."

"I need to see blood."

Shoving past him, Anthony frowned at the pizza cartons thrown around the kitchen and the beer cans littering the floor of the living room. A tee shirt was balled up on the coffee table, the fabric a greasy brown after three days of mopping up spills.

He chuckled. "Man, does this bring back memories." At Hugh's questioning look, he added, "Life before marriage. It was a toss-up who was the bigger pig—Blossom or me. Now Mary has us on a schedule—shopping day, cleaning day—we earn points for tidiness."

"So you're into bondage." Hugh kicked a beer can from his path. Truth was, it sounded nice. "How's everyone in town?"

Anthony's gaze filled with mirth, but he shut tight as a clam.

"Heard anything from Birdie?" Hugh persisted, surrendering the last of his dignity. "I thought she might leave someone, maybe Delia, a forwarding address."

"God, you're stubborn. Blossom was right. She said I wouldn't be here five minutes before you asked the magic question." Anthony tossed a paper plate from the couch, clearing a space to sit. "Birdie's great. She's still working at the restaurant, at least until the holidays are over. She's come into money."

"She's moved up to robbing banks? That's my girl. I knew she'd make something of herself."

"It's perfectly legit. At least the rubies are. Seems Justice intended for Birdie's family to inherit half of the gems. So Birdie's loaded. Theodora has a letter to prove it—straight from Justice's diary."

"Birdie found the rubies?" Stunned, Hugh dropped into his recliner. A few pretzels crunched beneath his ass, but his attention remained fixed on Anthony. "Where were they?"

"Theodora had them all along."

"So Birdie's still in Liberty?" Hope punched his heart, but he fended it off.

"Yeah, she stuck around. She can give you the details, assuming you have the sense to look her up." Anthony's expression grew serious. Switching topics, he asked, "If you've quit the *Register*, what are you planning to do? Finding work ten days before Christmas is a bitch. No one's hiring."

Hugh grunted. For now, he was content to leak money from his retirement account. Losing Birdie had put him into a bigger tailspin than he'd anticipated. Formulating a game plan for the future was impossible.

Without her, there *was* no future.

"I'm taking it easy for a few months." He couldn't admit he'd lost the taste for investigative journalism, and he certainly didn't have the courage to ask if the *Register* coverage had destroyed Birdie. Her life as a petty thief was no longer a secret. Why hadn't she been run out of town? "I'm thinking about moving South. Virginia or North Carolina. Start fresh."

"I need help during the holidays." Planting his elbows on his knees, Anthony clasped his hands. Something in his face put Hugh on alert and he prepared to get it, both barrels. "I don't mean to lay on the guilt, but you hurt my kid. Blossom thought you were back in Liberty to make her famous all over again. A big deal to an eighth grader."

Hugh suffered a pang of guilt. "I can imagine."

"She contacted kids from here to Tokyo about the article she thought you were writing. You should see what she put on Facebook. Madison Avenue's got nothing on her."

Hugh's guilt became excruciating. "She didn't."

"Welcome to the digital frontier, man. My kid starts bragging in cyberspace like she's headed for stardom and embarrasses herself on five continents. She got so much mail, asking when she'd upload the article that she pinned a DO NOT ENTER sign on her computer monitor. Now she won't touch the keyboard, and my kid lives for her computer. You've taken away the air she breathes."

"Oh, man." He was scum. The kind of scum buried at the bottom of a landfill. "Anthony, I should've played straight with you."

"Yeah? Were you going to do that *after* you nailed my ass to the wall?" When Hugh's jaw dropped, he added, "Birdie mentioned you were investigating me."

"I guess all's fair in love and war." Reconsidering, Hugh groaned. *No, it's not. Women always collect more chits.*

But he didn't have time to relish the irony of Birdie getting in the last salvo because Anthony's brows lowered threateningly. "Why did you think I took money from websites set up to save my kid's life? You crossed the line, pal."

Tormented, Hugh floundered in the thick silence. He'd quit the *Register* in a rage over what he'd done to Birdie. He'd tried not to think about how the news would affect Landon Williams, a broken man. What Hugh neglected to consider was the impact on Blossom. She was a kid, too young to comprehend why a trusted journalist would lie to her.

"I used Blossom to get to you." He let his head drop. "My life has turned to shit because all I ever cared about was the story. If people got hurt, it didn't matter. The news always came first."

"And now?"

"I don't know what I care about." It took effort, but he wheeled his attention back to Anthony. "I can't fix what I've done to your daughter. If there's anything I can do to make it up to her—"

"Start by taking a shower. And for God's sake, find a razor. It's pay back time."

He struggled to his feet. "How?" Then he remembered. "The business you mentioned?"

Rising, Anthony grinned. "You're running the place for me from now until Christmas." He slapped Hugh on the back. "It'll put a few bucks in your pocket. All things considered, you probably need the cash."

At the suspicion gathering on Hugh's face, he added, "Relax. You're going to love this."

* * *

In the parking lot behind the Gas & Go Hugh stamped his feet, which were numb from the cold. From the back of the semi parked at the south end of the lot, two men unloaded Christmas trees.

He still wasn't sure why he'd agreed to this. The commute back and forth to Akron would be a hassle. Anthony had offered the spare bedroom at his house, which Hugh had quickly refused—he still hadn't run into Blossom. The kid was notoriously mischievous. There was no telling what she might do if Hugh stayed in the house. He'd wake one morning to find he'd been hogtied in bed. Or worse.

Impervious to the weather, Anthony came out of the Gas & Go with his jacket flung open. He appeared alert and ready to face the day. Unlike Hugh, who was exhausted and depressed.

Longing clenched his heart. He still wasn't sure if he'd seek Birdie out. He'd never put things right, so why bother?

Anthony nodded at the men. "They'll have you set up in an hour."

"About the costume—"

"I'm done arguing. You're wearing it." Anthony hesitated, his expression sobering. "What's this about you calling Landon?"

Stunned, Hugh crossed his arms. He'd put in the call less than an hour ago. How fast *did* news travel in the small town? "Ralston should've given Landon an opportunity to comment before the article appeared. I wanted to apologize. His maid said he was out Christmas shopping."

"With Birdie," Anthony supplied, grinning when the information snapped Hugh's head up. "For a reporter, you really don't keep up. Landon's her father. He's got a paternity test to prove it."

"What?" Hugh reeled. "Landon's her father?"

"I'll give you the details when you get back."

"Where am I going?" he asked warily.

"Over to the Second Chance to calm the savage mob, my daughter included." Anthony frowned. "You didn't write the story but the women blame you. Or maybe they're baying for your blood because of what you did to Birdie. Either way, it's your problem."

"Oh, shit."

"The news story brought a horde of people to town last week, all searching for rubies. The antiques in the Second Chance weren't damaged but the wallpaper is torn and someone left graffiti on the walls." Anthony shook his head. Damn if he didn't appear to be enjoying himself at Hugh's expense. "Offer to have the carpets cleaned and the walls repaired. You might avoid Finney's skillet if you do."

Hugh doubted it. Finney was probably eager to bash in his skull. At least Birdie was AWOL. He wasn't prepared to see her until he came up with an apology.

Shuffling across the center green, he tried to compose the proper words to pacify the women. Through the restaurant's window, he spied a few customers seated in the dining room. Delia, her green hair flashing, was taking an order. Ethel Lynn stood arguing with Theodora while Blossom drowned them out with the ear-buds of her iPod.

He noticed a sign on the door, which looked suspiciously like Blossom's handwriting:

If you're looking for rubies, go away.
Their rightful owner has claimed them.

As the door creaked open, Blossom tossed down her iPod and nudged Theodora. Finney barreled through the swinging door from the kitchen with her wooden spoon raised to strike. Delia and Ethel Lynn seethed. Theodora's wrinkles firmed into a mask of rage, which she accented with an abrupt shimmy-shake of her shoulders.

They'd enjoy roasting his hide.

Run like hell.

But if he ran now, he'd never be able to show his face in Liberty again. Sorrow knifed him. He didn't have a future with Birdie, but he'd never find peace until he apologized.

Theodora jabbed her finger toward a barstool. He sat. *Take it like a man.*

Swinging his barstool around, she stood before him like a supremely enraged gnat. "Do you realize the fine mess you stirred up? If Blossom hadn't put the sign up on the door, we'd still be overrun with hooligans."

Mention of her brought a red-faced Blossom forward. "What about me?" She halted before him with her brown eyes watery. "I thought we were friends."

"We are. I'm sorry. Forgive me?"

She wrinkled her nose. "The jury's still out."

He looked around wildly at the women. "I didn't stop to consider how the publicity would affect all of you."

Delia shrugged. "I made out okay—treasure hunters leave big tips." Her pleasure faded. "Of course I nearly lost my best friend. I blame you. I was pissed off at Birdie for days, until I realized she'd stopped stealing money weeks ago."

Hugh stifled a groan. "She did?" Why hadn't it occurred to him that she was trying to go straight?

"People in town gave her an awful time," Ethel Lynn put in, fluttering to a standstill. "Natasha over at the bakery? She slapped her. What a terrible thing." To his astonishment, the old woman raised her delicate and heavily veined fists. "I have a mind to put you in your place."

In turmoil, he searched for something to placate the women. Not to mention Blossom—hell, was there any way to make it up to the kid? And the baker had slapped Birdie? Heartsick, he let the pain suffuse him, body and soul.

Finally, he took Blossom's hand. He'd set things right, starting with her.

"Blossom, I quit the *Register*," he said, a dart of relief skimming through him when she appeared ready to hear him out. "I can't write about you. Lying to you was wrong, and I'm ashamed of myself. No story is that important. Tell me how to make things right."

"Let me work for you."

"Selling Christmas trees?" An odd request, but he'd give her anything she asked.

"No, I want to work for you as a stringer," she said impatiently. "That's what it's called, right?"

"A stringer works for a newspaper, but I can't get you a job at the *Register* or anywhere else. You're too young."

Theodora nudged the girl aside. "She's talking about the rubies, fool. Birdie's trying to decide what to do with the money. If you ask me, Liberty needs a newspaper. Someone ought to report the goings on. Someone like you."

"You want me to open a newspaper with Birdie's inheritance?" Hugh nearly laughed but the women's displeasure stopped him cold. Carefully, he added, "I'm sure Birdie won't talk to me. Besides, there isn't any news to report."

Theodora whacked him on the knee. "Our farming community has news galore. The pig festival up in Bellrywood, the church supper next week—there's a lot of news."

Pigs? Church dinners? "I think we're getting ahead of our-selves." He scrubbed his palms across his cheeks. Was Theodora serious?

Behind the counter, Finney lowered her spoon. "All of you, ease up." When he glanced at her in silent thanks, she added, "It took some guts coming here to apologize. I expect you called Landon this morning for the same reason."

"Yes, I—" Hugh rocked back on the barstool. Did *everyone* know his business? "I understand he's out shopping with Birdie."

"He is. But don't bother yourself on his account. He doesn't want your apology."

From somewhere behind, a silvery voice added, "Actually, my father would like to thank you for bringing Birdie home to us. I would, too."

The attractive blonde had gone unnoticed in a corner of the dining room. She came forward now at a dignified gait, her tweed coat swaying and her diamond earrings flashing. Her stylish, platinum blonde hair brushed her ivory cheeks and he froze—he'd never seen her before but something in the turn of her lips, in the shape of her eyes, reminded him of the woman he loved.

"I'm Meade Williams, Birdie's half-sister," she said, her hand outstretched. Hugh shook her hand, releasing her fingers in stunned silence. "We never got the opportunity to meet last year, when you made Blossom famous. I was in Europe."

"You're Cat Seaver's daughter." Hugh swallowed down the regret barreling into his chest. Fate was forcing him to face all his demons today. "Fourteen years ago, I was the reporter who broke the story—"

"I know." Sadness pooled in her eyes.

The other women drifted away. Appearing satisfied when they were left alone, she seated herself beside him.

"I've learned a lot about my mother this past week," she said as if he were a trusted confidant and they'd been talking for hours.

She laid her hands flat on the counter and splayed her fingers. "Cat did a lot of good for Ohio. The day she drowned . . . Hugh, I'm sure it was an accident. She was arrogant, proud—not suicidal. She could be so dramatic. I think she was angry. The Trinity story could've uncovered her indiscretions."

"The article was about your father."

"Of course." Meade patted his forearm, a surprisingly welcome gesture. "My father . . . well, he's rather old-fashioned. He'd never damage my memory of my mother. Fact is, she took many lovers. They were always young men she controlled. You were the one I knew about. Unfortunately, you weren't the only one."

A shudder went through his chest. "She told you?"

"Right before she went out on the lake. She handed me the photographs of Wish, and my father with Birdie . . . and she told me about you. A young reporter with too many ethics who she hoped she'd destroyed. My father had already paid off one of her lovers to buy his silence. Once the story appeared in your newspaper, Cat was sure there'd be no way to stop the others."

"I had no idea." Relief washed over him. *I'm not responsible for her death.*

A shadow of a smile played on Meade's lips. "You've given my father Birdie, the daughter he'd lost. You gave me the sister I didn't know I had." She clasped his fingers and he couldn't stop himself—he held on tight. "If you hadn't investigated Birdie, there never would've been a story in the *Register*. She would've moved on."

"Once she found the rubies, she planned to."

"If she had, my father never would've healed. I owe you a debt of gratitude."

For proof, she kissed him lightly on the cheek. Drawing back, she playfully nudged his shoulder. "Now, go on. From what I've heard, Anthony has you working the Christmas tree lot. Don't keep him waiting."

CHAPTER 31

Fortunately Theodora's stuffed groundhog, Alice, and the gold pedestal upon which she perched, were missing from the dining room table. The dead rodent had been replaced by china set out on an appropriately colored, ruby red tablecloth.

"Alice is on the back deck," Theodora's daughter, Ruby, whispered. She placed a platter of barbecue chicken in Birdie's waiting hands and picked up the bowl of collard greens. "We'd like to give that poor groundhog a proper burial, but Mother won't hear of it."

Birdie followed Ruby into the dining room. "Name the time and place and I'll toss Alice into a shallow grave."

Ruby laughed. "Mother will tan your hide if she finds Alice missing." She placed the food on the table then gave Birdie a hug. "How are you doing? Still nervous?"

Of all of Theodora's children and grandchildren Birdie had met this snowy Sunday afternoon, Ruby was by far her favorite. Something of Theodora's fire was evident in her sandy brown eyes, but it was mellowed by the serene expression on her well-rounded face. She wasn't tall but she was a large woman, with every exaggerated curve and hill of her body created to give love and comfort. Ruby patted the faces of her adult children, squeezed her two brothers whenever they slipped into the kitchen to ask about dinner, and playfully smacked her two sisters on the behind as they finished at the stove and removed pies from the oven.

Birdie glanced into the living room. "I'm still nervous but I'm holding up." Her new relatives were crowded in small groups, talking loudly. They appeared galvanized by the savory aromas drifting from the kitchen, as if sweet potato pie and barbecue were stimulants for conversation. "It's a little overwhelming trying to remember everyone's name."

"There won't be a pop quiz. We're all just glad you're here." She took Birdie by the hand. "C'mon. Mother wants to show you something before we all sit down for dinner."

Intrigued, Birdie followed her down the hallway, away from the living room's revelry. Surprises no longer sent her looking for an escape route. Her past career as a petty thief didn't matter. Ever since she'd found Theodora waiting outside the cave, everyone had showered her with affection. She now knew her real father. Her older sister, Meade, in a stunning about-face, had taken to fussing and fretting over her. Theodora and Ruby and the raucous Hendricks clan were now the extended family she was proud to call her own. She didn't have Hugh, of course, but she'd learned to ignore the heartache. With so much family to treasure, it seemed ungrateful to wallow in self-pity because their relationship hadn't worked out.

With a wave of her hand, Ruby led her into a large bedroom sweetly decorated in pastel hues. Theodora's room? Nothing of the feisty matriarch's gun-toting personality was in evidence. A rocking chair sat in one corner, and the four-poster bed was decorated with a trove of lacy pillows.

Theodora marched out of the walk-in closet. "Here it is." She hefted a leather volume to the rocking chair and sat. She glared at Birdie. "Well, come on now. It's time you saw this."

Ruby nudged her forward. "Go. She's wants a moment alone with you." She left the room.

After she'd gone, Birdie settled on the rug at Theodora's feet. The volume resting in the old woman's lap was large, and it carried the faint scent of roses. The pages of parchment were golden with age, the edges painted with gilt.

"Is that Justice's diary?" Delighted, Birdie ran her finger across the soft binding as Theodora searched for something inside.

Finding it, the old woman smiled. "Now, you know Justice opened the Second Chance Grill. Back then it was called The Second Street Eatery. First restaurant in Liberty. People didn't think a colored woman should own a business, but our Justice didn't care."

"She had spunk—like you."

"She did at that."

It was more than spunk, really. Justice had lived in a world segregated by race, decades before women won the right to vote. It didn't matter. Freed from a life of servitude, she traveled north heavy with child and learned to compete among men. She built a good life because she was determined and knew she deserved better. She understood her own value, nurtured her talents and never gave up. She'd possessed courage, through and through.

Breaking the silence, Birdie said, "I want to be like her . . . and like you."

The comment sent dampness into Theodora's eyes. "Lord knows you are, more than you realize."

The possibility was heartwarming. "Do you really think so?"

"I do, child." Theodora turned the book sideways, allowing them both to view the bold cursive running neatly across the pages. "See here? Justice even wrote down some of her best recipes."

"Martha Washington's Candied Cake," Birdie read. She lifted her brows. "*The* Martha Washington?"

"How Justice came by the recipe is an interesting story. I'll tell you sometime."

"What else is in there?"

"Observations, her deepest thoughts, more recipes. The diary spans her whole life." With affection, Theodora pressed her palm to the open page. "Truth be told, this diary is a compass. Whenever my life was difficult, I used the wisdom inside to find my way."

Emotion glazed the explanation. Touched, Birdie said, "I could use a compass." After the mistakes she'd made she needed a damn road map, with every intersection in life clearly marked and posted. "I'd like to read the diary sometime, if that's all right."

"Of course it is. Justice had a heart of gold and more horse sense than anyone you'll ever meet. She can guide you just as she guided me." Theodora turned the page. Her expression soft, she added, "Life is never simple and it certainly isn't easy. But you'll learn, child. Justice will teach you, and I will too."

Eagerly, Birdie gleaned the page. The word *patience* leapt out at her; so did *love* and *kindness*. Theodora turned to yet another entry and she grabbed hold of the words, *my dreams won't matter if I don't persevere to give them substance.* Gems of wisdom were intermingled with common advice about raising a colicky baby and how to select produce for the expanding restaurant. The diary brimmed with good sense and sweet humor about surviving in a world that wasn't fair or simple to navigate, but was beautiful nonetheless.

"I like the part about dreams." Damp-eyed, she glanced up at Theodora. "I've never had any, unless going legal counts."

"Well, you've done that. Now it's time to stretch your arms wide and take in more of what the world has to offer." Theodora rose from the chair. "For instance, have you bought a Christmas tree yet? It's a good place to start."

Birdie struggled to her feet. "What does a Christmas tree have to do with fulfilling my dreams?"

Theodora carried the diary back to the closet. When she reappeared, her more taciturn expression was firmly in place. "You're a fool, child. You know that, don't you?"

"So you keep telling me."

"Then high tail it over to Anthony's Christmas tree lot tomorrow. Dreams have to start somewhere." She nudged Birdie from the room. "Might as well have yours with some tinsel and a star on top."

* * *

"You still haven't bought a Christmas tree?" Meade asked with faint distress.

Birdie refilled her sister's coffee cup. "Why does everyone care if I decorate for the holidays? It's five days until Christmas, too late to buy a tree for the apartment. Besides, I'm spending Christmas Eve at Theodora's house and Christmas day with you at your father's house."

"*Our* father's house," Meade said, winking at Landon. "Still, you should get one."

Landon patted his mouth with his napkin. "She'll purchase a tree when she's ready." In an oddly conspiratorial tone, he added, "All good things to those who wait."

"She's waited long enough!"

"Patience, darling."

What was the big deal? It wasn't like you had to get a tree to enjoy the holiday. Birdie's amusement vanished when the portly man at table seven glared. He began drumming his fork and knife. "Uh, we have to wrap this up," she said. "The natives are restless."

Meade gave a regal wave of her hand. "What you *should* do is sit down and dine with us. It's ridiculous for you to continue working here."

Birdie gazed heavenward. How many times had she explained that she couldn't leave Finney shorthanded during the holiday rush? They'd find a replacement in January when things slowed down.

"I'll think about my options next month." She nodded at the man waiting for her to take his order. "And stop bugging me about a Christmas tree. Even if I did want one—and I don't—I don't have ornaments to put on the thing. Enough already."

During the next few days, she wondered why she hadn't kept her mouth shut.

On Tuesday, three foil-wrapped boxes appeared outside her apartment door. The gift was from Meade, of course, a gorgeous sampling of gold stars and blazing red candy canes that looked good enough to eat. By Wednesday, her refusal to buy a tree reached the women of The Second Chance. Delia handed her a box of shimmering silver balls. Ethel Lynn presented two boxes of holiday lights.

And, on the morning of Christmas Eve, Finney cornered her in the kitchen as she was tying on her apron.

"Here." The cook thrust a large, hastily wrapped package at her. The Santa paper was crinkled at the corners. The red bow on top was coming loose. "Just so you know, I was at Wal-Mart before sunup. Lordy, there's nothing crazier than a store full of women the day before Christmas."

"You shouldn't have done this." Moved by the cook's generosity, Birdie gently set the box on the counter. "This is too much. Let me pay you back."

"No, you won't. What you *will* do is hightail it over to the Christmas tree lot. You're the only person in town who hasn't been there."

"Not a good plan. I don't *need* a tree." Sighing, Birdie tore off the wrapping paper. She'd done her best to remain upbeat throughout the holiday season, even though she'd become increasingly lonely.

She still missed Hugh. Foolish, sure, but she harbored the crazy hope he'd call. But if the phone rang, it was Theodora or Ruby on the other end, or Meade calling to chat. It was never Hugh. Chances were, he hadn't thought about her once since returning to Akron.

Pushing the thought aside, she peered into the box. Six packs of Christmas ornaments were crammed beside packets of tinsel.

For a fleeting moment, she imagined decorating a tree with Hugh upstairs, cozy in the apartment they'd shared. The thought sent a dull ache into her chest.

Resigned to obeying the cook, she untied her apron and hung it back up. "Okay, I'll get a tree right now. And thanks . . . for everything." She nodded toward the box. "Do you think they have anything small? Something I can drag back here without a forklift?"

Finney brightened. "Sure they do! If you want a four-footer, they'll fix you right up."

"Great. I'll be back in ten minutes."

Outside, Christmas carolers were converging in the Square's center green in the morning light. A soft snow was falling, dusting the shops and the evergreens with a froth of cheer. Wearily, Birdie trudged across the center green toward the Gas & Go.

Try to be happy. She had so much to be grateful for—Landon, Meade and Theodora's large brood, not to mention the women of The Second Chance. She had family right here in Liberty, people who welcomed her to their tables and showered her with love. If that wasn't enough, seventeen flawless rubies were tucked away at Liberty Trust waiting to be used as collateral to start a business once she figured out what to do. She'd start fresh, in her new hometown. Just like Justice had done.

She even had a nicely bound photocopy of Justice's diary, which Theodora and her daughters had presented as an early Christmas present. Settled in her apartment each night, she enjoyed reading about the freedwoman's life and her love for Birdie's ancestor, Lucas. The diary was full of sweet wisdom and gentle observations on how to live a good life. In so many ways it was a guidebook for the human heart.

So her relationship with Hugh hadn't worked out. Remaining glum seemed ungrateful, given all the new gifts in her life.

Before the courthouse, the carolers formed a jolly line. Their voices lifted, merry and bright. Trying for happiness, Birdie swiped at her eyes.

The Christmas tree lot was empty. The place was cleaned out; twigs and pine needles were packed into the surface of the well-trodden snow. Twenty paces off, a pathetically dressed Santa was heaving the last of the trees into a stack. Birdie pitied him. Something in the stoop of his shoulders gave the impression of someone who'd fallen on hard times. The suit he wore was about five sizes too large. From the back, the loose fit of the red velvet coat gave the impression he could use a decent meal.

Unaware of her approach, he worked slowly gathering up the forgotten trees. It struck her as a great loss, how the imperfect branches and the bent tops destined the greenery for something less than bright lights and tinsel. She began looking in earnest for a tree she could save.

Slim pickings—after a moment, she spotted a small tree he'd missed. "This one's a beauty," she called, from over her shoulder. Standing the fledgling upright she ignored the bare spots midway down where branches had broken off. "How much do you want for it?"

"Take it. We're closed," The man yelled back.

He crouched in front of the pile and she noticed the smudges on the back of his costume. The way he pushed the tree trunks close seemed a great effort, and her pity increased. When he drew a pack of matches from his pocket, she rushed over.

"Don't burn them. Wait until after Christmas." She stopped a few paces away, caught short by the way her entreaty froze his hands a second before the match ignited. "It's Christmas Eve," she added, as if the holiday explained everything. Embarrassed, she laughed. She really was sentimental. "The season of miracles, right? Leave the trees for now. Someone might come at the last minute to save them."

"Only a fool holds out hope," he said. No sarcasm in his voice—only pain.

Hugh.

The beard and the hat had rendered him unrecognizable. The costume hid everything but the despair in his gaze as it slowly lifted to hers.

"You *have* to hope," Birdie said from behind a glimmer of tears.

He appeared too overwrought to reply. Finally, he said, "Sometimes it's too late."

"Not if someone cares about you." Taking his hands, she helped him to his feet. "Because I was thinking," she added, "This town needs a crack reporter. Now that I'm rich, should I start a newspaper?"

It was enough to make him quirk a brow. "To cover pigs and such?"

"And the quilting club, the Rotary—Theodora says the county fair is a real thrill."

"You *will* need a crack reporter."

"Sure will."

He rested his hand on her waist, the only man she'd ever loved. "Birdie." He whispered her name like a prayer.

The emotions tangled inside her unwound and released, until there was nothing left but her love for him. He waited, stock-still, as she stepped into his embrace. Carefully, she pulled off the hat and the beard to reveal his bristled cheeks and midnight gaze.

She cradled his face between her palms. "Why didn't you tell me you were back?" A twinge of anger scuttled her pulse. "I've been miserable without you."

"It wasn't a good plan," he said, mimicking her oft-declared credo. Grinning, he trailed his fingers beneath her lips. "Can you forgive me? I love you. I can't live without you. I don't even want to try."

"I love you, too," she said in a quavering rush. Grasping the heavy velvet of his costume, she dragged his mouth to hers. But as he leaned in eagerly, she thought of something else. "When did you get back?"

He tightened his hold. "Last week. I'm sorry. I should've told you."

"Hugh!"

"I was still working on my apology. I couldn't go to the restaurant until I'd perfected it." He smiled then, sad and sweet, and relief spilled through her as the pleasure lighting his features banished the agony in his gaze. "So . . . about the job. I can be persuaded to sign on at your newspaper if you offer the right benefits."

Hungrily, she unbuttoned his tunic. Pleased, he took over the task. Wrapping the heavy fabric around them both, he snuggled her against his chest.

Birdie laid her head on his shoulder. "What sort of benefits?" she asked, closing her eyes. She was happy to stand here forever, enjoying the heat of his body melting into hers. "Name your price, Mr. Reporter."

Considering, Hugh brushed his mouth across her temple. "For starters, a second chance," he said, and her emotions soared. "Birdie, you've stolen my heart and made my life worth living. I don't deserve you, but I'll do everything in my power to make you happy." He lifted his head and looked off, glimpsing the future. "Do you think there's any commercial property for rent around here?"

"I have no idea."

"We should start looking. Newspapers need room. We need something big for the press."

Tilting her face, she assessed the excitement rioting across his features. "So you'll do it? You'll help me start a newspaper?"

"Theodora *is* right. Liberty needs one. I'd say we're up to the task." He sobered, his dark gaze filled with passion. "I love you, Birdie. We can make this work. Are you in?"

She glanced back at the center green, where families were gathering to hear the carolers. She didn't know the song that had burst on the air but it had a peppy beat, and she began tapping her foot. She'd learn the lyrics this year or next—it didn't matter when, as long as Hugh was here in Liberty beside her.

Trembling, she lifted her lips to his. "It sounds like a great plan."

THE END

ABOUT THE AUTHOR

Christine owned a small public relations firm in Cleveland, Ohio. Her articles and press releases have appeared regionally in northeast Ohio. Her short story, Night Hour, appeared in Working Mother magazine.

Christine closed the firm fifteen years ago after she traveled to the Philippines and adopted a sibling group of four children. She has been writing novels fulltime since 2004.

Please visit her at
www.christinenolfi.com

Follow her on Twitter at
@christinenolfi

Please turn the page for a sneak peek of *Second Chance Grill,* the next novel in the Liberty, Ohio series.

CHAPTER 1

Mary Chance feared she'd poison half of Liberty on her restaurant's opening day.

Not that she was responsible. Ethel Lynn Percible's cooking skills—or, more precisely, her lack of them—had Mary wishing she'd dumped antacids instead of mints in the crystal bowl beside the cash register. Perhaps the elderly cook hadn't poisoned anyone, not yet. But the historic recipes Mary hoped to serve were soggy, lumpy, undercooked or scorched to a fine black sheen.

She flinched as Mayor Ryan, a trim woman with a helmet of orange curls, rose from a table and snapped, "I hope you were a better doctor than you are a business woman." Storming past, she added, "You should've opened an emergency room instead of a restaurant—or better yet, both. *Then* you'd have a thriving business."

For a shattering moment, Mary connected with the mayor's frigid gaze. Like most of the town council, the mayor had ordered the opening day special—Martha Washington's beef stew. She'd received a concoction that looked like glue and smelled worse.

Turning the Second Chance Grill into a prosperous enterprise would be difficult.

In the dining room, the young waitress Mary had rehired looked frantic. Delia Molek was arguing with a customer beneath antique pewter sconces.

In contrast, Ethel Lynn was hiding in the kitchen. Given her culinary calamities since the first customer had arrived promptly at seven a.m., it was for the best. Maybe she suffered from opening day jitters. Maybe she *would* serve up savory meals once she got into the swing of things. The restaurant had closed for six months. Was it any wonder if Ethel Lynn's cooking skills were rusty? And, in the fervor of new ownership, Mary *had* overhauled the menu. She'd brought back recipes that hadn't been served in over a century. Surely the historic cuisine was to blame for the elderly cook's bad start.

Mary was wringing her hands when Delia marched up.

"He didn't leave a tip." The waitress nodded at the portly man fleeing out the door.

"And he'll never come back."

"Would you?" The waitress popped a stick of gum into her mouth and chewed thoughtfully. "So. Your first day is a train wreck. Guess what? We still have the dinner rush tonight."

Mary surveyed the patriotic decorations festooned throughout the dining room, a treasure trove of Americana harking back to the restaurant's inception during the Civil War. So many beautiful things, but they'd gone unappreciated. The customers had only noticed the glop on their plates.

Her heart sank. "There won't be a dinner rush," she said. "After the meals Ethel Lynn cooked for the breakfast and lunch crowds, we won't see a soul."

Delia approached the restaurant's picture window. "I hope Mayor Ryan doesn't burn up the phone lines scaring off our customers." She squinted at the courthouse anchoring the north end of Liberty Square. "Then again, she has a soft spot for Miss

Meg. It might stop her from passing legislation condemning this place."

"Maybe I should ask Aunt Meg to give her a call." Would long-distance lobbying work?

Delia slipped her order pad into the pocket of her apron. "Meg will fix everything," she said, grinning. The mirth on her face died when she added, "The mayor was sorry to see her go. We all were."

And sorry to see me arrive? "My aunt promised to come back and visit." With a brave smile, Mary ignored the curious look glittering in Delia's blue eyes. "She called last night—from Tibet. She's praying with the monks."

"Meg sure is eccentric."

Incorrigible was more like it. "She was planning to practice yoga then have a drink after the monks retired for the night." A shot of whiskey didn't sound too bad, at the moment.

"Makes her own rules, she does." Delia folded her arms. "She's also an open book, which you aren't. You never talk about yourself."

"I will, when I have something to say."

What she *did* have were emotions sorely in need of CPR. Not to mention a bank account on death's door after generous Aunt Meg handed over the restaurant then danced into retirement.

True, Meg's largesse was perfectly timed. Mary was eager to leave Cincinnati for a yearlong sabbatical from medicine. Slogging through her residency and working long hours in the ER had left her exhausted. Worse still, her grief over the sudden death of her friend and confidant, Dr. Sadie Goldstein, hadn't abated. She needed time to heal.

None of which was suitable to discuss with her employee, the gum-popping Delia. Excusing herself, she returned to the kitchen.

At the stove, Ethel Lynn fluttered. Her oversized apron swung in loose folds as she padded her fingers across the collar of her bluebell-patterned dress. The retro number was better suited for the Eisenhower era, much like Ethel Lynn herself.

"Is the lunch rush over?" she asked. "I'm ready if you need anything."

Mary hesitated. "Should I take over for a few hours?" she finally asked. "You look frazzled."

Ethel Lynn patted her wizened cheeks. "Oh, I'm fit as a fiddle."

Right. The woman was a bundle of nerves. Maybe she possessed the metabolism of a sparrow on amphetamines. Whatever the reason, she'd worried her way through the renovations after the historic restaurant changed hands. Ethel Lynn had perspired in her delicate way, lace handkerchief at the ready, as the dining room was repainted and the patriotic bunting hung on the picture window. Now they'd reopened to disastrous results and she seemed prepared to fret into a full-blown state of distress.

Which was never good for a woman on the far side of sixty.

Gently, Mary patted her back. "About your cooking . . . there've been a few complaints. Do you need another pair of hands in the kitchen?"

"Of course not. Didn't you rehire the staff?"

"I rehired Delia," Mary corrected. "When I called the other waitress, she refused my offer." The mysterious Finney Smith had blistered Mary with a few choice words before slamming down the phone. Shocking, sure, but who cared if they were short a waitress? "We'll find a replacement for Finney. Honestly, I can't imagine a woman like that waiting tables." Not unless the tables were in Sing Sing.

A squeak popped from Ethel Lynn's throat. Which was when Mary noticed that her lips were quivering.

"It's about Finney," she whispered, and something in her voice sent goose bumps down Mary's spine. "She wasn't a waitress, dear. Her job was—heavens to Betsy—a tad more important."

Mary's pulse scuttled. "What exactly are you saying?"

* * *

CHAPTER 1

Blossom's dad thought a lot about dying.

She supposed it was natural given all the pain, blood tests, and hospital visits they'd endured. Going through it, years of it, had changed him. It put lines on his forehead and doubt in his eyes. She'd watched the changes color him, as if he'd been a pencil sketch before the ordeal and was now bolded in by the blues and grays of his experience with cancer.

She wanted to tear up that picture, throw it into a trash can of unwanted memories. She'd heard for herself the word Dr. Lash used. *Remission.*

It was over. Finished. The word always made her happy. Then she'd think about her dad, stuck on his thoughts of death.

Which made her sad.

Pausing on Second Street, Blossom tugged the book bag's straps tight across her shoulders. Feeling self-conscious, she hesitated beside the large picture window. A drapey curtain patterned like the American flag had been hung by the restaurant's new owner.

She hooked a curl behind her ear and glanced down the street, like a spy afraid of being noticed. Which was stupid. She was a seventh grader at Liberty Middle School and knew everyone in town.

Before she might chicken out, she peeked in the window.

The place was empty. Blossom sighed. Then she swung her gaze to the long counter hemmed in by bar stools and her mood soared. Mary was there, all right.

Ducking out of sight, she leaned against the wall's rough bricks as the fizzy elation ran down to her toes.

Then she dashed across the street.

She ran diagonally through the park-like center green of Liberty Square. Maple trees wagged leaves in the breeze. The scent of freshly mown grass mingled with the sweet aroma of summer flowers.

Moving faster, she narrowed her concentration with an adolescent blend of purpose and amusement. Sure, her dad thought about dying when he ought to try *living.* Grown-ups did all sorts of stupid things. They acted as if death lurked outside the door waiting to take them away. Blossom knew it was a silly idea. Death wasn't a person dressed up like Darth Vader, cloaked in black and waiting to snatch you away.

Yet no matter how many times she reassured her father, he saw death as the enemy. He believed in it.

That was nonsense. Blossom knew with an eleven year old's certainty that death was outsmarted by good doctors and positive thoughts. Wishing helped, too.

Buoyed by the warm May air and her foolproof plan, she ambled across the hot pavement of the Gas & Go. Inside the garage her father clattered around the pit, working beneath a late model Toyota.

"Hey, there." She spotted the vintage oak office chair, her favorite, and dropped onto it. "How ya doin'?"

"Hi, kiddo," Anthony Perini called from inside the pit. "How was school?"

"Just counting the days until my prison break." She yawned theatrically. "Guess what? The restaurant reopened this morning. Been there yet?"

A rattling erupted beneath the car. "Too busy." Several bolts clanked into a tray.

"Go over and meet the new owner, Dad. She's nicer than Prissy Meade Williams."

"Don't start. All right?"

It was an old request. Meade Williams poised the biggest threat to Blossom's emotional well-being since she and her dad had high-tailed it out of the hospital last year. Rich and as plastic as a platinum haired Barbie doll, Meade was now upping the ante. The cosmetics entrepreneur filled her Mercedes at the Gas & Go so frequently she was probably siphoning off gas outside town and dumping it in a cornfield to keep her fuel gauge on empty.

Ditching the thought, Blossom said, "Meade will have you doing the goosestep to the altar if you aren't careful. You don't know women like I do. I *am* a woman."

"We aren't having this conversation again."

"Face it, Dad. If I don't give you good advice, who will?" The chair was equipped with casters and she wheeled toward the garage door. Sunshine dappled the quaint shops and the restaurant on the other side of Liberty Square. "The lady at the restaurant is real pretty. You've got to meet her."

Beneath the Toyota, a tool clanked then stilled. "Meet who?"

Blossom wheeled close, happy she'd caught his attention. "The lady—I think she's Miss Meg's niece. She's a real looker."

"If you say so."

"Aren't you interested?"

A grease-stained hand popped out from beneath the car and grabbed the air ratchet's snaking black hose. The hand disappeared underneath, as an ear-splitting, motorized whirring rattled through the garage.

When the tool fell silent, Blossom continued. "She has brownish-red hair down to her shoulders and green eyes. She's kinda shy. Like she's scared or something. She even fixed up the boring old menu. I'll bet the stuff she's making is better than your cooking."

"Hard to believe anyone cooks better than me."

"A lady like that must be a great cook."

"Whatever."

Frustrated by his lack of interest, she kicked away the bolts he'd thrown from the pit. "She changed the restaurant's name. It's now called Second Chance Grill. Her name is Mary Chance, by the way."

"Great."

"She's younger than you. Twenty-nine, thirty, maybe. She's nowhere near the old fart stage." *Like Meade.* "C'mon Dad—take me there for a sundae." Her father muttered a curse before climbing out of the pit. Plastering on a smile, she added, "You've got to see her."

When her father paused before her, she wrinkled her nose. He was grease monkey all the way. Droplets of motor oil dotted his curly brown hair. Oil glazed the side of his rather large nose. Beneath deep brown eyes, smudges of black made him resemble a boxer who'd seen too many fights. To top it off, he stank of eau de gasoline and perspiration.

"You're a stink pot." She pushed the office chair toward the garage door and the reprieve of springtime air. "And you're ruining your clothes. Geez, we'll never get the gunk out of your jeans. Not even with ten boxes of Tide."

Looking mildly offended, Anthony ran his palms down his filthy tee-shirt. "Why are you always bugging me about my clothes?"

"You're a good looking guy, that's all. Clean up once in awhile. Strut your stuff."

He gave her the quizzical look that meant she'd crossed the line of father-daughter relationships—a line she didn't think existed.

"I hate to point out the obvious but you need a date. Meade stalking you doesn't count." She rolled her eyes at the ceiling. "How long's it been? Can you remember the last time you had a date?"

"Not really."

"That's *why* she's got you in her sights. It's about damn time you found a nice woman."

"You shouldn't swear."

"You shouldn't make me."

She pulled her attention from the ceiling and leveled on his sweet, teddy bear gaze. It never failed to warm her when he looked at her that way. It also made her sad, the worry lurking in his eyes, the concern he tried to hide.

He'd had that look her whole life.

Crouching, Anthony held the chair's armrests to still her. "Blossom, the last couple of years nearly did us in. It's a miracle we survived. I can't imagine thinking about a woman or dating or—"

"You don't have to worry." She patted his greasy cheek. "We're fine."

The concern in his eyes deepened. "I know."

"Try believing it."

A weary smile lifted the corners of his mouth. "I'm trying."

He let the chair go, and she snatched the paper bag at her feet. Following him across the garage, she said, "I brought clothes. You can wash up and change."

"You what?"

She lifted the grocery bag. "Clean clothes. We'll go to the Second Chance for a sugar buzz."

He cocked a brow. "Shouldn't you be home, doing homework or something?"

"Got it done in study hall." She pulled out a pair of jeans and wagged them before his nose. "Can we go to Miss Mary's restaurant? Please?"

Her father leaned against the doorjamb, shaking his head. "Shit, you never give up."

She tipped up her chin. "You shouldn't swear."

He offered a lopsided grin. "You shouldn't make me."

* * *

Mary smiled in greeting as the now-familiar girl with the corkscrew curls entered from the street. She'd been peering in the window for days, an amusing state of affairs. A tall man in jeans followed. Hopefully they'd arrived for an afternoon snack that wouldn't put Ethel Lynn anywhere near the stove.

To Mary's eternal relief, the girl asked, "Do you have sundaes?"

"With twenty flavors of ice cream." She reached for the order pad as they slid onto barstools. "Would you like menus?"

The girl smiled broadly, revealing pearly teeth. "Naw, I'll stick to chocolate ice cream with chocolate sauce. And sprinkles, if you've got 'em." Light sparkled in her toffee-colored eyes. "I'm Blossom Perini. You're Mary, right?"

"I am. It's nice to meet you."

The man quietly studied her, sending a pang of discomfort through her. He had the most expressive eyes—almond shaped, and a deep, warm brown. Like Blossom, his hair was a darker brown, and curly. An older brother? Or Blossom's father? He had the well-toned build of a man who worked out, lending him a youthful appearance. Deducing their relationship with certainty was impossible.

Immediately Blossom cleared up the mystery. "This is my dad, Anthony."

Mary extended her hand. "Hello."

"It's a pleasure." He surged to his feet to give a handshake formal enough for colleagues meeting at a medical convention.

But he didn't let go after the obligatory three seconds. And he continued to stare at her. With a start, she wondered if an odd bit of food was stuck on her face. Flecks of ash from the sausage Ethel Lynn had burned? With her free hand she made a self-conscious swipe at her cheek.

Clearly aware of her discomfort, he released her fingers and jerked back. He continued to stand behind the barstool in what she decided was a state of utter confusion. She didn't know how to proceed, not with him staring at her and Blossom watching the interchange with ill-concealed mirth.

"Sit down." Blossom yanked on his sleeve and he dropped back onto his barstool. "Do you want coffee?"

The question drew Anthony's attention back to his daughter. When he nodded in the affirmative, Mary tried to regain her composure. She stole a glance at the mirror behind the bar—no smudges, no food anywhere on her face. What had he been gaping at? Surely she appeared presentable, if a little exhausted. Given the apologies she'd doled out all day long, who wouldn't look haggard?

Shrugging it off, she scooped ice cream then fetched the coffee pot. She'd just finished pouring when Anthony said, "So you're Meg's niece. How is she?"

"Traveling the world." His remarks were light, and much friendlier than his strange, first reaction and so she added, "My aunt's decision to turn over the restaurant came as a shock. I'd never visited—I should've found the time."

"I would've remembered if you had."

He seared her with a look and she stiffened against the sudden heat flushing her cheeks. Was he flirting? The possibility sent unexpected pleasure darting through her.

Steering the conversation back to safe territory, she said, "It's been a crazy week. I'm still sorting through the antiques in the storage room and cleaning things up."

"This is the oldest landmark in town, but Meg hadn't been turning much of a profit." Anthony took a sip of his coffee. "I'm sure you'll have better luck."

"I hope so."

An attractive grin edged onto his mouth. "I hear Ethel Lynn is still around." He nodded toward the kitchen. "Keep her on a short leash. She's . . . high strung."

Mary chuckled. "And as eccentric as my aunt."

"Eccentric? Wait until you get a load of Theodora Hendricks." Anthony warmed to his story. "Blossom will tell you that she's an old war-horse. Closing in on eighty, she thinks yellow lights mean 'hurry' and red means 'floor it.' She's a bit crabby and about four feet tall—she drives a sky blue Cadillac. If you see her barreling down the road, get out of the way."

His eyes danced, drawing a laugh from Mary. "Thanks for the tip. I'll watch out for her."

Behind her, Ethel Lynn fluttered through the kitchen's swinging door. "Now, Anthony, you know better than to frighten Mary with tales of Theodora's driving."

"She's had six fender-benders in the last year. Trust me with the numbers. I'm stuck working on her car, every time."

"You do bodywork?" Mary asked. *His* body didn't need any work. He was a glorious study of lean muscle and commanding height. Squashing the unwarranted thought, she added, "I mean, if you work on Mrs. Hendrick's car . . ."

"I'm a mechanic. The bodywork is a side business. Theodora is my best customer."

He shrugged and Mary decided she liked Blossom's father. He was attractive and sweet, and extremely protective of his daughter. Since they'd arrived, he'd reached behind his daughter's back several times to pat her affectionately or rub her shoulders. It was heartwarming to see a man so engaged with his child.

Anthony turned to Ethel Lynn. "Does the change of ownership mean you're retiring, too?"

Ethel Lynn tipped her head to the side. "I promised Meg I'd stay until Mary settles in."

"Meaning you'd *like* to retire?" Mary savored the thought of ridding herself of the fretful woman. Guilt washed through her— Ethel Lynn *was* Aunt Meg's closest friend.

Blossom, finishing her sundae, scanned the newly painted dining room. "I think Mary is doing great by herself."

Anthony nudged her shoulder. "She's Miss Chance to you." He gave Mary an assessing glance. "Or is it Mrs?"

"Dad, I told you—she isn't married," Blossom said, rolling her eyes at her father. "Well, *Miss* Chance, I like everything you've done to the place. Especially the new name."

The girl's enthusiasm was truly engaging. Mary winked at her. "I'm glad you like it," she said.

"Second Chance Grill. It's a great name." Blossom turned to her father. "Everyone deserves a second chance—right, Dad?"

Her inoffensive question drove sorrow into Anthony's gaze. Mary's breath caught. Both Ethel Lynn and Blossom missed the expression, vanquished quickly from his face. But Mary recognized it, a demonstration of intense pain deftly hidden a moment after it appeared. It was an emotion she knew too well.

Like Anthony, she'd learned how to hide the pain as soon as it surfaced. The sudden death of her closest friend, the loss of Sadie's calm presence and unwavering confidence—all the dreams they'd shared about building a medical practice together had vanished in an instant of horror.

Mary dispelled the memory before it gripped her heart. Well, she'd finish grieving before returning to Cincinnati. Once the Second Chance Grill was solvent, she'd get on with her life.

Drawing from her thoughts, she blinked. Then flinched—she was still staring at Anthony. Flushing, she pulled her gaze away. But not before his eyes grew dull with some confusing mix of emotion. Clearly he understood: she'd glimpsed his pain. His emotions were laid bare before her, a perfect stranger.

Her mouth went dry as his expression closed. Embarrassed, she stepped back as he rose and paid the check. Murmuring a farewell, he led Blossom from the restaurant.

They skirted across Liberty Square. "What . . . was that?" Mary whispered.

Ethel Lynn looked up with confusion. "What, dear?"

"Anthony was so upset when Blossom said everyone deserves a second chance." Why had the remark upset him? Trying to work it out, she asked, "What's the story between him and Blossom's mother?"

Ethel Lynn waved the question away. "Hells bells. Anthony dated Cheryl when they were teenagers. She got pregnant and he did the honorable thing by marrying her. Two years after Blossom came along, Cheryl fell for a guitarist and skedaddled off to Florida."

The explanation was depressing and all too familiar. "Does Cheryl visit Blossom?" Mary asked.

Ethel Lynn snorted. "Good grief, we haven't seen Cheryl in years. I doubt Blossom remembers her. Good riddance, I say."

"No wonder Anthony was upset by Blossom's comment. With a wife like that, he doesn't believe in second chances."

A perilous silence descended on the dining room, filling Mary with foreboding. Beside her, Ethel Lynn withdrew a lace handkerchief from the pocket of her bluebell-patterned dress.

"You don't understand," Ethel Lynn said, dabbing at her eyes. "Blossom has leukemia, dear. Last year she was so sick, we weren't sure she'd make it. The leukemia is in remission, thank God."

Mary's heart clenched. She'd watched children at Cinci General battle cancer. "And Anthony? How's he managing?"

On a sigh, Ethel Lynn shook her head. "He's afraid to believe in second chances. He's learned to live each day as if it's Blossom's last."